THE
AWAKENING

BOOK FOUR

THE AWAKENING

The Adventures of Cassandra Rho

PHILLIP MARTIN

Published 2024

Printed in the United States of America

ISBN: 979-8-9913998-1-4 (Hardcover)
ISBN: 979-8-9873344-9-2 (Paperback)
ISBN: 979-8-9913998-0-7 (eBook)

Cover design by Daniela Ivanova
Map art by Shaun Carroll
Edited by Fabled Planet
Design and layout by Teddi Black Design

For information, address:
Phillip Martin
Phillip@cassandra-rho.com
www.cassandra-rho.com

Books in the Adventures of Cassandra Rho series

A Witch Is Born
The Quest For Zolmex
The Barbarian King
The Awakening
Birthright (coming soon)

I dedicate this book to my sister Terri, who has overcome obstacles most would not. You are an inspiration to me! Stay strong and keep enduring. Love you!

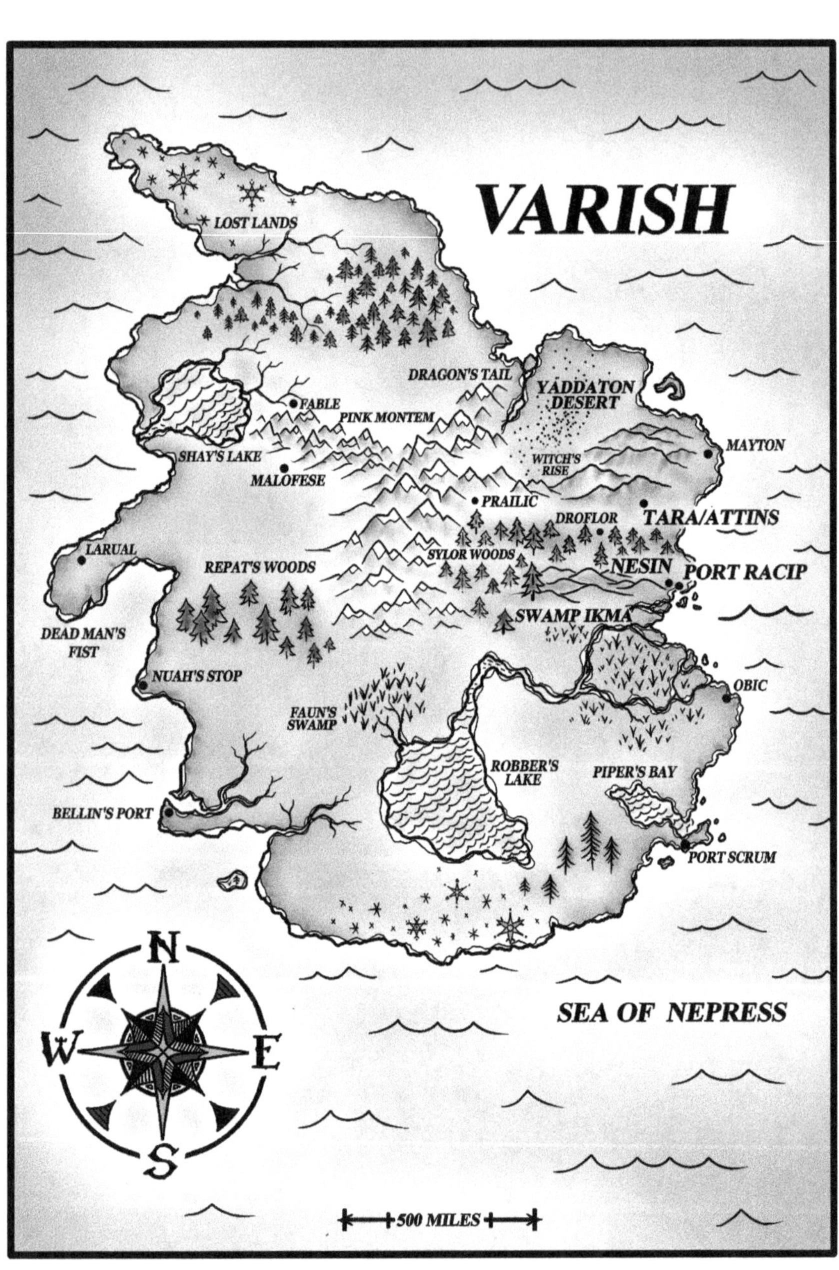

VARISH
LOST LANDS
DRAGON'S TAIL
YADDATON DESERT
FABLE
PINK MONTEM
MAYTON
WITCH'S RISE
SHAY'S LAKE
MALOFESE
PRAILIC
DROFLOR
TARA/ATTINS
LARUAL
REPAT'S WOODS
SYLOR WOODS
NESIN
PORT RACIP
DEAD MAN'S FIST
SWAMP IKMA
NUAH'S STOP
OBIC
FAUN'S SWAMP
ROBBER'S LAKE
PIPER'S BAY
BELLIN'S PORT
PORT SCRUM
SEA OF NEPRESS
N
W
E
S
500 MILES

Cassandra's World

The Allies

Cassandra Rho—The main protagonist. Cassandra is born an orphan with strange, mystical powers and a bizarre ability to control ravens.

Kessi Rho—Cassandra's sister. Kessi is pure of heart and as close to her god, Adlesk, as she is to Cassandra.

Greyson Kavince—Prodigy of the god Plath. Greyson has a hard time putting his friends' interests above his insatiable sexual appetite.

Binta Mulay—Cassandra's best friend and love interest. Binta cares deeply for Cassandra and will do anything to protect her.

Baxter Von Glord—Instructor at Victoria's School of Magic. Baxter is a powerful wizard and is madly in love with Cassandra, who is half his age.

Kringus Brahmore—King of Pelesea. Scarred by a duel with a red dragon, Kringus is a just leader who would do anything for his queen, Penelope.

Penelope Brahmore—Half-elven queen of Pelesea. Penelope's loyalty to Kringus and her city is unmatched.

Lady Victoria—Founder of the school of magic in Pelesea. Victoria is the most powerful wizard in her corner of the world, and Baxter Von Glord is her best friend.

Alleah Mansuell—Priestess of Sinnis. She is as blessed by her god as she is by exquisite beauty.

Daro, the ranger—Keeper of the Woods south of Pelesea. Daro is an ally to Pelesea and an admirer of Sasha De'Formen.

Von and Lenore—Elven cousins to Penelope Brahmore. Von and Lenore are loyal to Pelesea and extremely dangerous when using a bow.

Arrin Malik—Captain of Pelesea's army. Arrin is best friends with Kringus Brahmore and would give his life for him.

Sasha De'Formen—Ice carofex who befriends Daro. Sasha was born with god-like beauty (to the human eye), but the ice carofex find her hideous.

Jamison Oland—Steward of Pelesea when the royal couple leave the city to adventure. Jamison is madly in love with Binta Mulay and rescues her from servitude.

Breeston—Druid of Swamp Ikma. Breeston uses his power to summon powerful allies to defend the swamp and his friends.

Emiline—Elven vampire bride of Heinsvick. Despite her state of undeath, Emiline has a good heart and befriends Kessi Rho.

Mateon and Sitra—Married couple who befriend Cassandra. Sitra is a sleeth with snake-like hair and a gaze that can petrify. She and her blind husband, Mateon, live in the Yaddaton Desert.

Gophia—Culiem fairy. Gophia and Cassandra Rho become friends during their captivity in Yaddaton.

Spring Goodwright—Leader of the original New Order. Spring led the ill-advised charge to hell to destroy Marnelphion.

Leo—Member of the original New Order. Leo is known as the most powerful wizard ever to live and battled Marnelphion centuries ago.

The Villains

Ronnis D'Breeth—The orphanage administrator where Cassandra and Kessi grew up. Ronnis blames Cassandra for all his woes and is intent on exacting revenge.

Cass Ruben—Cassandra's nemesis from Victoria's School of Magic. Cass is Cassandra's rival in every way and loves to humiliate and torture her whenever the opportunity arises.

Matilda—High priestess of Marnelphion. She is determined to complete the prophecy that will summon Marnelphion back to the human world, requiring Cassandra's sacrifice.

Cerus the Grey—Demi-god, son of Gorl. Cerus is Matilda's cruel, blood-thirsty husband who craves battle over anything life offers.

Heinsvick—Vampire lord of Novafontera. Heinsvick is a powerful sorcerer whose arcane abilities have carried over to his state of undeath.

Barktuck Misol—High priest of Meshlor. Barktuck is good friends with Ronnis D'Breeth and assists him in his quest to capture and torture Cassandra Rho.

Vasheba—Powerful demon. Vasheba is Matilda's designated torturer and looks forward to spending an eternity in hell with her soul.

Marnelphion—Demon lord. Marnelphion is a god-like demon who intends to return to the human world to finish what he started nearly seven hundred years ago.

OTHERS

Kane, the lich-god—Powerful lich that discovered immortality. Rumored to be Cassandra's father, he seems to enjoy toying with her life.

Boz—Fire carofex mercenary. Boz is as dangerous as he is mysterious, and he hails from the monastery in Mecca-Loraine. He has never lost a fight or failed a mission.

Maltor—Vicious barbarian leader of the Serpent Tribe in the Yaddaton Desert. Maltor desires Cassandra Rho as a bride.

Inuentas, the Indomitable—Half-demon messenger. Inuentas warns the current New Order of the prophecy centered around Cassandra Rho.

Franklin Ruben—Cass's father. Franklin is a wealthy citizen of Pelesea who serves as an advisor to Jamison Oland and blames Cassandra Rho for his daughter's problems.

Malikai—Demonic sorcerer. Malikai uses his unique powers to assist Matilda and anyone else who doesn't mind paying a steep price.

PLACES ON TORLIA

Oldorburg—Small town where Cassandra and Kessi Rho grew up, located about eight hundred miles south of Pelesea.

Pelesea—Large city ruled by the just king and queen Kringus and Penelope Brahmore. Cassandra flees the evil of Oldorburg and begins life anew in Pelesea.

Novafontera—Dead city that Marnelphion cursed over six hundred years ago. It is located two hundred miles south of Pelesea and is the former home of the original New Order.

Godhomme—Small fortress of goblin hunters located near Pelesea.

Mecca-Loraine—Town located one hundred miles southwest of Oldorburg. Home to the fire carofex monastery and the priests of Meshlor who fled Oldorburg.

Farmer's Stop—A small farming community near Oldorburg.

Places On Varish

Port Racip—Large port city with two sets of leaders, one above ground, the other below ground. Neither vigorously enforce any laws.

Nesin—Mountain fortress home to Matilda and Cerus the Grey, near Port Racip. The fortress is a base for the Marnelphion priests and Gorl warriors.

Tara—Small community of Plath priests where Greyson Kavince grew up.

Attins—Small farming town at the foot of the mountain where Tara is located.

Swamp Ikma—Home of the mighty dragon Malebak and the druid Breeston.

Yaddaton Desert—Home of the desert barbarian tribes.

CONTENTS

PROLOGUE

Spring had taken hold of Pelesea, and many rare and beautiful flowers were in full bloom in the queen's garden. Penelope Brahmore, queen of the grand city and born of elven blood, had an affinity for rare plants, and the fragrance of those unusual specimens wafted through the castle grounds, especially in early spring as was the case in the fair city.

The light smell of flowers reached the far side of the castle grounds from which the gardens grew. There, in a small apple orchard, a humble cottage had been constructed for the king and queen's friend, Daro, the ranger. He was within the city but staying in the castle, leaving the cottage vacant. Therefore, the king and queen had invited Binta Mulay to stay at Daro's secluded home, and she had readily accepted.

Binta breathed in the fragrance of the flowers as she walked barefoot through the grass, smiling as it tickled her feet. Smiling had been foreign to her the last six months, but it was slowly becoming easier. She had stayed at the cottage for nearly four months, and that time had regenerated her soul a bit. Kringus and Penelope, the grand king and queen of Pelesea, had even sent for her parents, Wallium and Deb Mulay, who had lived at the cottage with her for the last month as she healed.

She had been through a lot since her friend, Cassandra Rho, had passed away in a horrific fire nearly half a year ago. Her heart had broken, and she had fallen into a deep despair. Cassandra had secretly been her love interest, and she missed her friend horribly. Then Greyson, her lover and the only one to know her true feelings for Cassandra, also left her. He had been gone so long now, on a journey to the other side of the world, that she assumed he was dead. Binta did not take smiling lightly, as it had been a chore for her since Cassandra's death.

Her loneliness and despair had led her to make a series of bad decisions, which eventually resulted in her working as a prostitute at the southern end of Pelesea four months earlier. The despicable Cass Ruben was the madam who forced her into such an unscrupulous lifestyle. She was an evil person and Cassandra's tormentor while the three of them had attended Victoria's School of Magic together the previous year. Cass's volatile relationship with Binta's friend made serving her all the more degrading and strangely gratifying.

One of her regular customers during her forced prostitution was a wealthy and caring man named Jamison Oland. He had reported Binta's predicament to the king and queen, who soon freed her. The king had exiled Cass from Pelesea, and now Binta finally felt safe and happy. At least, that is what she told herself. Her smile melted away as she considered it.

She found herself at Daro's bench, near a beautiful pond, facing the crystal-clear water, which now reflected the setting sun. She stood there a moment, contemplating her life. She wanted to be happy and genuinely felt better than she did a few months ago, but that old feeling of despair crept back into her thoughts most days, even now, as the beautiful sun began to set. Nights were the hardest, and that was when she missed Greyson and especially Cassandra the most.

Movement on the far side of the pond gained her attention. She snapped out of her thoughts to find her parents walking hand in hand there. Binta waved at her much-in-love parents and then sat on Daro's bench. Life was good now, she kept telling herself. Cass was gone, and she would soon return to her education at Victoria's School of Magic. Binta had been a fledgling wizard when she had met Cassandra there over half a year ago. Both students of magic immediately became friends and quickly grew close. Tears welled in her eyes as she understood returning to school would be hard. She would leave her parents, whom she had grown accustomed to living with again, and the school would only remind her of Cassandra.

She and Cassandra had been misfits at the school and in their lives before coming to Pelesea. Binta especially had felt alone before meeting Cassandra as she never fit in with other girls, tending to wear her makeup a little darker than was acceptable and indulging in piercings, which few seemed to understand or appreciate. She absently reached up, touched the small nose ring, and finally found the strength to smile again. It was Cassandra's favorite, and although her friend had never told her this, she knew in her heart that was the case by the way Cassandra always admired it. Her mind wandered further, and she recalled that night in Cassandra's dorm room when they had shared a kiss. Binta had instigated it on a whim because it had felt right. But after several attempts, the kiss became very passionate. It was safe to say she fell in love with Cassandra that night and was pretty sure the feeling was mutual.

Soon after, Greyson had been thrust into her life, and he had shown her the best sex imaginable. He was very well-endowed and had the lovemaking skills of a man much older than his nineteen years had shown. She sighed and hugged her arms to her chest. She missed Greyson and loved him very much, but that love was nowhere near what she had felt for Cassandra. She wondered how the two would have turned out had Greyson not gotten in the way.

She lost sight of her parents through the thick vegetation as they continued their trek around the wonderous pond. A fish jumped nearby, sending new ripples through the water. This place was paradise, and she should have been happy there. She dismissed the thoughts of Greyson and Cassandra. Her life was different now, and Cassandra and Greyson were a thing of the past. She would be starting school again, having a second chance at life, and she wanted to be focused. She would become a wizard—it was something she had intended to do when first arriving in Pelesea, and she would see it through.

Queen Penelope had visited with her months ago and assured her that Cass Ruben had been banished from the city. The banishment made her feel safe and, at the same time, disappointed. There was a sickness deep within Binta that she could not explain, one that had her obeying every order Cass commanded of her. The king and queen did not understand that the sexual acts that Cass had forced upon her were not entirely against her will. Actually, it was precisely what Binta had needed at the time to cope with her depression over losing Cassandra and Greyson. She was better now, but she bit her lip at the thought of those nasty things Cass had made her do. Her loins tingled at the torrid memories.

She felt an overwhelming desire to do bad things, sexually degrading things. She wouldn't care who witnessed those naughty acts, finding her addiction to pleasuring Cass too much to shake. She recalled the rough, dirty men she had been with during that brief time and the filthy things she had done with them. She desired that again in many ways. It was hard to remain focused. She closed her eyes and recalled her time of servitude to Cass. It was the best and worst time of her life.

"Binta Mulay," came the familiar greeting from behind her.

Binta jumped at Sammy's voice and quickly sat up. She turned and smiled at the approaching young man, quickly shaking the naughty memories from the forefront of her mind. Sammy was a castle servant and a little younger than she, perhaps sixteen years of age. He had been assigned to the cottage to look after her every need. He was her eyes and ears during her stay and had filled her in on many of the goings-on in Pelesea.

He walked up to her, smiled with a wave, and said, "May I?" and pointed to the bench.

Binta smiled, moved over, and said, "Of course."

He sat and took in the incredible sight before him. "Wow," he said under his breath.

Binta studied the young man, understanding his enchantment with the pond. She watched him from the corner of her eye, enjoying his reaction and welcoming his companionship. He was a lovely boy, and she would miss him when she returned to Victoria's school. Most of his family worked at the castle; she had learned that his mother and father were official cooks, part of a team of several dozen men and women. As Sammy pointed out, they were the most trusted people in the castle, and he would beam with pride every time he told her. She agreed with that statement and knew he was just as trustworthy as the royal couple had deemed his parents.

"So, did you kiss Stef yet?" Binta blurted out.

"No!" he responded, and his face became flushed.

Stef was his crush, working as a laundry maid in the castle. Binta had never met her but had heard a lot about her during her time at the cottage, through Sammy, and she enjoyed giving him grief over it.

"Please do not do that," he whispered.

"Do what?"

"Talk about her," he said excitedly.

"You talk about her," she replied, feigning confusion.

"Yes, when I am ready, and only about things I want to discuss. Kissing is not one of them."

"Kissing?" came a stern voice from behind them.

Sammy jumped up, and Binta thought he might faint at first, but he considerably relaxed when he saw Binta's parents approaching from their walk.

"Mr. and Mrs. Mulay, it's a nice evening for a walk," he said, trying to change the subject.

"And kissing?" her mother asked.

Sammy's face turned red, and he shuffled his feet. "I—"

"Said cooking," Binta interrupted. "Cooking, Mother and Father, not kissing."

"Oh," her father said with a smile and a wink to Binta so Sammy did not see.

"Yes, that's right. My parents made you something delicious: a pot pie and a cake. I put them in the cottage, along with some fresh fruits and vegetables," Sammy rambled, changing the subject.

"Very well, Sammy. Your parents have fed us well, so please thank them for us," her father said, patting the boy on the shoulder.

They moved off hand in hand toward the cottage. "Come along soon for dinner, Binta," Deb said over her shoulder.

"I'll be there shortly," Binta promised as Sammy retook his seat.

"I'm sorry, Sammy," Binta said warmly.

Sammy waved it off like it was no big deal and said excitedly, "I have news!"

"More stirrings in the castle?" Binta asked, becoming more serious.

For the last month, there had been a hushed excitement within the castle walls. The servants did not know anything in particular, but they could all sense a nervousness about the guards, and the royal couple seemed worried and distracted. Binta and Sammy had discussed things and had speculated what the fuss could be about, but to no avail.

"No, nothing has changed there. However, I believe there are positions available for two dishwashers within the kitchen. My parents will put in a good word for your parents."

"That is great news, Sammy! When I return to the school in a few weeks, they must leave the cottage. I'd hate for them to leave the city; I have grown accustomed to them being about."

"Don't say anything to them yet. I hope I will know something in a few days." The young man stood and added, "Well, I should be going, or they will wonder why my chores are incomplete."

"Of course. I will talk to you soon?"

"Soon," Sammy agreed with a nod and a smile.

He hurried off, leaving Binta alone. Her parents were inside the cottage by then, and the sun was beginning to set. Her smile slowly faded as she became lost in thought. Nights were the hardest because Greyson was not there to keep her warm, and they always reminded her of Cassandra because of their late study sessions in Cassandra's room. Also, Cedric, the disciple of Kane, had given Cassandra a magical cottage that was always dark and cozy. She had spent time with Cassandra and Greyson in the enchanted cottage as well. The nights were the hardest. She took a steadying breath, then followed her parents inside.

FRANKLIN RUBEN SAT AT A LARGE TABLE IN ONE OF THE THREE WAREhouses he owned in Pelesea. He was the father of Cass, Binta's tormentor, and one of the wealthier citizens of the great city, making his fortune via a grand fleet of cargo ships. His sturdy ships navigated the Sea of Nepress better than any other local merchants', making his enterprise very profitable with runs to and from Illid and even the wild lands of Varish. As was the custom, he was in the biggest, most comfortable warehouse after Cashmere, the boat named after his estranged daughter, had made a particularly hazardous run to the rough southern waters of Varish.

He sat at the head of the table, a blank expression on his face as the captain made his way into the warehouse, followed by half a dozen men carrying several large chests. Griswin, a crusty old wizard from the city's south side, where laws were sometimes not followed particularly well, joined Franklin. He was greedy and despicable but loyal to Franklin and could be trusted to appraise items Franklin's vessels found. Franklin trusted him because he paid him well and supplied his shop with many unusual trinkets and spell components, such as scarce herbs and mushrooms found only in Varish. Griswin was also spineless and feared Franklin and his prominence in the city. The greedy wizard licked his lips and watched in anticipation as the bauble-filled chests came closer.

On the other side of Franklin, and as far away from the unpredictable Griswin as possible, sat Jamison Oland. Jamison was one of the top ten wealthiest men in the city, a long-time friend of Franklin, and Binta's rescuer. He appreciated the finer things in life, from boats, food, liquor, and clothing to collectible items and magical devices. That was why Franklin had invited him to be witness to one of the most profitable hauls *Cashmere* had ever made. For once, Jamison was as eager as the fool Griswin and prepared to pay substantial gold if he found something he liked.

The captain handed over the ship's log and packing slips as his men hauled the chests and sat them on the table. Franklin handed the packing slips to Griswin, who took them and eagerly began scanning for items he might want to examine. Franklin set the logbook down without even opening it.

"And?" he asked the captain absently.

"Well, sir, we had a fine voyage. Six months at sea and nearly a full crew returned," the captain answered.

Franklin was distant and had been since the loss of his daughter. King Kringus had expelled her from the city months earlier when winter was harshest. Jamison had been indirectly responsible for that course of action. As was typical for him, he collected rare and beautiful women as much as any other luxuries life offered. When Cass had made him the offer of sexual pleasures in exchange for gold, Jamison had playfully taken her up on her offer, thinking it some strange joke. In the end, he had inadvertently discovered Cass was prostituting Binta at Poppy's Inn on the south side of the city. Jamison immediately fell for the exotic young woman. Binta was the most passionate woman he had slept with; she was young and full of sexual energy. He had become smitten that first night and had returned several more times to partake of Binta's incredible body. Their relationship had solidified into a routine, but Jamison became jealous of Binta's many other lovers. Soon after, he made his discovery known to Kringus, who had Cass arrested. Franklin did not know this part of the story; if he did, Jamison probably would not have been invited, and he would not have been allowed anywhere near Franklin again.

"Yes!" Griswin exclaimed suddenly, holding up one of the parchments. "Show me this one!" he said, waving it around.

The captain took it, and the old wizard pointed to the item he was curious about. The captain nodded to one of the men, who took it and began searching the chests for the item as the wizard looked on, rubbing his hands together.

"What could possibly be so exciting, Griswin?" Franklin asked with more than a bit of annoyance in his voice.

"You'll see!" was all the response he received.

Franklin gave a derisive snort and poked a thumb at the strange wizard. "You know, Jamison, Cass used to get this excited over magical items when she was younger."

"Yes, I've heard her tell stories of some of your finds."

Franklin chuckled and said, "I think she took a few pieces before I could have them inventoried and sold. I always turned my back on those indiscretions because she was far more valuable to me than any item."

Jamison nodded, letting the man talk about Cass and hopefully heal the fresh wound of losing her. It wasn't long before the talk turned to the ill-fated adventure concerning the hidden place Franklin called the cursed caves. Last fall, Cass and four others had adventured to the magical and dangerous catacombs. Jamison knew Binta had been part of that group and he had expected Franklin's anger in his delicate emotional condition to fall on Binta eventually.

"She stole some things from that fool Cassandra Rho, I believe. Powerful trinkets!" Franklin said with a chuckle.

"The one that died in the tragic fire?"

"Tragic? I only wish that I had set her ablaze. She deserved her fate, I say!" Franklin said, pounding a fist on the table, startling the men. They all stopped their search and looked to Franklin, who waved them back to their work.

"Five went on that expedition, four kids led by some damn fool priest that Cassandra Rho had dug up from the bowels of that cursed temple. I hear he died a horrible death out there, killed by bloodthirsty goblins. A fate I would not wish on anyone unless they were responsible for harming my Cass. Anyway, the four kids came back, all cursed."

Franklin counted on his fingers as he named each one. "Cass was near death, and to be honest, her true self died during that damned trip. The curse of that place changed her personality into an ungrateful, evil person. As you know, she took that out on the idiot, Binta Mulay, making the girl suffer for the evil done to her. I can't begrudge my daughter that.

"Cassandra Rho died in that fire; again, a well-deserved death. It is rumored Greyson Kavince is dead, having lost his wits and run straight over to Varish to die alongside his brethren. Binta Mulay is cursed in a way that is not as obvious. I hear the little whore was in love with both Cassandra and Greyson. Now, with them both dead, I hear she is quite daft."

Jamison bristled at that comment, having heard the ignorant words before from his dear friend. He hoped that as time passed, Franklin would forget Binta, but he was beginning to wonder if she would be the focal point of his ire since she was the only one remaining he could blame. Binta had been unreachable within the castle walls for the last few months. Jamison longed to see her and knew that he would soon, for he had learned she would attend the school of magic once more. He needed a way to win her heart, so he planned to shower her with gifts that only a young student of magic would truly appreciate. That was why he was there.

One of the men produced a hefty tome from the chest and laid it on the table. Griswin knocked the man out of the way before he could move. He silently cast a spell of detection and waved his hand over the tome, waiting as the spell took hold. His eyes widened, and a frown formed on his face. "This is not it, you fool!" he yelled at the sailor.

Griswin moved the tome gently to the side and shooed the other men away. He eagerly began the search himself. The others looked on as the wizard rummaged through the chests, neatly making stacks of jewels, gems, and coins on the table. Finally, he gasped and stopped, seeming to freeze in time. He slowly reached both hands into the chest and took out what looked to be an ancient book. Its yellowed pages stuck out from the worn leather cover and remained barely intact. The wizard laid it gently on the table beside the other baubles.

"What is it, Griswin?" Franklin asked.

Jamison stood to look at the item, and Franklin leaned over to see it better. The book looked like any other old tome and appeared to be nothing special.

"This, my lord, is the personal journal of the great wizard X'lor," Griswin said with a big smile.

Jamison had heard of the legendary wizard and had even obtained one of the quills the great man used to pen his spells. He did not know much about him, but he was rumored to be extremely powerful. Still, he immediately wanted the book for his collection, in particular, to impress Binta with it.

"Who is X'lor?" Franklin asked with a frown.

Jamison nearly chuckled as the wizard's eyes flew open in shock as if everyone should know the grand wizard X'lor. "He is the greatest wizard of all time!"

"So, what does this book do?"

"Nothing magical, I'm afraid; it is probably just filled with his notes and potential spells, but it is worth its weight in gold. It is far more valuable than I can afford, so I'm afraid I cannot purchase this wonderful item. However, if it pleases you, I can purchase a peek inside."

"How much?"

Griswin thought about it momentarily and said, "I can offer five thousand gold."

"For the book? That is amazing," Franklin said with the first genuine smile that had crept across his face in some time.

"No," Griswin said, his face wrinkled in confusion. "No, my lord, for a peek inside. The book will fetch ten times that."

"You want a look inside this old journal, and you'll pay five thousand gold to do so?" Franklin asked suspiciously.

"Absolutely."

"Deal, my friend."

A large smile widened on the crazed wizard's face, and he picked up the book and rubbed the old cover as if caressing a fragile vase or original painting.

"Why pay so much for a look inside?" Jamison asked.

"You wouldn't understand," Griswin said a bit defensively.

"Try me."

"Because legends say that only the most worthy of wizards can mentally observe the notes of X'lor. Those with weaker minds cannot take the view for more than a few seconds. It is a test of one's prowess. To be a wizard and to have looked upon the work of X'lor is to gain the favor of the gods of magic. It is a rare and wonderful opportunity."

"Then please awe us with your prowess." Franklin waved toward the unusual journal.

"But I have not paid yet, my lord."

"I trust you, Griswin; pay me after."

The wizard smiled and laid the tome on the table as the captain and crew gathered to watch. Griswin licked his lips in anticipation and looked around nervously. He cast a silent spell, waved his hand over the book, and then looked to Franklin, who nodded. The wizard returned the nod and slowly opened the book.

His eyes widened even further as he looked on, and a smile slowly grew on his face. Jamison knew better than to look directly at the book and held Franklin back when his friend began to stand to take a peek. A crewman was not so fortunate, and when he looked at the pages, he froze in place as if in a trance. His mouth dropped, and his chin seemed to elongate. The captain and remaining crew stepped back as the man's eyes began to smoke. Jamison and Franklin understood the danger, and they slowly walked back from the table, their eyes fixed on the crewman and the wizard, each fighting their own battle with the book.

The sailor let out a little scream for just a moment before he collapsed on the floor, smoke still wafting from his eyes. Griswin seemed not to notice anything as his eyes widened somehow further. His bottom lip quivered, and he let out a small moan that started low and slowly rose in pitch. He stayed that way for a long while until his hair began to turn white on the ends. He eventually closed the book with shaking hands. His eyes were impossibly large, with tears running freely down his cheeks. His hair had turned grey and brittle, and a weird smile stayed plastered on his face.

"Griswin?" Franklin asked, but the wizard did not respond.

"Wizard, can you hear me?" Franklin repeated.

The man eventually turned to regard Franklin and said, "Sey, I ma enif." He walked over to his seat at the table and took up the glass of water he had been sipping from. He wetted his fingers, then flicked the water into his drying eyes, which would never close again. He stood there briefly as the others looked on, occasionally splashing water into his wide eyes.

Franklin approached the table again and asked, "Griswin, your eyes?"

The wizard turned to him and said, "Tahw, I leef taerg."

"What?" Franklin asked.

The wizard took his water and left the room, and no one ever saw him again.

After he left, everyone was silent for a long while, and no one would go near the book. Eventually, Jamison went to it and gently locked the cover clasp.

He looked at Franklin and whispered, "I've got thirty thousand gold with me."

"Sold," Franklin said.

A Lady of Pelesea

T HE NEW ORDER MET IN THE LARGE BANQUET HALL IN THE castle of Pelesea for the third straight day, trying to come to terms with the details of the prophecy as it had been told to them by Inuentas, the half-demon messenger. In attendance were Kringus and Penelope Brahmore, the king and queen of Pelesea; Daro, the ranger from the southern woods; Victoria, master wizard and owner of Pelesea's only school of magic; and Arrin Malik, captain of Pelesea's army. Three New Order members were absent: Alleah Mansuell, high priestess of Sinnis, and Von and Lenore, the elven brothers of Nessor. Von and Lenore were on a diplomatic mission to Nessor and would not return until the end of summer, six months away. Alleah's absence was more problematic, for she had ventured to the harsh continent of Varish in search of answers to questions that the New Order now understood were more severe than any had imagined. Alleah had been correct in thinking that the evil activity was not just random acts of violence but part of the very prophecy they now discussed. Her suspicions had been accurate, and the group now wondered if it had cost them her life. Inuentas was also in attendance at the invitation of the king and queen. He sat at the end of the table, as he had the previous two days, ready to receive the multitude of questions the New Order might have.

Kringus brought the meeting to order by standing and clearing his throat. "Friends, we meet once more to finalize our plans to address the claims of our guest, Inuentas," he said.

Inuentas nodded his understanding. The half-demon sat comfortably; thus far, the friends had detected no lies concerning his tale. Kringus understood by looking at the creature that he was telling the truth. He had suffered a significant deception long ago and knew the telltale signs of someone who was not being honest. He didn't trust the half-demon, but he could find no reason to doubt his word. Kringus looked upon Inuentas, understanding that some might interpret his mannerisms as arrogance. He considered the man confident, not arrogant or untruthful, which bothered him the most about the creature. Inuentas knew they would not catch him in a lie because there was no lie.

Kringus continued, "And so we have called for our elven friends, Von and Lenore, from the northern city of Nessor, and they will arrive by summer's end. Upon their arrival, we will search out Alleah, and when she is once again by our side, Inuentas, the New Order will be whole once more and ready to move against this priestess named Matilda you have told us about."

Inuentas only sat silently, but Kringus could tell he disagreed with his words. After a short pause, Kringus continued, "Lady Victoria, have you been able to research and verify the story our guest has provided?"

Victoria stood and nodded to the king. "Yes, Kringus, I feel he is telling the truth."

Kringus noticed Inuentas's slight nod at her proclamation but remained silent. "So, you have found proof of this prophecy?" he pressed.

"We have found proof that a prophecy may exist but cannot confirm all of the details—"

"And you will not, my dear lady, without journeying to hell and asking Nezeratu himself," Inuentas interrupted.

The half-demon stood then, his tail wagging menacingly behind him. Kringus didn't like the creature much, but the queen was tolerant of all races, even those from the bowels of hell, and he respected that. However, that tail, the half-demon's black, pupilless eyes, and the tiny horns protruding from his forehead all unnerved the king. The worst was the man's shoes, supposedly made from human skin. Under normal circumstances, Kringus would never allow such an atrocity in his castle, and if they found the creature a liar, he would throw him out personally.

Inuentas turned his attention to Kringus and said, "And, Kringus, be advised, even when the elves return, and if you do find your missing friend, the New Order will not be complete."

"We've been through this before, demon; we are eight," Kringus said, his neck muscles flexing.

Inuentas bowed deeply and exaggeratedly, saying, "Don't kill the messenger, dear king, for I have told you repeatedly that the New Order must contain twelve members."

"We have never contained twelve," Penelope intervened before Kringus could lose control.

"Penelope, please understand the original New Order contained twelve members, and to fulfill the prophecy, yours must as well," Inuentas replied with a smile and a gleam in his eye.

Kringus did not like how Inuentas looked at his wife; his gaze showed a hint of recognition. He had witnessed it several times over the last few days, and although his patience was wearing thin with the presence of the strange creature, familiarity with his wife would eventually put his anger at a dangerous level.

"So, we are supposed to invite just anyone to join our cause so that we will have twelve members?" Kringus asked with more than a hint of anger in his voice.

"No, King, you are supposed to recruit people you can trust with your life," Inuentas countered, his tail suddenly becoming more agitated.

The two stared at each other silently, Inuentas matching Kringus's stare with equal intensity. Penelope put a gentle hand on Kringus's arm and was about to speak, but before she could say anything to defuse the situation, Daro said, "Sasha."

All turned to the ranger, who ignored them and continued to eat his breakfast. A smile crept across the half-demon's face, breaking the staredown with Kringus, and he nodded his agreement. "That is the first good idea this group has had since I've been here," Inuentas said.

"Who is Sasha?" Kringus asked.

"Who indeed," Inuentas said, flashing Daro a giant smile and retaking his seat.

Daro slowly looked up from his food to see all eyes on him. He wiped his mouth and said, "Sasha is a new friend, Kringus. I accompanied her to the catacombs beneath Novafontera to battle the demon there. She is skilled with a sword beyond most I have seen."

"Especially the one she now carries," Inuentas added.

"So, a ninth member?" Penelope asked.

"I would recommend her above anyone I know who is not already a member," Daro said.

"I have seen her in action, and I agree with the ranger; she would be a good addition," Inuentas confirmed.

"So, that would give us nine, and if Daro and Inuentas endorse her, I will allow her membership without even meeting her. So, where is she?" Kringus said.

"Well, that is a bit of an issue," Daro said.

When no one said anything and all eyes remained on him, he put his fork down and continued with a sigh, "She went home."

"Where is that, Daro?" Kringus asked impatiently.

"She returned home through the waterfall at Wolf's Crest."

"Wolf's Crest?" Penelope asked.

"Yes, a place in my woods where I first met her. She came from a different world through a portal, yet I am unsure how. She has returned home to rescue her mother," Daro explained.

"Great. So, we have another potential member, but do we need to find her also? This process is madness, Inuentas! By the time we gather everyone and add three more members, the time of the sacrifice will be upon us. What exactly do you propose we do?" Kringus asked.

"It is not my concern; I am only here to clean up the mess if the New Order fails to stop the summoning," Inuentas said, patting the hilt of the sword strapped to his waist.

Kringus had already heard the tale and understood that the half-demon's weapon was powerful. Inuentas had not told them much about it other than that it was attuned to the life essence of Marnelphion to banish him back to hell if needed. Inuentas was the required executioner, ready to fix the problem if Kringus and the New Order couldn't prevent the summoning. The whole thing seemed impossible, and Kringus was losing his patience.

"According to the prophecy, the New Order, consisting of twelve members, as the Order of old, must stop the sacrifice. There is no need to bring forth your army, and to do so will devastate your city," Inuentas explained.

"So you've explained to us," Kringus said. "And you expect twelve heroes to infiltrate a fortress of evil priests to stop this? How can we possibly go forth on your word without a supporting army?"

"Because to bring an army will be suicide," Victoria answered for the half-demon.

Kringus locked stares with Victoria, and he knew she was telling the truth. She had confirmed most of what Inuentas had told them already. With a sigh and a shake of his head, he said, "So, what is our next step?"

"We fill the New Order," Penelope said.

"Very well, so we find this Sasha person. Who else do we invite for membership?" Kringus asked.

"Baxter," Victoria answered immediately.

Kringus nodded his agreement. "That makes ten; who else?"

"Sheriff Max of Oldorburg," Arrin suggested. "He is young but carries himself well and can use a sword."

"He seemed inadequate the last time I faced him. Is he truly qualified to join in such a dangerous endeavor?" Kringus asked.

"I spent the winter in Oldorburg and can vouch for the man's heart. His skills with a sword may not be as advanced as some, but his heart is the size of a lion's."

"He will join us?"

"If we ask, I feel certain he will join."

"I trust your judgment on this, Arrin, as I have since I've known you. That makes eleven, so who will be our final choice?" Kringus asked.

"How about Greyson Kavince?" Penelope suggested.

"He is but a child."

"A prodigy," Victoria added.

Kringus was vaguely aware that both women in the group were quick to nominate and endorse the charming young man. The thought passed as quickly as it came, and Kringus nodded in agreement. "Very well; when we find Alleah, we'll invite Greyson to join us. That makes twelve."

The group sat silently for a while, and Kringus's attention fell on the half-demon again. He seemed arrogant to the king, yet he had only passed along the information he knew. Kringus's attention went to the sword strapped to Inuentas's hip and he understood the source of the creature's confidence. Something intangible about that sword made Kringus very nervous. After a few moments, Kringus noticed the half-demon looking at him with a sly smile. When they made eye contact, Inuentas offered a wink.

LATER THAT EVENING, KRINGUS AND PENELOPE PRIVATELY MET WITH Arrin in a study high in the castle proper. They had shared many private meetings over the last few days, discussing the most troublesome news that Inuentas had brought them.

"So, all of us agree on the potential new members?" Kringus asked.

"I feel good about the selections, my king, given my knowledge of the potentials," Arrin said.

"What if we go to find Alleah and Greyson, and they are lost to us?" Penelope asked.

"Lost?" Kringus asked.

"Yes, if they are truly gone or we cannot find them, we need a contingency plan. How long do we search, and where do we search? If they are gone, we will be missing two of the required twelve members."

"What constitutes membership, then?" Kringus asked. "A simple invitation and acceptance?"

"I believe so. What are you getting at, my husband?"

"We take alternates with us, knights of Pelesea's army, to accept membership if required," Kringus reasoned. Then, with an exasperated sigh, he added, "If any of this makes any sense, that is."

Penelope kissed him gently on the cheek. "It is hard to grasp, but the half-demon speaks the truth. Victoria and I have confirmed the prophecy. Well, as best we can."

Kringus smiled and looked deeply into Penelope's eyes. The love and support he found there were overwhelming. He was glad at that moment to have such a strong and loving friend as his queen. "I know. And I believe Inuentas, as far-fetched as the notion of twelve people going into a foreign land and invading a fortified mountain stronghold guarded by a multitude of evil warriors and priests is."

"Now, Kringus, you know you have an adventurer's heart, and you prefer the road to sitting here in the castle playing politics," Penelope teased with a smile.

Kringus could not help but smile, and he kissed her lips. They hugged, and as Kringus looked over his wife's shoulder, he made eye contact with Arrin, who was already heading for the door. His captain and good friend nodded and smiled, then quickly exited the study. Kringus slowly undressed Penelope, and they spent the remainder of the night making love and sleeping in front of the fireplace. Kringus's mind was wholly on his beautiful half-elven wife during their lovemaking. However, during the periods between their lovemaking that night, he worried about the world's future. After all, what difference could twelve people really make?

MATILDA STOOD ON THE NEWLY CONSTRUCTED LEDGE NEAR THE TOP of Nesin's rock fortress. She looked to the north, the destination of the priestess and her gathering entourage. Matilda thought deeply and closed her eyes as the warm spring sun washed over her. She knew now that they would find Cassandra; she only hoped the filthy offspring of Kane would still have her virginity intact. The priestess doubted that was possible in the company of the savage barbarians to the north, but her prayers had indicated otherwise. She believed Cassandra was alive and well and still a virgin.

She meditated on her prey again, opening her mind and focusing on her goal. It was difficult during the daytime, as her god, the demon lord, Marnelphion, gave her the most influential powers at night. During the day, those powers waned, but she still received positive assurance during the minor communion. She had nearly died when she had made her unholy journey to Novafontera over half a year ago. She had stood at the gates of hell, previewing her afterlife, where the demon Vasheba promised eternal pain. However, Marnelphion had deemed her worthy of leading this sacrifice and had breathed life back into her lungs. He had sent her back from the land of the dead and, in doing so, had transferred a touch of his essence into her soul. The boiling tar of Novafontera had seeped into her body, giving her powers no other mortal had ever received from the demon lord. Those powers allowed her to sense Cassandra's condition, and she was still alive. She was somehow still a virgin, and Matilda would need to act fast to capture her and bring her to Nesin.

She believed her new allies, Cass Ruben and Ronnis D'Breeth, had been gifts from her god. They were beacons in the world, helping her to reach her goal. The hate they had for Cassandra was uncontested and pleased her god. Both Cass and Ronnis wanted her dead and would assist Matilda in making sure it happened. She had captured Cassandra's sister, Kessi, tricking the vampire lord, Heinsvick, into turning her over for sacrificing. Unfortunately, the vampire had told her it was Cassandra, and she had believed him.

Matilda had panicked after learning the truth of that deception, understanding the trail to Cassandra was probably lost. Now, Marnelphion renewed her hope by blessing her with her two new allies. At one point, Cass had obtained a fabulous magical necklace attuned to Cassandra's life force. The magic had significantly faded, but Matilda had used one of the most potent abilities offered to her by Marnelphion to have it slightly replenished. It had been just enough to find Cassandra's location. She had used Kessi's blood to reignite the magic in the necklace once more. It had not lasted long, but the necklace's power had given her the location. Cassandra Rho was in the Yaddaton Desert with the barbarians, and Matilda would finally catch her. Matilda had traveled the world searching for Cassandra, only for her to end up about four hundred miles from where the search began.

The priests, and especially Matilda, had studied and prayed about the barbarians since their return to Nesin. There were many tribes scattered across the large desert, which would normally make finding Cassandra impossibly difficult. However, from their research, they determined there were only five major tribes that would most likely have her, and only two that were known for venturing out of the desert for raids. Of those two, the Serpent Tribe was the only one that was known for venturing over the sea for their raids. Matilda did not know how the savages had learned to navigate the water, or where they kept their vessels, but after much prayer and research, she determined that the Serpent Tribe was where Cassandra had to be. Also, after performing the ritual with Kessi Rho, using her pure blood to rekindle the medallion linked to Cassandra, the device indicated she was at the southern tip of the Yaddaton, exactly where the Serpent

Tribe barbarians made their home. So, that was where they planned to start their search.

From her vantage point, she could not see the gathering army far below but could hear Cerus instructing his men on the pending march to Yaddaton. They would leave soon and were taking all the warriors of Gorl with them. She looked at the scroll in her hand and smiled. The trip would be much quicker than Cerus knew. The scroll was a final gift from Malikai, the wizard who lived at the edge of the great desert they were traveling to. Once read, the spell within the scroll would open up a rift straight to the outskirts of Malikai's stronghold. From there, the trip to the barbarians would be swift. She ran her fingers along the rolled scroll, thinking of her last night with the wizard. She had paid for the scroll on her back and had paid well.

In preparation for their journey to Yaddaton to claim Cassandra, Cerus had hired soldiers to watch over the prisoners in Nesin's jails. Matilda and Cerus had gathered many captives for the summoning, and they were entrusting their care to a group of mercenaries. Cerus believed in them, but Matilda had her doubts. She did not want to lose her collection of sacrificial fodder. In addition to Cassandra, they would need 665 other sacrifices to summon Marnelphion. Kessi was one of over three hundred captives currently held in the prisons of Nesin, including three dozen women detained in her cell, which Matilda accurately believed to be virgins, and therefore powerful sacrifices. The mercenaries were only fifty-strong, but Cerus assured her the men could easily watch things while they retrieved Cassandra. Matilda would only leave one priest behind, one strong enough to control Emiline, Matilda's pet vampire, while they raided the barbarian lands.

Merrik was the second most potent priest in Nesin, next to Matilda, since Garyn had died at the hands of Greyson. She smiled at the thought of Greyson, the priest she had bedded on the night of the Harvest Festival in Attins. Their lovemaking had been thorough and passionate, and the young man was by far the most incredible lover she had ever experienced. Unfortunately, when Cerus and his men had invaded Attins and Tara the following day, the young priest declined to join their cause, and Matilda sentenced him to death.

Cerus had been enraged when he had learned of her indiscretion and had taken out his wrath on the young man, killing him in the temple of Plath in Tara. However, Cerus now believed Greyson to still be alive, claiming to have spotted him just outside the port city of Racip just east of their location. Her smile widened at the thought of one day possibly bedding Cerus and Greyson together. Greyson's survival of the ordeal at Tara, when he appeared to be burned alive in the temple, was a testament to his cunning and priestly powers. She secretly hoped that she could reunite with the young man soon. But for now, she had to focus on Cassandra, find her prize, and only then pursue her pleasure.

The men below erupted in cheers, and Matilda knew that Cerus had just finished his speech, one to motivate them for conquest. Warriors of Gorl did not need motivation, of course, and they would have to use their combat skills and more than a bit of cunning if they hoped to overtake the barbarians. This invasion would not be as simple as the one of Attins, when they had massacred or captured the defenseless citizens of that small town.

"My lady," came a voice from behind.

She turned to regard Merrik entering the newly constructed balcony. He looked the part of a priest of Marnelphion, with a shaved head and the dark robes of her god. "Yes, Merrik?"

"The priests have gathered, and the warriors of Gorl are ready. It is time to begin your conquest for Kane's spawn," he said with a bow.

The priests of Marnelphion totaled thirteen, and all but Merrik would make the journey. Matilda knew they needed all the priestly powers they could muster to ensure the quest was successful, but Merrik would stay and watch over things for her. She trusted his powers and ability to control Emiline and watch over the mercenaries.

"My lady, are you sure it is wise for me to remain behind?"

"Do you doubt my judgment, Merrik?"

"Of course not, but we will need—"

"No, we need you here. You are Emiline's caretaker in my absence. You have a rapport with her that none of the other priests do. I need you to stay here and watch over the prisoners."

"And Emiline?"

"Of course. And the vampire will be your greatest ally if something does happen. Deploy her at will and protect the prisoners at all costs."

"As you wish, my lady," Merrik said with a deep bow.

Matilda made her way through the mountain fortress and eventually approached the gathered crowd at Nesin's entrance. A fine horse waited for her there, as did the other priests, all mounted on their steeds and ready to travel. There was a giant war horse for Cerus, but it remained unsaddled as Cerus continued to address his men.

Cass and Ronnis waited nearby, next to their steeds. The warriors of Gorl, nearly three hundred strong, would all make the journey on foot. They formed up, and Cerus approached Matilda with a giant smile.

"Are you ready for the greatest conquest we have experienced thus far in our grand scheme?" he asked her.

"More than ready; I have chased the brat, Cassandra, across the world and back and want nothing more than to put her in a cage."

"And I am anxious to begin her tortures as you have promised," Cass added, walking her horse up to the couple.

Matilda turned toward the all-too-anxious and careless woman. No, not a woman, more of a girl, no more than nineteen. Matilda liked the idea of letting Cass administer the many tortures she had planned for Cassandra, but she would have to be on guard to ensure Cass wouldn't kill her most precious prize. She would be good on her word and allow Cass her fun because, without her help, Matilda would have never found Cassandra. She owed her and would see it through. However, if Cass couldn't control herself and became too aggressive with her fun, Matilda would have to put a stop to it. That was a concern for later. For now, she needed Cass and her unignorable powers.

So, she smiled and said, "Of course."

"Then let us go," Cerus said, mounting his horse.

He looked the part of the complete warrior, his toned muscles cording as he mounted the beast. Matilda noticed the appreciative stare that Cass gave him and understood she would have to let Cerus have his playtime with Cass soon. She would allow it, but she could not deny the jealousy she felt over the much younger and exotic-looking beauty Cass indeed was. She made her way to the front of the expedition, unrolling the scroll as she did.

"What are you doing?" Cerus asked.

"Making our journey a lot easier," Matilda replied.

"What magic are you enacting?"

"A gift from Malikai, one that will allow us to traverse hundreds of miles instantly."

"Malikai? We do not need his help!" Cerus bristled.

"Contrary, my husband, we need this help, and I intend to take it." Matilda completed unrolling the scroll. Before she read it, she looked back to Cerus, whose face was now flush with anger, and added, "Besides, I paid handsomely for this, and we wouldn't want that effort to go to waste, would we?"

The proud Gorl warrior said nothing and watched Matilda enact the magic on the scroll. The parchment disintegrated upon reading, but behind Matilda, a shimmer in the air started as a subtle wave and soon became an opening large enough for the small army to march through. Cerus looked on with disdain as Malikai's stronghold came into view. The portal would put them all within a few hundred yards of the wizard's front door.

Matilda mounted her horse, cantered beside her husband, and said, "Shall we?"

Cerus did not look at her and instead kept his eyes on the stronghold of the wizard he desired to kill. A hard swallow was the only response she elicited from him.

"Come now, don't be that way. I'll let you play with Cass as we travel. Will that appease you?"

He turned to regard Cass, who smiled mischievously. She had not heard Matilda's words, but to Cerus, Cass would be a just reward for the embarrassment he had suffered at the hands of Malikai. He nodded at his wife and said, "Let us be on our way."

The procession of priests and warriors made their way through the gate, taking a giant step toward capturing Cassandra Rho.

BINTA ONCE AGAIN SAT ON THE BENCH NEAR THE POND AT THE SMALL cottage. The view of the pond and the smell of Penelope's garden were terrific, as exotic flowers continued their blooming in the early weeks of spring as winter finally melted away. If what Sammy told her was true, Binta's parents would hopefully secure jobs within the castle soon. For the first time in many months, Binta was content.

She basked in the warmth of the evening sun, and she closed her eyes, imagining the next semester of school. She would return soon, and she could concentrate on her studies again. With Cassandra's death and Greyson sailing out of her life, things had been hard. She had come to terms with both events, and there would always be a special place in her heart for both of them. A sudden hand on her shoulder had her sitting straight and her eyes flying open.

"Sorry, I did not mean to startle you," a man said.

He was a little older than Binta and was a nice-looking yet rugged man. She had never seen him before, and the stern visage he wore spoke volumes.

She stood and said, "That's all right; I just didn't hear you approach."

"Of course not; if you had, I wouldn't be a very good ranger, now would I?"

"Ranger?"

"I am Daro, Keeper of the Woods south of here," he said with a bow. When he rose, he added, "Perhaps you've heard of Daro's Woods?"

"No."

"Fair enough. But now you know me, and I can only assume you are Binta Mulay?"

"Yes, why?" Binta asked, a little nervous at the fact he knew her name.

"I am here to inform you that I am moving into the cottage soon."

"When?" Binta asked nervously.

"When do you start school?"

"In a few weeks."

"Then."

"Why are you here now?"

"To be honest, I wanted to meet you. Kringus has told me a lot about you."

Binta's heart raced, and she said, "The king has spoken of me?"

"Yes, often. Kringus has allowed you to stay in my cottage due to your unique situation, correct?"

Binta was at a loss for words. Obviously, this man was important to the king and queen and spoke with them often. Why would he come to the gardens to talk to her?

She finally whispered, "Yes, I guess that makes sense. I am grateful for the king's hospitality and will leave the cottage soon enough. Thank you for letting me stay; I did not know you needed it."

"Unfortunately, circumstances have changed, and my stay in Pelesea has been extended indefinitely, so I will need the cottage when you have moved out. I just came to check on the status of it and my pond," he said with his arms extended to the incredible scenery around them.

"You think I would deface either?" Binta asked curiously.

"I trust the king's judgment but like to assure myself on such matters," the ranger said with a smile.

Binta smiled and nodded, taking in the beauty of the garden. "I understand that."

"Good, I will need my rest before …" Daro started but trailed off as if catching himself before telling her something secret.

He smiled and nodded, then turned to leave. His actions puzzled Binta, so she grabbed his arm as he turned. He looked at her hand, now on his arm, then made eye contact. She understood that perhaps this man did not like to be touched, but the annoyance that flashed across his face was short-lived. She released his arm.

"Sorry, but you can't say something like that and walk away."

"Is that so?"

"Yes, please explain your words," she said, not backing down.

At first, he stood there, expressionless, but eventually, he smiled when she just returned the blank stare. "You are a unique young lady living in a troubled world, Binta Mulay. Stay true to yourself for the sake of humanity. People like you are why the New Order exists and why Kringus so easily lets you stay on the castle grounds. The world is changing, so stay strong."

He stared at her again, but it appeared to Binta that he was looking through her as if his mind were elsewhere. "Perhaps in another lifetime, things will not be as complex, but not for people like us," he added.

He turned to walk away once more, and she moved to stand in front of him. "Wait. I want to know what you mean. The world is changing? You said you need rest? What is the New Order planning?" she asked rapidly.

Finally, he sighed and said, "Look, I am not supposed to tell you, but the New Order is looking for new members. Kringus will announce it soon enough, so I guess it's all right for you to know."

"New members? For what?"

"Sorry, I can't say anything else, but you will hear soon enough. Just wait for the king's announcement. And if you say anything to anyone about this, it will not be good for either of us."

"You are serious, aren't you? This doesn't sound good, Daro from the south. Should I be concerned?" Binta asked, nearing a panic.

She had just come to terms with losing Cassandra and Greyson, and now the ranger was forecasting that the New Order was dealing with something terrible on a grander scale. She didn't know much about the New Order but understood that the king and queen were members, as well as Lady Victoria. Her heart sank at the news, and she wished the ranger had never approached her. A few moments ago, she was blissfully unaware of any world issues. Now, she felt herself slipping back into the despair that had had such a firm grip on her months ago. That feeling brought a tingle to her loins, and the thought of wanting Cass back in her life flashed through her mind briefly.

Daro's voice interrupted her thoughts. "Are you all right? I did not mean to scare you."

She looked into his eyes but could not respond, her sudden feeling of loss and despair quickly slipping back into her mind and finding a place to nest. He grabbed her and said, "Listen, you'll be fine. Continue with your life at the school and take care of yourself. The world is a good place, and the New Order is proof of that. Kringus and Penelope have given you a second chance at life; do not waste it."

With a sincere smile, he turned and left, and she let him go this time. Binta's mind raced with all the new information she had just received from the ranger. She slowly sat on the bench and stared across the small pond at the setting sun, which usually gave her such joy. However, she didn't see it. She dearly missed Cassandra and Greyson suddenly. She sat there a while until the sun had fully set. She did not break down and cry until it was dark.

She returned home after sitting on that bench for many more hours. Her parents were worried about her but were relieved when she finally arrived at the cottage. She did not explain other than to say she had been walking. Her mind was suddenly jumbled, and she skipped dinner, offering her parents the excuse that she was not feeling well. She fell asleep almost immediately, and her dreams were very troubled that night.

BINTA AWAKENED WITH A START AND SAT UP IN HER BED. AS SHE reoriented to her surroundings, she realized her mother sat on the edge of her bed with a concerned look.

"Binta, you were having a bad dream. Are you all right, my dear?" she asked.

Binta noticed that the sun shone through the window, and she knew it was late. Her mother wiped her matted hair from her face with a worried expression.

"What is it, Binta?"

"Nothing, Mother, just a bad dream," she lied.

"Very well. I woke you because it's late, and a man from the castle came to see you."

"Daro?"

"Who?" her mother asked.

"Daro, the ranger?"

"I don't know who that is, dear. The messenger did not give a name."

"Messenger?" Binta asked, her mind still foggy from sleep.

"Yes, a courier from the castle gate came and dropped off a parchment for you."

That got Binta's attention, and she rose and didn't bother dressing. She went to the kitchen in her gown to find the sealed parchment. It was lying on the table where her dad sat with a suspicious look. She wilted slightly under his gaze, thinking she might be in trouble with the king. She was evidently the subject of conversation with the royal couple, at least on some level. Then she remembered Daro's words to stay strong and be herself, and they steeled her resolve. She picked up the rolled scroll and studied the wax seal. It read "JO."

"Who is JO?" her father asked.

Binta thought about it and could not fathom who it could be. She wondered if Daro was sending her more cryptic messages, but it didn't make sense for him to do so.

"I'm not entirely sure," she said, still staring at the seal.

"Go ahead and open it, dear; it looks important," her mother said as she started breakfast.

Binta broke the seal and unrolled the paper. It was penned in fancy calligraphy:

Dearest Binta,

I hope you are well and that this letter finds you in good spirits. I hope your time of healing within the castle walls has been productive. I have thought of you constantly since last we met. Alas, the guards have denied me access to the castle grounds time and time again. I long to see you, my love, to hold you, to kiss you, to ravage you. Let me show you how much I genuinely care by taking you to the finest tavern in Pelesea. I will be at the castle gates this evening as the sun sets. I hope you will be there so I can show you how deep my love for you indeed runs.

Jamison Oland

Binta let the parchment roll back into shape and dropped it to the table. Jamison had been a regular for her during her brief time in servitude to Cass. He was responsible for freeing her from that life, and she wasn't sure she appreciated that in her current state of mind. Daro's warning from the previous night rang out in her head again. The world was changing, and Binta needed companionship. She needed Cassandra. She needed Greyson. She needed Cass. She would settle for Jamison.

SHE WAS NERVOUS ABOUT MEETING JAMISON. HER FEW DAYS AS A prostitute seemed like a lifetime ago, and she was still coming to terms with that brief time. She had blocked some of it from her memory, but after her talk with Daro the previous evening, she remembered more and more. Sadly, she was remembering it fondly. She had been a prisoner to Cass, who treated her as such. But hadn't it been Binta's choice to enter into that arrangement? Worse yet, hadn't she enjoyed it, at least on some level? She didn't understand that, but she had always had a submissive nature, and Cass knew how to bring it out of her. She decided to meet Jamison, even though he was part of the memories of that strange time in her life.

She was happy to see him when she exited the castle gates. He arrived in a fancy carriage and stood nearby as she walked out. His face lit up when he saw her, which sparked an emotion she had not felt in a few months. Was it lust? The memories of Jamison mounting her and his endurance came to the forefront of her mind. He had been her favorite customer and a great lover during her days of prostituting. Not as good as Greyson, but few men were, she reasoned.

The carriage ride was initially awkward, as they acted like a couple of teenagers on a first date. The setting was new to them; it wasn't just about the sex. Jamison was in his early thirties, more than ten years her senior. He was handsome enough and charming in his own way; however, he was not nearly as good-looking or as lovely as Greyson. He wore expensive clothing and had styling products in his hair and mustache. His cologne was slightly overbearing, and the fragrance brought her back to those days a few months earlier when he paid to ravage her. The memory flashed through her mind, and a bolt of electricity shot through her crotch. She chewed her lip, tried to cast the memories aside, and focused on the evening. However, she was losing her fight against her lustfulness.

The conversation eventually became easier for them as the carriage ride proceeded through the ritziest part of Pelesea. Jamison made her feel comfortable because he had a way about him. He was worldly and well-traveled; she remembered that from her time with him. She felt special in his presence, as if he cherished her. She had not experienced that before, other than with the promising relationship she could have had with Cassandra. She appreciated that quality in him.

He took her to a fine tavern called The Pegasus, and she felt underdressed and unworthy of being there. She was glad she had found the energy to bathe before their date but felt intimidated in the fancy place. Jamison made her feel beautiful and comfortable in her skin, dark makeup, nose ring, and all. Soon, they were talking and laughing like old friends. She tried lobster for the first time and loved it. He fed her a steady stream of special elvish wine imported straight from the mountains of Nessor. She wasn't much of a drinker, but she loved it. By the end of dinner, she remembered why she had always liked him. He was a sweet person who seemed to care for her genuinely.

As he helped her into the carriage to take her home, she felt dizzy from the wine and nearly toppled backward. He caught her and held her tight. He stood behind her, and his arms felt strong and his embrace warm.

He breathed into her ear, "I desire you, Binta. Come home with me."

"I… I… shouldn't," Binta's foggy mind protested.

He pulled her hair from her neck and kissed her nape gently. She felt that familiar sensation in her loins, and she leaned heavily on him. Her mind buzzed with an excitement she had not felt for months. She remembered sleeping with Jamison the first time and how it had been more than just sex to her. Unlike the others who paid Cass for Binta's services, he had been gentle yet passionate. He had returned regularly, and the sex was always great. Her inhibitions melted away, and she spared no thoughts for Cassandra or Greyson at that moment. It was all about Jamison and how he could please her.

"Yes," she whispered.

His strong arms guided her into the carriage, and he leaned out of the cab and told the driver to take them home and not to the castle. When he pulled himself back into the carriage, he removed his jacket. He fell over her in a passionate kiss. Binta melted and let his hands roam her body, quickly stripping her of her clothing. He had her naked and took her well before they reached his home. That was where they were comfortable; sex was the centerpiece of their relationship. Binta's climax was quick and powerful. They put themselves back together long enough to exit the carriage, their clothing and hair disheveled. Binta giggled when she saw Jamison's usually immaculate hair standing straight at the back.

As they walked up the marble steps to his large house, she realized the size of the place, which cured her giggles. She sucked in her breath and stared at it wide-eyed. "What is this place?" she whispered.

"My home. And the place I will make love to you the rest of the night."

She tried to turn to him, but instead, he grabbed her face and kissed her hard before she could complete the movement. She kissed him back, and they stumbled inside. They lost clothing as they proceeded up the oak stairs but never stopped kissing. They didn't quite make it to the master suite before he took her on the plush carpet in the hallway. After their tryst, they lay together in each other's arms, panting. He put her hand on his chest, and Binta felt his heart fluttering, eliciting a smile from her as she stared deeply into his eyes.

"What?" he asked huskily.

"Nothing."

"Tell me," he asked again, propping his head on one arm.

"I don't want to be anywhere but here tonight. Thank you for bringing me into your world, Jamison," she said with a smile.

His face produced a smile that threatened to swallow him, and she thought she had never seen a more genuine reaction to her words. He kissed her again, carried her to his room, and tucked her in. They slept for a bit, but Jamison made good on his word and made love to her most of the night.

AS THE SERVANTS MADE BREAKFAST THE FOLLOWING DAY, THEY SIPPED sweet tea and cuddled on a plush sofa. Binta looked around at the finely furnished room, which Jamison called his breakfast room, and was amazed at the size of it.

"How do you do this?" she asked.

"Do what?"

"Have all of this?" Binta said, holding out her arms to encompass the room.

Jamison smiled and said, "I come from wealth. However, I also collect rare and beautiful things." He kissed her gently on the lips and winked. "I make a large profit on most items I collect," he added.

"A profit?"

"I find rare items and sell them for a large gain."

"How?"

"Let's just say I have a knack for it… and many connections." He stood and said, "If you like this, I have something to show you."

He took her hand and led her out of the room, stopping to tell the servants to warm their breakfast. Binta wore a nice, warm robe that fit her perfectly, provided by Jamison when they awakened. It was the most comfortable garment she had ever worn. He took her back to his room; she first thought he wanted to make love again.

"You are insatiable, but I am hungry," she said with a smile and a ruffle of his hair.

His hair still contained some of the styling oils he had used the night before, and it kept its wild look, making her giggle. He fixed his hair the best he could and smiled at her flirtatious nature.

He kissed her and said, "As much as I would like to ravage you all day, there is something I need to show you."

"What?"

"This way, my lady," he said, motioning toward the door to his room.

Binta gave him a puzzled look and shook her head. She entered his room, the same one she had spent the night in, and looked around. The bed was made, and their clothes, once strewn across the floor, were gone. The room was immaculate, like the rest of the house.

"Wow, that's clean. I—"

"No, the servants cleaned for us when we went downstairs; that is not what I want you to see," Jamison interrupted.

"What then?" Binta asked.

He turned to her, took her by the shoulders, and looked nervously into her eyes. He said, "Do you remember when we first met?"

"Of course," Binta whispered, becoming more intrigued with his strange actions.

"When Cass first strutted you around the tables at Poppy's Tavern, and all the patrons became quiet at the sight of you, including myself, you had my attention.

"You wore that skirt that was too small and gave us all a flash of your perfect body. At that moment, I knew I would pay whatever price Cass would charge to have you. When I finally had my turn, I feasted on your beautiful body, but then I discovered your soul was even more attractive. That is when you had my heart, Binta Mulay.

"It made better sense when I learned you were held against your will. I knew that a perfect woman like yourself would never choose such a degrading profession, so I had you freed from that awful place. I knew that someone so beautiful should not be kept hostage performing such filthy acts.

"Then, when the king rescued you from Cass's forced prostitution, you were given shelter at the castle. I longed to find you, to speak with you, to be with you. Although I am friends with the royal couple, I was not allowed in the castle, and it took some time before my message found you."

"Something has the king and queen on edge," Binta said, recalling Daro's words.

"What do you know?"

"Nothing, it can wait for another time," Binta said, realizing Jamison seemed lost in thought and very nervous. "So, why are you telling me this?"

"Because I love you."

He motioned with an arm to a door on the other side of the room. Binta looked at him curiously, trying to figure out precisely what was happening. She recalled Daro's words and panicked just a bit. According to the ranger, the world was changing, and those words haunted her as she made her way to the door. She immediately dismissed the thought; Jamison had been nothing but pleasant to her, and she had nothing to worry about. Still, something in the back of her mind screamed that this was wrong. She opened the door, and what she saw made her stop and stare, her mouth agape.

It was another room, slightly smaller than Jamison's bedroom and just as finely decorated. Another fancy bed was there with a canopy and accompanying veil. There was a closet with the door opened, revealing an entire wardrobe of expensive dresses. The vanity contained sparkling jewelry, including rings, necklaces, and bracelets. The room itself was more significant than anything Binta had lived in before, and the value of the items had to be worth a fortune.

Then she saw the large painting on the wall, a painting of her standing in the forest, wearing a beautiful white dress. It was well done and probably cost a small fortune. She immediately wondered how Jamison could have ever produced such an item. Wouldn't she have to sit for a portrait like that? Her mind reeled with many questions as she felt Jamison gently touch her shoulder.

"What is all of this?" she asked, her eyes glued to the portrait.

"It is all for you."

She turned to him, unsure what to say or do next. What could she possibly say? It was like a dream that she wasn't entirely comfortable with. Still, she could not deny that it was the most flattering and beautiful thing anyone had ever done for her. She was just an outcast back home, and that hadn't changed when she attended Victoria's school. No boy had doted on her then, and no man had ever acted like this toward her. So, why was this happening? The sex was great between them, but how could that lead to this kind of obsession?

"But why?" she whispered.

"Like I told you, I collect rare and beautiful things; you are my grandest find. Will you marry me, Binta?"

The question nearly knocked her over. How could this even be real? She studied his face, looking for a sign that he was joking, looking for anything indicating it was all some kind of strange dream. But his visage didn't change; she knew this was real. His face said it all; he was indeed in love with her, and how could she deny him?

"I… I don't know—"

He gently kissed her lips and said, "Don't answer yet."

He took her hand and placed a large diamond ring on her finger. She watched as if everything was unfolding in slow motion, unable to speak or move. The ring fit perfectly, and she held her hand to admire the sparkling diamonds.

"Just live with me in the meantime. Consider this ring a token of my sincerity, and if you decide to accept my proposal, this will be your world."

Binta couldn't speak for a long time and eventually lowered her hand. She looked him in the face, still stunned at what was transpiring, her heart racing with the possibilities. She wanted to say yes, but her thoughts went to Cassandra and Greyson. She had lost Cassandra, and a life like this would ease that pain and help her move on. If the rumors were true, Greyson was gone as well. The idea of living in her tiny dorm room at Lady Victoria's school suddenly seemed sad and lonely.

"My parents… I can't stay."

Jamison held up a hand to stop her, but she lost her voice, still trying to comprehend the strange turn of events. "I sent word last night to your parents, and they know you are safe. They are also coming here for dinner tonight to see that you are fine. Let's give them a glimpse of what life you could have."

"I still do not understand any of this, Jamison. We hardly know each other."

"However, we know each other well enough to make love all night long, remember?"

She could not deny his reasoning. She found him attractive, and he was a thorough lover for sure. But how could he be in love with her? They still hardly knew each other. What if she progressed down that path and Greyson returned? After all, there was no confirmation of his death. Did she desire Greyson more than Jamison, and could she make that choice if Greyson returned? She loved Greyson, but she could probably love Jamison as well. He loved her. She could feel it, and it was true; he had saved her from Cass's clutches. She owed him.

"Do not answer, my love. Not until I return."

"Where are you going?"

"I have business this evening, so you have the place to yourself. Your parents will be here for dinner, and you may discuss the issue with them if you wish."

"I can't possibly stay here," Binta said.

"Sure you can; I insist. Kleve will see to your every need while I am gone."

"Kleve?"

"One of my trusted servants who runs this place while I'm away."

"How long will you be gone?"

"I'll return tomorrow morning. If you decide not to stay, Kleve will see you have a passage back to the castle with your parents. However, I do hope you'll stay."

He took her hand and kissed the back of it. Then he hugged her tight and kissed her hard. Binta returned the kiss, but she kept her eyes open as she did, taking in the magnificent room. Her eyes settled on the painting once more. She couldn't help but feel more than a little uncomfortable.

LATER THAT NIGHT, SHE AND HER PARENTS ATE LOBSTER, AND JUST like Binta the night before, her parents had their first taste of the expensive dish and loved it. Kleve organized the meal, and several young women waited on their every need. Binta and her parents felt like royalty for a night and loved everything about Kleve. He was older, with thinning grey hair and a matching mustache, and was very kind to them. He immediately became a mentor and tutor as Binta was out of sorts and a bit overwhelmed.

After dinner, Kleve served tea and explained that tea time was a tradition with Jamison's family and that the lady of the house would do well to embrace that tradition. When Binta failed to understand who that was, he patiently explained with a warm smile that he was referring to her. So, she shared an invigorating fig and lemon tea with her parents. They loved it, and all had a second serving. They sat around the parlor digesting their meal and sipping their tea as the sun descended. It was all surreal for Binta, and her thoughts dwelled on the haunting portrait in her bedroom.

Her father interrupted her by saying, "What now, my daughter?"

Binta set her tea cup on her saucer, nearly spilling it in surprise. "What do you mean?" she asked.

"This," her father said, holding his arms out to encompass the fancy room.

"I don't know," she whispered.

"Are you in danger?" her mother whispered.

"No, of course not!"

"Then what is all of this? It is too sudden and suspicious for me to approve," her father said.

"Do you want to return to the castle with us?" her mother asked.

"What? Why?"

"Because we do not know this man, and neither do you," her father said.

Kleve came in then, and Binta was thankful for his timing. She was already overwhelmed with the turn of events, and with her parents doubting her, she was grateful for the interruption.

"Lord and Lady Mulay, would you like a tour of the house?" Kleve asked.

Her parents looked at each other, contemplating the possibility, but neither disapproved. When her father eagerly agreed, Binta knew they would be fine with her decision. However, she had no idea what that would be.

They toured the magnificent place and discovered several ballrooms, a spa, a splendid kitchen, an indoor greenhouse, several bathhouses, and countless bedrooms and studies. The place was overwhelming, and they were all at a loss for words when they reached the main foyer.

"I will give you some time to discuss the idea of Lady Binta remaining here tonight or returning to the castle with you. I will notify the driver that you will decide soon," Kleve said. He then bowed slightly and left them alone to discuss their options.

Her father took her hand to examine the ring and said, "So, this means you are engaged?"

"No. Jamison gave this to me as a symbol of his dedication."

"Did he ask you to marry him?"

"Yes, but—"

"Then you are engaged," her father said, cutting her off.

Binta was at a loss for words. Her father was right, although she did not want to admit it. She had not said yes but had accepted the ring. The whole thing had happened so fast that she hadn't realized that perhaps she was engaged.

Her mother interrupted her thoughts by saying, "So, you are engaged, and we are happy for you as long as he is a good man and you are content."

Her words struck a nerve and made the whole thing finally seem real. Was she going to continue down that path? She didn't love Jamison, but she knew she could learn to.

"So, will you return to the cottage with us, or is this your life now?" her father asked.

"We support you either way," her mother added.

Her father nodded slightly, which made Binta feel better. That was the closest thing she would get to approval from him. It made the decision to stay more effortless. She hugged her parents and watched the fancy carriage take them home. She was content with her decision, and so began the next stage of her life.

She spoke with Kleve for a long while that night, wanting to learn more about her future husband. After that lengthy discussion, she felt even better about her decision. Jamison seemed to be a perfect person in every way, almost too good to be true.

BAXTER SAT IN A COMFORTABLE CHAIR IN VICTORIA'S PLUSH OFFICE at the top of her tower. The spring semester was about to begin, and he assumed he was there to discuss the curriculum for the coming classes. The wizard sipped on a fine wine Victoria had given him as she pored over his notes for the coming semester. He knew she would approve; they had been through this routine for many years and knew each other perfectly. However, what she said next nearly knocked him over.

"Do you think Ralf can handle this workload?"

"What? The new instructor?"

"He has been with us for almost four years now, Baxter. Do you think he can handle your class load this semester? Maybe permanently?"

"What? Ralf is an herbalist; he can't possibly teach spellcasting!" Baxter said, sitting up in his chair.

"We may have no choice."

Baxter leaned back in his chair slowly, letting the words sink in. "Victoria, are you firing me?" he asked in disbelief.

"Hardly, Baxter. However, I do have some very important news for you."

"I'm listening."

"I have two things we must go over. They are life-changing events that will affect us greatly."

Baxter had rarely seen Victoria upset, but her solemn visage worried him. He realized then that this was not about him or a simple firing; something was wrong.

"First, the New Order is looking for new members, and your name came up immediately," Victoria continued.

"The New Order?"

"Yes, but before accepting our invitation, you must be aware of something. The world is changing, and the New Order is being called upon to defend it."

Baxter could not believe what he was hearing. He had come into the meeting thinking he would discuss his curriculum for the spring; this conversation was not something he had expected. "Victoria, if the New Order needs members to stifle a threat against the world, I will gladly join."

Victoria smiled and continued, "There is more to the tale, Baxter. Gathering new members is a serious matter thrust upon us suddenly."

Baxter nodded and said, "I understand. If you and the rest of the New Order deem me worthy, I will heed your call."

"I knew you would say that. We will swear you into the New Order by the end of summer, and Kringus will announce your name as a new member within a week."

"Kringus is addressing the city? Something big truly is happening if he is making a public announcement."

"It is, Baxter. There is a prophecy, one that Penelope and I have researched and believe to be true. At least, we have found no reason to doubt it."

"A prophecy?"

"Yes, a half-demon named Inuentas, who entered the city weeks ago with Daro, delivered the information. The ranger vouched for his character, regardless of his race."

Baxter did not miss the qualification of the half-demon. Few knew that Victoria was a half-demon, and Baxter was one of those few. He appreciated her honesty concerning her race, although he trusted her with his life.

"We have met with him for nearly a week now, asking him questions and verifying his tale, this prophecy that he believes in," Victoria continued.

"And you and Penelope have discovered no deviations to his story?"

"None. We cannot confirm some information, but we verified everything we could and believe Inuentas is telling the truth."

"So, what is this prophecy?"

"It was generated centuries ago by Marnelphion himself, soon after his banishing. He has been planning to return to our world since that day."

"The demon lord is coming back? Is that even possible?" Baxter asked in disbelief.

"Yes; according to the prophecy, on the 666th anniversary of the banishing, a sacrifice will occur at midnight to allow it."

"A sacrifice? And that is what the New Order must stop?" Baxter asked.

"Precisely."

"But that means we only have …" Baxter counted on his fingers, and his eyes widened. "We only have about a year and a half before the anniversary," he finally determined.

"Slightly less than that."

"What kind of sacrifice are we discussing, and how do we stop it?"

"That is the next part of this story that you will be amazed to hear. The sacrifices must consist of 666 victims, with the last being the most special. Without that last sacrificial victim, the summoning will not work."

"So, we eliminate the last sacrifice and effectively stop the threat."

"Yes, Baxter, that is what we have considered. Other possibilities exist, such as stopping the priests tasked with the summoning."

"Do we know who that is?"

"Yes; according to the prophecy, there is one priestess who is key to orchestrating the event. We believe she was here recently, right under our noses." Victoria sighed.

"Here? Why, and who is she?"

"Her name is Matilda, and that is all I know. However, we have reason to believe that she traveled with my father."

"Is your father involved in this?"

"Not directly, we do not believe. However, according to Inuentas, the half-demon, Matilda was here. The remains of two people we found in an adjacent room to where my father stayed were indicative of sacrifice. So, we assume that was his business here in Pelesea; he was her means of entering the city without being detected. They left the same way."

"So, Matilda was here in Pelesea, but why?" Baxter asked.

"She was after the special 666th sacrifice. That person was also here, and it is someone you know."

"What? The sacrifice was here as well? And we know who it is?"

"Yes, we know the identity of the last sacrifice, the one who will open the gate for Marnelphion."

"Who is it?" Baxter asked, hardly believing the events had unfolded in Pelesea without anyone knowing.

"You won't believe it."

"At this point, I'll believe anything."

"It's Cassandra Rho, Baxter."

The words sank in, and Baxter would have fallen to the floor if the chair had not been there to support him. The mention of Cassandra, the woman he had inadvertently fallen in love with, weighed heavily on his heart. The loss was still fresh, and the pain very real. He had lost her a few months earlier in a tragic fire, and he had struggled to deal with it.

"So, the threat is over, then. Cassandra is dead," he whispered.

"No, she is alive," Victoria said.

Victoria might as well have slapped him with those words. His eyes widened, and a smile crossed his face. He didn't care about the world's fate then; he was delighted to hear that Cassandra was alive. "How?" he asked, barely able to speak.

"It is an interesting story, and I will tell you all about it. So, back to the original question: can Ralf take your classes in the foreseeable future? I know of no one else who is qualified."

Baxter shrugged, and in light of the information, he suddenly found the spring semester unimportant. "Sure," was his curt and honest response.

BINTA HAD THE MOST BEAUTIFUL DREAMS DURING THE FIRST NIGHT alone in Jamison's home. Although he wasn't there, the large, comfortable bed was the softest she had ever slept on. Sleeping in a strange place still felt odd, but she drifted off and had no despairing thoughts like her last night at Daro's cottage. She was awakened by a bright light and squinted open her eyes to find Kleve opening up the massive drapes and letting the bright, warm sunlight in. She sat in bed, carefully holding the sheets to cover herself.

"Where is Jamison?" she asked.

"He has been delayed a few days, my lady."

"Is everything all right?"

"Of course. Delays happen quite often with Jamison's travels. Nothing unusual."

"So, why did you wake me?"

"Because now we have time to learn the etiquette required of a lady of your stature," Kleve said, approaching her and holding out his hand.

Binta did not understand the gesture and said, "I am not a lady of any stature, Kleve. I do not need any training in etiquette. I am only here because Jamison invited me to stay."

Kleve gave her a sour look and withdrew his hand. He took hers and held it up, making the morning light reflect from the large diamond.

"You wear Jamison's jewelry and his fine clothes," he said, swinging a hand out to the closet.

The door was open, and the beautiful clothing within made her bite back her words. She could not deny Kleve's observation, but this was all too fast for her to register. At that moment, she felt like getting up and returning to the small cottage in the castle gardens. But then Kleve held his hand out to her once again.

"What?" she asked, growing more flustered.

"A proper lady will not wear a nose ring."

"You want my nose ring?"

"Jamison would prefer it, my lady."

"But I do not," Binta said stubbornly.

Kleve continued to hold his hand out, demanding her nose ring. She matched his blank expression for a bit but finally caved. "Fine," Binta whispered. She took out the small ring and placed it in the palm of his hand.

She watched him stuff it into one of his pockets, and then he said, "And now, Rose will assist you with your morning bath and wash the odd makeup off your face."

A portly woman came in, wearing a giant smile and carrying some towels. "Good day, my lady. Are you ready for a bath?"

Binta didn't know what to say. Again, things felt like they were moving entirely too fast. She had worn her makeup the same since she was young. That and her piercings made her who she was, at least in appearance. And now Jamison wanted to change that? Her other option would be to walk away. She looked at the large rock on her finger and went with Rose after a few moments of reflection.

After her bath, Rose applied her makeup without a mirror so Binta could not see the progress or give directions. She sat patiently and let Rose work her magic. The woman talked nonstop, mostly about how a young lady should properly carry herself. Binta ignored most of it and tried to make sense of the unexpected and crazy path before her. Once Rose had completed applying the makeup, she dressed Binta in a beautiful red evening gown that was fancier than anything Binta had ever worn, added some jewelry, and pulled her in front of a full-length mirror.

What Binta saw took her breath away. The young, submissive woman, who just a few short months ago had been a local prostitute with a nose ring and dark makeup now resembled a princess. Rose had applied a generous amount of color to her face and lips, added a necklace and lovely earrings, and thoroughly brushed her hair. The result was more than she could have possibly imagined. She would not have recognized herself if she hadn't known it was her.

"Now, this is how a proper lady should look," Kleve said, entering the room.

Binta turned to face the man, unsure of what to say or do. Rose moved to stand beside Kleve as they both looked her up and down, nodding their approvals. Occasionally, Rose would move up and straighten out a wrinkle in the dress or fluff her hair. Binta felt like she wasn't even there, as if she were just some living doll made of expensive accessories.

"You've outdone yourself, Rose," Kleve said.

"Your turn, then?" Rose asked.

"Not yet. It would be best if you worked with the lady on posture and walking in heels the rest of the evening," Kleve said.

"Of course, how silly of me," Rose said. The woman then went to the closet and sorted Binta's shoes.

"Jamison will be pleased; you look stunning," Kleve said

"Jamison may be pleased, but what about me?" Binta asked.

"Are you pleased?"

She looked herself up and down in the mirror and half turned to the right and left to get a better view. She looked amazing and was truly happy with what she saw. It was as if her old self had been discarded, and she saw a new and improved version. She thought of her days with Cassandra and Greyson and knew she would leave that life behind if she continued with Jamison. Her heart ached, and despairing thoughts threatened to take over, especially with Daro's warning. She shook the thoughts away and told herself that she was happy. She convinced herself once again that she could love Jamison.

"Yes," she said.

Kleve smiled as Rose returned from the closet with several pairs of shoes for Binta to try on. Binta returned the smile, and it was genuine. She learned to walk in heels and carry herself properly for the rest of the day. In the two days following that, she learned to eat, speak, and converse like a lady. It was a lot of work, making her realize how little she knew about this life. She worked hard to learn everything Kleve wanted her to know. She was excited at how fast she learned to change her walk and carry her-self differently. Binta could not wait to show her new skills to Jamison; she wanted him to be happy with her. She had to admit then that the life of a Pelesea lady might not be so bad.

Still, the prostitute inside of her made her want to do bad things, dirty sexual acts that a lady of Pelesea would never consider. She saw through the makeup, fancy clothing, and pretty accessories. She knew what she was deep down inside, and occasionally, thoughts of Cassandra and Greyson surfaced. Those days were the hardest and loneliest.

ESCAPE

ASSANDRA COULD NOT SPEAK TELEPATHICALLY WITH THE FAIRY, Gophia. Still, she had communicated enough through her body language, using slight nods and eye contact, that the creature knew Cassandra would help her. Gophia was a prisoner to Maltor, the leader of the barbarian tribe to which Cassandra now belonged. The fairy had been a present from King Boskel of the Culiem Tribe, located in a part of the desert where the fairies were abundant, and had been offered as a gift to Maltor before the gladiator battles. Now Gophia hung in a cage by Maltor's throne.

The culiem fairies were magical, and Gophia had telepathically reached out to Cassandra for help. Unfortunately, Cassandra was every bit as much a prisoner as the fairy. She was not relegated to a cage but instead wore a metal collar with a chain attached to a wooden pole, one of several such poles that held up the massive tent Maltor used as a personal living space within the Serpent Tribe. Besides the collar and chain, Cassandra had been treated with care and had many luxuries, including lovely, silky clothes and pillows piled around the pole.

In truth, Maltor cared for her greatly and considered her a gift from the barbarian goddess, Strenna, because of the mark on Cassandra's hip.

The scar resulted from the branding Ronnis D'Breeth had given her with the pummel of his sword. The sword's handle appeared as a snake eating its tail, meaning her brand was that of a snake's face. Ronnis D'Breeth had hated Cassandra since wolves killed her adoptive mother, Unis Rho. He blamed Cassandra for the incident and, since then, had it in for her. His latest attempt at torturing her included the brand, unintentionally marking her as a gift from Strenna, the goddess of snakes.

When he had seen the snake brand, Maltor believed her to be a gift straight from the deity. He inadvertently saved her from Ronnis's torture, rape, and, most likely, her ultimate murder. For that, she was thankful. However, she was being held against her will and had been living among the barbarians for several months as a prisoner.

She had fought in a strange gladiator tournament a few weeks prior, somehow winning against incredible odds. Unfortunately, the winner gained the honor of marrying the king of their respective tribe. In this case, Maltor was Cassandra's prize, a winning she did not desire. Cassandra initially had no chance at the tournament, being a spell caster, not a fighter. But at Maltor's direction, the tribe shamans had given her a tremendous set of skills in hand-to-hand combat, which would typically take years to hone. She had learned them in the few days it took to conduct the ritual, and they were embedded in her memory as if she had known them for years.

In truth, she was quite dangerous with or without a weapon. Cassandra was thankful for that, but that skill set had come with two significant costs. First, to transfer those skills to her, the ritual required the sacrifice of a warrior who possessed them. In that instance, it had been Vixa, the female barbarian warrior to whom Cassandra had taken a liking. She hated Maltor for Vixa's death. Secondly, the shamans had stuffed cactus needles into her arms and gums. The cacti that grew in the desert were a natural arcane suppressant. That procedure had been painful, and the needle in her right forearm had broken in the last battle she had fought in the gladiator ring. The wound was healing but was still very raw and caused her significant discomfort.

Ultimately, Cassandra had survived the tournament using Vixa's melee skills, a little of her magic, and much luck. Although she could not decline her prize of queenship, she was thankful for avoiding the procreation tent, a guaranteed fate if she had lost, and a most horrible existence. As she recovered from her wounds suffered during the grueling contest, Maltor made plans for their wedding. Her arm was still on the mend, and the wound heavily bandaged, but the barbarian king was impatient, so the wedding day was upon them. However, Cassandra had formulated a plan, and Gophia was the key. They would help each other, hopefully resulting in freedom for them both. The chance was slim, but Cassandra was out of time. And so, she moved forward with the near-hopeless plan just hours before her marriage ceremony.

Three guards were in the room as two handmaidens quickly prepared her. They stripped her naked and bathed her, then dressed her in new, silky clothing befitting a barbarian queen. All the while, two of the guards watched the scene unfold, lewd expressions plastered on their ignorant faces. Jak, the third guard overseeing her care during Maltor's absences, genuinely cared about her well-being. He had never said much to her, but she trusted him. He turned his back to her as she bathed to prove the point. Perhaps she would have to exploit that trust to escape.

The barbarian handmaidens didn't say much or even bother looking her in the eye as they worked. They were older than her by a few decades and were tribe members, whereas she was not. Their reactions spoke volumes about the respect she would receive after becoming queen. It was just another reason she needed to avoid the ceremony. She would be nothing more than an outsider to most of the tribe and never a true queen. After dressing, they brushed her hair, pulling tangles roughly, disregarding any discomfort the grooming was causing. The next phase was for them to splash a pungent liquid all over her. They sprinkled it on her in fistfuls until she was reeking of the stuff. They didn't tell her what it was, and she dared not ask; she only assumed it was the tribe's perfume. When they finished, they stood her up and straightened some wrinkles in her clothing and tussled her hair in several places, then shared a nod, agreeing on a job well done. They bowed slightly to Cassandra and took their leave from the tent, never making eye contact.

Cassandra stood in disbelief, trying hard not to vomit at the stench. She noticed the other two guards smiling, and their expressions indicated they liked what the handmaidens had done. She paid them little attention and instead focused on Jak as he turned to face her. He wore no expression as he tended to do and merely nodded, letting her know he approved. Her chance was now, and she summoned him over with a wave. She would have to be clever since there were three guards. Jak was the key; she had to dispose of him first.

Before he could take the first step, a young boy entered the tent near hysterics. He went straight for Jak and babbled. It was such a fast interaction that Cassandra didn't catch most of it. He said something about the king's missing crown, and that was all it took for the three guards to become animated. Jak shooed the boy away and motioned for one guard to stay to watch over Cassandra and for the other to follow him. He exited the tent with the second guard close behind.

"Even better," she whispered, amazed at her good fortune.

"*Please help Gophia,*" came the tiny voice in her head again.

The fairy knew the time was right, and so did Cassandra. She glanced at the cage to find Gophia leaning her forehead against the bars, her tiny fists grasping them. The fairy looked at Cassandra pleadingly, and Cassandra nodded her understanding. She turned her attention to the remaining guard, who looked her up and down, remaining vigilant, but the lust in his eyes betrayed him. Her eyes wandered briefly to the axe on his belt. She had only used one once before, even though she was proficient in handling the weapon. She knew it would feel right in her grasp. Her prior use had occurred in this tent and with a different guard. She had defended herself against his unwanted advances, and according to Maltor, the man would never have children because she had wedged the weapon in his groin. She could easily do it again, which would spoil her escape plan. No, she had to be discreet for this to work.

She smiled seductively at the lone guard and beckoned him with a curled finger. He crossed his arms and stood firm, defying her call. "I will be queen soon and have never been with a man. Teach me how to kiss so that I may please Maltor," she said as seductively as possible.

The man stood firm and shook his head, but she noticed him glance toward the door as if to consider her offer. "As I said, I will be queen soon, and I'll remember your defiance. I may not have much power, but Maltor will not be happy to learn that you kissed me, whether you truly did or not."

The man uncrossed his arms then, suddenly angry. "You would lie, interloper?"

"No, I would lie as your queen, not an interloper. That is different. Now get over here," she ordered with as much conviction as she could muster.

The man checked the door several times, looking from her to the tent entrance, then slowly came forward. He was suspicious and not happy at being manipulated by her, understanding her threat for what it was. He was young, however, and probably believed her lie. And so he cautiously approached her, one hand on the hilt of his axe. As he did, Cassandra unfocused her vision to see the magical symbols, taking inventory of their abundance floating around Gophia's cage. The little fairy generated many symbols that Cassandra recognized and a few she had never seen. Those symbols assisted her in formulating spells. Few wizards had the power to do so, and anyone known to have the skill was labeled a witch or a warlock. She thought of the few spells she knew or had seen, trying to formulate one that would not injure the barbarian guard. She only thought of one that might suffice, although she had never cast it before.

She remembered the simple spell Cass had used against her, which commanded her to sleep. She closed her eyes momentarily and recalled the appropriate symbols, then reopened them to see the man unsheathing his axe. He was suspicious, and she would need to act fast. She sorted the symbols quickly and tried to piece together the spell; however, the cacti needles interfered, costing her precious time. She extended her right arm closer to the man and the symbols. She felt the magic gather in that arm since it no longer contained many vicious needles.

However, the guard cleverly backed up out of her range, and if she could not physically reach him to check for a key, everything was lost. Gophia came to life at that point, somehow understanding what Cassandra was doing. The little fairy let out a shrill shriek. It was instantaneous and loud, and the guard jumped with surprise, turning toward the sound and drawing his axe fully. Cassandra cast her spell when the man turned his back away from her and his attention elsewhere.

"Sleep," she commanded.

The guard swung and clipped Gophia's cage with his axe, sending it swinging. Gophia held on to the bars for dear life as she spun around. The man turned to Cassandra and stumbled, his eyes already drooping. He managed to whisper, "Devil magic," before falling to his knees, then face first to the sandy floor.

Shortly after, he snored loudly, and Cassandra jumped into action. Luckily, he had fallen forward and within Cassandra's range. She had to manipulate her crude leash a bit, but she could reach him and search what little clothing he wore. She looked for a key somewhere, assuming all the guards looking after her would have a set. It didn't take long to discover that was not the case, as the young man carried an axe and nothing more. She needed a key to her leash or the cage. After a brief look, her heart sank as she found neither.

"Are you kidding me?" she said aloud.

She looked up to Gophia, and the fairy now wore a concerned look as her cage slowly began to stop revolving. A new guard started to enter the tent, but before he could, someone called him away in a hurry. It was still chaotic outside, but her window of opportunity was closing. She stood and focused on the cage. She had read about telekinesis in the vast documents in the cellar of Victoria's School of Magic. That was an advanced spell, and she had never learned how to cast it. She had no choice but to try, so she began sorting through the various symbols hanging in the air around Gophia. She wanted to sort them as she remembered them penned in the great tomes she had perused.

She closed her eyes and focused, knowing her time was short. She could not recall the exact spell but could feel the many arcane symbols answering her call, changing order and shape to give her spell an effect. She was unsure if it was a telekinesis spell, but it was all she could do. She opened her eyes, and Gophia was the only one there to witness the phenomenon of Cassandra's eyes turning a bright, icy blue. It had only happened a few times before, and although she was not aware of the phenomenon, it only occurred when she focused her powers to great effect. She released the built-up energy through her right arm toward the cage, hoping her spell would somehow open the tiny door.

Instead, the cage shook violently, knocking Gophia down and making it swing wildly again. Cassandra growled in defiance as the cacti needles did their work once more to mute her abilities. They prevented her from calling out certain symbols, making the spell sloppy and unfocused. She released a final wave of powerful magic, focused on the cage door. Suddenly, it exploded, and Gophia let out a surprised squeal, shielding her face with her arm. The explosion created a puff of smoke, and when it finally dissipated, the door was missing, the hinges still glowing red-hot. Cassandra looked around the large tent and found the door on the other side, glowing red from the heat.

Cassandra was amazed at the effect, and her right arm pulsed with magical energy. She held it before her and examined it, her eyes slowly reverting to their natural blue color. Once Gophia caught her bearings, she fluttered quickly out of the cage and toward the tent door.

"*Cassandra is a friend of Gophia. Thank you!*" The fairy's voice echoed in Cassandra's head.

"Wait!" Cassandra shouted before the fairy could make her escape.

She flew quickly to Cassandra and fluttered in front of her face, her head pivoting nervously between Cassandra and the door.

"Wait, my new friend," Cassandra said calmly. "I helped you, and now I need your help."

The fairy scrunched up her tiny eyebrows in confusion. "*Gophia help?*" she asked doubtfully, looking over the chain attached to Cassandra's collar.

"Bite me," Cassandra said, presenting her arm to the fairy.

Gophia recoiled and shook her head. "*No! Gophia will kill new friend!*" Her tiny voice boomed loudly in Cassandra's head.

"No, Gophia, I'm immune to venom."

Other than branding Cassandra that fateful night all those months ago, Ronnis had somehow transferred part of the magic in that evil sword of his into her. Since then, she had twice beaten lethal venom, her body expelling it through the brand. Although the fairy was highly venomous, Cassandra hoped to defeat any venom the little creature injected her with. If not, she would die, which would be an escape for her anyway. Gophia continued to shake her head and look nervously at the door.

"Gophia, I have saved you; now is your chance to save me. Release me from my cage as I have done you. Please."

A commotion outside, followed by the sound of several barbarians approaching the tent, had the fairy fly into action. She took Cassandra's forearm and prepared to bite. She looked into Cassandra's eyes one last time as if verifying she really wanted to be bitten. Cassandra nodded and smiled.

"Go ahead, Gophia, I will not die," Cassandra said, trying to sound confident.

"*Gophia sorry,*" the fairy said, bit Cassandra hard, then flew out the tent door before anyone arrived.

The bite did not initially hurt, and it felt like a slight bee sting to Cassandra. She looked at her forearm to see the tiny puncture wounds and wondered if the bite would do anything at all. Perhaps she had misjudged what the fairy was capable of, and possibly her plan would be all for nothing. However, she could feel the venom pumping through her body and, as she suspected, felt it drawn toward the brand on her hip. The final step would be to convince Maltor she was indeed dead. With the empty cage and the bite on her arm, she knew Maltor would put together the scenario, but she would need to look dead.

She began to conjure an old spell that could help with such a thing when the pain in her abdomen had her doubling over. She fell to her knees and vomited what looked like very dark blood. It wasn't much, but it made her nervous. She tried to stand, but the pain in her mouth had her falling backward onto the pillows. She could feel the cactus needles, and they pulsed with the most intense pain she had ever known. She reached into her mouth to massage her gums and alleviate some of the pain. Nothing helped, and she moaned as the venom did its work effectively. Just when she thought it couldn't get any worse, her arms began to throb with a pain equal to that in her mouth. She held her arms in front of her and watched the skin on her forearms change to a deep black. The left one hurt worse; she assumed it was because it had more cactus needles remaining. She began to sob, unable to deal with the intense pain.

She lost the strength in her arms as they fell to her sides. All of her muscles became paralyzed, and she could even feel her heart slowing. Perhaps she was wrong in assuming her snake brand could defeat all toxins. The barbarians had warned her of the lethalness of the tiny fairies. It didn't matter; if she remained in the barbarian tribe, her life would be forfeited anyway, so death was a better alternative. Her breathing came in shallow gasps, and her vision began to fail. She thought she sensed more blood trickling from her mouth, but she wasn't sure. She couldn't even summon a hand to wipe it away. That was the last thought she had before the world went dark.

Greyson walked the perimeter of Breeston's property, deep in Swamp Ikma. The druid, Breeston, had housed Greyson and his two friends, Alleah and Chloe, for nearly two months. On an expedition to Tara, several hundred miles north of Ikma, Greyson and a troop of Sinnis priestesses were ambushed by Cerus and the evil warriors of Gorl. The worshippers of Sinnis and Gorl were sworn enemies, and now it seemed that only Alleah and Chloe remained from the more than forty sisters of Sinnis that began the journey. Greyson's god, Plath, was an ally to the worshippers of Sinnis and was part of the expedition meant to take him back to his home of Tara. The group never reached Tara because of Cerus's ambush, having been chased into the swamp, and there they remained.

Luckily, Breeston had found them before Cerus could, and the druid of Ikma summoned the lord of the marsh, the great dragon Malebak. The dragon had sided with Greyson and his allies and had purged Cerus and his men from its home. Cerus was the only one to escape the dragon attack, but just barely. Malebak had unleashed his powerful breath weapon, a cloud of large, killing flies. Since then, a host of the giant flies had lingered around the perimeter of Breeston's home, imprisoning Greyson and his two friends.

Greyson studied one of the flies, which clung to a tree. The creature was black, as black as the dragon that breathed it, and the size of a large mouse. Its legs contained many ridges for grasping its prey, and the devilish proboscis looked razor-sharp. It was an evil-looking creature that stared back at Greyson almost hatefully. He brought a hand up slowly to the beast, and it started buzzing its wings in response, calling to other flies in the area. Dozens flew from every direction, landing on the tree next to the calling fly. There, they walked and buzzed agitatedly, waiting for Greyson's next move. He slowly lowered his hand, and the creepy flies seemed to relax a little.

"Don't worry, my friend, their numbers diminish," Breeston said, clapping Greyson on the back and continuing past.

"They don't appear so diminished," Greyson argued.

"That is because the dragon is beginning its slumber again, and the flies make sure there is no threat to the swamp before Malebak fully sleeps."

"Can't you just tell him that we mean no harm to the swamp and only wish to leave?"

"I wish it were that easy, Greyson. Dragons like to take their time to decide things, so I assure you that time will be taken for Malebak."

The two walked further, constantly changing direction when encountering one of the strange flies. The insects reminded them when they reached their limited range from Breeston's cottage. So, they could walk the perimeter of Breeston's tiny home and nothing more.

"Ah, how about this one?" Breeston asked, pointing his magnificent staff toward a dead tree.

Over the last few weeks, they had searched for the perfect tree to carve a staff for Greyson, similar to the one Breeston carried. It was the most potent item the druid owned, and the priceless gem atop it that glowed with a purplish hue gave the staff its strength. Zeva, Breeston's wife, occasionally birthed the mighty rocks, attuned to Breeston, amplifying his druidic powers. Breeston had invited Greyson to sleep with Zeva almost immediately upon his arrival at the cottage, but Greyson had yet to summon the nerve to do so. Breeston had reasoned that if she birthed a gem for Greyson, it would be a conduit to his god, Plath, enhancing Greyson's powers. Greyson had glimpsed the path that led to her lair, along with the numerous slithering snakes found therein, and had readily declined. She was a sleeth, a race of humanoids with snake-like characteristics that were common in this part of the world. According to Breeston, all sleeth were born with a blessing and a curse. The blessing for Zeva was the production of the powerful gems, but Breeston would not elaborate on the curse.

They agreed that Breeston could carve the dead tree into a staff for Greyson as he pondered his choices. They lugged it back through the muck to Breeston's cottage so the druid could begin his preparations for carving and curing the wood. Greyson knew that Alleah and Chloe had set up a rudimentary altar for Sinnis and had just completed a prayer to their goddess, asking if their sisters were still alive. They were in quiet meditation, obviously listening for answers to that prayer; both women closed their eyes and breathed shallowly, hoping for an answer. Greyson took the opportunity to ogle Alleah. She was by far one of the most beautiful women he had ever met and was a very close friend. Her religious beliefs required her to remain chaste, and so a much-desired sexual encounter with her was not in his future. However, when given opportunities such as this to admire her perfect figure, he took them. Her shirt and pants were worn and muddy, and it gave her a sexually appealing look, in his opinion.

The two men passed them by and took the small tree to the back of the cottage where Breeston could do his work. He took a small axe and started sculpting the tree into Greyson's new staff. Greyson prayed to Plath and asked for guidance on their trek from Swamp Ikma. He knew the day was fast approaching, and they would get the chance to leave Breeston within a few weeks. By the time his prayer was over, Breeston had a good start on the staff and was shaping it with a carving knife.

"Welcome back," he said with a smile as Greyson's eyes fluttered open.

Greyson smiled at the cynical druid, understanding that he did not worship a god other than Malebak and did not spend his time in prayer. Greyson looked more closely at the handiwork and saw the staff already taking shape. He had never used a staff before, but he liked how Breeston's staff felt in his hands and knew that if he could channel his god through it, he would soon grow fond of it.

"Your time grows short," Breeston said, not looking up from his work.

"Before we may leave?"

"And to generate a gem," Breeston added.

Greyson knew the druid was correct. His fear of snakes and the mystery surrounding Zeva had him on edge. He had never turned down the opportunity to sleep with a woman before, but something about this situation seemed wrong. It wasn't the fact she was Breeston's wife, for he had lost his virginity at the age of seventeen to a married woman. No, he had slept with many married women, and Breeston was more than willing to be a cuckold. What gave him pause was the fact that Breeston would not disclose the nature of her curse. With a sigh, he relented. "Very well, I'm ready to give it a try." A smile spread over the druid's lips, and he nodded.

Later that evening, after they had eaten and were winding down for the night, Breeston led him to the trap door again. "Are you sure?" Breeston asked.

"Yes, but quickly, before I change my mind."

The druid opened the trap door, and the stench of swamp water wafted from the depths of the pit. It was dark, so Greyson summoned his powers from Plath to light the eight-sided star he wore around his neck, the holy symbol of Plath. The light bathed the bottom of the pit, and Greyson saw that water filled most of it. Many snakes swam in that water.

"Too late, I have changed my mind," Greyson said, backing away.

"Do not be afraid, my friend; the water is only waist deep, and the snakes are my children. They will not bother you unless you harm or threaten their mother," Breeston assured him.

"I—" Greyson began before Alleah entered the room with Chloe.

Greyson knew Alleah would disapprove of his decision, so he held his tongue when she entered. Breeston stood but continued to hold the trap door open. Greyson lost interest and now faced the two women.

"Greyson, I know nothing of the ways of sexual desires and mating rituals," Alleah began. "However, I support your endeavor if it will bring something as powerful as Breeston's gem into your possession. We could use that kind of power to help us find my sisters. If Breeston assures you it is safe, do it, for I trust him. Swallow your fears, for Sinnis will soon lead us out of this swamp."

Breeston turned to Greyson and flashed another smile, and Greyson knew his choice then. If Alleah approved the event, nothing except his fears would stop Greyson from following through. Alleah and Chloe joined Breeston in staring at Greyson, waiting for his answer. He felt uncomfortable under their gaze.

"I mean, it's sex, Greyson; you know you want to do it!" Chloe blurted out.

The group shared a laugh that eased the tension a bit. Still, Greyson wasn't sure that venturing into the snake-filled stagnant water was such a good idea. Eventually, he summoned the courage to approach the trap door once again. Alleah was quickly beside him as he lay on his stomach and thrust his holy symbol into the pit. She lay next to him to see into the pit as well. The light cut through the darkness, and many snakes were visible.

"I hate snakes," he whispered.

Alleah smiled, and he turned to face her. "It's not funny, Alleah," he said but barely hid a smile.

"What does Plath tell you, Greyson? If he blesses this joining, he will be with you, even down there," Alleah said, nodding to the pit.

"He has shown no sign that this is a bad idea. And now it sounds like you approve as well?"

"I think we need all the help we can get to survive this swamp and whatever we find once we exit it. Our friends may still be out there; if so, they need our help."

"So, this is not about me and my fear of snakes; it is about us?"

"Only if you obtain a gem. Otherwise, it is completely about you and your fear of snakes." She rose then, leaving Greyson to peer into the black water.

After a few moments, he spoke. "Breeston, how likely is Zeva to become pregnant if I venture forth?"

"She is always very fertile, especially this time of the year. Your chances are good, but it may take several attempts for her to birth a gem."

Greyson sat up from his prone position to look Breeston in the eye. The druid still held the door open for him. "Breeston, tell me, what sleeth curse is your wife inflicted with?"

The druid only smiled and said, "I am not at liberty to say; you must ask her."

Looking back at Alleah and Chloe, he slowly shook his head and climbed down the wooden ladder into the water. Once in the cellar, he regretted his decision, and when the multitude of snakes swarmed around him, he nearly climbed out. Instead, he kissed his holy symbol, prayed for strength to conquer his fears, and forged ahead.

True to Breeston's word, the snakes did not bother him but were constantly there, swimming in and out of the many holes in the muddy walls. The stench of the swamp was magnified there, underground, and he had to cover his nose with his hand to lessen the repulsive odor. After trudging through the water and nearly losing his boots to the sucking mud, he eventually discovered another light far ahead of him. He waded through the water, which remained waist deep, and moved toward the light. Eventually, he came to a set of stone steps, lit nicely by the light of several lanterns hanging on the walls at the top, where the area opened up, perhaps to the beginning of a room.

He stepped out of the water and onto the steps to better see the area. He had to take his time pulling his legs from the dark water because the mud underneath played tug-of-war with his boots. Once out of the water and on the steps, he had to avoid many more snakes that slithered away, some into the water and some under the steps. As he climbed them, the area opened into one large room filled with lovely furnishings: a large bed of fluffy pillows, a table with chairs, and a vanity. Many lanterns hung at various points in the room, lighting it nicely, with only the far corners of the room covered in shadow.

The ceiling was low, barely giving him room to stand, but the area was much nicer than he anticipated. So much so that he did not want to advance off the steps and soil the rugs with the muddy water dripping from him. He stood there momentarily, taking in the strange sight.

"Why don't you take off those clothes so you do not dirty my den?" came a seductive female voice from the right side of the room, within the shadow.

He strained his eyes and could vaguely make out a silhouette within. "Yes, my thoughts exactly," he said nervously. "However, please show yourself so that I may be more comfortable in my nudity."

He did not mind being naked. After all, that was why he was there, and he was sure Zeva knew it. Still, something screamed in his mind to use caution. He trusted Breeston, but it did occur to him then that perhaps he was being set up; maybe this was nothing more than a trap! The woman stepped out of the shadows as those thoughts swirled through his mind. The sight of her had him taking a step back and his jaw going slack. Out of the shadows stepped Alleah.

JAK WAS THE FIRST ONE TO FIND CASSANDRA, HER EYES WIDE AND staring at the tent ceiling, blood trickling from her mouth. The barbarian took in the scene, including the snoring guard and the empty and damaged cage. Before he could react, a cheerful Maltor entered the tent, wearing his lost-but-found-again crown.

"My dearest queen, all is fine. A jealous maid who didn't want an interloper for a queen stole the crown. I will have her hands removed—" he began but stopped abruptly beside Jak, the smile melting from his face.

"Cassandra!" he screamed and ran to her, cradling her head in his arms. "Find Grink, quickly!" he screamed to Jak.

Jak ran from the tent to find the tribal medicine man, and soon after, several shamans worked on Cassandra trying to heal her wounds. However, as soon as a healing spell washed over her and her blackened forearms turned lighter, the flesh immediately reverted to the sickly black hue. And no matter how much they healed, she never regained consciousness, her dead eyes staring off into space. A large crowd had gathered outside the tent, and many rumors had circulated throughout the tribe. The queen was dead.

"Nooo!" Maltor yelled and threw his crown, which he had so feverishly fought to find a short while ago.

He kicked at one of the shamans, connecting with the poor fellow's skull. The man fell face first into the sand and remained motionless. The other shamans, including Grink, were smart enough to flee the tent. Maltor turned his rage to the sleeping guard, who was then coming to. Maltor had forgotten the fool, but now that he sat up and stretched, he was the focus of the barbarian king's wrath. Maltor kicked the man in the ribs, sending him rolling away.

"What happened here?" Maltor roared.

The man, still trying to gain his bearings, looked around, and when he saw the dead form of the queen, his eyes widened. He pointed to her and said groggily, "Devil magic."

That earned him a punch in the face, and he fell back with his arms up as Maltor loomed over him. "If it was dark magic, then why is she dead? She would not kill herself; the fairy escaped and bit her!"

The guard looked to the empty cage, then at Cassandra, genuinely perplexed. When no answer came, Maltor unsheathed his great sword. "No, my king, please! I—"

Maltor's great sword, plunging through his chest, cut off the guard's last words. As the man slid to the ground, dead, Maltor's anger was temporarily sated. The barbarian king heard the murmuring from the crowd outside the tent, and the anger rekindled within him. With a guttural cry, he heaved his mighty sword out of the tent, clipping a man who stood too close and nearly impaling another. The crowd disbursed in a panic, and Maltor grasped the dead guard's axe. He turned to the giant pole holding up the tent, the very one Cassandra remained collared to, and with a mighty roar, began chopping.

"My king," one of the younger guards began, but Jak waved him off.

As the man stepped back slowly and eventually out of the tent, all the guards followed, except for Jak. He had guarded Cassandra since Maltor had first found her, and he had a responsibility to protect her, even if that meant protecting her dead body. He produced a key and went to her, kneeling next to his enraged king, who continued to scream and hack at the massive pole. The timber creaked as the thick pole began to strain against the barrage. Jak slowly unlocked Cassandra's collar and picked her up in his arms. Maltor paid him no mind, so distraught that he did not register the action. Jak carried Cassandra's still form out of the tent shortly before it collapsed, burying Maltor and finally silencing his roars.

A few days later, as several carpenters worked on setting a new pole to hold Maltor's tent, a caravan formed to make a trip to the burial lands located to the south of the desert. The barbarians did not bury their dead; instead, they dumped the bodies and let nature take care of the cleanup. A trip to the burial lands was ordinary among the barbarian tribes, especially now for the Tribe of the Serpent, Maltor's tribe. Along with Cassandra and a few of the tribe who had recently passed, including the guard Maltor had murdered, nearly a dozen other interlopers from the procreation tent, where some of the captives had not survived the harsh environment, were stacked in a camel-drawn cart to make the journey. There were three carts in total: one to hold the members of the tribe, one to carry the interlopers, and one to hold the precious body of Cassandra.

Maltor led the procession on a camel alongside his top advisor, Jozerah. Grink and several of the shamans also came to give rites to the dead tribe members and a unique offering to Strenna, their god, to accept Cassandra's body. A dozen guards escorted the small caravan, but none were needed as there were few hazards along the way, and no tribe would interfere with the trek to the burial lands. Each of the five barbarian tribes had their own burial sites, and the Serpent Tribe had one that snaked the southern edge of the desert. Due to the smell, the burial grounds were nearly a day's travel by camel, so Maltor had much to discuss with his advisor along the way. He was still in a foul mood, and Jozerah was now bearing the brunt of the king's ire.

The intense heat of the Yaddaton Desert affected them very little, the skin of all the barbarians brown and glistening in the sun. The shamans covered the dead bodies with thick cloths to keep the sun from expediting the decaying process. As they traveled, Maltor's anger grew. To have his queen taken from him so suddenly after what he had gone through to get to that point enraged him.

"Boskel is to blame," Maltor said through gritted teeth.

"What, my king?" Jozerah asked.

"Boskel. His fairy killed Cassandra."

"Yes, but that was unintentional—"

"He is to blame!" Maltor roared before his advisor could finish speaking.

"How could he have known?" Jozerah dared to press with Maltor's foul mood. "Besides, he had nothing to do with the fairy's escape, correct?"

Maltor eyed him suspiciously, stealing Jozerah's bluster, so they rode a bit longer without speaking. Maltor's rage slowly consumed him, but he said nothing else. Instead, he stewed on the event, clouding his thoughts with anger and revenge. They eventually reached their burial ground, which was nothing more than a sea of dead bodies, with hundreds of vultures in the branches of nearby trees awaiting a fresh meal. The bodies already filling the sea of dead were picked clean, and now the hungry birds eyed the caravan intently. A few still picked at the bleached bones of the dead and took flight when the barbarians got too close, settling with the other hateful birds in the trees.

Maltor eyed them with disgust and anger but understood their part in the burial system. He recalled Cassandra's battle with the warrior from the Vulture Tribe fondly. She had defeated that opponent and even coaxed a vulture under her opponent's control to peck out her eye. Cassandra was Maltor's prize, one he would never replace. The cart with the interlopers was dumped, with no regard to how the various bodies landed in the sea of dead, stiffening limbs sticking this way and that. Next, they gently laid the three tribe members on the interlopers. It was tradition for the true barbarians of Maltor's tribe to enter the afterlife ahead of others, so they presented their bodies first to the vultures so they did not have time to linger and decay.

Grink said a few words over them and sprinkled their bodies with various spices and oils. According to the shaman, the items would ensure a safe journey to the afterlife. After the brief ceremony, the shamans came to stand before Cassandra's cart. She looked stunning, wearing the same gown Maltor would have married her in. Maltor himself had cleaned her face of the dried blood and vomit that was there when they found her body. Handmaidens had covered her discolored arms with powders so her color appeared more natural. They applied some of the cover around her lips, as well, since her mouth had also begun discoloring in the same fashion. Even in death, she was beautiful to the proud barbarian king, and this showed on his face. All those witnessing the ceremony could see that her passing truly saddened him.

He bent and kissed her lips gently, then whispered in her ear, "I have lost you now, my wife, my prize, my gift from Strenna. I send you with honors to the afterlife and will avenge your death. Go, my beautiful bride, and know that we will be reunited in the fields of Strenna one day."

Grink handed him a veil, and he placed it gently over her face. The strong king appeared to be on the verge of tears, but he swallowed his sorrow and turned his face into a visage of anger. He watched as two young men of the tribe came to place her in the burial sea, but he stopped them and picked up the body himself. If he had not been so grief-stricken and with plans to avenge Cassandra's death dancing in his head, he would have noticed how limp her body still was as rigor mortis had indeed not set in. Perhaps if the men had carried the body or the shamans had been able to get closer, someone might have noticed the shallow rise and fall of her chest.

Maltor placed her gently in the ditch of the dead atop the three freshly buried members of the tribe. Grink gasped but did not react beyond that, although the act of burying an interloper on top of tribe members was blasphemy in his eyes. After all, Cassandra was never an official member of the tribe, although she had almost been their queen. Jozerah gave the shaman a stern look, and Grink looked to his feet, understanding the silent threat.

As the shamans prayed to Strenna, Maltor whispered to Jozerah, "When we return, we go to war."

"What? With whom?" Jozerah asked.

"Boskel and the Culiem Tribe."

"To avenge this?" Jozerah asked, waving a hand toward Cassandra's still form.

"Yes," Maltor said, eyes boring holes through his advisor.

"As you wish, my king," Jozerah said with a bow. "I can have the warriors ready to march within three days of our return."

"Two."

"My king, it will take—" Jozerah began before he saw the look on Maltor's face. He bowed and said, "In two days. They will be ready in two days upon our return."

Maltor nodded, then solemnly watched the remainder of the ceremony, nearing tears multiple times. The proud king had not shed a tear since he was a child, and that fact would stand when they eventually left. Once the shamans climbed out of the pit and Maltor inspected the body of his queen one final time, the barbarians headed home. None noticed the small butterfly-like creature fly out from under one of the wagons and flitter into the sea of bodies as they left.

"WHAT TYPE OF MAGIC IS THIS?" GREYSON ASKED, STANDING ON ZEVA'S steps, water dripping from his clothes.

"Is she not your desire?" the fake Alleah said.

"Of course, but you are Zeva, are you not?"

"The one and only."

"Then let me see you in your natural form."

"Why? If this is your desire, will this not allow you to pleasure me more fully, not to mention the enjoyment you will receive?"

Greyson began to argue the point; after all, he preferred to know what a woman honestly looked like before having sex with her. Of course, he had never seen a sleeth, and perhaps that was the curse; maybe she was not attractive. However, the more he considered it, the more he agreed with her. She looked and sounded like Alleah, so this would be a marvelous fantasy for him. Perhaps he never really needed to know her actual appearance, he reasoned; he just needed the gem. His groin began to tingle with anticipation at what delights the sleeth might be able to give him. He started unbuttoning his shirt. Zeva smiled and walked to the pillow bed, where she lay down and patted it for Greyson to join her. Soon, he was nude and walked the remainder of the steps.

"Impressive," Zeva said, admiring his nakedness.

He stood before her, his hands on his hips, looking her over. He knew what he saw was an illusion, but it was perfect. She even smelled like Alleah, which completed the package. As far as he was concerned, it was Alleah before him, not Breeston's wife.

"Now, Alleah, I will finally have you," he said with a lewd smile.

Playing the part, Zeva bit the tip of her finger seductively and said, "My god forbids me to be with a man, so I am but a virgin."

She knew Alleah was a virgin as well? That impressed Greyson and added even more to her elaborate illusion. He wondered if his friend's anatomy would be accurate once he removed the sleeth's clothing. How could she know all those details concerning Alleah?

As he considered those things, Zeva said, "Be gentle."

Greyson fell over her and began kissing her hard, something he had always wanted to do with the true Alleah. Even her kisses tasted sweet, and soon, his hands explored her body and began removing her clothes. They made love; it was everything Greyson had dreamed, and Zeva was highly passionate about her lovemaking. She reminded him very much of the one night he had had with Matilda, and to add to the similarity to that night, Zeva was insatiable. He was a thorough lover, but he had a difficult time keeping up with her that night. Finally, after many hours of lovemaking, they collapsed into each other's arms, exhausted. Greyson drifted off to sleep a delighted and content young man.

GREYSON AWAKENED SOMETIME LATER TO AN AWFUL SMELL THAT reminded him of rotten fish. He slowly opened his eyes and blinked away the sleep, trying to gain his bearings. It took him a few moments to remember he was in Zeva's bed. He would have smiled at the thought of their affair, but the odor was too strong. He realized that Zeva was asleep, her head on his chest. Her hair was a greenish hue, and when he looked down at her, the smell almost had him retching. The smell was coming from her!

He moved to push her off him and rise but realized that his arms were tied to eyehooks in the wall. He struggled to move his legs only to find them fastened to another set of hooks on the floor. He tried to break free, but the binds were sure, and the effort aggravated his injured shoulder where Cerus had stabbed him with his spear over a year earlier. His effort awakened Zeva, who sat up, still naked, and stretched her spindly arms.

"Good morning, lover," she purred and kissed him.

Her breath smelled worse than her hair, and he tried to turn his head to avoid the kiss. However, she held him still with incredible strength and forced her tongue into his mouth. Now, her authentic taste overwhelmed him. It was the worst sensation he could imagine, and he gagged several times as her tongue danced with his.

She eventually broke the kiss and sat up, and he finally got a good look at her. Her skin was as green as her hair, and she had many warts and moles on her face, most with long hairs protruding from them. She had prominent, bushy eyebrows, and her teeth were yellowish-brown. When she stretched, he noticed large tufts of hair poking from her armpits, and her arms and legs were thick with coarse hair as well. She was absolutely the most repulsive woman he had ever met.

"I thought you liked my kisses," she pouted.

"You, no! Alleah, yes!" he screamed out in a panic.

"We made love for a very long time last night, and I am highly fertile this time of the month. There is a good chance I am pregnant," she purred.

"No!" he screamed.

"But wouldn't you like one of those rare gems that my loins can produce, just like Breeston?"

"No, I have changed my mind; I do not want one," Greyson said, nearing a panic attack.

"But that is the whole point of you being here, is it not? I can make things interesting for you. I recently gave birth to a new nest of Breeston's children, so I am still lactating," she said, straddling him so her breasts were in his face.

He noticed that her breasts had many hairs growing from the nipples and green milk leaking from them. She held one up to his face, and he turned his head to avoid it. Again, she forced it back and pulled on her right nipple, spraying his mouth and face with green milk. The odor intensified, and he nearly lost his last meal.

"Please… Zeva, you must release me," he choked between gags.

"Nonsense, we must make love all day today to ensure that you impregnate me. After all, I need more children, and you need your gem, remember?"

"No, Zeva, I cannot perform for you," he said honestly, still trying to catch his breath as the sticky milk dried on his lips and chin.

She got off the pillowy bed and went to one of her vanities. After rummaging through her drawers, she came back with a small container. Greyson was thankful for the reprieve because the smell nearly vanished entirely while she was on the other side of the room. However, it grew as she returned, making his stomach churn again.

"Please, Zeva, I cannot."

She unscrewed the cap of the small container and dabbed two fingers inside, pulling them out coated with a white cream.

"I thought you might act this way, so I have a way to make you comply."

"I cannot, Zeva, I—"

He stopped mid-sentence when she grabbed his manhood and began rubbing the lotion on it. "Wait, what are you doing?"

"Getting you ready, my lover," she purred.

The lotion did not hurt as he suspected it might, and the fondling felt nice. As his body absorbed the lotion, his member responded fully. Soon, he was erect and ready for them to continue their lovemaking.

"That's more like it," she said, climbing atop him.

"Breeston!" he screamed as he entered her.

She cut off his screams with a hard kiss that had him gagging again. She was insatiable, just like the night before, and the lotion allowed him to orgasm many times before finally giving out. It was very late that night before Zeva let him rest, and the only food he received was the green milk from her breasts, which she assured him was nutritious. He was a prisoner and feared she might never release him. With the help of her special lotion, his manhood betrayed him. They made love for the next two days with few breaks in between. He was physically spent when, at last, she finished with him.

"That should be enough," she said with a smile as she untied him after the third day.

"Enough?' he asked, donning his clothes quickly once he was free of the binds.

"To produce a gem. I am pregnant, that I am sure of. The gem may or may not transpire. I will send word through Breeston once I know, and if not, we can try again," she purred.

He gagged and dry-heaved at the thought and limped toward the stairs as quickly as possible. His sore groin made it a challenging walk, and the swamp water burned him there once submerged. He hardly registered the snakes swimming around him while returning to the trap door.

Zeva called out after him, "Come back to me, lover, if you'd like to have another go at it. You are most welcome anytime."

He finally retched fully, spewing green milk into the water, making him retch even harder.

THE VULTURES SWOOPED IN FOR THEIR MEAL BEFORE THE BARBARIANS were out of sight. That was the way of Yaddaton; the barbarians brought their dead, and the vultures greedily ate them. Gophia was there to shoo them away from Cassandra; although the spices and oils the shamans had placed on her helped repel them some, it was a chore the little fairy had a difficult time accomplishing. The vultures were hungry, always so, and she was small. However, Gophia wanted to give Cassandra a chance if she was alive. The little fairy didn't believe she could survive the potent venom from her bite but had risked her life to make the journey to the burial site in case there was a chance of her living.

Her new friend hadn't moved and appeared dead to Gophia. Still, she would keep her safe for as long as possible. Gophia was far from home and needed a friend, and she trusted Cassandra. So, the fairy remained vigilant. The hateful birds wanted to begin their feast with Cassandra since she was atop the stack of bodies, but when they tried, Gophia hissed at them and shooed them off as best she could. Still, they were relentless, and she was small and not very intimidating. They did move on to the lower bodies, pecking and tearing at them and pulling them from the pile. The disruption of the stacked bodies made Cassandra slip further into the stinking mass of decay. Gophia could do nothing to prevent that, and the smell of rotting flesh and the relentless assault from the vultures made it difficult for her to stay.

Eventually, exhaustion from fighting with the birds overtook her. She slept atop Cassandra's still form, intending to leave if she had not stirred by the next night. She shed a tear as she slept, saddened at the apparent loss of her friend.

SHE AWAKENED EARLY THE FOLLOWING DAY AS THE VULTURES RETURNED to their feast. One had already started on Cassandra's little finger, eliciting a groan from the woman. To Gophia's surprise and delight, Cassandra was not dead! That renewed the fairy's motivation to protect her new friend. She screamed and hissed at the vulture, which eventually hopped away with a flap of its wings. The creatures grew more daring as the day went on, moving in to peck at Cassandra, each strike drawing blood and making Cassandra moan slightly. Gophia tried to awaken her, but the woman was non-responsive. So, she fought the birds as best she could, but it was a losing battle.

By late that evening, Cassandra was bleeding from multiple pecks but remained unconscious. The stench was nearly unbearable for Gophia as the bodies had bloated under the hot sun for almost a day and a half. Several dead vultures lay in the vicinity—Gophia had resorted to biting them. It was not pleasant to taste the filthy birds, but it was the only way to truly protect her friend. She grew tired and could not continue the fight much longer. That second night, she tried desperately to awaken Cassandra, but to no avail. She eventually slept, tired, hungry, and very thirsty.

THE FOLLOWING DAY, CASSANDRA AWAKENED TO THE SOUND OF A skirmish and an unbearable pain in her arm. She opened her eyes after days of unconsciousness to a blinding sun and the smell of death all around her. She did not recall where she was or how she had arrived there, but a flock of angry birds in the open desert surrounded her. Her fuzzy mind initially thought them to be the ravens coming to take her to the afterlife. After all, she felt like she was dying, with a burning in the pit of her stomach and all of her extremities aching. That was especially true for her left arm, which felt like it was splitting open. She was aware of the pain, although her dulled senses tried to register what her eyes saw: a whirlwind of feathers and beating wings surrounded her, followed by a familiar shriek or a hiss. She would also occasionally feel a stab of pain in her hand or leg, but nothing to compare to the pain she felt in her left arm.

As she slowly came to, she realized the birds were not ravens at all but vultures. Worst of all, they were eating her! She saw little Gophia trying to prevent their attacks, swooping this way and that, biting and hissing at the birds. The pain in her arm significantly subsided as the fairy chased away the bird perched there but then had to hurry away to chase off another one at her feet. The fairy was protecting her, but where were they? She slowly remembered the ruse to escape the barbarians and how Gophia had bitten her and then fled. But the fairy had returned to help her; that was obvious. But where could they be? With the overwhelming stench of death and the many vultures, she soon realized she had made it to the sea of death. She had escaped the barbarians, but her situation was dire, and she was now exposed to the dangers Yaddaton had to offer.

The vulture alighted on her left arm and began feeding there again. The pain returned, an excruciating pain that got her attention as she fully regained her senses. She summoned the energy to lift her head and study the creature. To her horror, she saw it pecking away at her darkened fore-arm, actually pulling the cactus needle from her arm and tossing it aside so it could get at her flesh. The pain had her nearly blacking out again, but she managed to half sit and shoo the bird away. Her movement caused the birds to take flight and also caused a wave of nausea to bubble up inside her. She turned to the side enough to throw up a dark pool of blood and venom. However, the movement caused her to slip further into the various bodies that served as her bed.

The soft, bloated bodies quickly parted with her tumble, moving aside as she sank further or rupturing and emitting a decaying gas. Her hand plunged into a decomposing body, furthering her sickness. The fall was not far, but the pain that wracked her body was nearly unbearable. She retracted her hand, but not before it closed around something solid, something metal. She retched some more, and the smell permeated her, engulfing her. She tried to move, but the effort only made her sink into decaying flesh even more. Her hand held tight to the metal piece, unaware of the action.

"Cassandra, we must leave at once! I cannot fight the nasty birds; they hurt Gophia and Cassandra. Gophia tired." Gophia's voice suddenly squealed excitedly in her head.

Cassandra's weary mind understood the words of her tiny protector, and she renewed her struggle to be free of the dead bodies. It took many moments, and she dry-heaved many times in the process, but no more blood came up, and she considered that a good sign. Eventually, she was free from the tangle of bodies and the birds, who seemed to lose interest in her as she crawled out of the gully. The birds swarmed in once she was away from the dead, bloated bodies, tearing and pecking at the rotting flesh. Cassandra collapsed at the edge and fell on her back, the sun roasting her again. She hurt all over and understood her pain to be from multiple sources: wounds from the birds pecking her, severe sunburn, and remnants of the strong venom still in her system all fought against her.

As she lay there, catching her breath and trying to recover from the intense pain, Gophia flittered over to her and landed lightly on her chest. The little fairy looked about as bad as Cassandra felt, her hair matted to her face with sweat, her skin burned a bright red, and she panted heavily. The two sat like that for a moment before Cassandra smiled weakly. Gophia returned the smile and hugged her neck, making a purring-like sound. Cassandra knew the fairy had saved her life, but they were not out of the woods yet. They needed shelter from the sun and desperately needed food and water, especially water.

As they lay there, just a few feet from the sea of dead and the feasting vultures, Cassandra finally became aware of the metal object in her hand. She did not remember grasping it and had no idea how long she had held it, but she was reasonably sure she had obtained it from one of the bodies deep in the pile of decaying flesh. She slowly brought the item up to her face and was astonished to see a medallion in her hand, the broken chain indicating that it had once been a necklace. It was a perfect sculpture of a wand with a trail of stars, the unmistakable holy symbol of Gella, her goddess.

GREYSON EMERGED FROM BREESTON'S CELLAR, SHAKEN AND ANGRY. He let the cellar door slam shut and staggered out of the cottage to find Breeston putting the final touches on the staff he was carving for him.

"What did you do?" he moaned through gritted teeth, then gingerly sat on a log beside the druid.

"I see you met Zeva," Breeston said with a chuckle.

"You should have told me," Greyson moaned, adjusting his injured crotch.

"Would you have gone to see her if I told you her curse, that she is the most hideous and repulsive woman alive?"

"Of course not!"

"Then I have done you a favor."

"How is that a favor, Breeston? I have never been more repulsed."

"Yet now you may have that elusive gem that will bring you closer to your god."

"Even so, I am not returning to fetch it. It is not worth it."

Breeston chuckled, even more so when Greyson had to stand because sitting was causing him too much discomfort. "I have a salve for that," the druid announced.

"Good, I need all you've got."

"I'll fetch it," Breeston said, standing and heading for the cottage door. "Here, feel it out and see if it is to your liking," he added, tossing Greyson the staff.

Breeston went inside, leaving Greyson to look over the staff. The wood was dark, almost black, with streaks of grey running its length. The druid had sanded it smooth, and Greyson ran a finger along it. At the top was a tangle of small branches that had been fashioned into a nice little cubby for a gem to fit, assuming he would have one before he left. He didn't hold out much hope for it, and he certainly meant what he had told Breeston: he would not venture into that cellar again.

He heard Alleah and Chloe returning from their daily food gathering. Their mood was light, and he heard Alleah's beautiful laugh before he saw the duo. Greyson moved gingerly to a spot to get a better look, using the staff to assist him. He immediately liked the feel of it and was surprised at how little it weighed.

He forgot about the staff when he glimpsed the two women carrying the large basket of mushrooms that would serve as their dinner. By her looks, Alleah had recently bathed, a rare treat in the forsaken swamp, and she looked stunning. Images of her lustful expressions he had experienced as he plowed into her flashed through his mind. Of course, he knew it hadn't been Alleah, but he held on to that memory as accurate, and it caused a stirring in his groin.

"She gave you that, right?" Breeston asked, suddenly behind him and nodding toward Alleah.

Greyson adjusted his injured manhood and nodded slightly, never taking his eyes off Alleah's perfect face.

"Well, at least that's something," Breeston said, handing him a small cup of salve.

He walked back into the cottage as Greyson slowly rubbed the salve into his groin. It did feel better almost immediately, and he whispered his reply long after the druid had left. "Absolutely," he said, still watching Alleah intently as she and Chloe cleaned the food they had found, unaware of his presence.

The Tome

SASHA DE'FORMEN HAD NOT RETURNED TO HER HOMELAND AS SHE had told Daro she would. It was not by choice, however. She had discarded her necklace; the one Clade instructed her to wear so he could monitor her time in the human world a month ago, tossing it into the water near the falls. She had expected him to open the gate immediately to confront her. He had not. Her home was in the land of ice called Glacies, and she was an ice carofex, a race similar to humans in appearance but with a powerful command over ice. She had befriended Daro, the ranger, during her time in the world of humans, and he had even helped her defeat the demoness so she could obtain what she had come for: Iustia, the wonderous sword of ice. She would not have been able to defeat such an enemy without his help or that of the surprising vampire lord, Heinsvick, who had lost his life in the process.

She had abandoned Daro shortly after the battle with the great demon, as Clade, her master, and Presin, her uncle, had ordered her to return to the falls with the sword. From there, they would open the gate to her world so she could return. Instead, she had discarded the necklace and hastily created a fake Iustia, using the powers of the actual sword to create a near-perfect replica. She intended to use the fake to barter for her mother's life. She held Iustia up before her eyes, studying the wondrous item. She would gladly trade it to Clade for her mother's release, but she knew in her heart he would not honor his word. No, she would have to barter with the fake Iustia and hope they didn't see the true nature of the replica sword.

She had to keep the copy in the cool water because it was made entirely of ice, and the chilly water was the only thing cool enough to keep it frozen. Although Iustia was also wholly made from ice, the magical properties in that sword held it together, no matter the temperature. It was an artifact, but the fake was not, and it would melt quickly in the heat. She understood the danger in that as the weather changed in the strange human world, and she felt the uncomfortable bite of the heat as spring came on in full. She was not familiar with what spring truly meant or what exactly it was. However, it had been nearly a month since she had tossed the necklace, and during that time, the ice and snow surrounding the cave behind the waterfall were melting.

It had been far too long for Clade to react to the lost necklace. Why the delay? Was he still able to watch her even without her necklace? Did he know of her plan to barter for her mother with a sword as fragile as a melting icicle? He had warned her he would come for her if she tried to flee, and he obviously knew she had the sword, so what was the delay? Discarding the amulet implied she was fleeing, but still, there had been no gate. All she could do was wait and hope the gate would eventually open. In the meantime, she would keep the fake sword whole by leaving it in the cool water and using the powers of Iustia to keep it from melting.

Clade was smart, and the long delay in opening the gate made her nervous. She felt insignificant and dreaded facing Clade alone. Sasha had thought of Daro often since they parted ways, and she wished he were there, for she sorely needed an ally. However, she had to try to save her mother. The risk was worth the effort to free her from the horrible ice carofex of Glacies. She wanted her mother to taste the freedom the human world offered. Sasha drifted off and dreamed of her mother. She couldn't remember anything about her, but she was kind and beautiful in her dream, not ugly like Sasha. That made her smile.

The next day was hot, and she ventured out of the cave only to take a quick bath and wash her clothes in the large river where the falls spilled. She searched for her favorite food, the fruit Daro called apples, but could find none. Instead, she rationed what little food remained from Daro's stores. She had visited his small cottage a few weeks earlier and took most of the remaining food, knowing that he wouldn't be there to eat it and wouldn't mind if she helped herself. Now that the food was almost gone, she had to ration it. Once it ran out, she'd have to find food, meaning leaving the waterfalls. She did not intend to do that if she could avoid it.

After her refreshing bath, she returned to the small cave behind the falls where she had lived for the last month. She carried her clothes in and laid them on some rocks to dry. She knew something was wrong almost immediately, and she turned with a start to find Clade emerging from the cave recesses, followed by two monstrous dibolicies, also referred to as ice demons. The creatures were tall, nearly eight feet in height, and made of ice. Red, beady eyes glowed from within their faces. The beasts had maws filled with icy teeth, and razor-sharp icicles hung from their arms. They commonly served only powerful carofex, and the fact Clade had two under his control was a testament to his prowess. They moved to flank her as Clade walked to stand before her.

"Dear Ugly One, why are you naked before me? Do you have no shame?" he asked, diverting his gaze to the cave ceiling.

"Don't call me that. I am not as ugly as you would have me believe."

"Did the humans lie to you and say you are beautiful, dear? They are hideous creatures, so they naturally find you attractive. You are the same ugly person that walked out of Iciale months ago," her uncle, Presin, said, walking out of the shadows to join Clade.

He had a smirk on his face, and worse, he had Iustia. She hated him at that moment of arrogance. She glanced at the hiding spot where she kept the sword; it was not there. She had let her guard down long enough to bathe, and now they had the weapon. There would be no bargaining for her mother's life.

"Ah, yes, Iustia is back home where it belongs. Did you truly think you could keep it from us, Ugly One?" Clade asked, holding out his hand for the sword.

Presin grinned evilly and bowed to Clade, offering the sword with both hands. The older priest took it and marveled at the blade as it sparkled in the light creeping through the falls. Sasha wanted to reply that she had no intention of keeping the sword, but that would have been a lie. Men like Clade and Presin would detect such a lie because they were masters of deception. With her attention on the glimmering blade, she didn't realize the ice demons had moved closer. She was a warrior, one of the best that Clade had ever developed, but the beasts used a natural ability to move silently, and she didn't see them until it was too late. They were suddenly close, and each grabbed an arm and held her tight, their grips vice-like.

"And now, for your punishment, child. We will take you back to the sewers, and you will suffer the heater before being thrown back into your cell," Clade said with a wicked smile.

"No, please," Sasha whispered.

The heater was a device the evil priests of her home of Castle Iciale had developed to emit a tremendous amount of heat. They would strap their victims to a chair underneath the heating unit and leave them there for days. To an ice carofex, it was the cruelest and most extreme torture imaginable.

"Oh, yes, dear, but I will not kill you for your deception because you have succeeded in your quest, and I have what I wanted. However, I will send you back to your sewer home, and perhaps one day, you can serve me again. First, we will reapply your ice mask, child," Clade said, bringing his hand up before her face to fashion a new mask.

She had worn a similar mask all her life until they released her to come to this world. Her heart broke as she considered wearing it again. With her spirit thoroughly crushed and resigning to the fact her life was forfeit, that the slight reprieve was over, she made her desperate request: "Do with me what you will, but please release my mother."

It came out as a pathetic squeak, and the two men nearly burst out laughing immediately. She knew the answer before either of them could calm themselves and respond. They would not free her mother, and she would not get to meet her. Sasha's heart broke at the terrible thought, but then Presin said something that seemed much worse.

"I killed your mother right after you were born, Ugly One. She embarrassed the family by spreading her legs for an ugly human, then gave birth to a hideous child. She died for that mistake while you were but a few days old," he said, chuckling.

Tears welled in her eyes, and she looked at the floor, stunned but unsurprised. She had failed to see the lie, and now she was caught in that web of evil once more. She had lost her sword, her freedom, and Daro, her only true friend. She was a fool.

"Hold her still while I make a nice mask to cover that hideous face," Clade said to the dibolicies.

Their strong arms held her tighter, but she made no effort to struggle or break free. She was caught, and she deserved what was to come. She didn't care anymore. So, when Clade's hands moved to the side of her face, and the frost started to pour forth, she accepted her fate and felt the familiar ice mask begin to take hold. However, before it could truly begin, it ended. A loud clap of thunder reverberated through the cavern, deafening Sasha and throwing Clade against the far wall. Her hair danced wildly from the electrical charge and it took her a moment to register the event as the next few moments were complete chaos.

She saw Clade's smoldering form lying still near the cave's far wall. She could not tell if he was alive, but his entire body spasmed uncontrollably from the sudden strike. A lightning bolt must have entered the caves, but she did not understand how that was possible. She turned to regard movement from the cave entrance and was overjoyed to find Daro and another man there, holding a wand pointing in her direction, the apparent source of the attack on Clade.

A smile found its way onto her face, replacing the despair. But before she could greet her new friend, an excruciatingly intense pain shuddered through her back and chest. She vaguely heard Daro scream but couldn't hear his words. She looked down and saw a large, blood-soaked spear of ice sticking out of her chest. An ice demon had stabbed one of its forearm icicles through her back. She assumed it must have barely missed her heart, for it did not instantly kill her, but she understood she was as good as dead. The wound was mortal, and the pain shuddered through her body. She felt herself cry out, and then the creatures released her arms, which flopped down uselessly at her sides. She hung there, impaled on the creature's arm like a trophy catch hauled in by a demonic fisherman. Then the beast grabbed her by the hair with one arm and pulled its other arm away, removing the giant sliver of ice from her back. It then tossed her like a rag doll into the cool water.

The water quickly became clouded with her blood, but she barely felt the pain of the wound. That scared her more than anything. But in that near-death moment, she regained enough of her senses to understand her friend had returned for her and Daro was in trouble. Few could fight dibolicies individually, but two would prove very difficult. She tried swimming back to the falls, which seemed so very far away. Her body did not fully answer her call to swim, and she awkwardly half-floated and half-swam toward her goal. Her arms didn't seem to function correctly. Her only hope would be to find her hidden sword in the water. She'd had foresight enough to switch the swords before her bath. If Clade had retrieved the sword she'd left with her things, which was fake, that would mean Iustia was still hidden in the water, near shore.

She struggled mightily to make her way to the spot. She could not see well with all the blood darkening the water, and her vision became filled with dark splotches. Her body was shutting down, and she almost gave up as she struggled with the waterfall's current. Her lungs began to burn from the lack of oxygen. She felt numb and hopeless, but the sudden sound of another lightning blast made her move again. She gave it her all, not for herself, but for Daro and, more importantly, her mother.

BAXTER AND DARO HAD USED VICTORIA'S MAGIC CARPET TO FLY FROM Pelesea to Wolf's Crest Waterfall, where Daro had first met Sasha. They hoped to find her quickly, but Daro seemed doubtful, so Baxter didn't hold out much hope. They planned to find her and convince her to join the New Order. If she accepted, Daro and she would return to Pelesea, while Baxter would continue to Oldorburg to extend the same offer to Max, the town's sheriff. Daro had tried to tell him of the character and extraordinary beauty of Sasha De'Formen during the trip, but he had paid little attention to the ranger. In truth, his thoughts rested solely on his lost love, Cassandra Rho.

Baxter had been overwhelmed and jubilant at learning Cassandra was alive. She had not died in the fire, but no one knew what had truly happened to her. The queen believed that Boz the carofex was directly responsible for the deception of her death, as well as her kidnapping, and Baxter agreed that was the most feasible story. But what had happened to her since then? His heart raced at being reunited with her. He had never had a chance to discuss things with her after that magical kiss. Did she like the kiss? She had kissed him back that day, so he assumed so. Did she feel the same about him as he did about her? He had to find the answers to these questions, which he had thought were lost until now.

So, when he landed the carpet outside the waterfall and Daro spotted fresh tracks leading into the cave behind them, he quickly followed. When he entered the cave, he was stunned to see a woman he could describe only as physically perfect, restrained by some ice-like creatures. She was beautiful enough to catch him off guard, but what made the situation more startling was the fact she was naked. Her body was as perfect as her face. Daro was right; if this was Sasha, she was absolutely the most beautiful woman he had ever seen. His mind tried to absorb everything about her, especially her nakedness, and his gawking delayed his response to the dangers before them. Baxter was stunned for a moment until Daro went into action. The ranger drew his swords and charged at the creatures, so Baxter drew his wand. That was when Baxter realized two strange-looking men were also standing near the woman. Luckily, the deafening sound of the falls masked their entrance, and no one seemed to notice their arrival.

It looked to Baxter like the giant ice creatures were the most dangerous foes. However, as he aimed with his wand, he discerned that the real villains were the two men standing before the helpless woman. His instincts told him to focus on one of them. One in particular looked to be performing a spell, and Baxter was confident it would harm her if he allowed its completion. He could not allow that, so he took aim at the man and hit him squarely with a bolt, flinging him hard against the cave wall, where his body spasmed and smoked. Baxter heard Daro scream in denial and looked to see one of the ice creatures driving a spike of ice through the woman's back. The amount of blood that instantly gushed from the wound and trickled from her perfect mouth told Baxter all he needed to know—the wound would kill her.

Daro advanced on the creature that had impaled his friend and engaged it in combat, his swords flashing in fantastic precision. The beast had easily flung Sasha into the water, where the churning from the falls turned it a dark red, and Sasha disappeared. Daro's anger played out, and he fought brilliantly against the giant beast, striking it several times and taking chunks of ice with each hit. However, he seemed to be doing only minor damage, and Daro was barely dodging the monster's deadly swings. The beast ignored Daro's stinging hits, and they only seemed to enrage it. Baxter was torn between the reddening water where the creature had tossed Sasha and the battle raging before him.

He stepped toward the water, but Daro yelled his name and broke him out of that trance. He turned to see the second ice creature approaching the battle, which would quickly overwhelm the ranger. "A little help, here!" Daro yelled.

Baxter quickly summoned the energy for a spell. Soon, three magical darts left his finger tips and slammed into the second creature's face. It growled in pain and turned toward him. It roared and took several giant strides his way. Baxter calmly pointed his wand and called forth a mighty stroke of lightning that smashed into the creature's open mouth. The beast didn't fly across the room like the man had, but it stopped as shards of ice flew all about the area and black smoke rolled from its maw. The lower half of the monster's jaw hung awkwardly, and as the smoke cleared, Baxter could see that few teeth remained. The red, evil dots that flickered within its eyes slowly faded, and the creature fell to the ground dead.

That seemed to inspire Daro as he doubled the intensity of his attacks. Baxter had never seen such a fantastic display of swordsmanship as Daro's blades became blurs. Daro's attacks hit more often than they missed, but the wounds he was causing seemed superficial to Baxter. He wondered if Daro's slashing swords could even harm the ice creature. The ranger was much faster than his opponent, but he was tiring and narrowly dodging the beast's swinging arms. From witnessing Sasha's apparent death, Baxter knew what would happen if the creature caught Daro. But because the combatants moved so swiftly, he could not summon another lightning bolt for fear of hitting the ranger. An idea occurred then, so he holstered the wand and quickly gathered his components to cast a spell to assist Daro.

SASHA EVENTUALLY FOUND THE SWORD, AND TO HER DELIGHT, IT WAS Iustia. She grasped it and let the extraordinary power flow through her. Sasha summoned the power of the magnificent weapon to heal her wound, and she felt it closing almost immediately. The relief was exquisite, and after regaining her strength, she quickly crested the water, taking in a giant gulp of air. Her burning lungs received the much-needed oxygen, and the sword continued to heal her. Sasha was in bliss momentarily, and she shut her eyes as she basked in the sensation.

The sounds of battle rang out around her, and she knew Daro needed her. The sword completed its healing cycle, and Sasha breathed deeply. With the exhale, she prepared herself mentally for the fight. She wasn't fully healed, but she would not die from the wound; she just hoped she was strong enough to help her friends.

She opened her eyes to find Presin standing before her, up to his knees in water, the fake Iustia leveled at her throat. She realized she was kneeling before her uncle. She knew right away that the evil man had made two significant errors—first, he believed his sword to be the authentic relic, and second, he could not see her arms with everything below her shoulders submerged. He did not realize she held Iustia and was feeding off its energy. The smirk on his face told her that he had no clue how much danger he was in.

"I'm glad to see you are alive, Ugly One. I have many tortures awaiting you in the sewers of Iciale. Now get up, and let's go home."

He grabbed her by the arm to pull her out of the water while leveling the sword at her neck with his other hand. He seemed surprised when Sasha stood and brought forth Iustia as she did. His eyes widened, and he fell back, sitting hard in the water. She noticed his eyes grow bigger as the water rolled off her naked form, and her mostly healed wound came into view, no longer bleeding.

"I don't think so, Uncle, for I have the artifact you seek. The weapon you hold is nothing but a fragile piece of ice."

"How?" he sputtered, leveling the fake sword her way.

"I understand how you could make that error," she continued, ignoring his question. "The swords look nearly identical. However, Iustia doesn't like you and will never accept you as its wielder. So, you'd still be doomed even if we exchanged weapons."

"I am your uncle, and you will obey my commands, child! Drop that weapon; it does not belong to you," Presin said, standing and backing out of the water.

Sasha ignored him but slowly advanced from the water, peripherally keeping an eye on Daro as she did. Daro and his friend engaged with the lone dibolicie and seemed to have the situation under control—she knew she could focus on the task at hand. A smile crept across her beautiful face as her eyes became crystal-like, reflecting the light in the cave and making her seem powerful. With Iustia, she indeed was.

Presin recognized this as well and, in a moment of panic, took the ice sword and hurled it like a spear her way. Sasha didn't flinch and held up her hand, catching the sword telekinetically and holding it in midair, easily manipulating the ice that comprised it. It floated before her, and Presin's eyes seemed to pop out of his head. With a flick of her left hand, the sword shot across the cave. Presin's turning head seemed to take several moments to catch up with the movement, and his mouth hung agape when he saw the destination of the fake sword, for there was Clade, the most powerful man in Castle Iciale, standing again, trying to recover from the lightning attack that would have killed most men. He had somehow regained his feet, but now that effort was for naught as the fake Iciale struck him in the chest.

His face and hands were red from the lightning bolt, his hair stood on end, waving crazily about, and the hilt of the ice sword protruded from his chest. To his credit, he did not fall but staggered toward the open portal that would take him back home. Presin had a similar idea and wanted nothing more to do with Sasha. He sprinted toward the falls, where Clade stepped through. Sasha was not going to let her evil uncle escape, though. She knelt, put Iustia in the water, and called for the sword's power to freeze water. It did, turning the water to ice all around her and making a straight line of freezing liquid form to the falls, where it spread quickly, freezing the falling water before Presin could run through. The booming sound of the falls became a trickle, and Presin reached the wall of ice and began pounding on it, calling for Clade's assistance. Sasha advanced.

BAXTER NEARLY LOST HIS SPELL WHEN SASHA EMERGED FROM THE water. She was alive, appeared uninjured, and was armed with a unique-looking sword. Baxter's mind barely registered the icicle-shaped weapon as he transfixed on her god-like features. Her face was perfect, and her eyes, now sparkling like diamonds, only enhanced her beauty. Then there was the rest of her, completely nude and on display without a hint of modesty. Her skin was a faint blue color now, and Baxter didn't know if that was from the loss of blood or the cold temperature of the water, but that slight change in her skin also added to her beauty. He almost stopped his chant, which would finalize his spell to assist Daro, as he became entranced by her extraordinary beauty.

"Baxter!" Daro yelled, breaking him from his trance.

He somehow maintained the spellcasting and returned to the matters at hand. Daro was dodging now more than he was attacking, his swords being used more as shields than weapons. He barely dodged a savage swing by the ice demon, but the creature was backing him into a corner. He feigned an attack to the right but quickly cut back to the left, trying to escape the trap. But then the beast did something neither expected and breathed a ray of dangerous frost. Daro managed to duck the attack, but it knocked him off balance, and he stumbled back into the wall. Inches away, the frost breath froze to the cave wall and spread like an expanding spider's web. Daro pushed himself off the wall before the ice could reach him and renewed the fight for his life.

"Any day now, wizard!" he yelled between swings.

Baxter's spell went off perfectly; it was the first time he had cast it under duress. He had witnessed the spell the previous winter when the goblin shamans had used it against the warriors from Godhomme. It would increase the temperature significantly in the area where Daro fought and, hopefully, give the ranger an advantage over the ice creature. Of course, Baxter had made a few modifications over the goblin spell, focusing the temperature on metals and hopefully allowing Daro's swords to cut through the ice more easily.

"Your swords, Daro, they will be more effective now. Use them quickly; strike the beast while you can still hold your weapons!"

"What?" Daro shouted back, but even then, his swords began to smoke.

Baxter summoned a few more biting magic darts and slung them at the beast, hitting it about the face and distracting it so Daro could freely attack. He knew the ranger's prowess with his swords, and any distraction would do the trick. And it did. The beast roared in protest and swatted at the stinging magic. At the same time, Daro dropped to his knees and plunged a sword into the creature's belly. It sunk to the hilt, and Daro released it. Baxter watched as the metal turned a bright red inside the beast, melting it inside and out. Daro had to toss his other sword to the ground, but no fight remained in the beast as it fell over and writhed in agony. The temperature continued to increase, and the beast began moaning pitifully as it melted. Soon, it was still, and the sword glowed through the ice carcass.

"Wow, that went better than I expected," Baxter said with a proud smile, placing his hands on his hips and nodding appreciatively.

"Ow! Ow! Ow!" was Daro's only response.

Baxter turned a concerned glance to the dancing ranger, who was gingerly removing his belt, which now contained a glowing buckle, a sack of coins, and a few other metal trinkets. Baxter watched in amazement as Daro threw his belongings around the cave to escape the spell's effect. Baxter lost interest quickly, having become enamored with Sasha again. He watched her stalk her prey, the lone, terrified man.

She had her back to Baxter, and he became mesmerized by her hips. She was female perfection at its finest, and he was powerless to do anything but admire it. The fact that she had her sword at the ready didn't faze him, and if she were in battle and needed him, he probably wouldn't have realized that either. He swallowed hard and watched.

He never even heard Daro rush past him, continuing his chant of, "Ow! Ow! Ow!"

The metal rivets, buttons, and snaps sewn into the ranger's clothing were red-hot and shining brightly. Smoke billowed from his clothing as he dove into the cool water to offset Baxter's potent spell.

PRESIN TURNED TO FACE SASHA, AND IT WAS THE FIRST TIME SHE HAD seen anything but arrogance on his face. Abject fear replaced that arrogance now as he held his hands before him, and they smoked with the power of frost. "Stay back, Ugly One… I mean, Sasha," he stammered.

He was afraid, and Sasha understood that to be a good thing. He should be frightened; she was one of the most potent warriors from the gladiator pits in the sewers of Iciale. With the sword, her powers were far beyond that. She knew without a doubt that she could kill this slime of a person that stood before her. The vision of her mother murdered by his hands had her swinging away.

He brought a hand up before the strike, forming a small shield of ice that Iustia smashed to bits. As Sasha followed through with her swing, he issued a ray of ice that would have hit her square in the chest. However, the ray bent and changed direction halfway there, called by the mighty sword of ice. It hit the blade, and the sword absorbed it, glowing with power, which made Sasha's eyes sparkle all the more. Presin backed away until the frozen waterfall cornered him, and fear splayed across his desperate face.

"Sasha, please!"

She ignored his pleas and swung again with Iustia. He brought both hands together this time and formed a thicker, more protective ice shield. Sasha understood that enchanted ice comprised the sword and that no form of cold would hinder its attack. It sliced through the barrier as if slicing through butter and cut a deep gash in Presin's hand. He screamed and fell to his knees, holding the bleeding palm toward Sasha.

"Please, my niece, show mercy! I am your flesh and blood, and I beg your forgiveness."

His words stayed her hand. As much as she wanted to avenge her mother and strike down the abomination that was before her, she could not kill Presin. The fight was over, and he would never harm her again. There was no need to kill him, and she did not want that blood on her hands.

She lowered Iustia and said, "Go home, Uncle, and never bother me again. If you do, I will kill you. I am staying in this world, never to return to the world of ice. Go there and bask in whatever life you desire, but remember, I spared your life this day, so maybe do the same for someone else. Soften your heart, and change your ways. There is joy in the world if you seek it out."

With a wave of the great sword, the iced-over waterfall shattered, and the water poured again. There before Sasha was the portal waiting to take Presin home. She turned and walked toward her friends, the sparkle in her eyes dimming and the bluish hue of her skin fading as she drew less power from the sword, the threat over.

BAXTER WATCHED THIS AS IF IT WERE IN SLOW MOTION. SASHA WALKED straight for him now, and he couldn't think straight. His thoughts became jumbled, and he could only focus on her face, the most beautiful face he had ever seen. Cassandra was his true love; she was the one he desired, but looking at the goddess before him made him lose focus. Until he saw

Presin moving up quickly behind her, dagger raised above his head for a downward stab into Sasha's back. She was unaware of him, and her guard was down. He stumbled for words momentarily but finally managed to yell, "Sasha, behind you!"

At the same time, he summoned a quick spell that would do no real damage to her attacker but one that might buy her some time. It was a simple spell similar to the one he had performed nearly a year ago when he had first met Cassandra in the Happy Harpy tavern. Instead of a heatless flame, however, he summoned sparkles in the air that sizzled and popped in front of Presin, distracting and blinding the man instantly. That was enough for Sasha as she spun around with her weapon, slicing through the air behind her.

Presin stopped and held his dagger in the air, still above his head, the attack freezing him in place. The movement had caused Sasha to kneel, and there she stayed, sword ready for her uncle's attack. Presin's eyes were wide, and his mouth moved as if he were trying to speak, but all that came out was a strange clicking sound. The dagger fell to the cave floor, and his decapitated head soon followed. As the body fell, Sasha stood, once again lowering her weapon.

Now snapped from his trance, Baxter approached, keeping one eye on the portal, expecting more of the ice creatures to spill forth. Instead, it diminished and closed, leaving just the falls. He saw Daro climbing out of the icy waters, his hair dripping and his clothes smoldering.

"What happened to you?" Baxter asked.

Daro gave him a derisive snort and walked past. Baxter shrugged and followed. Soon, they were standing beside Sasha, looking down at her dead uncle.

"I didn't mean to kill him," Sasha whispered.

"You had to; he would have killed you," Daro reassured her.

She turned to regard them both, not ashamed of her nakedness and not trying to cover her face as she had when she first met Daro. She hugged the ranger and cried, letting out all of her emotions for her mother and now her uncle. She dropped Iustia to the ground, and Daro held her tight. Baxter rummaged around his pack, found a blanket, and handed it to Daro. Once Sasha controlled her emotions, they broke the embrace, and he offered her the cover.

She wrapped herself in it and said, "Thank you, Daro, for coming back for me; you saved me."

She kissed him on the cheek. Somewhere deep in Baxter's mind, he felt a pang of jealousy. He did not understand it, for he loved Cassandra and wanted no one else. Being around Sasha was confusing, and he wanted her attention. He cleared his throat. Sasha turned to him, and he lost all sensibilities.

"And you," she said, walking to stand before him. "You saved me as well, and I offer you my gratitude."

"Yes," was all that Baxter could think of to say. When he saw her confused look, he knew he had to clarify. He shook his head and said, "I love Cassandra."

Sasha turned to Daro and asked, "Are all the people of this world I meet going to do this?"

Both Daro and Baxter replied simultaneously, "Yes."

A SHORT TIME LATER, THE THREE SAT AROUND A ROARING FIRE AT THE mouth of the cave, Sasha having dressed and Daro undressed. The ranger's clothes were close by, drying nicely near the warm fire. Daro sat wrapped in the blanket now as the cool spring evening was quite chilly, especially for someone who had taken an unpleasant swim in the still-icy waters. Grey, Daro's wolf friend, joined them and sat close, rewarded with the occasional toss of food as they shared a meal. Sasha and Grey got along splendidly as Daro and Baxter watched her intently. Her interaction with the wolf was mesmerizing, especially for Daro, who had rescued the wolf long ago from a hunter's trap when he was just a pup.

"You're both doing it," Sasha said.

Daro and Baxter simultaneously looked away and focused on their food, Daro even reaching to ladle out more soup. Sasha grabbed his wrist, and he slowly made eye contact with her. Baxter, who had just stuffed most of a biscuit in his mouth, froze and slowly looked up, crumbs falling from his lips.

"It makes me uncomfortable," she said.

Daro sighed and glanced at Baxter, who shrugged and coughed, spraying biscuit crumbs into the fire. Sasha released Daro and sat back until the coughing fit was over. Daro just smiled and shook his head through the episode. Once he regained control, Baxter apologized for the outburst, his cheeks flushed.

"Neither of us wants you to feel uncomfortable," Daro replied. "Your beauty, fair Sasha, simply overcomes us."

Sasha sat unconvinced, waiting for him to continue. Daro had told Baxter about this very routine when he first met Sasha. Daro had strong feelings for the beautiful woman and had ever since laying eyes on her. According to Daro, Presin and the others from her home had told her all her life that the human blood in her made her ugly, and they had treated her as such. Sasha had even told Daro about a strange ice mask she had worn her entire life until coming through the gate in search of her mighty sword.

"You are not ugly, Sasha—" Daro began but was cut short.

"No, not at all!" Baxter interjected.

Daro looked at him sternly, and Baxter shrugged, his face reddening again.

"Contrary to what your uncle there has told you, your beauty exceeds anything we have ever witnessed," Daro added, nodding toward the falls where Presin's lifeless body rested. Neither of the men missed Sasha's wince at the mention of her uncle.

"Then it is a curse, either way. If every man I meet will act like an idiot as the two of you do, how am I supposed to exist in this world?"

"I'm afraid I have no answer for you, my friend. Yes, you can view it as a curse, and I understand your reasoning if you choose to do so. However, I am truly honored to be in your company," Daro said.

The ranger blushed as he realized Sasha and Baxter were looking at him strangely now.

Baxter smiled and said, "And Victoria thought I was bad."

"What does that mean?" Daro asked, stealing a slight glance Sasha's way.

"What my friend here is trying to say is that your beauty is stunning and—" Baxter began.

"What?" Daro suddenly yelled and craned his neck to look outside. Sasha and Baxter both followed his gaze, and everything was quiet. If the ranger had heard someone call, neither of them had.

"Be right back," Daro said, standing quickly and struggling to hold the blanket around him.

"No one is there, Daro," Sasha said, but the ranger ignored her.

He had taken a few steps toward the cave door when Grey stood and playfully stepped on the blanket with both front paws. Daro didn't notice and, in his haste to leave the cave, lost the blanket. He never looked back but continued his trek outside and into the cool breeze, his backside on full display as he did.

Baxter chuckled, but when he looked back at Sasha, she was not laughing. That quieted his giggling fit quickly. "As I was saying, Daro loves you. That should be evident," Baxter said.

"No, I don't," Daro replied from outside. Baxter smiled, picturing the naked ranger outside the cave, listening to the conversation.

"No one has ever loved me, Baxter; therefore, it is not evident. I truly don't know what love is," Sasha replied, ignoring Daro.

Baxter nodded and stood, gathering Daro's clothes. "I should get these to him; they seem dry enough."

Sasha smiled, but before he could turn and leave, she said, "You mentioned earlier that you love Cassandra."

"Yes, I do."

"Who is she?"

Baxter smiled and lost himself in thought. She was many things: an orphan, a witch, a loner, a fighter. Cassandra was a sweet but misunderstood person with whom he had fallen madly in love. He wasn't aware of the stupid look that washed over his face, but Sasha gave him a quizzical look. "What?" he asked.

"If that is what love looks like, I don't want anything to do with it."

"A little help, wizard." Daro's voice drifted into the cave, interrupting the conversation.

Baxter shook his head, saying, "Cassandra is the reason we are here."

He left Sasha to digest those words as he took Daro's clothes to him. Sure enough, he found the ranger standing behind a tree outside the cave, Grey lying at his feet. "Why did you say that?" he asked as soon as Baxter was near.

"I thought she should know the truth."

"The truth is, I like her and thought she'd be a perfect fit with the New Order."

"So, you don't have feelings for her other than that?"

"Of course not," Daro said, putting on his mostly dry pants.

"She said she likes you," Baxter lied.

Daro stumbled over his pants leg and nearly fell, catching himself awkwardly on the tree. He looked at Baxter and swallowed hard, unable to speak.

Baxter looked at him with raised eyebrows and said, "Uh-huh, you are in love."

Baxter walked back to the cave, and Daro called after him, "Did she say that?"

"Nope."

"Then why did you say it?"

"To find the truth, and I did."

Daro's silence spoke volumes, and Baxter smiled, knowing he was right. He and Daro were quickly becoming friends, and he enjoyed teasing him, especially where Sasha was concerned.

Baxter entered the cave again and found Sasha standing over Presin's body. He approached gingerly, knowing that her uncle's death had been difficult for her. When she saw him, she wiped away a tear. He stood beside her and she said, "I must bury him."

"I will help."

"We will help," Daro corrected, entering the cave, fully dressed and holding his boots in one hand. "Let me slide these on, and we'll find a place for him."

THE THREE FOUND A NICE PLACE NEAR THE RIVER TO BURY HER UNCLE. None of them were devout worshippers of any particular god, but Baxter said a few words, and Sasha shed a few more tears before it was over. They went to Daro's nearby cottage but stayed up most of the night talking about the new events they had discovered concerning the prophecy centered around Cassandra. When the moon was already past its zenith and falling slowly from the sky, and the fire burned low in Daro's cottage, only Sasha and Daro remained awake. Baxter was curled up on the sofa and snoring lightly.

"So, this Kringus fellow you speak of, he has taken your word that I am a suitable fighter for your group?" Sasha asked.

"Yes; Inuentas backed me up, he also believes in you. We are desperate for members we can trust with our lives. I told Kringus we could do just that with you."

"I owe you everything, Daro, so naturally, I accept your offer."

Daro smiled and nodded. "We will travel back to Pelesea, where Kringus will swear you in as a new member." The smile faded from his face as he thought a little further along and added, "However, it will be dangerous. Ending this prophecy is not your cause, and this isn't even your world, for that matter. Are you sure you want to do this?"

"As I said, I owe you my life. If you and Baxter had not returned, I would already be in the sewers, most likely under a large oven, to be tortured for years to come. You have saved me from that." Sasha leaned in close.

Daro swallowed hard and nodded. With Sasha close, he lost his voice.

"And, without you, I would never have found Iustia."

"Or apples," he added.

She laughed, and it sounded like an angel's laugh to him. When she stopped, she agreed. "Yes, and apples. I owe you a lot."

"I don't want you to join for those reasons. I need you to be committed to the purpose of our journey," Daro said nervously as Sasha remained too close.

"I am committed, Daro, not just to you as a friend but to the people of this world. The ones I have met far outweigh the carofex and are worth fighting for. This is my home now, and I will fight for it. Fighting is all I've ever known, and I am quite good at it."

"I know," he whispered.

Sasha leaned in closer so their faces were inches apart. Daro swallowed hard again. "Kiss me," she whispered.

"What?"

"I've never been kissed, never been loved. Kiss me so that I might experience it."

Daro slowly raised a hand and brushed her cheek with the back of it. Just touching her was electric. He moved in and kissed her lightly on the lips. They briefly broke the kiss and looked into each other's eyes before kissing again, deeply and sensually.

When they broke the kiss the second time, Sasha stood and said, "That was nice, thank you."

"Yes, it was. Where are you going?"

"To your bed, to sleep. We must travel to Pelesea tomorrow, so I need rest."

Daro got up to come along, but she touched his chest. "No, my friend, you sleep here tonight."

At that moment, Daro felt like a feather could push him over. "You didn't like the kiss?" he managed to squeak out.

"I absolutely adored it and will treasure it forever. I ask for small steps here, ranger. I have never been with a man, nor have I ever considered it. However, I could get used to kissing you."

She smiled and left him standing there, entering his room and shutting the door behind her. His heart beat in his chest as he stared at the door for a long time. Baxter's snoring stopped briefly as he turned over but soon began again.

Daro smiled and whispered, "You are right; I love her. Now I know how you feel, and it is exquisite. Don't worry, my friend; we will find Cassandra and bring her home."

Daro turned himself in after that but did not find sleep for a very long time. When he did, he dreamed of Sasha, and the dreams were grand.

THE FOLLOWING DAY, THE THREE PARTED WAYS AS BAXTER RODE THE carpet to Oldorburg to meet with Max, the town's sheriff, to discuss membership into the New Order. Daro and Sasha started the trek to Pelesea, which would take nearly a month on foot.

"I will visit Oldorburg and catch you well before you reach the city," Baxter said.

"Good luck to you, Baxter, and be careful," Daro said.

"Always. I am sure I will see you soon."

He commanded the carpet to rise and fly swiftly to Oldorburg. Daro and Sasha waved until he was out of sight. Then they turned toward each other, and Daro quickly became lost in her eyes.

"Well, we should—" he began before Sasha kissed him deeply.

When she broke the kiss, he stared at her, his eyes wide and a silly smile on his face.

"I like kissing you," she said.

And so, the two began their journey to Pelesea, not hand in hand as Daro truly desired, but things were progressing. They learned much of each other during the trip, sharing stories of their past, and they were quite giddy, as new love tends to make people. They did not consummate their budding relationship along the way, but to Daro's delight, the woman with goddess-like beauty liked to kiss—a lot.

BINTA WAS HAVING A MOST SPLENDID DREAM, ONE CENTERED AROUND Cassandra. They were together again, sitting in Cassandra's dorm room, studying magic and discussing the idiots Cass and Jabell. Life was once again whole for Binta and full of hope, and a kiss promised great things to come. She relived that kiss in her dream and could even smell the faint aroma of the perfume Cassandra used to wear. The dream was so intoxicating that the world's reality hit her hard when she awakened to a full moon outside her window. She was sleeping alone in a strange bed, in a strange house. The worst part was Cassandra wasn't there, and as the dream faded, so did the echo of Cassandra's laugh.

She tried so hard to fall back to sleep, to restart that most beautiful dream where it left off. But she could not, so she threw off her sheets and got out of bed with a frustrated huff. She walked to the open window, the cool spring air giving her a slight chill. As she stood in her nightgown, viewing the large backyard of Jamison's manor, her thoughts reeled back to the moments before she kissed Cassandra. They were looking out the window, and it had been a cold night. That sudden flash of a memory had her heart aching. She turned away from the window and made her way downstairs.

She told herself to hold it together, to appreciate the beautiful possibilities Jamison offered her. However, by the time she reached the kitchen, she was silently crying. Binta could no longer restrain the grief, and the black cloud of despair again fell over her. She sat on the floor and cried, letting it all out. Since Cassandra's death, she had been an emotional mess, and she needed to cry. She lost track of time, but she knew she had sat there for a long while, and as her crying tapered off to sniffles, Binta finally looked up to behold something she never expected: a raven stood on the large kitchen table!

"How did you get in here?" she whispered. "Are you a sign from Cassandra?" she added, nearing tears again.

The bird cocked its head a couple of times, studying her as she slowly rose from her sitting position on the floor. She tentatively made her way toward it, hoping it was a messenger from Cassandra and it would tell her she was fine and everything would be all right. It flapped its wings as she approached but made no sound. She stopped in her tracks as it fluttered a bit, and once it settled down, she took another step. It let out a caw and took flight, startling her. It flew into the darkness of one of the many hallways, and suddenly, she understood this was no ordinary raven. It had come with a purpose and was leading her somewhere.

Her heart raced as she followed it down the dark hall. Was the bird a sign from the grave? Was it Cassandra reaching out to her, perhaps still alive? She followed as quickly as possible, but she could not see well. Binta saw a small light spilling into the hall from a cracked door but saw no bird. She followed the light, quickening her pace as she got closer. When she arrived, she saw a feather on the floor lying in the crease of light.

She bent and retrieved it; it was black as night, the feather of a raven. She slowly pushed the door open, her eyes wide as saucers. Inside, she saw what appeared to be a study with a warm fire smoldering in the fireplace. Bookshelves with many books filled the place. There was an oversized comfortable chair before the fire, and a smoking stand next to it. She entered the room and subconsciously closed the door behind her. It was warm inside, and she could smell the faint hint of pipe and brandy. She liked it in the small room and could only guess it was a special place for Jamison to come when he wanted to be alone. However, there was no raven there.

The bird's caw had her jumping and looking toward the sound. She saw no bird, but she noticed a slightly crooked bookcase. Her heart beat faster as she approached the bookcase to find it revealed a dark passageway behind it. She had discovered a secret door! The raven's call came from within. Her mind didn't register that the opening behind the bookcase was far too small for the large bird to fit through. It took all her strength to open the secret door, and when she finally did, she found herself at the entrance of the dark hallway. She could not tell how long it was or where it led, but the raven was in there somewhere, and she intended to follow.

A small lantern was hanging on the wall alongside a lighting stick, which she lit in the fireplace to bring the lantern to life. As the light spilled into the passage, she heard the raven call again, and it sounded a long way off. She didn't want to lose the bird, so she hurried along, hoping to catch up to it. The passage wasn't long, and soon, she found herself in a storage area with many bookcases and rows of shelves. Tomes and scrolls filled most of them, with the occasional chest or bag. There was even a bookcase that contained wands, which appeared to be magical, such as the one she saw Baxter use against the goblins. There were also three suits of armor and a wall full of swords and other weapons. It was storage for valuables, and she guessed that most of them were magical.

She was awestruck, her mouth agape as she took in the incredible sight. She temporarily lost all thoughts of the raven until she heard it call out again, making her jump. She turned sharply toward the sound and saw a pedestal standing in the corner of the room with a wooden box atop it. There was no sign of the raven, but the raven's cry most assuredly came from that direction. She held the lantern before her, trying to get a better look, and slowly advanced. As she got closer, she noticed that the box had a lid with a lock. She saw, to her delight, that the lock was open.

She set the lantern on the pedestal and removed the lock. She looked around to ensure no one was there; something tugged at her conscience, telling her what she was about to do was wrong. The raven's cry echoed in her head, and she knew she had to proceed because if this had something to do with Cassandra, she was determined to discover it. She slowly opened the wooden lid to find a large book inside.

"A spellbook," she whispered excitedly.

The book was old, and the pages looked yellowed and brittle. Binta wasn't confident it was a spellbook, but it reminded her of the books she and Cassandra used at Victoria's school, only this one was much older. She undid the cover clasp and took a deep breath. Binta knew that opening an old tome, especially one that was probably magical, was one of the most dangerous things a person could do. She had some knowledge of magical items, but not enough to defend herself if the tome was protected or even trapped. Her curiosity got the better of her despite the alarms going off in her mind. She opened the tome.

She stood motionless for a long while, studying the first page. Her eyes froze open and refused to blink. Eventually, tears ran down her cheeks. A million thoughts flashed through her mind in those moments of bliss and pain. Random thoughts from her life surfaced from the far recesses of her brain, then were gone just as quickly. Most of the memories she recalled and treasured, such as Cassandra's kiss, some she had forgotten and was joyed to relive, and others she didn't recall. Her life rolled through her mind in a matter of moments, and she could suddenly remember many things she had forgotten. All her senses seemed to magnify at once, and she felt like a sixth sense was awakening from deep inside her. She felt like her mind would explode, and at the same time, she felt an inner peace.

She stayed locked in that position for a very long time, unable to move or call for help. As the changes continued to take hold in her mind and her senses waxed and waned, the one thing she could fixate on was the book's first page. Whether she was dying or something worse, the page that was so obviously causing this issue was the one she currently had her eyes locked on. As the whirlwind of feelings and thoughts and painful memories barraged her, she could not pull her eyes away from it. She could not understand precisely why it was happening, but all she knew was that the page was completely blank. No words or symbols adorned it, and she couldn't understand how the tome was doing this to her if she hadn't read any words or seen any symbols. Tears splashed onto the blank page from her quickly drying eyes. Soon after, the taxing effect of the tome took hold of her, Binta's world went dark, and she knew nothing more.

Nearly two weeks later, Baxter caught up to Daro and Sasha about one hundred miles southeast of Pelesea. To their delight, Max had come along for the ride, sitting in front of Baxter on Victoria's carpet. Baxter spotted them waving, so he lowered the carpet beside them. When they were at ground level, hovering about five feet from the newly sprouting grass and flowers, Baxter noticed the stupid look on Daro's face, a look Baxter had worn far too often around Cassandra. A pang of jealousy shot through him again, but he was in love with Cassandra and happy for his new friends. So, he lost the jealousy immediately.

"Daro! Sasha! I knew I would catch you before you reached Pelesea," Baxter said.

"Well, we can't all have magical, flying carpets, wizard," Daro said.

"True, my ranger friend. Trust me, though, this is the only way to travel," Baxter said, patting the rug.

Daro laughed, but as the laughter died down, all eyes were on Max, who sat dumbfounded, his eyes locked on Sasha.

"Not again," Sasha said.

"I am Daro, Keeper of the Woods and ranger of Pelesea," Daro said, extending his hand and breaking the young man's trance.

Max jumped off the carpet and grasped hands with the ranger. "And I am Max, Sheriff of Oldorburg."

After a warm smile and a firm handshake, his eyes moved immediately back to Sasha, who stood next to Daro with a disgusted look on her face. Max seemed not to notice. "And you must be Sasha? Baxter has told me—" Max began.

"Has told you what? That I have god-like beauty?" Sasha interrupted.

"Well, yes—"

"And do you agree?" she interrupted again, taking a step toward the young sheriff.

"I do, my lady," Max said, standing his ground but his face turning red.

Sasha stood before him now, and the man seemed to melt being that close to her. Baxter thought he might crumple to the ground and slink away. But Max stood firm and kept eye contact with her. Baxter understood that Sasha had to be getting tired of this behavior from every man she met, and he began to worry about what would happen when they reached Pelesea. He was also guilty of the rude behavior and was glad she was not focused on him as he again stared at the beautiful woman.

"I find you rather attractive as well, Max, but that is where it stops. There will be no more gawking, whether you think I see you or not. Like the way Baxter is looking at me now."

All three turned to Baxter, and he could feel his face growing warm. He cleared his throat and looked up to the clouds, knowing Sasha was correct; she had spotted him being an idiot once more. He cussed himself on the inside and found focus on Cassandra. He could not wait to begin their adventure to find her, and that was what he centered his thoughts around as Sasha slowly turned her ire back to Max.

"Understand, Sheriff of Oldorburg?"

"Yes, of course. I am married, and I don't think—" Max stammered.

"Besides, I like kissing Daro, understand?"

It looked like Max had been slapped across the face with that last remark, and he looked over to Daro, who winked at the young man.

"I do," Max said and nodded, looking between Daro and Sasha. A smile finally crept across his face, and he nodded to Daro, who returned the smile and winked once more.

"I spent five days at Oldorburg, informing Max of the plans. He was gracious enough to let me stay in his home, and I had the honor of meeting his wife, Tanna, and his toddler, Sade," Baxter said.

"I have to say that I am most honored to be considered for membership by this amazing group," Max said.

"It was Arrin who referred you. The king has taken his word that you are pure of heart and full of courage," Daro replied.

The mention of Kringus made the sheriff smile even wider. "And how goes King Kringus, anyway? The last time we saw each other was on opposite sides of the battlefield."

"Not many people can say that and live to tell about it," Daro said.

"He spared my life so that I could change the face of Oldorburg," Max said, fondly recalling the event.

Even Sasha understood what that interaction with the king meant to the man, and she smiled at him and nodded, letting the awkwardness of their meeting fade and accepting Max into their group.

"And he has done just that; I was impressed with the new leadership in Oldorburg. Although Tanna probably makes most of the important decisions," Baxter said.

When Max turned a stunned expression his way, it was Baxter's turn to share a wink. The gesture had the four laughing heartily, and all tension washed away. They shared some small talk for a bit, but they eventually found themselves on the road to Pelesea a short while later. Both Daro and Max suggested that Sasha ride the carpet with Baxter. Daro got an elbow in the ribs and an explanation from Sasha that she required no special privileges simply because she was female. So, Max had climbed back atop the rug, and they started off. Baxter kept the carpet hovering beside his friends as they did. Their mood was light as they made the trek, and the tales were plentiful, especially from Baxter, who told them all he knew of Cassandra. Von and Lenore would return from Nessor soon, and the New Order would officially leave on their quest shortly after. By the end of summer, the New Order would be on their way to defeat the looming prophecy.

The quest was a grand and important event at the forefront of their thoughts. Baxter had a bad feeling that if the four of them understood what they were getting into, none would have been quite as optimistic as they were on that warm spring day. As it was, they traveled merrily along, and Baxter tried to share their joy but struggled. Max was excited to see Pelesea and meet Kringus again, Daro's attention was solely on Sasha, and Sasha was just happy for her new life and eager to help. Only Baxter seemed aware of the pending dread. He longed to see Cassandra again, but he wondered how many of his friends would die in the effort to find her.

Maltor's War

Cassandra's delirium worsened by the hour, and now every step she took in the thick sands of Yaddaton took great effort. Her mind was barely conscious of her movements as the sun beat down, baking her already burned skin. Dried vomit adorned the front of her gown, and she stumbled and fell often. The culiem venom from Gophia's bite still worked through her system, and the snake brand on her thigh still expelled some of the potent venom. She fell to her knees and retched once more, which turned out to be nothing but a long, dry heave, her dehydrated body having nothing left to expel. She took in her surroundings once the fit played out. There was nothing but sand and an occasional rock or cactus, then just lots and lots of sand. She spotted Gophia beside her, a worried expression on the little fairy's face as she wrung her hands together.

"Gophia, why are you still with me?" Cassandra whispered between cracked lips.

"Cassandra is my friend," Gophia answered telepathically.

Cassandra wasn't sure how long ago they had left the burial sea from which she had crawled. Gophia had stuck with her and had tried to protect her. Cassandra knew this but felt it was a losing battle. She could not go on much further before the desert took her. Cassandra brought her left hand up before her, which still grasped the holy symbol of Gella, the broken chain dangling from it. She noted how black her forearm was; even her hands and fingers seemed discolored. She knew that wasn't good and that she desperately required healing. But a more immediate concern was the sun; if she didn't find shelter or fresh water very soon, she was as good as dead.

"You should go home, Gophia. You have freed me, not only from Maltor but from the vultures. You have repaid your debt to me twice, and I appreciate your effort. I will always remember you for it, my friend. However, I do not want you to die out here with me."

Gophia fluttered around Cassandra's face, gently touching her cheeks with tiny hands. Cassandra closed her eyes and enjoyed the slight breeze the fairy's wings generated, temporarily providing a little bit of relief from the relentless sun.

"Gophia will find help. You stay. Rest."

Cassandra smiled weakly and nodded. She knew the end was near, and she didn't want Gophia to witness her death. Perhaps it was best if the fairy went looking for help, holding on to false hope. Cassandra lay face down in the sand, then turned her head to the side and again brought Gella's medallion to her face. It was hot, but she barely noticed the burning sensation in her fingers.

"Gella, my goddess, I am sorry for forsaking you. If you find a way to help me survive this, I will be devout in my worshipping of you. If you allow me to live, I will return the favor with a lifetime of fealty," she whispered, then kissed the medallion.

Gophia flew away quickly, and Cassandra watched her new friend until she was out of sight. It warmed her heart to know the fairy had stuck with her and fought off the vultures at the sea of bodies. She was faithful to Cassandra; even now, as Cassandra approached death, the fairy did her best to keep her alive. Cassandra closed her eyes and focused on the incredible heat. She had no hope to contend with it, and she couldn't beat the Yaddaton. It had her in a death grip, and she felt powerless against it. She smiled at the thought of escaping Maltor; this fate was better than what she would have experienced with the barbarians. Eventually, sleep took her, and in her delirium, Cassandra understood that she might never wake up again if she answered the call of that darkness. She had little choice.

It didn't take long for the desert predators to become aware of Cassandra's still form. Without Gophia there to protect her, she was in grave danger. Gophia had been gone only a short time when the first such predator approached; in her delirious state, Cassandra was only vaguely aware of its presence.

FAIRIES ARE TINY, AND THEIR WINGS CAN ONLY BEAT SO FAST AND FOR so long. Gophia found a spot to rest a few miles south of where she had left Cassandra. She sat in the shade of a large rock and within a clump of desert grass. The shade provided needed coolness for the culiem fairy, and because of her weariness from the long journey, she quickly fell asleep.

She awakened hours later with the sun sinking from the sky. It took her a moment to realize where she was and shake the sleep away. Gophia flew into the warm evening sky and looked all about. She saw no one who could assist them, so she returned to Cassandra. Gophia had been gone a long time, so the fairy flew as fast as her little wings could carry her.

When she finally arrived at the rocky area where she had left her new friend, she discovered Cassandra was missing. It didn't take the fairy long to figure out what had happened as the spot where Cassandra had collapsed now showed a trail leading to the east, looking as if something had dragged her friend through the sand. More concerning were the large footprints and tail tracks that moved with it. Something had taken Cassandra away, and whatever it was, it had probably killed her by now. The fairy was heartbroken.

"Gophia is stupid!" she shouted. The outburst startled her as she usually did not speak, much less shout, preferring to communicate telepathically instead. "I will find you, Cassandra, my new friend. Stay alive; I am coming," Gophia whispered, then took flight, speeding away as quickly as possible, following the giant tracks.

CASSANDRA DREAMED OF THE DARK MAN, A POWERFUL AND VIVID dream. She found herself once more in the room with Zolmex. The blue topaz at the top sparkled from the sunlight that poured forth from the windows. Her father, the dark man, was there, motioning with an outstretched hand toward the artifact. As she always did, she approached the table where it lay. She knew what would happen when she reached for the artifact but could not control her movement. When she did reach out, the image changed as it always did, and she found herself at the sea of dead once more.

This time, instead of standing on the shore and watching the vultures take flight, she lay atop the river of bodies. She could smell the decay and feel herself sink into the bloated corpses, the smell and feel of rotting flesh overpowering her as it had when she crawled out of the barbarian burial ground. She felt herself moving, floating down the macabre river. Her stomach churned from the odor and the movement. She did not feel pain until she began to float, and then everything hurt. She managed to snap out of the dream long enough to understand it wasn't a dream. Instead, some smelly creature had her by the leg, dragging her.

The beast was as large as an elephant, a strange creature she had studied in school but had never encountered. It was a giant lizard, and in her delirium she could not recall if it was venomous. It mattered little, for she hadn't the strength to fight it. Her leg was in its mouth, and it dragged her swiftly through the sand. It was fast for its size, and Cassandra could do little to inhibit its speed. Her arms dragged limply above her head as she slid across the hot sand. She couldn't summon the energy to move them, and even the thought of doing so made her cringe in pain. She thought of yelling for help in case Gophia was near, but she could not even speak.

She was nothing more than a meal, and death was imminent. That was acceptable to her. She had narrowly escaped dying over the last few months. She had endured kidnapping, torture, branding, beatings, stabbings, and drowning, and had barely avoided being raped several times. What was this life for? She held on to Gella's medallion with limp arms that refused to work correctly. Cassandra held it as tightly as possible with weakening fingers as it dug grooves in the sand behind her. She prayed to her goddess as she drifted off again. She knew Gella had saved her from the sea of dead, had given her the strength to escape the vultures, hence the medallion she now possessed. But it wasn't enough, and now Cassandra was ready to meet her goddess and enter the afterlife.

THE LIZARD GENTLY RELEASED CASSANDRA'S LEG AND BELLOWED loudly. It was just outside its lair, a giant hole in the sand at the base of a mound of rocks. The bleached bones of several animals it had recently eaten lay scattered about the entrance. It moved slightly away from her and bellowed again, louder this time. After a few moments, it came back and sniffed Cassandra. It pawed at the sand beside her, pushing sand atop her with its giant claw. It did not bury her; it just flung a couple of clawfuls of sand at her. It smelled her again and bellowed some more. Eventually, a figure crested the dune near the rock outcropping the lizard called home.

"What is it, Grog?" the man called to the lizard.

The creature hissed in response, and a smile spread across the man's face. He was human, with dark skin from living in the desert his entire life. His white robes covered his body to block the sun's effects and repel the sand during storms. He usually wore a bandage wrapped around his face to keep the sand from his mouth and nose, but he had unwrapped it before cresting the dune, just in case Grog was in trouble. His teeth were bright white when he smiled at his lizard friend, contrasting his face perfectly. The man's eyes were pupilless and nearly as white, blind since birth. He carried a large wooden staff as a walking stick and a weapon. He sensed something was not quite right, and the smile faded from his face. He made his way to the lizard, which continued its hissing sounds, along with an occasional clicking from deep within its throat.

"Show me, my friend," the man said, gently placing his staff against the lizard's side.

The creature moved slowly so the man could follow him, which he did, keeping the staff against the lizard so the beast could serve as a guide. When Grog stopped near Cassandra, the man used the staff to continue his walk, gently sweeping it out in front of him. He poked Cassandra, testing her with several small taps with his stick. Understanding it was the body of some unfortunate creature, the man knelt. He used his hands to identify what type of animal Grog had brought home, and his eyes widened when he quickly discerned the body to be that of a human.

"Oh no," he muttered. "This better not be a barbarian, Grog, or we'll have the whole of the tribes upon us."

The creature clicked once in response, and the man gently found Cassandra's left arm and raised it, feeling for a pulse. He couldn't see the blackened skin or he probably wouldn't have bothered. However, she moaned when he moved her as the effort caused her severe pain. Her wrist was tiny and the skin too soft for the Yaddaton.

"This woman is no barbarian and is surely not dead," he muttered. "Good job, my friend."

He dug in his pack and produced the fruit that Grog loved dearly, the reward the lizard expected for such a worthwhile task: a giant lemon nearly a foot in diameter. Grog gently took the treat into his mouth and sauntered away blissfully. The man strapped the staff to his back and knelt again to pick up Cassandra. A hissing sound from the side, and not so far away, froze him. He knew his lizard friend's hisses, and this wasn't one of them.

"Hello?" he said, turning toward the sound.

"*Cassandra is my friend,*" came the telepathic reply.

Startled initially, the man remained frozen until a smile slowly formed on his tanned face. "A culiem fairy?" he whispered.

When no response came, he said, "I am Mateon, and I am no enemy of Cassandra, little one. As a matter of fact, if we do not move her inside, she will die within the hour."

Gophia fluttered to land on his shoulder and spoke through her telepathy again. "*I am here to bite if you hurt her.*"

He smiled and stood, his large arms easily picking up Cassandra's lithe form. "Understood, little friend. Now let us proceed; my home is close. Of course, I cannot see without my staff, so please inform me if I am about to run into a rock or fall into a hole."

In response, Gophia made a purring sound and guided Mateon on the few occasions he came near to stumbling over a rock. The man knew this part of the desert as he'd lived there a long time and was never really in danger of faltering. Soon, the terrain became very rocky, with large boulders jutting out of the sand and many smaller ones littering most of the area. Still, Mateon had no problem navigating the desert terrain, and soon, they arrived at a small cottage made of stone.

"Sitra, eyes shut!" he yelled, stopping about fifty yards from the entrance.

"*Why stop? Cassandra needs shade,*" Gophia said.

"Because you will die if I don't make the necessary arrangements," Mateon answered, then yelled again toward the home, "Sitra, eyes shut!"

Soon, a beautiful, slender woman appeared at the entrance to the cottage, wearing a blindfold. "I am here, Mateon; I have concealed my eyes," Sitra answered.

He brought Cassandra the rest of the way and entered the tiny home, which contained one large, furnished area and a few side rooms. Gophia flew around nervously once they entered but stayed close to watch what the couple would do to Cassandra. Mateon laid her still form gently on a bed in one of the side rooms and produced water from a waterskin in his pack. He gently lifted Cassandra's head, her neck limp and lifeless, and eased the water into her thirsty mouth. She managed to swallow a bit and coughed up just as much. Mateon considered it a good sign that she was animated at all. She showed little life, and he knew she was in trouble.

"I hear fluttering; we are not alone," Sitra said.

"There is a third being with us. Our patient is named Cassandra; her friend is a culiem fairy who is close by. Hence the reason for the blindfold."

"*Gophia*," the fairy said telepathically to both.

"Listen, Gophia, I have some skills at healing, but I must be able to see your friend. Do you understand?" Sitra asked.

"*Yes, Gophia understands, but why hide your eyes?*"

"I am sleeth-cursed. Anyone gazing into my eyes runs the risk of turning to stone," Sitra said, turning to address the fairy while Mateon forced Cassandra to drink more water. "Can you close your eyes tight? Do you trust me enough to do so?"

Gophia thought for a moment and looked at Cassandra's still form. She shut her eyes tight, covered them with tiny hands, and said, "Yes."

Once she received the fairy's approval, Sitra removed her blindfold. Although Mateon could not see, Sitra's gasp at viewing Cassandra's broken and dying form spoke volumes. "Oh, Mateon, I'm unsure I can help her."

"It's bad?" Mateon asked.

"Yes, but I will try. Please fetch my medicine kit."

Mateon nodded and left the room. Sitra sighed and examined Cassandra's extremities. The sleeth was not a healer and only dabbled in medicine. Cassandra needed a priest, maybe several. It would be a trying night for all four of them.

Maltor sat on a large rock deep in the Yaddaton Desert. He had declared war on the Culiem Tribe, specifically their king, Boskel, and now sat on the field of battle, the shamans attending his injured arm. A deep gash ran from his elbow to the back of his hand. Maltor barely felt it, his anger with Boskel blocking out the pain. The skirmish had ended with Maltor suffering the grievous wound, but not before killing a dozen men, including one of Boskel's captains. Now, as the shamans attended and wrapped his arm, his men scoured the area for survivors and looted the dead of the Culiem Tribe.

A young barbarian named Grems hurried up to the king and knelt. Maltor was in no mood for bad news, and Grems surely understood the chances of death from delivering such. The king had quickly called his men to war and had invaded the Culiem Tribe's lands shortly after burying Cassandra. He tasked the young messenger with counting the dead after each skirmish. And so, Grems waited for his king to initiate the conversation. The battle was the second skirmish in two days, the first two of the war that Maltor intended to win quickly by surprise. The king locked a stern visage on Grems until the shamans finished their work.

Then he finally spoke. "How many warriors of the Culiem Tribe have fallen today?"

"Nearly a hundred, my king," Grems said, raising his head to look his king in the eyes.

"And how many fairies?"

The question took Grems off guard, and he answered honestly after a slight hesitation, "None accounted for or seen during the battle."

"How many men did we lose?" Maltor asked.

"Nearly two dozen, my king."

Grems nervously awaited Maltor's reaction, and eventually, the barbarian king rose calmly from the rock and examined his bandaged arm. He breathed deeply, then released it slowly, staring hard at the kneeling messenger.

"With the numbers you gave me yesterday, we have killed nearly two hundred of their warriors already and with only three dozen losses of our own."

"That is correct, my king."

Maltor nodded and motioned with his hand for Grems to rise. "Walk with me," the king said.

Grems rose, and they walked through the carnage. Smoke was thick in the air as several nearby structures burned. They walked around the battlefield, observing the shamans healing the wounded and other warriors tasked with piling the dead.

"The Culiem use wood from the fairy trees to build homes, unlike our tents," Maltor said, pointing to the nearest burning structure.

Grems nodded, already understanding that to be the case.

"These structures were nothing more than outposts, the edge of their kingdom. You know what that means?"

"No, my king."

"We will be upon their homes soon enough. We must continue our strike quickly, and if they show no resistance, we will swarm them in but a few days. I want all their homes burning three nights from now."

"Glory to you, my king," Grems replied with a slight bow.

"They stole Cassandra from me, and now I will repay them by wiping them out completely."

Jozerah approached through the thick smoke, his face bloodied and his massive chest glistening with sweat and blood, some his own, most of it his enemies. He and Maltor clasped hands when they saw each other, and the three stood together and took in the scene.

"Another victory, my king," Jozerah said.

"Of course, the Culiem were unprepared, but they will regroup in their homes. We cannot allow a delay, so we must gather and treat the wounded, then continue our push."

"I like the way you think, my king," Jozerah said with a smile.

Maltor turned to Grems and said, "Scout ahead. Take two runners. By morning, I expect you to tell me the status of the Culiem Tribe. I will smoke them out if they have crawled into their holes."

"Yes, my lord," Grems said with a bow, then trotted off to recruit runners.

"And if they cower in their homes?" Jozerah asked.

"Go to Jak and the archers; have them utilize this night to prepare their arrows. Have them wrap their arrowheads in oiled cloth. We will rain hell upon them, and I will have Boskel's head as a trophy."

Jozerah nodded, and the two warriors watched the men scurrying around the battlefield as the sun set, the reality of Maltor's claims already within reach. The attacks had been too quick for the Culiem Tribe to respond. Maltor intended on keeping it that way. They would march before dawn.

MATILDA AWOKE TO THE SUN JUST CRESTING THE HORIZON. THE PRIESTS of Marnelphion and the warriors of Gorl had camped at the edge of the Yaddaton Desert and expected to be within striking distance of the barbarians within a day or two. It wasn't the sun that woke her, but the sound of Cass trying to silence her panting and moaning. Matilda rolled over, and sure enough, Cass was with Cerus, straddling him and grinding herself on him as she had done the previous two mornings. She could make out Cass's silhouette in the dim morning light, her demon wings fluttering slightly. Matilda allowed the tryst and secretly enjoyed watching her husband please the insatiable woman. It gave Cerus a sense of power over Matilda, and she needed him confident, as her time recently with Malikai had shaken his fragile ego. Her prize was within her grasp, and she needed him to be focused.

She reached a hand to her crotch and played as Cass quickened her pace and soon was in the throes of her latest orgasm. Cerus flipped her over and took her in a missionary position. Matilda could see her husband's muscles flex and the sweat glistening on his chest as the sun grew brighter. Cerus plowed into the young woman, and Cass loved it. Later, Matilda would find scratch marks on his back, scratches he had made sure she saw. Soon, he spent himself, and Matilda silently climaxed with him, stifling her moans by biting her lip. She pretended to sleep as the two lovers kissed, and Cass returned to her bedroll. As the morning watch woke the men, Matilda waited for Cerus to settle beside her.

As the small army began their day, a scout entered the camp and found Matilda. He was out of breath and seemed on the edge of hysteria. He was a young Gorl warrior, and he took his job seriously. His name was Jest, and Matilda liked him. She saw a different potential in him. He wasn't like most of the other Gorl warriors; he was not as bloodthirsty and was more level-headed. He was the perfect scout, and with Cerus's permission, she used the young man for this excursion.

"My lady," he said, panting and trying to catch his breath.

"Calm yourself, Jest. Let us gather breakfast, and you can tell me your scouting report while we eat," Matilda suggested.

She thought he might just burst right then, as he obviously had something important to say. She calmly produced food from her pack and shared it with the young man as they sat on a dead tree. Cerus soon found them and approached with his shirt off, which Matilda knew was for her benefit.

"What have you found, scout?" Cerus asked Jest.

"Husband, we are about to partake in breakfast. Would you care to join us? Surely, you need your energy after exerting yourself this morning."

Cerus smiled and grabbed one of the biscuits, hungrily scarfing it down. He remained standing and eyed Matilda with a smile.

"So, speak, warrior of Gorl," Cerus demanded with a mouthful of food.

Jest glanced at Matilda, who nodded for him to proceed. "The barbarian tribe is close, within three days by foot. They …" Jest trailed off and looked down at his food.

"Be at ease, Jest. What have you discovered?" Matilda pried.

"The Tribe of the Serpent is at war."

"What? With whom?" Cerus asked.

"We think another tribe. Their forces focus on the northwest, and their tents remain mostly empty. Now is the time to attack, my lady."

"How many soldiers remain in the tribe?" Matilda asked.

"Not many, maybe two hundred, maybe half that. Most are women or infirm males. Their king has left them vulnerable."

"Any sign of Cassandra? She would stick out from them; her blond hair and fair skin would be easily identifiable," Matilda prodded.

"I saw none that fit her description."

"We should approach from the southeast, as the terrain appears rockier on that side of the desert, and it will give us cover," Cerus said, and he nodded in that direction.

"You have done well, Jest," Matilda said with a smile. "And, yes, Cerus, lead us in the route that will provide the most cover. Rally your men; we should leave soon."

Cerus smiled, wiped his hands together to rid them of crumbs, and then marched off, barking orders to his men. Matilda was happy with the report and informed the other priests of Jest's news as the warriors of Gorl began breaking camp.

ANOTHER SCOUT NAMED BRAYLEN APPROACHED JEST AND WHISPERED, "Did you tell her?"

"Of course not," Jest said. They watched the camp stirring now like an ant nest. "Besides, Cerus and Matilda are happy with the report, and there is no need to ruin it."

"That old barbarian woman spotted us; I just know it."

"She was too far away to kill, and so we ran. No one will believe the old hag's story anyway. There is no need to ruin Matilda's mood with such news, so we won't."

They watched the excited interaction between Matilda and the other priests. They were all anxious to be this close to catching their prize. Jest cleared his throat uncomfortably and gently tapped Braylen's chest. "Come, let us find Cerus and see where he wants us to scout this day."

THAT EVENING, AS THE SMALL ARMY SET THEIR CAMP ON THE SOUTH-eastern side of the desert where the rocky outcroppings provided an excellent opportunity for them to rest, Jest once again sought out Cerus. Matilda was in prayer—the priests of Marnelphion usually prayed to their demon lord after sunset. The priests were deep in meditation and were not to be disturbed. However, when Jest delivered his unusual news to Cerus, the leader of the Gorl army interrupted them.

He poked his head into the tent to find Matilda softly chanting with her eyes closed, sitting on the sandy floor and holding hands with the two priests on either side. They, in turn, held hands with the priests next to them and so on, forming a circle. Cerus, despite his bluster, froze when he took in the scene. He needed Matilda's attention but dared not interrupt her chant. He didn't have to wait long for her reaction as Matilda's eyes flew open, and she looked displeased with his appearance.

Before she could ask, he blurted out, "Matilda, I have news that cannot wait."

"We are in prayer," Matilda said as the other priests opened their eyes and turned to Cerus.

"I have something else for you to pray about," Cerus said.

So, Matilda ended the prayer and told her disciples of Marnelphion to read from their unholy tome until she returned. She escorted Cerus out of the tent and walked a few yards away so that they could speak in private.

"You know I cannot be disturbed now, Cerus."

"You'll thank me for doing so."

"Then speak what is on your mind, my husband," Matilda said with more than a bit of annoyance.

"Jest has returned and says he has found a burial ground less than a day away from our current position."

"Wait, a barbarian burial ground?"

"By all accounts. Most are skeletal remains, but there are some new bodies, fat and rotting, and being picked over by the vultures."

"These must belong to the Tribe of the Serpent. How ironic and delightful at the same time," Matilda said happily. She kissed Cerus and said, "My prayers will run long this night. Try not to play with Cass too long; I will need your warm embrace when we finish." She turned and reentered the tent.

Cerus, understanding he had plenty of time to couple with Cass, looked around the camp and eventually found her sitting with Ronnis D'Breeth. Cerus found little use for the strange man wearing the white mask. He approached the two, who seemed to be in deep conversation. Ronnis looked up first, and Cass turned to regard Cerus, a sexy smile creeping across her pretty face.

"Hi lover, where is Matilda?" she said, standing and moving close to him.

"In prayer," Cerus answered, never taking his eyes off Ronnis, who remained seated and staring at him. The way he sat perfectly still and looked upon him unnerved Cerus.

Cass stood on her toes and whispered in his ear, "Do you have time to play?"

"Always," he said, his face remaining emotionless and locked in a stare with Ronnis.

Cass didn't recognize or address it as she turned to Ronnis and said, "We will continue our discussion later; Cerus and I have work to do."

Ronnis nodded but did not move otherwise. Cass took Cerus's hand and started away. Ronnis held the gaze with the annoying Gorl leader until the last possible moment, and Cass eventually gained enough of his attention that he broke the hateful stare. Ronnis sat perfectly still until the couple was well out of sight, then he crept off to his tent to temper his anxiety. Cerus was fast becoming an issue. Why he had a problem with him was beyond Ronnis, but he decided then that he would alleviate the situation if he found an opportunity. After all, Ronnis was a lord, and not a petty fool to be taken lightly.

He withdrew the Adder and closed his eyes, communicating with the mighty sword. He silently relayed his plans for Cerus, and the sword approved. He then sent his visions of what he would do to Cassandra once they had her. They would catch the brat soon, and he and Cass would finally play with their prize. He planned on playing hard, and the Black Adder was very pleased.

Matilda and her contingent of priests prayed all night, asking Marnelphion to grant them the power to overrun the barbarians and claim their prize sacrifice. Jest's sighting was not a coincidence; at least, Matilda did not think so. It was the perfect opportunity to summon the ultimate army—a throng of undead. Matilda had never animated that many dead before. Still, her god was the master of the undead, and if all the priests participated, especially given the nature of their quest, she was sure Marnelphion would answer their prayers. By morning, they were ready and confident they could accomplish the task. An army of undead was at their fingertips; if they could raise and command them, they would overrun the barbarians quickly.

By early that afternoon, they discovered the sea of dead, the end that contained the older bodies, all picked clean by the vultures and other scavengers. Matilda was amazed at the sight as they walked the seemingly endless river. Cerus ordered the men to camp between some large rocks near the river. He walked with Matilda, Jest, and another priest named Boscoe.

"Does this pile of bodies have an end?" Matilda asked Jest excitedly.

"Yes, eventually. We estimate at least two thousand bodies, though there could be more because they are stacked," Jest said.

"How do you know they are stacked?" Cerus asked.

"Because at the other end of this strange river is where the barbarians have recently dumped their dead. You can see they stacked them at least five deep there."

Matilda turned to Boscoe and said, "Send word to our brothers and sisters that we must sleep the rest of this day because tonight, we will perform the ceremony."

"And tomorrow, we march your undead into the village of barbarians," Cerus said.

"Yes, and take Cassandra Rho once and for all," Matilda added.

"On one condition, my wife," Cerus said, suddenly looking solemn.

"What is that, my dear?" Matilda asked, stopping and looking into Cerus's eyes with more than a bit of concern.

"I lead the warriors of Gorl ahead of the undead filth. My men get to fight; the undead can clean up what we begin."

Matilda snorted and waved her hand at Cerus. "Yes, yes, that is fine, Cerus. Now, let's find the end of this magnificent burial ground to understand better what we have here."

She nodded to Boscoe, who took his leave to relay Matilda's message to the brothers and sisters of Marnelphion. Soon after, the three made it to the river's end, or the beginning, depending on how you viewed it. There, the air was rank with the smell of rotting flesh. Jest covered his mouth with his hand, but the scent did not affect Matilda or Cerus. They moved up close to the pile of bodies to confirm that there were stacks, four or five high at the end.

"What is that?" Cerus pointed to a faded set of tracks leading out from the bodies' tangle.

The three of them went to the trail, which continued southeasterly. It was barely visible now, the wind having blown most of it away, but it continued over a dune and out of sight.

"It looks like a person staggered away," Cerus said.

"How long ago?" Matilda asked.

"A few days at most."

"So, you mean someone walked out of that pile of corpses?" Matilda asked incredulously.

Cerus stood and noted where the tracks began. The wind had blown away most of the first steps, but they undeniably came from the sea of dead bodies.

"It sure looks that way," he confirmed.

"Jest, follow them and see where they go."

"Take two other warriors with you. If you have not reached the end by nightfall, return and report what you know," Cerus added.

Jest bowed and left them. Matilda and Cerus shared a curious look, and then Matilda said, "Let me know what he finds; I am resting now until nightfall."

CERUS WATCHED HER GO, THEN LOOKED AT THE WINDBLOWN TRAIL. He eventually shrugged and turned back toward camp. With the camp set, the priests slept until dusk. Just before they awakened, Jest and his small scouting party returned and found Cerus.

"So, what did you find?" Cerus asked.

"The trail goes for a while, then it looks like whoever or whatever was making the tracks met something more formidable and was dragged away."

"In which direction?" Cerus asked.

"To the east. We didn't follow them then, not wanting to find the larger creature. Should we have?"

Cerus thought about it for a moment and shook his head. "I find this curious but not worth any more of our time. You have done well, Jest. Now, you find some supper, and tomorrow, we march into the barbarian homeland."

Jest bowed once more and then took his leave. Cerus stared east at the many rock formations that way. Although the tracks made no sense unless someone had risen from the dead and walked away, he made a mental note of them in case they needed further exploration.

LESS THAN A DAY'S TREK FROM THE SEA OF DEAD BODIES AND THE army of Gorl, Sitra worked feverishly on Cassandra's broken body, trying desperately to save the woman. She gingerly picked the needles from her forearms, trying hard not to tear the damaged skin any more than it already was. Her wounds there were black and swollen, and each little movement Sitra made with the needles elicited a small moan from Cassandra. Sitra had some experience with healing minor wounds but was not a healer. There was no time to find one because Cassandra would not live long enough for that. Her still form lay on a soft bed of cloth, stripped naked so Sitra could discover all the woman's wounds.

"How is she?" Mateon asked, appearing at the door to the small room.

Sitra sighed and said, "Not good. I give her about a fifty percent chance to live."

"That is not very encouraging," Mateon said.

"No, it is not. I wish I were more proficient at healing; I feel like there are so many things wrong with the girl that I'm not sure I can fix."

"Like what?"

With another frustrated sigh, Sitra said, "There are cactus needles lodged in both arms and her gums. The skin around her injured forearms, and around her mouth and especially her gums, is black."

"The skin is rotting?" Mateon asked with alarm.

"No, I don't think so. Cassandra does not smell of rot, but I think she has been poisoned, which is the cause for the discoloration, almost as if the poison aggravated her existing wounds."

"Poison?"

"Yes, very strong and potent. I found a bite mark on her arm."

"Was it the size of a culiem fairy bite?" Mateon asked, catching on.

"Precisely," Sitra agreed, then stopped what she was doing and asked, "I assume the fairy is not here?"

"No, she rests easily in the small bed I made for her. She is dehydrated, and maybe a little sun poisoned."

Sitra turned at the confirmation that the fairy was not around, not wanting to turn the little creature to stone accidentally. Sitra was a sleeth, her curse the gaze of stone; her beauty was her blessing. She had beautiful green eyes that no one had seen and lived to tell about, and her skin was as perfect as an angel's. Small snakes comprised her hair, which writhed when she was excited. However, at a distance, they looked like long hair, which she usually had tied in a ponytail. She looked hard at Mateon, his pupilless eyes unable to see her lethal gaze and protecting him from it. She was worried about her patient and wanted him to understand she might not live. She was also curious as to what had happened.

"You said the fairy was with her when you found them and was protecting her?" Sitra asked.

"Yes, without a doubt, the fairy was looking after her."

"Then why the bite?"

"None of it makes sense to me, Sitra," Mateon said, shaking his head.

"She is young, Mateon, too young to have all these wounds."

"The cactus needles make me think she escaped from the barbarians."

"Yes, but who escapes from the barbarians? You are either enslaved to them or killed. There is no escape. But besides the needles, there are other curious wounds."

"Oh?" Mateon asked curiously.

"Yes, her ribs are very black on one side, as if she were injured there recently as well. I have a feeling more than a few were broken. Also, there is a knife wound in her back, but it seems to be a little older and is more of a scar. The skin is not black around that wound, which supports my theory that it is older than the other injuries."

"Yes, that is strange; the poor girl has been through a lot."

"But the strangest thing on her is this," Sitra said, moving to Cassandra's right hip and examining the brand.

"What is it?" Mateon asked, unable to see where Sitra referred to.

"A brand of a snake head."

"From the Serpent Tribe?"

"Hardly. Have you ever known the barbarians to brand their slaves?"

"I can't say I have," Mateon said, rubbing his chin. "Very curious."

"Yes, but there is more," Sitra said, wiping Cassandra's hip with a towel.

"More? Another wound?" Mateon asked, not seeing the attention his wife was giving the brand.

"No, the brand, it leaks."

"Leaks?"

"Yes, it is leaking what appears to be raw venom. Not as much as when we first found Cassandra, but it is somehow expelling the poison from her system."

"I have never heard of such a phenomenon," Mateon said, shaking his head.

"Neither have I, but I am witnessing it. As you know, a culiem fairy is not necessarily that poisonous. What makes the fairies so deadly is the magical nature of their bite. They inject a little dose of poison, similar to a snake, but the magic that comprises it—"

"Keeps it producing more poison over the next few weeks," Mateon finished for her.

"Precisely," Sitra said, "which means two things: the bite was recent, and the brand is expelling the continuous production of the poison. The venom is keeping her very ill, but the brand is saving her life."

"And you think she has a decent chance at surviving this?" Mateon asked.

"As I said, it is a fifty-fifty chance for her. With the poisoning and cactus needles, along with being very dehydrated and sunburned, she is in terrible shape."

There were a few moments of silence before Sitra finally said, "Well, it's going to be a long night; I had better get to work. I don't know how I'll get those needles out of her mouth, and when I get to that part, I will need your help. Go and sleep a bit while you can."

"Yes, my dear," Mateon said with a loving smile. He left the room but stopped and said, "I would like to know what kind of incredible journey this young woman has been on. With this many wounds and the fact she is so young, the tale would have to be amazing."

Sitra thought about it momentarily and replied, "With any luck, we'll hear that tale."

Mateon left his wife to her work and stepped outside in the cool evening air to sit with the sunset and smoke his pipe. He would find little sleep that night as Sitra continuously needed assistance until the sun rose the next day.

Deeper in the Yaddaton Desert, most of the buildings of the Culiem Tribe burned as evening set in. Maltor's men searched for survivors but found none. The place was full of food, supplies, and weapons, but the tribe had fled. Maltor stood at the edge of the village and stared hard at the clump of trees nearly one hundred yards away. He saw no movement but knew King Boskel and his men were there hiding.

"Cowards," he said to Jozerah, who stood beside him.

"Why would they not fight?" Jozerah asked.

"They know what they did and fear my wrath," Maltor said through gritted teeth.

"What shall we do? They are one of the stronger tribes of Yaddaton."

"Take their supplies, then burn their buildings. We will flush them out and slaughter them," Maltor said.

"As you wish," Jozerah said, then bowed and left to relay those orders.

Maltor stayed and kept his hard stare focused on the woods, his arms crossed over his massive chest, a symbol of fear for any of the Culiem Tribe who gazed upon him. All around, his men pillaged the Culiem structures and gathered all valuables into a large pile. Maltor had already decided he would enslave any survivors of the Culiem Tribe, and they would carry the booty back home. His thoughts drifted to Boskel's four wives. He decided as he stood there to take them as his own. Four wives for Cassandra were not enough, but it would be a start.

Soon, Jozerah had the archers preparing more arrows tipped with oil-soaked strips of cloth. They stockpiled them near their king, quickly accumulating a large pile before the sun fully set. Eventually, Jozerah stood beside Maltor once more.

"What do you think their next move is?" Jozerah asked.

"They are cowards, and Boskel knows what he has done. He is spineless, so I predict they will do nothing."

"This is strange behavior; I've never known Boskel to be a coward," Jozerah said.

Maltor turned to regard his commander and nodded. "But they have sat and done nothing as we pillage their home. It burns to the ground, and Boskel cowers in the trees, knowing he murdered my queen. His jealousy exceeds his cowardice."

Jozerah said nothing, but Maltor understood his commander's feelings based on his lack of words. He knew that some of the tribe questioned Maltor's attack on the Culiem Tribe, but he was glad that no one openly opposed him on the decision. Cassandra Rho was just an outsider, generally treated with no rights within his tribe, but she was to be his queen. She had his heart, and Jak seemed to care for her genuinely. But it stopped there, as his people quickly forgot the respect she had earned in the Queen's Tournament. Maltor knew that no one else felt the sting of losing her like he did. Yet, they followed his command to attack and eliminate the Culiem Tribe.

"So, what of the fairies?" Jozerah asked, snapping Maltor from his contemplations.

"You refer to when the fairies eventually attack because the barbarian tribe is too cowardly to fight their own battle?"

"Aye."

"I have already thought of this and think that will be their next move. I have called for Jak, the finest archer we have. He is our weapon against the fairies if they attack," Maltor said confidently.

"Jak? I do not understand how one archer will fend off a swarm of fairies, my king," Jozerah said.

"You will see, my commander, in time."

Jozerah smiled, nodded, and left it at that. Soon, the sun set, and only the smoldering flames of the burning buildings lit the area. Maltor had a large bonfire set in front of him, close to the supply of arrows and with the archers nearby to be called upon if needed. Jozerah had retrieved Boskel's polished, wooden throne and brought it forth for Maltor to sit on, placing it near the bonfire. Jak was nearby, as were Jozerah and Grink, the head shaman. They waited, taking turns watching the woods for an attack.

No attack came that night, and as Maltor rose from an uncomfortable sleep, two sentries approached from the south end of the camp. They had a young boy, no older than ten, with them, who looked scared and tired. They walked up to Maltor, and the two warriors bowed while the boy fell to his knees, overcome by the presence of his king.

"Why are you here, son?" Maltor asked.

The boy was slow to answer, so one of the sentries nudged him with his foot. "I come with news, my king," the boy responded, lifting his head to look Maltor in the eyes.

"You have come a long way, and at the moment of my glory, boy; this news better be important," Maltor said.

"He claims to be from our tribe, my king, and he claims to be sent by Bolin," one of the sentries said.

"Interesting. I left Bolin in charge with a small contingent to protect our home."

"Yes, my king, but he sent me here as quickly as I could run. An army masses to the south, my king, nearly three hundred strong," the frightened boy said.

Maltor shared a concerned glance with Jozerah and said, "Boskel? How could he have reacted so quickly and countered our attack?"

Before Jozerah could speak, the boy said, "No, my king, not a barbarian army. They are interlopers."

"Interlopers?" Jozerah repeated.

The boy only nodded vigorously, his unkempt locks bouncing about his shoulders.

"Are you hungry?" Maltor asked.

The boy nodded, and Maltor motioned to the two sentries and said, "See this boy fed, then send him hurrying back to Bolin."

"Yes, my king," one responded as they both bowed, and each took one of the young boy's arms and helped him up.

Before they could hurry him off, Maltor raised his hand to stop them and stood before the young barbarian. He towered over him, and the boy craned his neck to look at him in the face. It appeared to Maltor that the youngster would have fallen over if the two strong warriors had not held him up.

He bent and said, "You have done well. Take this, go to Bolin, and tell him I received his message. Tell him not to attack but only defend. We will not be gone long."

Maltor then placed one of his necklaces around the boy's neck. "This will let Bolin know you speak the truth. Also, for your great service to the Tribe of the Serpent, that is yours to keep."

The boy's eyes widened, and he looked the necklace over. Polished stones and teeth, two commodities within the Tribe of the Serpent, comprised the necklace. He was at a loss for words and could only stare at the jewelry in amazement. He looked up to Maltor with tears in his eyes and nodded again. Maltor motioned to the guards with a wave of his hand, and they took him away.

"Do we return?" Jozerah asked.

Maltor thought about it for a moment and shook his head. "They are a mere three hundred and not a threat. We will disburse them easily when we return. But our work is not done here, my friend." He clasped Jozerah on the shoulder and added, "And I am pushing this quest along now. It is time for us to wipe them out, and I will take Boskel's head as a trophy and display it proudly outside of my tent once we return."

"I do not doubt your words, my king."

"Then let us finish this and be home," Maltor said, and they turned their attention again to the nearby woods.

Maltor instructed Grink to gather the shamans, then had Jak and the other archers nock an arrow and be ready. The shamans converged on their king, all five working in unison to prepare a spell for Maltor that would give him complete immunity to poison, albeit briefly. As they summoned their magic, Jozerah gathered the warriors of the Serpent Tribe to be ready for the call to charge. The mighty army was soon waiting in anticipation as Maltor emerged from the huddle of shamans, now protected from the fairy venom.

He walked halfway to the trees, his massive sword strapped to his back and a single bottle of oil in his hand. Close behind came the army of men, led by Jozerah, and behind them were the shamans. Only the archers remained at the smoldering bonfire, arrows ready and under the command of Jak. Maltor stopped about fifty yards short of the trees and studied them, his men stopping in unison. They were quiet, too quiet for the experienced barbarian king. He suspected an attack, so he raised the bottle of oil in the air, a sign for Jak to light the tip of his arrow, which he did. Jozerah and the barbarian army waited for their king's next move.

Finally, Maltor yelled loudly enough to startle the birds in the trees, and they took flight. The yell was long and guttural, a sign to all opposing men that Maltor was enraged and ready to die for his cause. A barbarian in such a state was dangerous, especially if he commanded an army of fifteen hundred men as Maltor did.

When the yell finally died, its echo remained within the woods, carrying throughout and stirring anything living or hiding within. And as Maltor assumed, that included the men of the Culiem Tribe. After a few moments, it was clear that the Culiem Tribe wouldn't move from their hiding spots, assuming they were there at all. The thought of a smaller army sitting at his doorstep back home did not sit well with Maltor, and he needed to end this confrontation quickly to return to his people.

"Boskel, the Coward, murderer of my queen, come out, and let's end this!" Maltor yelled.

Not a sound came back to him, and his men shifted anxiously from foot to foot. Jak's arrow burned too long, and he had to toss it and light a replacement. When no response came, Maltor took his boot and dug a large circle in the sand with it, then stood in the center.

He called to Boskel once more, "A challenge circle has been drawn, Boskel—a fight to the death. Come out and fight or suffer the title of a coward the rest of your days!"

That elicited a reaction—a swarm of fairies poured out of the woods toward Maltor. His men took a step back nervously, understanding the danger of the bites those little creatures could deliver. That initial shock was soon replaced with worried murmurs as the barbarians of the Serpent Tribe became agitated, not wanting to witness the quick death of their king. Jozerah calmed them the best he could and assured them that they could trust in their king.

Maltor stood perfectly still in the center of the circle. He had expected such a cowardly move and had come prepared. The challenge of the circle, known throughout Yaddaton, was a ritual of honor passed down through the centuries. If one barbarian challenged another this way, it was considered an act of cowardice to decline. If accepted, the two warriors would enter the circle until one surrendered or died. Quite often, both men perished in the brutal ritual. It was not uncommon for kings to battle this way, but before accepting the challenge, an assault was not unusual. If Maltor died in an attack by the fairies, Boskel could claim the little creatures attacked before he could accept the challenge. However, Maltor had expected such a move, so he only smiled as the fairies closed in.

As the little creatures got within twenty feet, Maltor suddenly flung the bottle of oil into the air straight for the center of the fairy swarm. Jak was ready, and as the bottle flew into the air, he quickly got a bead on it and fired; the fairies dove under the bottle, understanding they could fly under the hurled item and get to their prey. Jak's shot was perfect, and his flaming arrow struck the bottle of oil, shattering the glass and spilling and igniting the oil.

The resulting rain of fire fell upon the little fairies, catching most of them in flight, burning their butterfly-like wings instantly, and making them plummet to the ground with a trail of smoke. Three made it unscathed and focused on Maltor, who was just a few feet away now, unmoving with arms crossed over his chest. The Culiem Tribe trained the fairies to attack in coordination, and the little creatures took their job seriously. They rarely failed.

Maltor did not move as the three landed on him and savagely bit him. The little creatures understood one bite would kill Maltor, so when all three bit him hard, one on his arm, one on his shoulder, and one on his chest, the fairies assumed that would be the end of the mighty king. The venom didn't take effect; the powerful magic of the shamans provided Maltor immunity. Maltor calmly plucked the fairy from his shoulder, and the creature knew it was doomed. It attacked his finger, biting him hard and drawing blood, trying to free itself, until Maltor bit off its head and spat it to the ground. He then flung the headless body away and reached for a second one.

The fairies weren't dumb, and when they noticed the venom having no effect and then witnessed the brutal death of their friend, they flew away, back to the woods and out of sight. Maltor stood confidently, most of the fairies squealing and burning in the sand just out of the circle. A few moments later, Boskel emerged from the woods, and a smile creased Maltor's bloodied lips.

He stepped back, deeper into the circle, inviting his opponent to join him. Boskel was a large man, similar in stature to Maltor but at least ten years his senior. He wore a thin shirt and loincloth, and when he exited the trees and came fully into the morning sun, he stopped and removed his thin shirt. He was muscular, and his massive chest bore the scars of many past battles. He held out his right arm, and two men, large warriors themselves but small compared to their leader, came from the woods carrying a mallet. It was made of wood, like the buildings, large, and, Maltor guessed, very heavy. It looked well used, and the sizeable square head of the weapon was stained crimson. The men dropped it at Boskel's feet and bowed.

Boskel smiled and easily lifted the weapon with his right arm. He casually rested it on his shoulder and walked confidently to the challenge circle. His warriors came forth from the trees, armed and ready for battle. The barbarian rules dictated that no matter how the battle proceeded, a king's army surrendered when he lay defeated at his opponent's feet. All understood these rules, so very few kings challenged each other in this fashion.

Maltor's anger with Boskel was great, so he ignored the possibilities; he was too enraged to lose and confident he would win the fight.

When Boskel finally stepped into the circle, and the two armies converged around it, moving to within striking distance, Maltor said, "And so my challenge is accepted by King Boskel, Coward of Yaddaton."

"I accept the challenge from Maltor, the Betrayer of Yaddaton," Boskel answered, then added, "Name your challenge and your price, fool."

"I challenge you to a fight to the death," Maltor said confidently.

There was some murmuring from the Culiem Tribe and more than a few gasps from both sides. Boskel only smiled and said, "And your price?"

"Your bride."

"Which one?"

"All of them," Maltor said through gritted teeth.

This answer erased Boskel's smile, and his face became red with anger. His men began murmuring and grew agitated by the request.

"Your price is high and that of a fool," Boskel replied.

"No, my Cassandra is worth more than all four of your wives. But I will take them and your head and leave satisfied that I have served justice upon your tribe," Maltor said. "Also, I will require ten strong men from your tribe to carry the treasures back that we have confiscated from your homes."

"You are a bigger fool than I first thought, Maltor, the Betrayer. My people have been at peace with your tribe for decades, and now you throw that away. You will pay a hefty price for such arrogance."

"We shall see! Do you accept my price, old man?" Maltor asked confidently.

"I accept, and now I name my own."

Maltor nodded, remaining on the far side of the circle, his arms crossed over his chest, and his giant sword strapped to his back.

"When I defeat you, I will take over as the leader of your tribe, and there will no longer be a Tribe of the Serpent."

Maltor didn't flinch, but his men began protesting loudly.

"All of your warriors, women, slaves, and possessions will become part of the Culiem Tribe once I smash your skull in with my mallet!" Boskel roared, and his men cheered.

The warriors of the Serpent Tribe eventually increased their grumblings into screams, shouting curses and shaking their fists in the air at the warriors of the other tribe, who eventually returned the favor. The shouting and name-calling lasted a while, and Maltor's resolve remained firm. He waited patiently until the verbal exchange between the two tribes finally died down. His posture remained confident, and his visage locked on Boskel. He heard little of the shouted insults as his mind pictured Cassandra, his bride. He had sacrificed Vixa for her, witnessed her fighting prowess in the gladiator pit, and lusted after her body. Ultimately, he fell in love with a perfect specimen of a queen, regardless of the fact she was an outsider. Then he pictured her lifeless body, the tiny fairy bite on her arm. Boskel had stolen it all away. Maltor knew without a doubt that the old king had planted the fairy to kill Cassandra if she somehow won the Queen's Tournament. His rage intensified.

"I accept!" he roared, and both armies grew utterly silent.

He drew his massive blade and began to walk the circle's perimeter, weapon at the ready. Boskel did the same and started walking in the same direction, his mallet prepared to strike. They circled several times, and with each pass, they got closer, carrying out the ritual of the challenge circle precisely as intended. Finally, when they were within striking distance, Maltor uttered a guttural scream and attacked, swinging his blade with the precision of a master swordsman. He was the ultimate warrior in the Serpent Tribe, deadly, fast, and strong, and the most proficient at swordplay. He was confident that his skill level would have Boskel on his heels quickly, with the old king using the cumbersome mallet as a weapon. The weapon of fools, as his father called it.

But he didn't expect the shamans of the Culiem Tribe to enhance Boskel's power. Maltor's shamans had helped him fight off the fairies' venom, while Boskel's had blessed him with the strength of Strenna. Similar to the ritual of the Warrior's Heart performed on Cassandra, several men had to sacrifice themselves for the enchantment to take effect. Boskel lost two minor shamans, one of whom was his nephew, to bless him with the strength of a giant. Maltor did not understand the impressive level of strength until the melee began. And, when they clashed, the first strike of the circle challenge, the two tribes engaged.

Jak had the archers ready, their arrowheads burning, and when the two tribes began their battle, he signaled for the archers to let fly their arrows. They did so in unison, all hitting the trees and some igniting the woods where the rest of the Culiem Tribe hid. Soon, smoke filled the air, and the women, children, and infirm fled those woods, along with hundreds of fairies. The shamans of the Culiem Tribe turned their attention to the fire, producing magic to extinguish it. Jak knew that he could not focus his attacks on the shamans since all the barbarians of Yaddaton worshipped the same goddess, and he could not mow down the women because the queens had to be among them. So, he did the only thing he could: he ordered the archers to toss down their bows and take up their swords. They did, and they rushed into battle for the honor of their king. And for Jak, the additional honor of their dead queen.

Boskel's swift parry met Maltor's mighty swing. Maltor did not expect the large man to be able to move that quickly with the heavy weapon, and it caught him off guard. When Boskel swept the mallet back on the follow-through, Maltor had to suck in his gut to avoid taking a hit in the ribs. Boskel was swinging the mallet as easily as if it were a dagger. Maltor then understood that magic enhanced the king of the Culiem Tribe, and he was in serious trouble.

The two armies came together like ocean waves breaking against rocks as they squared off again. Men died or became mortally wounded on both sides, yet not one slipped into the circle. The circle was an age-old tradition, and the competition could not be interrupted once it started.

Maltor hardly noticed the commotion outside the circle; he had to maintain total concentration against his dangerous opponent. As the battle raged around them, the two kings within sized each other up, and neither noticed the smoke wafting through as the forest burned nearby. Boskel came on suddenly with a brutal attack, with Maltor dodging and parrying. He managed to turn away one strike, and the force of the impact had him nearly lose his weapon. His arm tingled for many moments afterward. He decided then that he would dodge the attacks until the old king's magical powers waned or he found an opening.

Boskel smiled confidently and came on with several feints, his smile growing wider as he played. The larger weapon easily turned aside any attack Maltor attempted. The game proceeded for a long while, and neither king could connect with their attacks. Boskel showed no signs of weakening or slowing. Meanwhile, hundreds of men died in battle just feet away. Maltor saw this now and understood that time was against him. They outnumbered his men, and the warriors of the Culiem Tribe were indeed hearty. The longer he stayed within the circle, the greater the chance they would slaughter his tribe. He would not be able to wait for Boskel's power to fade. And so he tried a different strategy, going on the offensive, hoping that his speed and stamina would find an opening and wound the old king.

He attacked with a flurry of strikes, some powerful enough to throw Boskel off balance just slightly, but after many such attacks, he had scored no hits on the hearty king, who seemed greatly winded from the effort. Boskel smiled and eased his stance, giving Maltor a moment to recover.

Boskel swung his arm about to the carnage outside the great circle in the sand and said, "Take a look, Maltor, Betrayer of Yaddaton. More of your men die with each passing moment. You will lose. You can see that now, so I will allow you to beg for mercy. Beg me, and I will stop the slaughter of your men. They will live and become my subjects as they join my tribe."

Maltor looked around and could not disagree with the old king. His anger had blinded him, and he found himself in a dire situation he could not win.

Boskel smiled and added, "Your ignorance has cost your tribe enough; do not let it result in your death and the loss of more of your men. Your tribe is lost, but I can spare your life. Throw down your weapon and beg me, and I will consider your plea."

Maltor lowered his gaze to the sand. Once accepting the challenge, no proud warrior dared surrender in the circle. It was a fight to the death, but Maltor knew that the longer this lasted, the more of his men would die. It was a desperate situation for the proud king, and Maltor pondered doing what Boskel desired, only to save his men. But as his eyes surveyed the sand, he thought again of Cassandra and how she had fought against impossible odds to become his queen. She could not have hoped to win against any of her opponents in the queen's challenge, but she fought anyway and won. Maltor raised his gaze to meet Boskel's smirk, and Cassandra's lifeless body flashed before his eyes. The rage took over, and he regained his strength, focus, and stamina. With a bloodthirsty scream, he attacked mercilessly.

His sudden outburst caught Boskel off guard, as he obviously thought Maltor would surrender. Maltor took the offensive, smashing his sword against the mallet's handle as Boskel managed to get the weapon in line for a parry at the last moment. Metal rang out, and sparks flew as Maltor's blade clashed with the enchanted wooden handle of Boskel's mallet. That, accompanied by Maltor's war-like screams, slowly caused the battle to dwindle. It started with those warriors closest to the kings who turned their attention to the circle. Still, it spread outward until the warriors from both tribes separated and realigned themselves on their respective sides of the circle. Bodies lay strewn about, some dead, some men moaning in pain, and an abundance of blood stained the yellow sands of Yaddaton.

Maltor noticed the stoppage in fighting, which, along with Cassandra's visage, drove him to greater heights. He let his skills take over, muscle memory taking over from thinking. His quick jabs and swings were natural as he kept old Boskel off balance with a fury that few had ever seen. He refused to let himself grow tired, refused to lose. One hit forced Boskel to lower the head of the mallet and fall to one knee, presenting an opportunity for Maltor, who quickly took advantage. He swung at Boskel's right hand, slicing through bone to take two of the king's fingers.

As Boskel screamed in pain and surprise, Maltor pressed the attack, wanting to end the confrontation quickly. Boskel wouldn't accept defeat that easily and quickly rose to meet Maltor's barrage. He took a stab in the shoulder for the effort.

Maltor's stab into Boskel's shoulder was deep and solid, and he thought the fight would end then, but Boskel surprised him by taking an aggressive stance and swinging powerfully and accurately with his deadly weapon. Maltor felt like he had awakened a giant and did all he could to dodge the blows. He knew that even one such hit would be lethal, so he dodged, dove, and ducked all about the circle, trying to tire the enraged Boskel. To his disappointment, it looked as if Boskel was not tiring nor losing his enhanced strength.

One particularly close swing forced Maltor to parry awkwardly, and the strike dislodged his weapon. The sword flew out of the circle, and the warriors closest by had to dodge the missile to avoid its cut. Now, Maltor was weaponless. Leaving the circle meant surrender, so retrieving his weapon was not an option. Likewise, his men could not touch the sword for the same reason. He would have to win without a weapon. And still, Boskel attacked, swinging the mallet like a toy. Maltor tried to close, to lessen the effectiveness of those swings, but he knew that grappling with Boskel would be like wrestling a giant. However, that was his only option for success, so he ran in after a mighty swing.

Boskel must have expected such a move and managed to backhand Maltor hard across the cheek. The swing was awkward and did not connect fully; however, with the magical strength Boskel possessed, it knocked Maltor onto his back. He was momentarily stunned but stubbornly shook the cobwebs away just in time to see the mallet coming for his head from an overhead chop. He rolled to the side just a moment before impact, and the strike blasted sand all about the area and left a small crater. Maltor tried to regain his feet, but Boskel was faster, swinging his massive weapon to keep Maltor off balance. So, Maltor continued to roll this way and that to narrowly avoid it.

Although both barbarian kings were tired and Boskel had lost much blood, neither seemed to be slowing until Boskel clipped Maltor on the hip. Maltor had finally made his feet, but the effort cost him. The impact had him fly across the circle to land on his back at the edge, and he briefly saw all the men there, no longer fighting but watching the spectacular battle. He did not have time to consider their actions as Boskel lumbered over for the kill. Maltor was now immobile, believing he suffered a broken hip, even though the hit he took had not been solid. Luckily, Boskel was winded, and the loss of blood had him in a weakened state. What the old king meant to be an overhead smash from the mallet resulted in Boskel falling to his knees beside Maltor and bringing the mallet down awkwardly and off balance toward Maltor's head.

Maltor was able to grab the weapon handle and stop what little momentum the swing possessed. He and Boskel grappled for control of the mallet. Boskel had the strength advantage, but missing two fingers on his right hand made it difficult to maintain his grip. The two struggled that way, and Boskel brought himself forward, leaning on the weapon and driving the handle slowly downward toward Maltor's throat. The old barbarian looked crazed and desperate as he licked his dry lips in anticipation. Maltor could not hope to hold off the press of the weapon, and it would eventually crush his throat.

Slowly, the mallet descended until it was slightly touching Maltor's windpipe. Boskel put more of his weight on the handle, pushing with all his might as Maltor strained to keep it off his throat. He was losing that fight, and soon he would lose everything. He could see Boskel struggle with his right hand as the blood-soaked handle was slippery, and it made grasping the weapon difficult. As it pressed further onto Maltor's throat, slightly cutting off his breathing, Boskel's hold with his right hand wavered for just a moment. Maltor took the opportunity to summon his remaining strength, to press back against the weapon's handle, and slowly lift it.

He focused on Cassandra, his inspiration, and understood he had to avenge her. He was the king of his tribe, partly because his strength was unmatched in most of Yaddaton. And so, he strained and pressed, and the weapon lifted, slowly at first but gaining momentum as he began to win the battle of strength. He could see the panicked look on Boskel's face as he realized, too, that somehow Maltor was winning the fight. In desperation, Boskel slammed his head forward to headbutt Maltor.

Maltor saw the attack and moved the weapon handle just enough, manipulating it easily with Boskel's tentative grip from his right hand. So, instead of Boskel shattering Maltor's nose with the attack, he slammed his forehead into the mallet's handle. Maltor felt his opponent's grip momentarily loosen from the weapon. In response, he thrust the handle into Boskel's face with all his might. It connected with a crunch, and Boskel fell face first into the sand and began to moan, then turned on his back, bringing his hands to his bloodied, broken nose.

Maltor used the weapon as a crutch to lift himself off the sand. A sharp pain shot through his wounded hip, and he could not put any weight on that leg. He screamed the pain away and, after a few moments, found himself half standing and half leaning on the upturned mallet for support. He knew he had little time to work with Boskel as the old king struggled to shake the cobwebs away and reorient himself. So, Maltor did what he had to: he set himself and ignored the pain in his hip as he summoned the strength to lift the mallet over his head, readying it for a downward chop. He noticed peripherally that hundreds of barbarian warriors from each tribe stood just a few feet away, watching the epic battle. He struggled to maintain his grip on the heavy mallet and his balance with the wounded hip. He did look up briefly to see Jozerah and Jak standing side by side just outside of the circle, their weapons bloodied and their expressions in awe of their king.

He nodded and screamed, "For Cassandra!"

The mallet came down, Boskel's eyes growing wide in anticipation as he realized he was about to die. The giant mallet slammed into the old king's chest, shattering his sternum and most of his ribs. Maltor fell over from the effort, and none of the warriors made a sound or movement. Boskel was wheezing as blood poured from his mouth; he stubbornly clung to life.

Maltor crawled over to his wounded opponent and clasped his hands around the king's throat, strangling what little life remained in him. With his magical strength finally diminished, Boskel had little energy left to pry Maltor's hands from his throat. Maltor made sure the last thing King Boskel saw was the rage in his eyes as he strangled the life from him. Soon, the king of the Culiem Tribe was dead, and Maltor's men gave a grand cheer.

The warriors from the Culiem Tribe stood down as Grink and the other shamans healed Maltor. His hip would never be the same, though, and a slight limp would follow him from that day forward. He would live the remainder of his days in pain because of the injury, a reminder of his dead queen, Cassandra. However, he left the circle with everything he requested: four brides, ten strong warriors, all the treasure and supplies from the homes of the Culiem Tribe, and the head of King Boskel. He had avenged Cassandra's death.

THE AWAKENING

INTA'S LIFE REPLAYED IN HER MIND, EVERY DETAIL FROM HER earliest days, memories she had forgotten, and some she did not remember. She even recalled some of her first days in the world, memories that she should not be able to relive. She watched them play out in one long stream and continue chronologically from infancy. They stirred many emotions: happiness, sadness, love, and loneliness, to name a few. Her favorite parts of this replay of her life were the memories of her parents when she was young. They were so loving and cared for and nurtured her, yet they could not keep her from becoming the outcast she eventually became.

She watched intently as her childhood days slowly melded into her early teen years. She recalled her first kiss. It was from a young boy whose name she had long forgotten but now remembered—Charlie! He was cute and friendly, and she felt comfortable around him. They kissed, which was nice, but she knew it was not her favorite kiss. No, her kiss with Cassandra meant so much more to her. She was so focused on the moment with Charlie that she did not want to skip ahead to more recent days. Cassandra's kiss could wait a bit. She wanted the scene to play out to see how much she had forgotten about her life. She was fascinated by the glimpse but nervous about what she might find as it proceeded. She watched her kiss with Charlie unfold and then saw his hands touch her without her consent. Soon after, he was running away, his nose bleeding. It was a funny memory, and she liked it.

Her schooling was important to her parents, who insisted she go, although they had never received an education. She had gone as they told her to; she was a good child, after all, but the feelings of loneliness and not belonging from that time in her life came flooding back to her. She had no friends, and other children teased her. She had forgotten how or when the teasing had started, but reliving the memories had it all rushing back to her. Charlie and his friends had begun the teasing. She assumed he was mad and embarrassed about the bloody nose, and she appreciated that now. He was compensating for being rejected.

The teasing intensified as time went along. Binta had always been a loner, but in those early teen years, when her body was changing and her emotions were high, the years she needed a friend there were none. During that time, she received her first piercing, not by choice, but at the hands of Charlie's girlfriend. She had also forgotten her name and most likely had just blocked out the horrible person, but now she remembered—Kima. The evil girl pretended to take a liking to Binta, and they quickly became friends within a few days of meeting. Binta remembered falling hard for that feigned friendship. She had not known about Kima's relationship with Charlie. Kima had earned so much of her trust that Binta followed her without question.

So, when Kima suggested they see a friend and get their noses pierced, Binta readily agreed. Kima had promised to pay the fee, so they snuck off that night for their first piercing. Binta recalled her parents having issues with her staying overnight with someone she had only known for a short time. They did not know much about Kima, but she seemed pleasant, and Binta vouched for her. She pleaded with them and convinced them that the girl was her best friend. Looking back, she knew they had let her go because she had no friends. They loved Binta enough to allow it, but she could see the worry on their faces as she left with Kima that evening. They knew it was too good to be true, and soon Binta would, too.

That night, Kima led her to a trap instead of a bonding experience as she had expected. Five other girls, Kima's real friends, had met them in an abandoned warehouse and held her down while they painted her face with dark makeup. They called her a tramp and a whore, all the while giggling as if they were discussing boys or other things teenage girls usually discussed. Binta had not cried then, but as she recalled the tragic memory, she felt the sadness well up inside of her. After the makeup, they had pierced her nose, and it was the worst pain she had ever felt. They shoved a sharpened stud in her nostril and left it to bleed.

Instead of letting her go, humiliated and injured, Kima took it a step further. She had her friends pull up Binta's shirt, and she pierced both her nipples. It hurt, Binta recalled, but she also felt the sting now as she relived the vivid memory. And then they left her there, lying on that table. She hadn't cried as they walked away laughing. Instead, she wiped her bloodied nose and just lay there, understanding the betrayal and letting it sink in. She had no friends, and she never would. However, she had Kima to thank for awakening something deep within her that night. Being held down and having her breasts manipulated had stirred up mixed emotions, ones that she felt keenly now. After the bullies had left, Binta had put her hand down her pants and had masturbated. She climaxed quickly and forcefully. Then she got up and calmly walked out of the warehouse and back home. She hated what they did to her but loved the sexual charge she received from them dominating and hurting her.

She took the piercings out of her nipples once she reached home, which hurt and bled a lot, but after cleaning the dried blood from her nose, she took a liking to the nose ring. She also enjoyed the dark makeup after wiping some away and toning it down a bit. From that day forward, she wore the piercing in her nose and the dark makeup to match. She shocked Kima and her friends when she showed up at school that way, and they never bothered her again. From that day forward, most of the kids at school shunned her. She was secretly a submissive from that point as well, wanting to be dominated and longing for it to happen sexually. She lived that night many times in her head, but it was not a bad experience. Every time she thought of how it felt to be held down and dominated, she became aroused.

She fantasized about someone nasty, like Kima, holding her down and abusing her sexually. A few years later, she got her wish from her parents' friend. She recalled that night with mixed emotions, and as the scene played out, she mostly felt aroused by it. Her parents had left her with a trusted family friend, as she was sick that day and stayed home from school. She was not ill but hung over from the effects of experimenting with alcohol the night before. Too embarrassed to tell her parents, who she understood now would have been lenient, she had lied and told them she was sick.

Her parents were poor and could not miss their shifts at the mill, as low-paying as it was. So, they had asked Freland to remain with her in case she took a turn for the worse. Her lie had unintentionally set up the scenario she had been dreaming of. Freland was her parents' age. He had always seemed nice, though she did not know him well. Still, she had not been alarmed by his presence as her parents left that morning. They told her Freland would stay and watch over her as they went.

She quickly went back to sleep that morning, wanting to take advantage of the day off and recover from the hangover. At some point, she awakened, and Freland was standing over her. He had a strange look on his face and had one hand down the front of his pants. Before she could react, he quickly threw the blanket from her and pulled her roughly over his lap. She was wearing little and knew he could see more than he should. She did not move and did not resist as he began spanking her. She was only fourteen and just beginning her journey to womanhood. She knew she was too young for sex, but the idea that he would forcefully take her virginity excited her.

Freland yelled at her, accusing her of playing sick and disrespecting her parents. The spanking was hard and furious but mostly sex-charged. Thanks to Kima, she loved it. After the spanking, his anger seemed to play out, and he even seemed sorry for administering such a radical punishment. He rubbed her stinging bottom, apologizing for his outburst. That eventually led to a kiss and him rubbing different areas. Binta half-heartedly tried to fight him off, but there was no stopping the monster as he took her virginity. And again, she liked it. Afterward, he threatened her, telling her never to tell anyone what had happened, and she gladly agreed. They had sex regularly, most mornings in a field along her path to school. The pattern continued for months afterward until the husband of a woman he was bedding murdered Freland in a bar fight.

Greyson came to her mind as she recalled her time with Freland, because he sexually dominated her as well. However, she would not let her mind wander forward; she wanted to savor the memories. Greyson was to come in the replay of her life; she was confident in that, but she wanted to focus on her earlier memories, so she pushed Greyson out of her thoughts, just as she had Cassandra.

Schooling was rough on her as she endured bullying but focused on her studies and excelled at them. The other kids were so cruel to her that by the time she reached eighteen years of age, her parents sent her to Victoria's School of Magic in Pelesea. She knew little of magic, but it was a place her parents could send her to get a fresh start.

She did not know it then, but the vision unfolding before her revealed that the money to send her to the school came from Freland. He had left her gold and jewels at the time of his death a few years earlier. Her parents had not told her about it as they thought it a strange bequest. Despite their humble existence, they had used it in her best interest and had not taken a single item from it. She loved them all the more for it.

Then Cassandra Rho came into her life. She was an outcast, like Binta, and they made friends easily. It was the first friend Binta had ever really had, and soon, Binta found herself in Cassandra's room night after night, studying. The only thing Binta really studied during those times was Cassandra. She studied her face: beautiful blue eyes, pouting lips, golden hair, and perfect teeth. Binta had never been attracted to another woman before, and it took her some time before she realized that was what was happening with Cassandra Rho—she was falling for her.

Then the kiss, her favorite kiss ever, had occurred. Binta had instigated it, but by the time they had finished it, Cassandra was an equal participant. She left Cassandra's room that night happy and content but then crossed paths with Greyson Kavince as he left the school. Binta did not know it then, but something about him had her stomach in knots. Now, as she recalled the memories, she understood that Greyson was a predator similar to Freland. He was not evil, but a user of women, so she had fallen for him. The sex was incredible, and she was soon putty in his hands.

The hardest part was telling Cassandra about him. Binta knew she hurt her with the news, but she physically belonged to Greyson at that point, although her heart belonged solely to Cassandra. She supported Greyson's attempt at seducing Cassandra, thinking it was a perfect compromise. She fondly recalled the night Cassandra and she had slept together naked, awaiting Greyson's arrival. That night alone with Cassandra solidified Binta's feelings for her. Unfortunately, Greyson had never arrived, and so sex with Cassandra eluded her.

Then there was the quest, the failed adventure for Cassandra's birthright. The death of Cassandra's mother followed the quest; she was hanged by the evil men in Oldorburg. Her heart broke at remembering that event, as she knew Cassandra's heart indeed had. She wanted to console her friend after such horrific news, but she never got the chance, as Kringus had jailed Cassandra for treason.

Then she remembered the fire! The disaster had taken Cassandra from her before they could develop their relationship and build on that beautiful kiss. She distinctly recalled the smell of burning flesh as she stared at Cassandra's charred body in the street in front of the jail. Her bright white teeth were the only perfect thing left on her once-perfect body. Of course, as she watched the scene unfold now, something struck her profoundly. She had been too distraught to see it before, but they were not Cassandra's teeth! She knew Cassandra's every feature, including her marvelous teeth, and the teeth of the burned corpse were not Cassandra's.

She pulled herself from the vision and made herself awaken from the deep slumber, her heart pounding in her chest. She did not know how long she had dreamed of her life events, but it seemed like a very long time. Either way, her discovery that Cassandra was probably alive ended that amazing recollection of her life. Binta blinked away the sleep and tried to find her bearings. She was in a beautifully decorated large room and did not initially recognize it. She sat up with some effort, dizziness nearly taking her, and looked around. A large window was open, the drapes flapping in the warm breeze and the sunlight spilling into the room.

She slowly recalled where she was and whispered, "Jamison." She remembered the raven she followed into Jamison's study and the secret passage leading to the tome. "The Tome of X'lor," she whispered breathlessly.

She realized then that a small bell was within reach on the bedside table. She turned to look at it. It crossed her mind ever so briefly that she was aware of the bell before she even noticed it. She took it up and rang it, and soon, she heard footsteps in the hall outside the room. She knew she was in Jamison's room, and she turned to regard the open door to her right that led to the room he had designated for her. There, she saw the unusual picture Jamison had commissioned of her hanging in its usual spot. She stared hard at it, and it felt like she was looking at herself in the distant past. Binta felt different now. She felt—

The door burst open, and Jamison came in with Kleve behind him. Both wore astonished expressions and just stared for a moment. Then a smile spread across Jamison's face, and he rushed to her. "Binta, my love, you are awake!"

"I have been asleep?" she asked.

"For nearly a month of days; we were afraid …" He trailed off and looked to Kleve.

"We were afraid you'd never awaken, dear," Kleve finished for him.

Jamison hugged her tightly, and she reciprocated but pushed him away quickly, understanding that time was of the essence. "Jamison, you must summon the carriage; I need to meet with the king… no, with Instructor Baxter, right away," she demanded, pulling back the sheets and standing for the first time in a long while. She was unstable on her feet, the dizziness returning, and Jamison took her by the elbow to steady her. The look on his face revealed to her that he was worried.

"What?" she asked.

"You should remain in bed until I summon a priest."

"Why? I feel good. Actually, I feel better than I ever have," Binta said truthfully. She closed her eyes and focused and soon overcame the dizzy spell.

"You have been bedridden for weeks, my love."

"Yes, which is why I swayed when I stood, but I am fine."

Jamison did not release her and only gave her a concerned look. She focused then on him and found she could sense his thoughts somehow—not read them, but she could sense his true intentions. He loved her. She smiled at the revelation and hugged him again.

She whispered in his ear, "You care about me."

He broke the hug, brought her to arm's length, and said, "Of course, I love you."

She studied his face for a moment and smiled. She knew without a doubt that he did love her. "Good, then fetch the carriage; I must see Instructor Baxter immediately."

"Binta, I refuse! I found you nearly four weeks ago, lying unconscious in my storage chamber at the foot of the Tome of X'lor. No one has ever read that book and lived to talk about it," Jamison said.

Binta considered his words and understood he was scared for her. She recalled viewing the book, and it did not contain any writing. She remembered the feeling of being transported in time and space and how her mind seemed to expand and grasp all sensations around her as she viewed the blank page. The experience had opened parts of her brain she had never used. She now understood more about the world, even how the tome had fabricated the raven to lead her to it. It had preyed on her despair, the deep, dark despair that had lived in her since Cassandra's death, and the tome showed her the error of that despair.

Her smile grew even more substantial, and she hugged Jamison once more. Then she turned to Kleve and said, "Fetch Rose. I need an outfit, and then fetch a priest because Jamison thinks I need one, although I do not."

Kleve began to speak but stopped, a look of confusion upon his face. He looked to Jamison for guidance, who nodded in agreement and shrugged. Kleve left to do just what Binta had ordered. When he was gone, Binta looked at Jamison and held up her hand, the ring comfortably on her finger.

Jamison said, "You accept?"

Binta smiled and said, "I wear your ring, but we must discuss the engagement later. For now, I must get ready."

"Why? What is so urgent about meeting with Baxter? And what is there to discuss? I love you and—"

"I love you as well, Jamison, although not as strongly as you love me."

"What? How can you know that?"

"I think it's the tome, Jamison."

"The tome? What about it?"

"It has enhanced my perception of… of everything! I strongly feel your love and am fast falling for you because of it. But first things first—I must see Baxter."

Rose burst into the room with a broad smile and said, "Lady Binta, you have awakened!"

The portly woman rushed over and gave Binta a warm and sincere hug. Binta smiled at Jamison as Rose gushed over her, and then she took Binta by the hand and led her to the giant walk-in closet. Binta shrugged and put up no resistance.

Jamison stood where he was by the window and yelled out, "And what of Baxter?"

"She is alive, Jamison!"

"Who?"

"Cassandra Rho!" Binta said, sticking her head out of the closet with a giant smile. She was quickly pulled back in by Rose, who began the task of finding suitable clothes for a lady of Pelesea. Jamison crept forward, deep in thought.

"The one who died in the fire?" he asked, and by the time he asked it, he was in her room and near the closet.

Binta poked her head around and was about to yell across the room to him, but his proximity startled her, and she jumped a little, giving him a view of her near nakedness as Rose searched for a dress, busy rummaging through the many specimens in the closet.

Binta covered herself and smiled playfully. "Yes, except she didn't die! Cassandra is the part we need to discuss later about our engagement."

Before Jamison could respond, Rose pulled Binta into the closet and scolded Jamison for being inappropriate while the lady dressed. Jamison scratched his head and returned to his room, absorbing the strange communication. He plopped down on the bed and whispered, "Cassandra Rho?" Rose shut the door, and Binta giggled from within.

KESSI AND SABRINA HAD FINALLY DEVISED AN ESCAPE PLAN TO BE FREE of Matilda's clutches. The chance of success was minimal, but it was their only choice. After miraculously regaining her memories, Kessi had told Sabrina and her other cellmates who she was and why she was there. Heinsvick, the vampire lord, had sent her, brainwashed into thinking she was her sister, Cassandra, the grand sacrifice Matilda so desperately desired. Heinsvick's mind control had succeeded initially, but the ruse eventually failed. Heinsvick wanted his bride, Emiline, returned, which Matilda had promised once he delivered Cassandra. Since he could not find Cassandra, he used the next best thing: her brainwashed sister. But during that exchange, Matilda betrayed him by refusing to give up his precious bride, so Emiline remained her pet. It was an incredible story of Kessi willingly sacrificing her life to save her sister. She was disappointed that she had failed but was just as disappointed that Emiline was not free from her servitude to Matilda.

Kessi's friends listened intently to her story, wide-eyed and amazed. They had each been taken captive by Matilda to prepare for the sacrifice to Marnelphion, but none had a story like Kessi's. And when she described the horrific demon that Matilda had summoned, the others knew they had to escape. Kessi confirmed that Matilda planned on sacrificing them all, using their blood to open a gate to hell to summon forth the demon lord Marnelphion. However, she also emphasized that Cassandra was the chosen sacrifice and that her blood would be the catalyst to open the gate. Without Cassandra, the summoning would fail.

And so they sat in their cell just after breakfast, planning their escape once more. Kessi had regained her memories a few months earlier, and they had formulated the plan then. Now, they perfected it as best they could.

"So, let's go over this once more," Kessi said.

"Again?" Kimmie asked. "We have gone over this for two months now and have done nothing to implement it." She sighed.

Kessi smiled and took Kimmie's hand. "I know it's frustrating, Kimmie, but I have had to work at this to ensure I remember everything about my past. We'll get only one chance."

"Only if we are careful, and we all know the plan. So, let's go over this again, and then again tomorrow and the next day and however long it takes," Sabrina, their elected leader, added.

Sabrina was the first abducted when Cerus and his men overran Attins. She had been an easy target, dressed as a virgin for the Autumn Festival, a holiday for the women of Attins to conceive. She had planned to do just that, to bear the offspring of the prodigy from Tara. Sabrina never had the chance to meet the young man named Greyson Kavince and had indeed not lost her virginity. Instead, the evil priests of Marnelphion had taken her here and placed Emiline in the adjoining cell to watch over her. That was over six months ago, and now the number of women in the cell had grown to three dozen. Kessi had been the last and the most crucial piece added, but Sabrina was looked to as their moral leader because she was the first to arrive.

"So, we know that Cerus and Matilda have left Nesin, and possibly most of the priests and warriors of Gorl have followed," Kessi said.

"How can we be sure?" Natasha asked. She was another of Kessi's cellmates who had been there a while.

"Well, we can't. But as we've discussed, only the one priest keeps coming to feed us and check on Emiline," Kessi explained.

"That man gives me the creeps," Sara whispered.

Sara was the youngest of the prisoners, only sixteen years of age, and Kessi liked her the most because her name reminded her of her mother.

Sabrina looked at her sternly and added, "He gives us all the creeps, Sara. He is an evil man who worships a demon. Suffice it to say, if Matilda did not task him with our safekeeping, it is hard to tell what he would do to us."

"Especially to Kessi," Sara added, then looked apologetically at her cellmate.

Kessi only offered a smile and sighed. "Yes, he is an evil man with evil thoughts, and we can see them etched across his face. We will use his evil desires and intentions against him, though. He will be the catalyst to our escape plan."

"Are you sure there is no other way?" Sabrina asked.

"None that we have come up with," Kessi said, shaking her head.

Since they discovered Matilda and Cerus had left Nesin and the lone priest, Merrik, was tasked with watching over them, the attention he gave Kessi seemed to grow. He was interested in her, and she had decided to use those lustful desires against the man. She had purposely made more eye contact with him the last few weeks, shared an occasional smile, and glanced away whenever their eyes met. She had no experience in the art of seduction but was acting the part of the shy virgin perfectly, hopefully fueling his desires.

"So, what is next?" Natasha asked.

"Next, I continue to make nice with the priest, and we somehow reach out to Emiline," Kessi said.

"The vampire?" Sara asked nervously, then glanced to the coffin in the adjoining cell.

All three dozen turned to regard the coffin, each expecting the volatile vampire to burst forth. When nothing happened, all eyes were eventually back on Kessi.

"Yes, as I've said before, I must speak with her privately but have had no chance over the last few weeks. I must find a way to reach out to her. Without Emiline, none of this is possible."

"In summary, Kessi will continue seducing the weird priest and eventually draw his attention so Emiline can attack him from behind. We take his keys, free ourselves, and have Emiline guide us out of the fortress," Sabrina said.

"Then what?" Kimmie asked. "If we can convince the vampire to help us, overpower the priest, and fight our way out, what then?"

"Then you go home and warn others of what transpires here," Kessi said.

"And if we have no home to go to?" Sabrina asked.

Kessi noticed that more than a few looked her way, awaiting an answer, and it broke her heart to realize that most of the young women with her were now homeless and without a family to return to.

"Then you are welcome to join me," Kessi offered.

Their plans after escaping were something they had not discussed, and Sabrina immediately grew curious at Kessi's answer. The two had grown close, and Kessi knew Sabrina had no home to return to now, but neither had discussed what they would do if they escaped the evil fortress.

"Join you?" Sabrina asked.

"I plan on stopping Matilda, and I technically have no home to return to, either. I am an orphan, remember?"

"Yes, but you have a mother and a sister to return to, Kessi," Sabrina reminded her, then added, "And what can you do to stop Matilda, anyway?"

"Yes, I have a mother who is hopefully safe on the other side of the world and a sister who, to my knowledge, is still hiding. If I follow Matilda, and she happens to find Cassandra, I will be there to help."

"Help how?" Natasha asked.

"I will help any way I can. Adlesk will guide me, and I will use my god-given powers to sabotage any efforts they make, help free the people they enslave, and cause Matilda grief at every turn she makes. All I know is that I must stop them because the world's fate rests on them. They cannot be allowed to continue with their evil plan."

"I will join you," Sabrina said.

"Are you sure? It will be a dangerous endeavor, and I don't expect you to risk your life to help," Kessi said.

"None of us should be expected to do anything, but we have a decision to make. You have given us a plan of escape so that those of us who have a home can return to it. For the rest of us, you have given us a chance to live, which is no small thing," Sabrina said.

"Yes, we are all dead anyway if we can't find a way out of here," Natasha added. "I'll join you in your cause. I'm not a priestess, but I can fight. I used to beat up my brother back home when we were younger; surely I can take a creepy-looking old guy like Merrik!"

They all shared a laugh, and when it quieted down, Kessi nodded and said, "Thank you all. If we get out of here, I'll accept all the help I can get. First things first, though, we must escape Nesin. To do that, we must communicate with Emiline."

They all turned to regard the silent coffin again, and the sight stole some of their bluster.

BINTA AND JAMISON SAT SILENTLY IN THE CARRIAGE AS IT RETURNED home. They had just visited the school, and Binta had learned that Baxter and Victoria had taken the semester off. Instructor Von Hueven informed Binta that Victoria and Baxter had business at the castle. He had told her he did not expect them back until possibly next spring. So, now they sat in silence as Jamison's driver slowly guided them through the bustling streets of Pelesea. Jamison looked out the side window, deep in thought. Suddenly, he realized Binta was staring hard at him.

"What?" he asked, shifting uncomfortably.

"You know something about this."

"You are right, and yet, I'm not sure how to tell you, my love."

She took his hand and said, "If I am to live with you, wear this ring, and prance around in these pretty dresses like a snobby rich person, then you need to level with me."

"You think I'm snobby?" he asked and seemed mortified.

She smiled and leaned in and kissed his cheek. "Actually, I do not, but I feel and look like a snob."

His expression turned serious, and he took both her hands and said, "No, never. You look stunning in that dress, and I find you to be more beautiful than ever when you wear it. You are a natural beauty and have taken Kleve's training without complaint. We have found a perfect lifestyle that complements your beautiful soul."

She could not help smiling as he leaned in and lovingly kissed her. He then sat back, and Binta could see he was looking for a way to tell her something. He knew details concerning Victoria and Baxter, evident by the look on his face, though she knew that if she consciously focused on it, she could scour his thoughts and find out what was behind their mysterious absence. The thought startled her, though. Whatever had happened when she read the Tome of X'lor had changed her. She felt so alive, it was true, but also very aware of things, as if she possessed a higher intelligence than before reading the old book.

It was Jamison's turn to break her from her thoughts. "What is it, Binta, my dear?"

She shook away the thoughts and scolded herself for even thinking of reading Jamison's mind. She might be able to use her mind differently now, but she had no idea what new skills she possessed. The possibilities excited her and terrified her. Although tempting, she knew she could not act on her impulses to invade someone's mind. Especially the people she cared about; they were too important to be treated that way.

"I just feel funny, you know, trying to catch my bearings since—"

"The Tome of X'lor," he finished for her.

She nodded, and he sat back in the seat.

"I should never have brought it home. I bought it to entice you but never thought it would lure you in and make you peruse its cursed pages. I'll burn it!" Jamison said, becoming more agitated as he spoke.

"You bought it for me?"

"Yes, but I did not know it would harm you, and for that I apologize."

Binta smiled warmly and said, "Do I look injured, Jamison?"

"No, of course not."

"And didn't that priest you sent for confirm that there is nothing physically wrong with me?"

"Yes, but—"

"But nothing, Jamison; I am fine, and no apologies are required."

He thought about that for a moment and studied her face. She knew he would never do anything to harm her, and his guilt was obvious. But as he studied her, some of that guilt seemed to disappear, and he relaxed a little. A smile crept across his face, but worry was there; something was on his mind.

So, she asked again, "Something troubles you, so tell me what it is."

"Very well, but I do not know all that much," he said as a shadow crossed him.

Binta became concerned and took his hand. "Tell me, why is Baxter staying within the castle?"

"I'm not sure of the full story there, but something is changing in the world, my love. Something bad, I fear."

"What do you mean, Jamison? I was not unconscious for that long, right? I mean, what has changed since I read the tome?"

Jamison smiled and said, "It was changing well before that. The New Order has decided to assemble once more."

"Assemble?" Binta asked.

She recalled the conversation with Daro, the ranger, at the castle's cottage, and suddenly, that conversation did not sit well with her. His words haunted her then as she put some of the story together. "The New Order is assembling and looking for new members," she said absently.

"What? How do you know that?"

Binta shrugged and offered a smile. "Daro, the ranger, hinted that was the case. But you cannot tell anyone; no one is supposed to know."

"You spoke with Daro? When?"

"Before you showed back up in my life while I stayed at the castle's cottage. He seemed distant and disturbed, like you on this ride home."

He smiled and said, "I am disturbed; I feel something awful is happening."

"But you don't know exactly what?"

"No. However, we can find out together."

"What? How?" Binta asked, intrigued.

"Tomorrow night, I have been invited to the castle for a special announcement. I would like for you to go as my guest."

"A special announcement? Daro said there would be one soon. But you said the event was by invitation only. Is the king not announcing this to the city?"

"No, not yet, but soon. Tomorrow is a private meeting for the city's leaders and wealthiest citizens. They have something big to announce, which must be serious."

"And Baxter is a new member of the New Order?"

"Again, I do not know anything about this Baxter fellow. Why is he so important to you?" Jamison asked.

"He is a friend. He protected me from Cass and helped me find a safe place after you saved me from Poppy's Inn."

"So, is he a romantic interest of yours?" Jamison asked nervously.

"Of course not. Baxter is an instructor, but we both took the loss of Cassandra very hard," Binta said, slumping back in her seat.

"Cassandra Rho? There is that name again," Jamison said, shaking his head.

Binta could not respond as she thought back to recent interactions with Baxter. She had always suspected he had a romantic interest in Cassandra, but in hindsight, it was evident that Baxter was in love with her. Binta had witnessed the kiss they shared on the dock the day Kringus jailed Cassandra. Still, she had put that out of her mind, hoping Baxter had done it in desperation to save her friend. She had been too far away to tell for sure, and the many ravens flying around the area obscured most of the view. In the end, Cassandra had died before Binta could discern any information from her about Baxter's kiss. But she could discover the answer to that question now because Cassandra was alive!

It was all clear now—Baxter loved Cassandra and had for a while. Like Greyson's, Binta had assumed his infatuation with her friend was born from lust. After all, he was twice her age. Her thoughts and memories were clear now, thanks to the strange tome. She did not doubt that Baxter loved Cassandra every bit as much as she did, and maybe more. All those awkward exchanges she had shared with Baxter made sense to her then. Binta gasped and covered her mouth as she recalled the rumor circulating in the school that Baxter and Cassandra had slept together. She always thought that was a lie fabricated by Cass and her idiot friend, Jabell, but now she wasn't sure. Binta vaguely heard Jamison call her name, so she made eye contact with him. She realized then that it was not the first time he had done so. She shook her head and blinked away her thoughts.

"What?" she asked.

"We need to talk about Cassandra Rho," he said.

"Yes," she silently agreed, still processing the revelation about Baxter.

She thought again of the brief time after Greyson sailed out of her life, how she had tried to run the temple of Plath for him, and how Baxter had checked on her. She was his closest link to Cassandra, and he felt compelled to protect her during those dark days. A gentle hand on her knee broke her thoughts again. She looked at Jamison and saw the concern there.

"What?" she asked a second time, struggling to keep her mind from wandering now that she could think so clearly.

"We are home," Jamison said. He opened the door and jumped out of the carriage. He extended a hand to help Binta down and said, "Come, I'll have Kleve make us some tea, and we'll talk things over."

She nodded and took his hand, and as promised, they had some tea and talked. At first, they spoke of the event at the castle the following evening, but the conversation quickly led to Cassandra.

"Why is Cassandra so important? You said she is alive; does that mean she did not die in that awful fire? You obviously thought she was dead and have now found out differently?" Jamison asked.

"Cassandra is an important part of who I am. I will tell you everything, but I want you to be open-minded about our relationship."

"Of course, my love."

She wasn't sure if he was ready to hear what she had to say, but she knew it would be best to say it before things progressed. And so she decided to be honest and tell him everything. "I met Cassandra at Victoria's School of Magic. We entered the school during the same semester and had a few classes together. I liked her immediately, and we hit it off quickly. Soon, I spent each evening in her room studying. During those nights, we bonded and discovered we were similar people with similar backgrounds.

"As the weeks passed, I grew closer to her, and she seemed to respond in kind. I felt bad for her because she fretted over her family's safety. My heart went out to her, which only strengthened our friendship. Victoria's school is quite large, but it seemed like Cassandra and I were the only ones there for those few weeks. It was one of the best times of my life."

"And Baxter was a professor, you said?" Jamison added.

"Yes, a professor at Victoria's school, and Cassandra and I shared his class on spellcasting. He was, and is, a great professor."

Binta could see the jealousy cross Jamison's face, but it did not last long, and a look of nervousness quickly replaced it. He was insecure about her; their relationship was new, and he was concerned about where the conversation was heading. She continued, though, understanding that she had to express her feelings for Cassandra before continuing her romantic path with Jamison. It would hurt less now than in a few months if the truth would indeed bother him.

"And he had feelings for you?" Jamison asked, not able to hold back any longer.

She shook her head and said, "No, not me, but in hindsight, I feel he loved Cassandra. A rumor circulated in the school that he and Cassandra had slept together. Cassandra denied it, and Baxter did as well, announcing to his students that the rumor was a lie. However, I wonder now how much truth there was in that rumor. Perhaps they didn't sleep together, because I don't think Cassandra would have lied to me. However, perhaps they kissed, and someone saw them and started the rumor. Perhaps someone witnessed more than that."

Binta chewed her bottom lip, lost in thought, until she caught Jamison looking at her. His confused visage said it all. "You were jealous of her. You liked Baxter?"

He still didn't understand, so she continued with a shake of her head, "No, Jamison, I was jealous of him."

He sat there momentarily, his brow wrinkled in confusion, but then the light appeared somewhere in his mind, and his eyes widened. Before he could speak, Binta continued, "Yes, I fell in love with Cassandra. When I broached the subject of the nasty rumor circulating the school, and she denied it, I took my chance."

"What did you do?"

"I kissed her. Lightly at first to see how she would react, but then more assertively and passionately when she didn't seem to mind. She responded well to the kiss, making me so happy."

"So, you are gay?" Jamison asked, his shoulders slumping.

"You have made love to me many times, Jamison. Do you think I'm gay?"

"Well—"

"Well, nothing. The sexual chemistry we share is one of the things I love about us. Do you deny it?" Binta asked sternly.

He smiled and shook his head. "Of course not."

"Good, then you know I am not gay."

"Then what are you?"

Binta thought about that for a moment and said with a smile, "Adventurous!"

"So, you experimented with Cassandra, but do you love her?"

"It was more than an experiment, Jamison; I fell deeply in love with her and still am. We just never had the chance to advance our relationship. You must be able to accept the fact that I am in love with another woman."

There were a few moments of silence as her words sunk in. Then Jamison finally said, "So, what happened? I mean, you have never spoken of her before. I recall Franklin Ruben mentioning her, but not in pleasant terms."

"Of course, that man doesn't like anyone but his beloved Cass." They both chuckled, and Binta took another sip of her tea before saying, "Greyson happened."

"Who?"

"Greyson Kavince, a young priest I met the night of my kiss with Cassandra. He charmed his way into my life and kept Cassandra and me from advancing our feelings and exploring our new relationship. He is the real reason Cassandra and I never slept together."

"You did nothing more than kiss her?"

"We fooled around some, but not much more than kissing and touching. We slept naked and cuddled one night but did not have sex. Looking back, the anticipation of sleeping with her caused knots in my stomach. Especially in anticipation of that night, which was the most amazing, even though we did nothing but cuddle."

"You wanted more from Cassandra and fell in love with her, but did you choose this Greyson person instead?"

"Not exactly. He exploited our feelings for each other and had the wild idea of the three of us sleeping together."

"And?" Jamison asked nervously.

"Well, it didn't happen, but Greyson and I were a couple until just a few weeks before you and I met."

"And Cassandra died," Jamison said, recalling the tragic event.

"She died in the jail fire, but I have recently discovered that she did not actually die."

"How do you know this?"

"I can't explain it other than I feel my mind has awakened, Jamison. I think the tome has given me the ability to think very clearly and see things in my past that I missed. I know Cassandra is not dead because I can recall the teeth of the corpse that was supposed to be Cassandra. They did not match her perfect smile. I just realized it while I was sleeping off the effects of the tome."

"You want to find Baxter and tell him she is alive. Why?"

"Well, he treated me so kindly after her death, and I knew he took the news hard, so I wanted to relieve his pain and share the joyous news. Now, I feel jealous because he is obviously in love with her, Jamison."

"And, should I feel a pang of jealousy?" he asked with a sheepish smile.

"Of course."

That took him back a bit, and his smile quickly faded. Binta let that settle in his mind and took a long draw from her tea before continuing, "I want to find her. No, I must find her!"

"Then what?"

"Well, that is what all this conversation is for. It all leads up to this moment. I know you are a good man, and your feelings for me are true, but can you handle the fact that I love Cassandra?"

"What? Of course, I can. I love you, Binta Mulay."

"I know that," she said, taking his hand and looking him in the eyes. "But can you handle the fact that I long to hold her again, to kiss her, to taste her, to make love to her? Can you accept that?"

She squeezed his hand, and he squeezed back meekly, and his eyes told her he was unsure of what she was asking.

"Jamison, when I find her, I want us to invite her to live with us."

"What?" he asked in surprise, pulling his hand away. "It is not proper, Binta, we cannot—"

"I am not proper and never will be. There are things you do not know about me yet. Not bad things, just things that are not normal. As you discover them, I'm hoping you will love me all the more for them. I know you are capable, but you must forget this image you want to create of me. I can dress in these fancy clothes, wear your jewelry and makeup, and walk like a lady, but on the inside, I am far from that. I am a former prostitute who loves sex and loves another woman."

He slumped back in his chair as if she had slapped him, and his eyes darted about as he absorbed the information. She gave him all the needed time and refilled their tea cups before he spoke. "So, are we to wed?"

"Possibly, but Cassandra would need to still be in the picture. I want her to live here with us if she accepts the invitation. I want her to share everything that Greyson wanted us to share."

"Which means—" Jamison began before she cut him off abruptly.

"Yes, sharing our home, food, clothing, and, most of all, bed. But more than that, I want to share our lives with her."

"This is all so strange, Binta. How can we just have another woman living with us? It is just not…" He trailed off, but she finished the sentence for him.

"Proper? I have asked you to forget that word when thinking of me."

She took another sip of her tea and stood, smoothing out her beautiful dress, and walked up to him. She sat on his lap and played with his hair.

"Is this proper, Jamison?"

"No," he whispered huskily.

"If I told you I want you to take me right here on this table, would that be proper?"

"Absolutely not," he breathed.

"I'm never going to be proper, Jamison. Can you still love me?"

He said nothing, but his look, so loving and full of lust, said everything. He kissed Binta hard, picked her up, and carried her to their room. They made love off and on and lounged there for the rest of the day. Binta knew then that everything would be fine between her and Jamison, and he would grow to accept her wishes. She knew he would readily agree to them once he saw Cassandra. And so, her thoughts drifted to her lost friend and how to find her. She would not rest until she did.

THE NEXT EVENING, JAMISON AND BINTA MADE THEIR WAY INTO THE castle to attend the meeting called for by the king and queen. They were dressed appropriately for the occasion: Jamison in a nice surcoat and cloak, carrying a fancy gold-tipped cane, and Binta in a lovely red dress and some light yet expensive jewelry. She was stunning by all accounts, and she had to half-heartedly fight off Jamison's sexual advances as she got ready, reminding him of how important the night was. So, as they walked into the castle, led by a single guard, Binta became a little self-conscious.

She could hear the crowd's murmur in the banquet hall, which made her nervous. Attending banquets full of rich people was not a life she had ever known, and she felt like she stuck out. She recalled the night Kima and her friends painted her face; she had never been more of an outcast then. She felt that way as they neared the hall, and she knew that everyone would see through the pretty clothing, jewels, and makeup to see the genuine person she was. Jamison picked up on her unease as they turned the corner and entered the grand banquet room. She gasped at the sight and stopped, forgetting to carry herself like a lady and stand properly.

"You will do fine; you are stunning," Jamison whispered in her ear.

They stood there for a bit, taking it all in. He let her take the time she needed to orient to the amazing scenario.

"You know, a month ago, I wasn't even allowed through the castle gates to visit you, and now we are guests," he said.

"Why, what changed?" she asked.

He shrugged and said, "A month ago, the king and queen had just learned of the changes the world is undertaking, and now they have a plan, one we are about to learn."

He put his hand on the small of her back and guided her to a reserved seat near the front of the room. It was right before the raised dais where two thrones sat, one slightly smaller than the other, obviously the chairs for the king and queen. Before reaching the table, the guard escorted them past other round tables decorated with fancy white tablecloths, expensive cutlery, and plates. The high ceiling also had four large chandeliers, each with two dozen oil lanterns burning. She took in the massive room and the wealthy people who mingled, and it took all her willpower not to panic. They all stared at her—not her and Jamison, just her. She knew by the looks on the men's faces just why they were staring. She was uncomfortable from the moment she walked into the place.

Jamison pulled out a chair for her, and she sat properly, as a lady should, precisely as Kleve had taught her. Jamison took the seat next to her. The guard bowed and left them, and a servant was quick to come and offer them wine. Binta did not want any, but she knew it was the appropriate thing to do, so she took a glass. Before they could get settled, someone called Jamison's name.

He waved, stood, and leaned to her ear, saying, "It is Franklin Ruben. Will you be all right by yourself for a moment?"

"Of course," she said, forcing a smile.

In truth, she wanted to be alone but not on display like she was, for she felt all the eyes on her, and she did not like the attention. She was thankful that Jamison did not call the pompous man over, because she had no use for him. Also, she knew from Jamison's remarks that the man did not care for her or Cassandra. Jamison left her at the large table by herself and she slowly sipped the wine and took in the crowd.

Jamison was not far from her, and she could always retrieve him if uncomfortable. He seemed fully engaged with Franklin, and their discussion seemed important. She was so entranced with the sight that she never saw a man walk up to her until he finally spoke. "Binta Mulay?"

She turned to see Baxter standing before her, his eyes wide as saucers. He wore his usual pants and shirt, not dressed up like the others. He did not appear as a powerful wizard, but Binta knew better. Her face erupted into a large smile, and she stood quickly, nearly knocking over her drink. She was almost as tall as he was in her heels, which made him seem younger, almost childlike, with the silly look he wore.

"It is you!" he said as she hugged him.

Victoria was seated at the other head table and raised her glass in a toast to Binta, who smiled and waved back. Then Daro caught her eye as he entered from a side door, which she assumed Baxter and Victoria had just entered from. He made eye contact with Binta, and even though his expression was hard to read, she knew he was shocked to see her made up, and he might not have even recognized her. Behind him was someone who had Binta catching her breath: a shapely woman who wore a veil over her nose and mouth, concealing most of her face. The uncovered part hinted at a great beauty that competed with the gods. It was Binta's turn to stare as she was no longer the most beautiful woman in the room.

"Sasha De'Formen," Baxter said, now gawking at the woman as well.

"What?" Binta said, half listening as Daro and Sasha sat next to Victoria.

"That is Sasha, Daro's friend."

"She is—" Binta began, but Baxter finished her thoughts for her.

"Beautiful," he said, and he even licked his lips a little.

His actions took Binta off guard, and she turned to him with a smile. His face immediately turned red, forcing him to turn from Sasha and face Binta again. She knew it was the only thing he could do to break the trance he was in with Sasha.

"I heard you were staying in the castle," Binta said after she had his full attention, though she could not help but steal a peek from time to time at Sasha.

"Yes, obviously associating with the New Order now," he said, extending an arm toward the table where Victoria, Daro, and Sasha were now involved in a deep discussion.

"That is a far cry from teaching magic, Instructor Von Glord."

"Please, call me Baxter. You look stunning, Binta; I did not even recognize you! Your time at the cottage and, more recently, with Jamison has done wonders for you."

"Yeah, I feel great, but I'm no Sasha," she said teasingly.

They both turned to look at the stunning woman, and Binta realized that the entire room was watching Sasha. Binta thought it ironic that just moments earlier, it was her that everyone seemed to be looking at.

They turned back simultaneously and said in unison, "I have something to tell you."

Binta gave him a sideways look, finding his behavior suddenly strange, almost antsy. Then she knew without a doubt, as she could sense his emotions as if they were spilling out of him for her to reference.

With a gasp, she said, "You know."

"Know what?" he asked and swallowed hard.

He appeared on the verge of tears, and soon, her eyes were watering as well. At that moment, she knew this man loved Cassandra as much as she did. She would not spoil that moment for him; instead, she vowed to support him as he obviously was going to take up the search to find Cassandra. She would use his feelings for her gain, and when they found Cassandra, she would let her friend decide if she wanted to be with Baxter or her.

"That Cassandra is alive," Binta said with a smile.

"Yes! How did you know that?"

Her heart beat out of her chest when he confirmed she was correct; Cassandra was not dead! "That is a story for another time, Baxter. How did you know?"

"The New Order discovered it from a strange source, to be sure. You will learn the details as the night progresses," he said.

"You are a member of the New Order?" she asked.

"Well, not officially, but I think an invitation is pending."

"That is a great honor, Baxter. What does Cassandra have to do with the New Order?"

"It is complicated, but they will go after her, Binta."

"When? Where is she?"

"Soon, and they are working on how to find her," Baxter said excitedly.

"I want to help."

She could tell that Baxter was confused by the request. His reaction was not unexpected; she was just a student of magic and not a very good one, after all. However, he did not know the skill set she had obtained from the Tome of X'lor. In all fairness, she didn't either, but she knew she could assist the New Order if they let her. He smiled and nodded.

"Well, I need to find my seat so we may begin the festivities," he said.

"Yes, that table there is filling up nicely."

He turned to regard the table. Arrin, the captain of the king's army, and another younger man Binta did not recognize had joined the others, filling all the seats except one, which obviously was reserved for Baxter.

He blushed a little and smiled. "We will speak again soon. I want to find Cassandra as badly as you, and that process starts tonight."

They hugged briefly, and then Baxter returned to the New Order table. She retook her seat and observed the occupants of that table. They had a specific chemistry, and all joined in the discussion, but Binta could read the concern on their faces. She took a deep breath, focused, and sensed their dread. They knew something of great importance and were about to share that information with the few people in this room. She felt honored to be a part of it but dreaded the forthcoming news. More importantly, she panicked at the thought that Cassandra was somehow lost and mixed up in this. The New Order should be searching for her, not having banquets.

Her thoughts were interrupted by the arrival of Jamison and Franklin. Once Cass's father saw Binta, his eyes widened, and he approached her. "Well, well, Jamison, what have we here? I am Franklin Ruben, my lady," he said, taking her hand and kissing the back of it.

"I know. I am Binta Mulay," she answered with a fake smile.

His brow wrinkled in confusion, and it looked as if he were trying to recall something important. "Mulay… Mulay… have we met?"

"Franklin, this is Cassandra Rho's friend, one of the adventurers who accompanied Cass into the mountain a few months ago," Jamison explained.

Franklin gasped as he recalled who Binta was and released her hand immediately. "You are not what I expected. I heard you were daft."

"Do I look daft to you, Lord Ruben?"

Her words had him puffing out his chest in defiance, but he shook his head. "No, of course not; you are by far the fairest woman here."

"Then you haven't seen Sasha De'Formen yet," she said dryly.

"Who?"

"You will discover she is the most beautiful woman in this room, as will you, Jamison. I am quite interested in how you will react to her exquisite looks."

The men took their seats, and Franklin looked around, obviously trying to spot the mysterious woman Binta had mentioned. It did not take him long to find her, and when he did, his mouth dropped open, and he stared hard. Binta almost expected him to drool. Of course, Jamison acted similarly to Franklin, but he at least tried not to gawk at the exotic woman. Binta knew Jamison did not want to disrespect her, which she appreciated. However, she watched as every man and most women in the room continued to have their gaze drawn to Sasha, the woman with the god-like beauty.

Eventually, four other people joined them at the table, giving them seven filled seats. The newest arrivals were some of Pelesea's wealthiest people. Sam and Tori Velt were a young couple, and Sam had inherited the family distillery located at the city's eastern end when he was still a teenager. Now in his late twenties, he had developed an annoyingly smug quality about himself. Binta did not care for him but immediately took a liking to Tori, his modest wife. Raul and Odessi Franz were a little older and originally from Varish. The rumors said that Raul was once a swashbuckling pirate who made a fortune stealing gems and jewels. He denied those tales but ironically owned three large jewelry stores in Pelesea. Binta cared little for either and made sure not to mention the fact that Raul was one of her clients at Poppy's Inn during her brief time as a prostitute. She recalled his skill at sex was about as weak as his personality. Luckily, he didn't seem to recognize her, but she caught him several times staring at her lewdly from the corner of her eye as the night wore on.

It was obvious to Binta that the six other people sitting at this table were the wealthiest citizens of Pelesea, with the other tables filled with those who were slightly less rich but just as stuffy in Binta's eyes. She tuned out the conversation they shared, not interested in the markets of Pelesea nor the horses, ships, and buildings they owned. Jamison played the part of a wealthy citizen whose interests included politics and commodities. Deep down, she knew he cared for those things but was not as pretentious as the others at the table. Binta knew this was a lifestyle she would need to embrace to be Jamison's love interest and potentially his wife. That didn't mean she would have to accept these idiots as friends.

After an eternity, a sentry asked for everyone's attention and for them to rise, then introduced the king and queen. A thunderous cheer greeted their entrance, which included applause from the New Order. Binta fell in line with them, not just because it was the proper thing for a lady of Pelesea to do, but because she genuinely liked the king and queen. They had saved her from Cass and treated her kindly, even allowing her to stay on the castle grounds. They were genuinely good people.

They were both dressed modestly, unlike the vision one would have of royalty. Kringus wore a silk shirt and pants, while Penelope wore a beautiful but modest green dress. They donned their crowns, and Binta assumed it was because it was an official event and not because they wanted to. They stood momentarily near the thrones, waving to everyone in the room until the applause eventually died. Then they sat, and everyone waited for the king to speak.

Eventually, Kringus said in a booming voice that seemed to echo through the large room, "Welcome, distinguished guests of Pelesea. The queen and I have invited you here this evening to hear the special announcement concerning our fair city and the New Order. Unfortunately, the news Penelope and I have to share with you is unpleasant. Therefore, we have invited you, the wealthiest citizens of Pelesea, to this meeting so that we may hopefully hedge any panic and answer your questions in an intimate setting. We will announce the important information before we eat, not to ruin your coming meal, but for us to eat in solidarity once the discussion has ended. This same announcement will be made publicly in one week, and we are hoping by that time, you, the merchants of Pelesea, can circulate some of this information to the public subtly so it will not come as such a shock."

"This seems bad," Franklin whispered to the others at the table, who all nodded in agreement.

Kringus stood so all could see him, and Binta found his behavior genuine and caring. The king had no obligation to stand, but he cared for his people and wanted them all to see him. She noticed his massive chest straining against his silk shirt and the hints of scar tissue sticking through the top. The legend was that he had been badly burned on his neck, chest, and maybe in other places, and there was a story behind the nasty scars. As she watched him, she understood without a doubt that the story would include Kringus performing a heroic deed. Binta considered him a true hero, worthy of being called a king.

"I'll get right to the point—our city is facing a potential risk, which doesn't just apply to Pelesea but to the world as a whole. These are dangerous times for our world, requiring its inhabitants to band together to stop the evil that now threatens us. The New Order has answered the call and is assembling and expanding its current membership. We expect to be whole by the end of the summer and will begin a quest that will take us, including the queen and myself, from the city for an extended period."

There was some murmuring throughout the room, and Kringus let it play out before eventually patting his hands in the air to calm them. Once it had quieted down, he continued, "This is a holy quest orchestrated by the gods, or more accurately, the demons and devils that plague the world. There seems to be a demonic prophecy that predicts the coming of the demon lord, Marnelphion."

There were various reactions in the room, some gasps, even a few cries of denial, and whispers of disbelief. Binta cringed at the shocking responses that some people denied the king's words, and she waited for the honorable king to react. He continued his speech as if he hadn't heard the crude remarks, and no one responded as Binta expected. She looked around nervously, still hearing a few people belittling the king's message. Still, no one reacted. She could not find the source of the negativity, and soon, it quieted down as the king's message seemed to quench the doubts. She looked behind her briefly and saw all faces focused on Kringus as if the rude comments had never been spoken. She shook it off and tried to focus on Kringus's speech.

"The New Order will leave by the end of summer in an attempt to stop the prophecy. I will tell you what I know about this prophecy and why the New Order is reacting quickly. Afterward, I will bring forth the messenger, who we have investigated and interrogated thoroughly. His message is credible, the best we can tell, so we believe what he has told us. His introduction may startle a few of you because he is a messenger from hell, sent by a rival demon lord of Marnelphion named Nezeratu."

There was chatter in the room then, and Kringus patiently waited for it to die. Once the shock of the news played out, he continued, "This messenger, a half-demon, speaks truthfully according to our sources, and the New Order trusts his word. Therefore, we expect you to as well."

Kringus's forcefulness gained the attention of those gathered, but their nervousness remained. Binta thought about how well the king and queen had planned this meeting. The news they offered was terrible and so intense that if delivered improperly, it could start a widespread panic in their city. That was evident as the small gathering, although warned that the news was terrible, was highly agitated. And again, she heard more of the negative and hateful comments made by several nearby people, although no others reacted. Regardless, she considered the king and queen clever in letting the smaller group in this room absorb the information with the plan of filtering it slowly to the citizens of Pelesea.

"This messenger, named Inuentas, has given us the following information concerning the prophecy: Marnelphion will be gated back into our world to rule, murder, and torture the human race if the New Order doesn't intervene. The summoning will occur on the 666th anniversary of his banishing, sometime early next fall. We have less than eighteen months to stop it, which we are confident we can do. The prophecy states that the offspring of Kane, the lich-god, will be sacrificed as the 666th offering. No other sacrifice will succeed in opening the gate; without Kane's child, it will not succeed. Therefore, we must eliminate the risk and remove the child of Kane from the equation."

There was more unrest among the guests, but Kringus's words seemed to give hope that the New Order could stop the threat. The city folk of Pelesea could stand to be without their monarchy for a little while if that meant it prevented a demon lord from roaming the world. Binta's heart raced as she realized precisely how Cassandra played into this. Her suspicions were confirmed when she glanced at the neighboring table and saw Baxter staring at her. His nervousness told her all she needed to know: Cassandra was the child of Kane!

As Binta tried to wrap her head around this information, Kringus continued, "So, the New Order will embark on a mission to defuse the situation when the elven brothers, Von and Lenore, return from the north. I'm not sure how many of you remember the old stories of the original New Order, but there were always twelve members of that group. That has not been the case with our New Order, which has no official power and only eight members. According to Inuentas, the New Order must grow to twelve members, like in the old days, and they alone will venture out to end the threat. According to him, we must not take the army of Pelesea, for it is unnecessary and will only hinder our progress. Therefore, we will venture out, twelve strong.

"We have invited three of the four new members we have chosen to join the New Order, and I am happy to announce all have accepted. We have not been able to deliver the invitation to the twelfth and final member because he is currently not in Pelesea. We feel confident he will accept the invitation once we find him on our quest and will have a temporary twelfth member until then. The missing member we speak of is Greyson Kavince, who is doing some reconnaissance work in Varish with Alleah Mansuell, a current member of the New Order. Until we find those two missing members, the cavaliers Erik and Marcus will fill in. Once Greyson and Alleah rejoin us, the cavaliers will step down and return home. We must keep our member count at exactly twelve, or the prophecy could work against us.

"Three others have already received the invitation and have accepted. I will swear them in as new members during the public announcement in a week. I will call their names now, and as I do, they will stand and face you so that you can recognize them as the newest heroes to our cause."

Binta heard little of this as her mind kept processing that Cassandra was the center of the grand and evil prophecy. She remembered those few wonderful weeks when they were students at Victoria's school and how life was so much simpler then. How could Cassandra be the center of this horrible event? More importantly, how could Binta not assist in the search to find her? And the New Order believed Greyson was alive? And he was going to be invited to join them? Her thoughts were interrupted as the room broke out in applause. She looked over to see Baxter standing and waving to the gathering, all cheering. Then she heard Kringus's words as he introduced the other members.

"Max Smithston, Sheriff of Oldorburg," Kringus said, as the young man at Baxter's table stood and waved to similar applause.

"And finally, Sasha De'Formen."

The exotic woman was hesitant to stand but reluctantly did so, holding her veil with one hand to ensure it stayed and waving briefly with the other. The people applauded Sasha, but most seemed mesmerized by her appearance, and rightfully so, Binta thought.

Then Binta heard the man behind her say loudly and clearly, "Take off the veil, honey!"

She turned to regard him, and he applauded the new members, like everyone else. He briefly glanced her way and said, "You too, gorgeous. You take that sexy little dress right off so I can see what's underneath."

No one seemed to hear his obnoxious comments. Only then did Binta realize the man wasn't speaking the absurd thoughts but was thinking them. Had she read his mind? She turned back and continued with the applause, registering what had just occurred. It dawned on her then that it had been thoughts she was reading when she heard the whispers against the king! It had to be a side effect of the Tome of X'lor. She had a sense of her new awareness, such as when she focused on Jamison's thoughts and received a premonition of what he was thinking. However, hearing someone's thoughts without even trying was entirely different.

The three new members eventually sat down as the applause slowly died. Binta's heart was racing, and she felt flush. She was warm to the touch, like she was running a fever, and needed fresh air. She didn't know if it was some strange effect of the tome or just processing the information that Cassandra was involved in the prophecy, but she was suddenly ill.

"Also, in our absence, we have named a steward to run the city. This person is someone we trust, and he will have a team of advisors to support him while we are gone. The decisions of the steward and his advisors carry the same weight as if they came from the queen and me. I will swear in the steward and his fellow advisors next week with the newest members of the New Order. I'll let my lovely wife introduce these special people to you," Kringus continued.

The king offered a hand to Penelope, who took it and stood, and the room erupted in applause again. Kringus sat and seemed happy to no longer be the center of attention. Binta closed her eyes and rubbed her temples, feeling ill. Jamison recognized her distress because he draped an arm around her and asked if she was all right. She waved him off with a smile, not wanting to draw attention to herself or interrupt the queen.

"The new steward of Pelesea is someone Kringus and I are close to, and we feel comfortable leaving the governance of our city in his hands. He is among the most honest, trustworthy, and kind people we know. He was our first choice for the temporary position, and he gladly accepted our invitation," Penelope explained.

As she spoke, she looked directly at the table where Binta and the others sat. The attention worsened Binta's condition as she quickly realized the steward would be someone sitting beside her. When Penelope finally announced Jamison as the new steward, and the applause began once more in earnest, there was a ringing in her ears. Jamison stood and waved to the gathering. It all happened slowly for Binta as the queen introduced the advisors, consisting of the other three men at the table: Franklin Ruben, Sam Velt, and Raul Franz. They all took their turns standing to be recognized. Binta could hear many murmuring voices during that applause and couldn't tell if they were spoken or thought. When the room quieted again, the ringing in her ears stopped, and she felt herself cooling off. Whatever fit had overtaken her was subsiding.

"Are you all right?" Jamison asked.

Binta smiled the best she could and nodded. "Steward?"

Jamison shrugged and said, "Kringus and Penelope asked me; I would never turn them down."

Penelope continued her speech. "Kringus and I are grateful to all of you who have volunteered, whether for membership into the New Order or to run the city's affairs while we are away."

She walked near the two tables where the advisors and the New Order sat with a large, appreciative smile on her face, and Binta thought she had never seen a more beautiful woman. As soon as that thought crossed her mind, she glanced at Sasha before realizing she was doing it.

"And we will now introduce you to the person responsible for enlightening us on this horrible prophecy. He is a being from hell, but one that has given us a chance to stop this prophecy. We will bring him up here and let you ask any questions you have of him. Again, as Kringus has mentioned, he is a half-demon, and he may be off-putting to some of you because of his race, and in all honesty, he was to some of us at first. However, his words ring true, as Victoria and I have gathered information concerning this prophecy to confirm his story. Also, please note that Inuentas fought alongside Daro and Sasha to defeat a demon in Novafontera, which we think may have been Marnelphion's spy. We trust him and consider him an ally. I present to you Inuentas, the Indomitable."

The crowd grew deathly quiet and Binta listened for the thoughts her newly powerful mind might register. They didn't begin anew, and she heard the loud clicking of bootheels hitting the marble floor. Binta turned with everyone else to watch the half-demon make his way from the back of the room to the front to stand before the king and queen. By then, Penelope had retaken her seat, and Inuentas bowed deeply to each of them before turning toward the crowd.

His black, pupilless eyes scanned the room, and there were a few gasps as the attendees drank in his strange appearance. Binta noticed his skin had a reddish hue, and the two small horns protruding from his forehead were as black as his eyes. His barbed tail flicked behind him, almost nervously. Binta did not feel comfortable being that close to the creature and was concerned for the king and queen's safety. She relaxed when she considered the number of sentries standing at the ready as well as the proximity of the New Order. Of course, she had heard that Kringus and Penelope were masters of weaponry as well. Still, as the half-demon surveyed the room, that uncomfortable feeling in the pit of her stomach remained.

"Good evening, citizens of Pelesea. I stand before you as an ally of your city. The words that the king and queen have told you this evening are true concerning me and the prophecy. I am here to answer any questions you may have."

There was a long pause as Inuentas stood waiting for a question. His tail seemed to flick back and forth as an agitated cat's might. After a few moments of uncomfortable silence, Kringus butted in. "Do not be afraid to address Inuentas. He is no enemy here, and he has the answers to your questions. So, please ask now if you have any doubts about his story."

Inuentas nodded in agreement and flashed a wide smile as Kringus spoke. To Binta, that smile seemed evil and insincere.

A man on the far side of the room stood, a large man in his mid-forties, wearing spectacles and shuffling nervously from foot to foot. "I have a question," he said.

Inuentas walked toward the man, those strange boots clicking as he did. At first, it looked like the man would run away, but he managed to hold his ground, and when Inuentas stood before him, the half-demon motioned toward the front of the room. The man stared at Inuentas, eyes wide, but eventually nodded. As they walked to the front, Inuentas put an arm around the man's shoulders and spoke softly.

Once they were at the front, Inuentas stood beside the more prominent man and said, "This is Brock, and he owns a feed store in the southern part of the city. He has tonight's first question."

Inuentas stepped back and waited for the man to speak. Brock looked around nervously and eventually made eye contact with Kringus, who smiled and nodded. That seemed to give him the courage to continue. "Mr. Inuentas, I wonder, since you are a demon, why have you come to warn us about an invasion from a fellow demon? It seems to me that you are betraying your kind, and quite honestly, that makes it hard to trust you."

The man gulped as Inuentas stood there and smiled, his tail waving menacingly about. Eventually, the half-demon motioned for Brock to take his seat. The large man did not need to be asked twice and hurried back to his chair.

"A good question, and one that has a perfectly logical explanation," Inuentas said, clapping his hands together loudly.

Some people near Inuentas jumped at the sound, indicating to Binta that none of the people in this room seemed comfortable around the creature. Binta agreed as she had a bad feeling about the fellow, especially those strange boots he wore. There was something about them that made her highly suspicious.

"There are several layers of hell, all inhabited by evil creatures and haunted by tortured spirits. There is nothing good I can tell you about the place, but it has been my home for many years now, and I understand it. So, trust me when I say I come from the highest level and the most civilized part of hell. There, evil has rules, but I assure you it is just as evil as the lowest layer. My master, Lord Nezeratu, lives in a palace, like some of you, perhaps. Again, he has servants and money and is calculating with his plans like most of you. However, I assure you he is evil; some would also consider me evil. I wish I could tell you differently, but I don't care about you."

Inuentas stopped there as a hushed murmuring filled the ballroom after his blatant claim to care nothing for the human race. Binta could feel the tension, and the half-demon let it play out, standing there and wagging his vicious-looking tail.

Finally, once the whispers died, he said, "And my master, Lord Nezeratu, cares nothing for you or your world. In that sense, you are fortunate because he does not want to rule you or even be here. However, his jealousy of Marnelphion is why I am here and is the reason you have hope. Nezeratu will not stand for the filth to rule the human world. His pride will not allow that to pass. That is why he sent me to deliver what information we know and to give the New Order instructions on how to stop the summoning.

"Furthermore, I have a skill set that earned me these magnificent boots, this powerful sword, wealth, and a grand reputation. I am an assassin and here to clean up the mess if the New Order fails. So, instead of fearing me, you should bow before me, even praise me! I am here to ensure you won't live out your days under the rule of Marnelphion."

Binta could tell the last of Inuentas's words struck a chord with the king as his neck muscles flexed, and he made brief eye contact with Penelope. The king did not seem to have such a high opinion of the half-demon.

"What is this Marnelphion capable of?" Franklin Ruben yelled out.

Inuentas walked up to the table and stood before Franklin. Binta noticed he looked straight at her and kept his gaze on her as he did. She felt highly uncomfortable under the creature's watchful eye but read no evil thoughts from him. She was relieved when he finally turned his attention to Franklin.

"Murder, torture, rape, genocide. Whatever thoughts you had as a small child, or perhaps even now as an adult, about what a demon is, Marnelphion is it. He is the purest essence of evil, and trust me when I say you do not want him here," Inuentas said.

Franklin nodded and gulped. Inuentas smiled in response, then locked stares with Binta again. He held that awful gaze with her for many moments before finally walking away. There were a few more typical questions, such as people asking for assurances that Nezeratu or a similar demon lord wouldn't follow the lead of Marnelphion and invade the world, how the sacrifice was performed to open the gate, or what Kane had to do with the prophecy. Ultimately, the people learned to trust Inuentas but to fear his story. Binta knew he spoke the truth, and she knew that Cassandra was in danger. By the time the questions faded and it was time to eat, Binta had formulated a plan to join the New Order. The mission was too important; she could not just sit back and not help.

When the questions finally died away, Kringus invited Inuentas to join the New Order's table, which he graciously accepted. He bowed and took a chair a young servant boy had brought him. Binta noticed it was Sammy, the young man she had befriended during her stay at Daro's cottage. She saw him deliver the heavily padded chair, then exit through a servant door and into the kitchen. She could only imagine his thoughts dwelled on Stef, his love interest. Binta recalled the lighthearted kidding she had barraged him with after discovering his secret. Things seemed so simple then and it seemed a lifetime ago. Now, the burden of the world was her focus, not some notion of puppy love.

"With the questions out of the way, let us eat together. I will ask Eldrick to pray, then the queen and I will join you in this marvelous feast," Kringus announced.

Eldrick, the elder priest of Censah, made his way to the royal couple, who stood between the New Order's and Jamison's tables. The priest was old, and Binta knew him from the temple when she had unsuccessfully tried to become a follower of Plath. He was dressed in priestly robes, wore a strange hat, and carried a tall staff. He was on display, Binta realized, as the people needed a sign of goodness to offset the evil story they had just heard. The old priest said a prayer and retook his seat.

Kringus clapped his hands twice and ordered, "Bring on the food!"

There was cheering as he and Penelope made their way to the middle of the room, found empty chairs at separate tables, and took their seats. They were mixing with their people and increasing morale. Binta wished one of them had sat at her table but appreciated and respected their actions. She was sure everyone expected them to sit near their thrones at the front of the room, but they had done the opposite, surprising their subjects and gaining their love.

The food was delivered by cart, with three servants and one cart per table. One servant supplied the food, one provided the drink, and the third worked the cart around the table until they had served everyone. Binta recognized her parents on the far side of the room, tending one of the tables. They were employed within the castle, bringing a smile to her face. She wanted to go to them and hug them and kiss them but did not want to cause a scene. She was so proud and so happy they were there.

She beamed with pride until she heard Raul say, "I remember you now, you little tart. You are a prostitute."

She nearly dropped her drink and turned to the repulsive man to lash out. She stopped when she saw the look on his face and knew that he had not spoken out loud. He sat there with a lewd expression, his beady little eyes undressing her, familiar with her nakedness. She quickly turned away, and the ringing in her mind returned briefly. She overcame it and focused on her food. It was lobster soup and quite tasty. She had eaten food from the castle while staying at the cottage but never a meal prepared by the castle chefs.

And so, the night grew long as the meal ended and the servants retrieved the dishes. Binta even spoke briefly with Sammy, and he was very excited to see her. He was not allowed to talk long but assured her that he would tell her parents she was there and that she was very proud of them. Soon, only the two main tables remained, but without Sam and Tori Velt. They had excused themselves after the meal, Tori stating that her meal did not sit well with her after the upsetting news the "devil" had delivered.

Jamison spoke intently with Franklin and Raul, and although she did not hear ignorant thoughts from Raul's mind anymore, he stared at her with those beady little eyes every so often. The only thing that kept Binta chained to the table was Raul's wife, Odessi, who tried to maintain a conversation about clothing, especially Binta's dress and the fabulous jewelry she wore. Binta knew nothing about it and cared even less, so she only smiled and nodded at the woman's comments. When Odessi was finally distracted by a server filling her wine glass, Binta snuck away.

She steeled her resolve and walked straight toward Kringus, who was now standing at the New Order table, speaking to Lady Victoria. Max and Baxter seemed to be engrossed in the conversation as well. Binta knew this was probably her only chance to talk with the king; most guests had left, and Jamison would be ready to return home very soon. She almost lost her nerve as she approached, and the conversation abruptly stopped when Victoria looked her way.

Kringus turned to regard her, and she could tell at first that he had no idea who she was. She was overwhelmed by the man's stature as he turned fully toward her. He was muscular and handsome, and she wondered briefly how he and Penelope were intimate, with him being so massive and her being so petite. She bit her lip thinking about that and just stared at him momentarily.

Kringus eventually recognized her and said, "Binta Mulay?"

"Yes, my king," she said and curtsied just like Kleve had taught her.

"My, you look stunning tonight. Who are you with?"

"I am with Jamison, my lord."

"I see. You have certainly changed from that broken young woman who came to my court a few months ago."

"Thanks to you, my king, and I want to thank you for letting me stay at Daro's cottage. Your kindness has allowed me to start life anew, which is quite wonderful."

A genuine smile spread across the king's face, and he nodded. "I am glad to help those that need assistance. Stories like yours give the queen and me great pleasure and are the foundation of what Pelesea is truly about."

Binta smiled and nodded. She wanted to get to the point of joining the New Order in their quest to find Cassandra before something awful happened to her. At that moment, she realized how Cassandra must have felt when the king had waited to make his trip to Oldorburg. Binta wanted action now, just like Cassandra had wanted an immediate rescue of her family, which took too long to begin and cost her everything.

"Binta?" Victoria asked, breaking her from her thoughts.

Binta looked to those seated at the table. All eyes were on her, and she realized that she must have been daydreaming and that Victoria had probably called to her more than once.

"Yes, Lady Victoria?"

"Baxter and I heard you had a health scare and did not start classes when they opened."

"Yes, that is true."

"I will send word to the instructors to allow you late entry. You must still make up almost a month's work, but I will allow it."

Binta thought about that and realized that none of them, except perhaps Baxter, understood how she felt. She decided it was time to make it clear. "No, my lady, though I appreciate the offer. Schooling can wait, and quite possibly forever."

Victoria and Baxter looked confused, and the king began to turn and walk away to give them privacy now that the conversation had turned to Binta's schooling. Binta gently touched his arm, stopping him.

"I'm sorry, my king, but I came over here to speak with you, and I want you to hear what I have to say," Binta said, moving her hand quickly away.

"Oh?" Kringus replied, then downed his wine and sat the glass on the table.

"Yes, I have changed."

"I agree with your assessment, Miss Mulay," Kringus said.

"No, I am no longer a wizard or a priest or anything of the sort. I have newfound powers."

"What are you speaking of, Binta?" Victoria asked.

"My illness, Lady Victoria. I assume Jamison did not go into details about what happened?"

"No, he said that you grew ill and were bedridden for a few weeks. Is that not the case?" Victoria asked.

"Yes, that is exactly what happened. However, it was no mystery illness; there was a justified reason for me to grow ill."

"And what is that?" Kringus asked, now intrigued.

"I read the Tome of X'lor."

"The Tome of who?" Kringus asked, his brow wrinkled in confusion.

"X'lor," Victoria answered, standing up. "Jamison," she said, breaking him from his conversation and waving him over.

Victoria walked up to Binta and looked her in the eyes, studying her as if she were looking into her soul. "And how do you feel now?" she asked.

"Good… for the most part."

Jamison arrived then with a concerned look and asked, "What is wrong?"

"You did not tell me she read the work of X'lor."

"Yes, you are correct, but I did not think it too important. The priest said she is in fine health."

"The priests can't help her," Baxter said before Victoria had the chance.

He was beside Binta then, studying her eyes as Victoria had. The situation had escalated, and Binta had not expected this reaction from the wizards. When she regarded the king and the concerned look he wore, she understood that her chances of assisting the New Order were quickly dwindling.

"I feel fine!" Binta said, louder than she intended.

"For now," Victoria said.

"You know something of the tome?" Kringus asked Victoria.

"Yes, it is legendary, my king," Victoria said. "X'lor wrote several of these works, which are highly dangerous, even sentient in nature."

"What do you mean? The book can think for itself?" Kringus asked.

"Yes, it lures in the weak-minded to devour their thoughts. In some rare instances, it preys on those with unusually heightened feelings."

"Such as despair," Binta whispered.

Victoria nodded and said, "Yes, despair; the deep despair you felt probably called to it."

"And the tome answered back," Baxter added.

Victoria turned to Jamison and said, "Where is the tome now?"

He had turned as white as a ghost and swallowed hard. "It's in storage, locked away. I plan on destroying it so this won't happen again."

"You cannot," Baxter said.

Victoria nodded and said, "We must deal with it delicately. Take it to my school tomorrow, and I will meet you at my tower. I will hide it away inside until we resolve this prophecy. Then Baxter and I, along with the other instructors, will determine how to rid you of this curse."

Jamison nodded his agreement. "Yes, of course, my lady."

"What will happen to Miss Mulay?" Kringus asked.

"Yes, tell me she will be fine," Jamison added.

"I do not know. I've never seen anyone survive the reading for more than a few hours."

Binta watched them fret over her and saw how scared it was making Jamison. She knew he was already feeling guilty about exposing her to the tome, making it worse. She had to put a stop to it.

"I feel fine!" Binta finally blurted out, drawing the attention of the queen and the few guests who remained.

Binta looked around, and the stares made her angry. She had intended to ask the king if she could join his group to assist in finding her friend. Now, she felt like a freak and understood they would never grant her permission to join them on the holy quest.

Victoria gently took her by the shoulder and said, "Binta, you may feel fine for now, but the side effects can be devastating. Stay within the castle tonight, and let Baxter and me watch over you."

Penelope joined the group, as did the rest of the New Order, and Binta felt the fool. She had felt perfectly fine since awakening from her deep slumber. Now Binta doubted her newfound awareness, especially after the numerous thoughts she had inadvertently read during the evening. Could she control what the tome had done? Was Victoria right? Would she fall ill from the effects?

"Who is this X'lor?" Kringus asked.

"X'lor?" Penelope repeated anxiously.

"He was a great and powerful telepath. He dabbled in the arts of the mind, something well beyond wizardry or even witchcraft. His powers were a sixth sense, and he could use them to dominate those who opposed him," Victoria explained.

"He was a tyrant, ruling his people with the threat of violence and dominating any subjects with his mind who did not conform," Penelope added.

"How did he do this?" Kringus asked.

"No one is certain," Victoria answered. "There have been several students of X'lor who have followed his teachings and have become telepaths, just not as powerful as he. Some rumors suggest he was a fallen god, but no one has confirmed that."

"It is a rare feat to accomplish this state of mind. Telepaths are rare and dangerous. Not only to others but to themselves," Penelope said.

"So, you know of these telepaths?" Kringus asked the queen.

"Yes, I've studied them but never encountered one."

"Well, perhaps now you have," Baxter stated, nodding to Binta.

They all stared at her, even Jamison, and she felt like an outcast again. She concentrated immediately on her mind-reading ability, not wanting to unintentionally pick up on their thoughts. She didn't want to know what they thought at that time. Her head began to ring again, and she rubbed her temples until it was gone. Once it subsided, she discovered she was sitting with Victoria kneeling beside her, looking up at her face, continuing to study her eyes.

"How much of the tome did you read?" Victoria asked.

"What? I don't know, I can't remember," Binta answered honestly.

"Stay here at the castle, share my room tonight, Binta. For your safety," Victoria said.

Binta noticed that everyone was standing around her, watching the scene, and she felt like a fool. There was no way they would let her go now; Victoria considered her damaged goods, so Kringus would never allow it. She was also not going to stay in the castle under supervision while Cassandra was out there somewhere in the world, in mortal danger. Binta calmly stood and smiled. Victoria stood with her, and they all took a step back. Binta felt like a freak, like many other times in her life, but she would not falter; she would be respectful like a lady of Pelesea should. She curtsied to Kringus and Penelope.

"No, I will spend the night at my new home with Jamison," Binta answered.

"Binta, perhaps you should—" Jamison began.

"No! I am going home. I feel fine. As a matter of fact, I feel better than fine; I feel amazing."

There was silence in the large room, and she saw Sammy hiding in the corner. She could see the fear on his face even from that distance. She had to get out of there.

"My king and queen, thank you for a wonderful evening, and I wish you the best in finding the child of Kane," Binta said.

Both nodded grimly, and the silence only made Binta more anxious. "And good luck to all of you," she added toward the New Order.

She made her way to the back of the room and heard Jamison say a few brief words to the group before catching up with her. The guards at the doors opened them for the couple to exit, and another guard met them there to escort them out of the castle.

"Follow me, please," he said. Binta and Jamison fell in line behind him as they walked down the hall.

"Binta, please, will you not reconsider?" Jamison asked her nervously.

"I am fine, Jamison."

"Not according to Victoria. Perhaps you should stay."

Binta stopped and said in no uncertain terms, "I said no, Jamison, and I do not wish to discuss it further. If we get home and I grow ill, you may take me back to Victoria. For now, I'm going home and going to bed."

The guard waited patiently, and when it looked like the spat ended, he continued escorting them through the magnificent halls, passing many other hallways with guards posted at each. They passed many relics along the way, but neither Binta nor Jamison registered them. Works of art, suits of armor, and weapons adorned the walls, but they were too distraught to recognize the relics for what they were. She had admired them when they first entered but thought nothing of them then; she wanted out of the castle as soon as possible. Binta felt a presence in a particular corner as they approached it and could sense someone there.

Before she could consider the unusual feeling, she heard a familiar voice in her mind: "*Binta, you are correct here. Do not let them sway your course. I will be at Hailee's Tavern in the northern part of town at noon tomorrow. Meet me there, and I will give you hope for your condition. I will show you the road to power. I will give you what you need.*"

She never saw who it was but thought the voice was Inuentas's. As they passed the shadowed area that seemed to be the source of the communication, she saw those black boots shining slightly in the recess, confirming her suspicions that it was indeed him.

They finally arrived at the castle gate, and the guard bade them a nice night. They boarded their carriage and spoke little on the way home. Once they arrived, Binta quickly undressed and went to bed. Jamison was so concerned for her well-being that he could not sleep and instead sat by her bedside as she tossed and turned. Binta's sleep was very restless that night, and she woke regularly. Each time she did, Jamison was there watching over her. The love she felt from him kept her in check that night and allowed her to sleep in small intervals at a time. She knew she needed rest; meeting with Inuentas the following day would be taxing, and she needed to be sharp for it.

ALLIES

"THE FLIES HAVE FINALLY DISBURSED IN FULL, WHICH MEANS Malebak gives you permission to leave," Breeston said over breakfast.

Alleah and Chloe shared a knowing smile, and Greyson could not suppress his excitement about the news. They had been in the swamp for nearly four months, and all were anxious to leave. Alleah and Chloe longed to avenge their sisters' deaths. From the stories Chloe had shared, there was little chance Cerus had spared them. Greyson wanted to leave the place so Breeston's insatiable wife, Zeva, would no longer ravage him. He had been below to see Breeston's sleethian bride almost daily for a month. She had worn many disguises to hide her appearance, but he knew her ugliness and had witnessed it many times during that month. His crotch was sore, and he was done with the whole scam. Breeston had promised him a power stone she would birth in his honor. Instead, she had given him a nest of snakes to call his children. Zeva repulsed him in more ways than he could count. It was time to leave.

"Although, I hate seeing you go; I get so few guests out here," Breeston continued.

The table was deathly quiet as the three visitors from Pelesea ate their meal, heads down with no eye contact.

"Also, Greyson, I'm sure Zeva will birth a gem for you soon. It has taken longer than usual, but it happens without fail; you will have that gem soon."

Greyson began to speak, to tell Breeston he would not spend one more night with his hideous wife, but Alleah beat him to it. "I am sorry, Breeston, but we must be on our way," she said.

"Yes, I agree. We appreciate the hospitality, but we are on a mission that has been compromised and delayed for far too long," Greyson confirmed, while Chloe nodded so hard that Greyson thought her head might fall off.

Breeston sat back in his chair, wiped his mouth, and smiled. "I knew I would not be able to convince you to stay, but I must admit, I will miss you."

No one spoke, and the druid crossed his arms over his chest, studying each guest. Finally, Greyson asked, "What is it?"

"You will need a guide out of the swamp, right?"

Greyson smiled and said, "Absolutely!"

They laughed slightly and agreed that Breeston would escort them out of the dangerous swamp. His next question caused some confusion: "Where are you going?"

It was a simple and obvious question for a guide to ask, but Alleah's answer was not what Greyson expected. "Port Racip," she said.

Greyson looked at her in stunned silence and realized the women had planned on that course long ago as Chloe wasn't surprised by Alleah's request. He had been preoccupied with his bedding of Breeston's wife and, therefore, had not been privy to the plans. However, his heart was not in that course, which was not part of their mission.

"Port Racip?" Greyson asked and locked his gaze with Alleah.

Chloe stopped chewing and looked first to Greyson, then Alleah, and she froze, waiting in anticipation of what was to come. Greyson knew by her actions how much the trip back to that port meant to them. And so, he knew there would be no compromise even before Alleah answered.

"Yes, Port Racip. Our sisters were lost there, and there we must go to find the trail and free them," Alleah answered.

"What if Cerus is there waiting for us? What if we walk right into a trap, Alleah? Chloe has already confirmed that there were no survivors."

"Cerus could not have survived the attack from Malebak, so we'll hope that Cerus is dead and his band of evildoers have left the port."

"Hope?" Greyson asked incredulously.

"What will you have me do, Greyson, leave them there to be raped and tortured and eventually killed?" Alleah asked a little more sternly.

"Of course not, but—"

"But what? What would you do if they were your people, if this were Darian or the high priests of Plath?" Alleah interrupted.

Greyson sat back and let the words sink in. She was correct; they owed it to the sisters of Sinnis to at least go back and try to find them, regardless of the repercussions. A smile crossed his face, and he said, "I would go to Port Racip."

Chloe smiled and resumed chewing her food. The love that he saw in Alleah's eyes told him in no uncertain terms that she truly appreciated his fast resignation to her predetermined course.

He resumed eating, and Alleah and Breeston soon followed suit. After a few silent moments, Greyson added, "After we rescue your sisters in faith, we go to Tara."

"Deal!" Alleah and Chloe said in unison.

And so, they decided to pack their things and leave the following morning to return to Port Racip. Greyson felt good about the course after considering Alleah's words. He understood that they owed it to any potential survivors of their adventuring party to go and at least verify their fate. There was no greater priority and Tara could wait. But as he dwelled on those thoughts and refocused on his food, a door creaked open in the back of Breeston's tiny cottage, the one leading to the trap door and Zeva's lair. They all turned to regard the sound and gasped when they saw a spitting image of Alleah walking through the door. She was naked, dripping swamp water, and holding a large green gem, but otherwise, she looked identical to Alleah.

"Zeva! She did it, Greyson!" Breeston said proudly, holding an arm toward the magnificent gem.

Greyson's eyes locked on that gem, and he could feel the power of Plath pouring from it like an unseen wave of energy. His eyes watered as he regarded it, and he truly felt the presence of his god, like how he felt meeting the angel who maintained Plath's holy caves so long ago. Up to now, that had been the most memorable moment of his priesthood, but this was something special. He froze in awe as Zeva presented the gem to him. He began to push back from the table and run to Zeva, overjoyed with the gem's creation. But then his eyes shifted slightly to regard Alleah. The look she gave him chased away those good feelings, and he swallowed hard. He noticed Chloe was staring at him with her mouth hanging open. Only Breeston accepted the vision of his wife as appropriate and admired the sight of a naked Alleah, slowly nodding his approval. Greyson swallowed hard once more and forced himself to make eye contact with Alleah again, to find her eyes narrowing even further. He smiled and shrugged, for what else could he do?

MALTOR AND HIS MEN ARRIVED HOME TO THE CHEERS OF THOSE HE had left behind to defend it. They roared their approval all the louder when he presented the head of King Boskel, his harem, and the many spoils of war. He placed King Boskel's head on a stake outside his tent as promised, then called for a bath. Maltor was not one to bathe often, especially in the dry summer months, but since spring was in full bloom and the water just plentiful enough for bathing, he called for one to wash away the filth of war. A natural spring in the center of their community served as a bathing hole, and a large tent covering it created the bathhouse for the tribe. Maltor invited the returning warriors, and they all lounged around in the warm water, letting it ease into their bones and cleanse their wounds.

Maltor's hip ached, and lounging in the water, which quickly became filthy, eased the pain even by barbarian standards. He relaxed at the edge of the giant bathing pit, leaning his head back and enjoying the water and the buzz of excitement his men shared concerning their victory. His brides, named Teena, Lorkai, Benala, and Ylfi, were on full display, naked and sitting on the edge next to their new husband. He had spent time with them on the trip home, and although none individually or even together could replace his dear Cassandra, he was happy with the arrangement. He learned they were submissive to his demands and would follow his every whim, following the rules of war precisely as intended.

So, he rested comfortably, his eyes closed, and let the warm water ease his wounded hip. His brides would lightly splash water on his half-submerged chest every so often or sprinkle water over his head, wetting his hair and letting the filthy water run down his face. He listened to his men's stories of his heroics in the challenge circle against Boskel, each greeted by cheers and hails to their king. He occasionally responded with a smile and raised his hand, eliciting more cheers. Through it all, he kept his eyes closed and enjoyed the water. He was happy to have Cassandra's murder avenged but tired and still heartbroken over her death. He would sleep well that night after christening his tent with his new brides.

His thoughts and meditative state were interrupted when Bolin's voice sounded behind him. "My king, we must speak."

Maltor cracked open a tired eye and craned his neck to see his commander standing behind him, fully armed and with a nervousness about him.

"Bolin, come into the bath. Join us in our celebration," Maltor said.

As Bolin undressed, Maltor sat up more fully and waved Jozerah over. His general waded over to one side of Maltor as Bolin entered the bath on the other. Maltor turned to Benala and motioned for her to massage his shoulders. He was happiest with her thus far, and she was slowly becoming his favorite bride. Her technique at massage was excellent, and he decided he would reward her that night by bedding her first.

Maltor closed his eyes again and said, "Speak, Bolin. What is it that is so urgent you dare to interrupt my celebratory bath?"

"Forgive me, my king, but I wish to discuss the small army gathered in the south," Bolin said.

"Ah, yes, you sent the messenger, and I told you not to worry about a gathering of three hundred outlanders. Did you not receive my message?"

"I did, my king, but they have shamans."

"Shamans?" Maltor asked, cracking open an eye to regard the man.

"Yes, I sent spies two suns ago."

"And what did you find?" Maltor asked, waving off Benala's massage, lying back against the sandy bank again.

"We counted nearly three hundred men, protected with leather armor and carrying spears. Also, a dozen shamans gathered in a circle near the sea of dead, appearing to pray to their god."

Maltor opened both eyes fully and sat up. "Why are they gathered around the burial grounds? Have they disturbed the bodies? Have they disturbed Cassandra?"

"We do not know why they gather, but they have not disturbed our dead, at least not as of two suns ago."

Maltor pondered this for a moment. The idea of a small army of outlanders that close to his home did not bother him as much as the fact they were camped near their burial ground, a holy place he did not want to be defaced, especially with Cassandra recently buried there. He decided that it would be best to eliminate the annoyance quickly so his tribe could heal from the battle with Boskel's tribe and his heart could mend from the loss of Cassandra.

"Jozerah?"

"Yes, my king?"

"Take a thousand men tomorrow and march for battle. Take Jak and the archers with you, Bok, and a few of the lesser shamans. Wipe them out and take prisoners as needed, especially for the procreation tent if any are fair enough," Maltor ordered.

"It will be done, my king," Jozerah said.

"Bolin, you go as well so you can point out the shamans for Jak to barrage with arrows," Maltor added.

"Yes, my king."

As Maltor enjoyed becoming acquainted with his wives that first night home, Jozerah gathered the best warriors of the tribe for the trip the following morning. True to Maltor's suspicions, Benala performed well in the bedroom and quickly became his favorite lover. All four brides were young and attractive, and possessed a specific skill set that was most pleasing to the barbarian king. He understood why Boskel kept those four as trophies and was happy to take them for his pleasures. As he slept, perfectly content and with his harem snuggled close, his dreams were centered on Cassandra and the hole her loss had left in his heart.

Two days later, Matilda's scouts delivered the news that a sizeable barbarian army approached. The priests had prayed for over a week, asking Marnelphion to grant them the power to raise the barbarian dead to heed their call. Matilda stood with Cerus, Cass, Ronnis, and the scout, Jest, looking to the north, where the barbarian army made its way closer.

The other priests still sat in a circle, feigning a ritual to call to their god, one they had completed three days prior. The undead lay perfectly still in the sea of dead, awake and listening to Matilda's commands.

"And you say they will reach us by midday?" Matilda asked Jest.

"Yes, my lady. We have little time to prepare," the scout answered.

"We are warriors of Gorl and are always prepared," Cerus said, eyeing the young scout sternly.

"Yes, of course, I mean no disrespect," Jest stammered.

"You're a warrior of Gorl and one of my men, so act like it," Cerus berated him. "My men are in position and prepared for battle," he said to Matilda.

"According to the scouts, your men are outnumbered three to one, my husband."

"And I trust my men in five-to-one odds," Cerus snapped back.

"Against seasoned barbarians?"

Cerus thought about it momentarily and answered, "Perhaps four-to-one, then."

Matilda smiled and let it go. She nodded to the scout, who returned the nod and quickly took his leave. She looked to the horizon in the direction the barbarians were marching from. Nothing was visible, but there was an undeniable sense of an approaching force. She closed her eyes and basked in the morning sun. This day could be the day she finally had Cassandra Rho in her grasp; this could be the day of her greatest accomplishment.

"Are we even sure these are the savages that have Cassandra?" Cerus asked, breaking her daydream.

"What do you mean?" she asked.

"Many barbarians populate Yaddaton; this is only one tribe."

"I will comb the desert and wipe out all of them if that is what it takes. Ultimately, I will have Cassandra Rho, my dear husband."

Cerus smiled and said, "I do not doubt your words or confidence."

"Look," Ronnis said, pointing to the horizon. They all turned to regard the sight, just in time to see hundreds of barbarians crest the dunes to the north.

"That army looks bigger than yours," Cass said to Cerus in amazement.

"Larger, yes, but not nearly as disciplined as my men, I assure you."

"They will overrun us," Cass gasped in response.

"We will see," Matilda said and left the group, walking over to the remaining priests still sitting in a circle, feigning a ritual.

The three watched her go, and although they could not hear her, they witnessed her giving explicit directions to her priests. When done, she had a young servant bring her a horse. She mounted it quickly and made her way back to them.

"Do they understand the meaning of parley?" she asked.

They all looked to the horizon, where hundreds of barbarians lined up on the top of a dune. They were about one hundred yards away, watching them intently. The sea of dead snaked along the bottom of the hill of sand, with the circle of priests just beyond it. Matilda, Cerus, Cass, and Ronnis stood nearby, the only other visible members of their party.

"Your men are ready?" Matilda asked.

"Should you even question that?" Cerus said with a confident smirk.

"They know the signal?"

"Of course, as long as your priests do their job."

"Are you ready, masked one?" Matilda said, turning to Ronnis.

Cerus and Cass turned to Ronnis, who slowly removed his mask and handed it to Cass. "To capture Cassandra Rho? I have never been more ready."

Matilda offered him her hand, and he laid his head in her hand, which puzzled Cerus and Cass. To their astonishment, he slowly transformed into a large black snake, an adder. His arms folded to his sides and melded with his body as his legs morphed. His sword, the source of that transforming power, melded with the snake form, as did his clothes. Soon, the deadly black snake, the new form of Ronnis D'Breeth, slithered over Matilda's arm and around her shoulders, his tongue flicking against her neck. He continued down and curled in her lap.

Cass clapped her hands, squealed joyfully, and said, "What a nice trick!"

"What kind of magic is this?" Cerus asked in amazement. "I have never known the masked fool do anything but get in the way. Still, I do not understand his purpose among us, but I am impressed by the trick. Who is this masked friend of yours?"

"He is not my friend, just someone who hates Cassandra as much as I do. I had no idea he could shape-change," Cass said, just as surprised by the turn of events.

"Either way, this is where he will prove his worth," Cerus growled.

"And now I'll meet with their leader," Matilda announced.

"I should go with you," Cerus insisted.

"No, from what I know of these savages, they will consider me weak because I am female. We will use that belief against them and bait them into attacking. It is the perfect trap, my husband."

MATILDA STROKED THE SNAKE ON HER LAP AND SMILED AT CERUS. HE nodded and watched as she spurred her steed on around the river of death, cutting around the side where the barbarians had laid Cassandra to rest just a few weeks earlier. She trotted toward the large dune where the army of barbarians watched her progress. Cerus stood with his giant spear at the ready, watching proudly but nervously as his unpredictable wife approached the barbarians.

"Perhaps they will kill her, and I will have you all to myself," Cass purred, rubbing a hand over Cerus's massive chest.

He grabbed her hand forcefully and pried it free. He clenched his jaw as he locked stares with his lover. Eventually, his visage softened, and he kissed her knuckles. "No, she is my wife, and I enjoy her around. Besides, it is more fun to ravage you while she lies nearby; it feels good to be on this side of the cuckolding."

Cass smiled and tossed Ronnis's porcelain mask onto the sand. She and Cerus intently watched as Matilda made her way to the line of barbarians. The stage was set, and all the barbarians needed to do now was take the bait.

JOZERAH AND BOLIN, THE ONLY TWO BARBARIAN WARRIORS WHO HAD made the trip on a camel, stood at the front of the anxious and agitated barbarian line. They watched as one rider came forth to their position. The barbarians did not frequently war with interlopers; their only experience in fighting them came from their invasions, and those usually ended in a massacre. They shared a puzzled glance, and Bolin shrugged.

"One comes forward, alone and without weapons," Bolin said.

"And where are the others? The scouts said they were three hundred strong, but I only see a handful of the fools sitting in a circle near the burial ground," Jozerah added.

"Perhaps they have gone for reinforcements?"

"Then we will slaughter those who remain and take the female back to Maltor as an offering. Perhaps the outlanders will understand they are not welcome here," Jozerah said.

"She has stopped," Bolin added.

Jozerah regarded the female rider who had stopped halfway up the large dune.

"She waits for something," Bolin said.

"And so I will go and pluck her from her mount and take her back. Ride to Jak and tell him to have the archers ready. Tell him to focus his attack on the large man near the burial grounds and the circle of defenseless shamans near him."

"And what of the female near the large one?"

"Spare her if possible, and we will take two trophies to Maltor."

Bolin nodded and rode his camel down the line toward Jak and the archers. Jozerah turned back to the lone female on the horse. He was a veteran of many battles and countless invasions, and he sensed something was wrong with the scene before him. Whatever it was, he wanted this confrontation over quickly. They had the advantage, and he did not intend to lose it. He spurred his steed ahead and toward the woman. He did not advance threateningly but approached leisurely, mimicking the interloper.

❦

MATILDA WATCHED THE LONE RIDER COME FORTH AND UNDERSTOOD that this man was the group's leader. He didn't look like a barbarian king and probably wasn't. She took her right hand and grabbed Ronnis at his thickest part. He coiled around her wrist lightly as they had practiced in private after she had discovered his shape-changing power. She kept him in her lap, hidden from the approaching savage, but noticed his tongue darting along her inner thigh as he waited in anticipation. She understood a snake used its tongue for smell, not taste, but either way, Ronnis was smelling or tasting her. It was perfectly perverted, and she allowed it to continue.

She focused on the approaching barbarian and noticed the others on the ridgeline growing antsy and restless. They wanted nothing more than to charge her, to kill her and her allies. She understood it was in their blood, and she knew the barbarian leader was baiting her. He approached casually, but when he was close enough for Matilda to smell him, she acted, quickly summoning a purple but harmless flame in her left hand. This action caused the large man to reach for the sword strapped to his back. The other barbarians began shouting at her and waving their weapons in her direction. Obviously, the barbarian people did not appreciate her dark magic.

"Hold, savage, or I will use my magic to melt the skin from your bones," Matilda said.

The man froze with his hand on the hilt of his sword and narrowed his eyes threateningly. If he called her bluff and came forward, she would quickly kill him, but she needed information about Cassandra. After all, her purpose there was to learn of her whereabouts, not to kill the savage people who had taken her.

When he didn't answer and slowly moved his hand away from his weapon, she continued, "Wise decision; you are smarter than you look. Perhaps there is hope that you will live through this confrontation."

"Your devil magic cannot win, outlander; it only shows your weakness," Jozerah said.

Matilda scoffed and said, "You are one magnificent specimen, I will admit. Muscular and handsome, but those magnificent muscles cannot save you from my wrath, barbarian. You move against me, and I will kill you well before you can draw that clumsy blade."

It was Jozerah's turn to laugh, and when he finally regained his composure, he said, "You are not only a weakling but a female, inferior in every way. I will defeat you here today, then drag you back to my king, where you will serve in the procreation tent."

"Before you try something that stupid, I need information, filthy savage. I have come for Cassandra Rho. Where is she?" Matilda asked, the serpent's tongue still tickling her thigh.

The sudden change in Jozerah's face told Matilda everything she needed to know—these barbarians held Cassandra, or at least knew where she was. His confident smile disappeared, and the stunned expression he wore spoke volumes. He knew Cassandra Rho! Matilda smiled, relieved she had found her prey so easily.

"Thank you, Marnelphion, for your wisdom and relentless desire to find the spawn of Kane," Matilda said, laughing hysterically at her good fortune. "Now tell me where she is, and you will not die first this day." Her laugh suddenly died away, replaced by a stern scowl.

Jozerah didn't move, and Matilda could tell the barbarian warrior struggled to maintain his composure. She meant to say something to keep him in check, something that would make him think twice about drawing his weapon. Before she could speak, he drew his sword and prodded his camel into action. Matilda was disappointed but knew this would be the eventual outcome of any attempt at a civilized meeting she meant to have with the savages. And so, she waited for him to close the twenty yards that separated them and made no move to flee, draw a weapon, or cast a spell. If this one knew of Cassandra, so did the others. She could persuade the other warriors to inform her about her prey if she killed this one. Matilda decided to set a proper example for the other savages. Their leader would die.

Jozerah let out a howl of triumph and moved his camel to Matilda's right so he could swing his mighty sword with his right hand. Matilda didn't know if he would try to strike her down or only wound her and take her back to his king, as he had said, and she didn't care. When the warrior was close enough to make his stench unbearable, she snapped her right arm toward him, tossing the adder that coiled her wrist. As practiced, Ronnis released his grip and flew toward the surprised savage. The barbarian was startled by the projectile, and he barely registered the attack as Ronnis, in snake form, landed hard on his chest, quickly wrapped around him, and bit at his neck and shoulders.

Jozerah's camel kept running strong, but as the barbarian reacted to the attack by dropping his sword and grabbing the venomous snake, he took several more bites on the neck and arms for his efforts. The barbarian pulled off the snake and tossed it away. However, the venom was thick in his veins by then. Matilda watched, amused, as Ronnis hit the sand and slithered into an outcropping of nearby rocks. He had done well.

The barbarian reached up and grabbed at his wounded neck as his camel ran harmlessly by Matilda. He half fell, half jumped from his mount and thrashed in the sand. Matilda had the notion to trample him under her horse but thought better of it. He could die more slowly from Ronnis's bite, and she preferred that fate for the arrogant warrior. Besides, the barbarians on the top of the dune were now shouting war cries and charging down it. Also, a volley of arrows was already coming her way, and she did not have time to toy with the poisoned barbarian.

She spurred her horse into a gallop, easily outrunning most of the arrows, although a few hit the sand beside her and one stuck in her mount's backside, causing it to whinny in pain and nearly buck her. But Matilda held on tight as the horse galloped past the sea of dead, and she had a hard time stopping it once she reached Cerus, who helped to slow down and eventually stop the frightened mount. The injury to the horse was not bad, so Cerus let it go once Matilda was off. By then, the priests were up, looking out past the sea of dead and to the rushing throng of barbarians quickly making their way toward them. Matilda noticed they were already casting their spell to counteract the next volley of arrows. She could feel the undead army lying at her feet, stirring and awaiting her call. Everything was working out perfectly, and she could not suppress a smile.

As she subconsciously gained command of the multitude of skeletons and zombies lying in the sea of dead, the other priests joined their powers to create a mighty yet temporary buffeting wind that quickly caught the second round of arrows and threw them harmlessly aside. The army of barbarians kept running down the dune, and the only ones left on the ridge were the archers and one lone warrior on a camel. Matilda assumed this one to be the second in command, and she made a mental note to keep that one alive long enough to pry Cassandra's whereabouts from him.

She watched in amusement as the archers reloaded for another volley. Before they could release their arrows, the men of Gorl, who had buried themselves in the sand at the top of the dune, emerged quickly and threw their spears at the barbarians who remained atop the dune. The priests had used their powers to summon light gusts of wind to bury the Gorl warriors and cover their tracks before the barbarians arrived. To the pleasant surprise of the Gorl warriors, the barbarian archers had remained behind and were easy prey to the evil men, who outnumbered them six to one. So, as the first wave of Gorl warriors rose from the sand and threw their spears, killing a great deal with the surprise attack, the second wave rose and charged, keeping the spears tight and viciously attacking before most of the barbarians could draw their swords.

As THE MASSACRE UNFOLDED AT THE TOP OF THE DUNE, THE SEA OF undead rose to meet the wave of barbarians charging Matilda and Cerus. The hearty warriors of the Serpent Tribe were only a few feet away from the sea of dead, preparing to leap the ten-foot ravine, when the undead army rose quickly to meet them. The zombies were the few that still had meat on their bones, and these creatures were quick to rise and leap upon the savage warriors, raking with their claws and biting with their elongated teeth, both characteristics given by the transformation from death to undeath. The skeletons had no flesh remaining on their bleached bones, but their teeth and claws were just as sharp as the zombies', and their bloodlust was equally powerful. Marnelphion blessed the undead creatures with super speed and agility, and they quickly overwhelmed the army of barbarians.

Bolin witnessed both attacks from the back of his camel and was stunned briefly as his mind slowly realized the danger they were in. They had under-estimated the interlopers, and it was evident Maltor would lose this day. He had just witnessed Jozerah's demise and the ambush on the archers by the savage interlopers, but the sudden rise of their dead quickly turned the tide of the battle. Now Maltor's army of a thousand strong warriors was outnumbered by two to one. There was no hope of winning this day, and many barbarians would die. He did the only thing he could at that point: turn his camel and retreat. He had to return to Maltor and warn his king of the devil magic these interlopers possessed. He took a spear to the thigh as he went but ignored the pain and urged his camel to greater speeds. Soon, he was out of range and could no longer see the battle at the bottom of the dune. As he sped away, the screams of the dying barbarians haunted him.

To their credit, the barbarians fought well and destroyed many undead creatures, but the sheer number of the unnatural beasts eventually over-whelmed them, and they retreated up the dune. However, the men of Gorl had quickly defeated the archers at that point and charged the retreating barbarians, catching them between their proficient spears and the vicious undead. The Gorl warriors quickly overwhelmed the savages, instantly killing the barbarians or wounding them so the undead could catch them and rip them to shreds. Only a few dozen made it past that awful trap and fled on foot behind Bolin.

JOZERAH WAS STILL ALIVE WHEN THE RETREATING BARBARIANS MADE their way up the dune. With a shaking hand, he produced a small waterskin from his side, one filled with the newly acquired antidote they had taken from the Culiem Tribe. The antidote was strong enough to cancel the effects of the vicious fairies, so the barbarian leader figured it would save him from the snake's venom. He drank it down and convulsed for a long while as the undead ran past him and jumped on the backs of his fleeing men. He did not register most of those awful moments as his men died by the hundreds. The antidote did save him, and he would regret that later.

IT WAS NOW OR NEVER FOR KESSI AND HER FRIENDS. SHE AND HER cellmates knew that something was amiss, that Matilda and Cerus had left the cavern fortress of Nesin. The usual guards had disappeared, replaced by men they had never seen before. They wore swords on their hips, whereas all the men following Cerus carried spears. They were not worshippers of Gorl, nor were they priests of Marnelphion. Something was different. They had a window to try their desperate plan, and it was unknown how long it would remain open. It had been several weeks since the guards had changed, and Matilda and Cerus could return anytime.

Kessi anxiously watched as Merrik, the only priest they had seen in weeks, unlocked the far door to Emiline's cell to let the two slaves carrying food to Kessi's cell enter. Per their discussion, Kessi was up against the cell bars, alone, letting her ripped dress hang dangerously low, revealing a lot of skin. The other women remained at the back of the cell, as was protocol.

Merrik noticed her immediately and even stopped his brisk walk when he saw her. He had that familiar look she had received frequently over the last month. It was somewhere between anger and lust, and it frightened Kessi. She pressed on, though, knowing Merrik and his apparent desire for her was their only way out of the prison. The two slaves obediently stopped and looked at their feet, waiting for Merrik to begin walking once more. Inevitably, they started shifting uncomfortably because of their proximity to Emiline's coffin. Eventually, Merrik continued his trek to Kessi's cell with the slaves in tow. He never broke eye contact with Kessi, and as he unlocked her cell door, she noticed he drank her in like a thirsty sponge. The man was neither discreet nor sorry for how he looked her up and down.

He opened the door and let the two emaciated servants enter and set up the dishes and serving platters on the cell floor. Merrik stood before Kessi. She was scared and did not like how he looked at her, but she told herself this wasn't for her; she was doing this to free her cellmates and ultimately save her sister. And so, she forced a sexy smile and didn't dare cover anything that the repulsive man might find interesting, even though she could feel her breasts nearly falling from her torn blouse.

She then forced herself to speak, finding the courage to appear flirtatious. "I am Kessi."

"I don't care."

The response put her back on her heels because it was not the one she expected. She tried to play it off and continue the charade. "You should," she responded.

He leaned in close and covered her hand, which grasped a cell bar, with his own. A wicked smile crossed his face, and he squeezed her hand hard. She tried not to grimace, but the pain was intense. To her credit, she showed no emotion and held his gaze as if nothing were wrong. His eyes looked her up and down once more, and as the slaves finally finished their work, he released her aching hand. She dared not move it for fear of him calling her bluff.

"I know what you're doing," Merrik said.

"And what might that be? I've seen how you look at me, how you've been watching me these last few weeks." Kessi leaned in closer so that her face touched the bars. "I need a man, and you're the only one I see that's worth my time."

She really had no idea what she was doing and had never seduced or wanted to seduce a man in her life. Yet, she thought she was doing a pretty good job, especially after he swallowed hard in response to her last comment. The priest seemed to be struggling with what to do next. The two servants stood obediently with their heads down as the priest tried to determine his next move. Suddenly, with surprising speed, he moved into the cell; it was so quick that it startled Kessi. One of her cellmates yelled in surprise as Merrik grabbed Kessi roughly by the arm and escorted her out of the cell.

Sabrina rushed up to the bars as the door slammed shut. Merrik worked the key and locked it behind him. The evil priest looked up to see others approaching behind Sabrina, and although none of them spoke, he must have realized how his actions looked. No doubt afraid of the consequences of harming one of Matilda's virgins, he loosened his grip on Kessi's arm and swallowed hard once more.

"I am taking Kessi to speak with her in private; she has information she wishes to share with me," he explained.

"Yes, and I will speak for a bit, then I will return unharmed, I am sure," Kessi added, trying not to let the panic show in her voice.

All the women in the cell looked at each other nervously, then their eyes widened, and they stepped away from the bars, transfixed on something behind Merrik and Kessi. The slaves shrieked, and Kessi turned to see them running for the far door where guards worked to open it. And there, standing next to her coffin, was Emiline. Merrik turned with a start and released Kessi, grabbing his unholy symbol, the skull of Marnelphion that hung around his neck, and presenting it to the vampire.

Emiline hissed and brought her arm up to cover her eyes as Merrik screamed, "Back, you undead filth, back into your box!"

Kessi stepped between the priest and Emiline, shielding the vampire from the symbol. Her back was to Emiline, but she felt safe, having dealt with a much more powerful vampire in Heinsvick.

"Emiline, Heinsvick sent me to rescue you; please help us!" Kessi said without turning to the vampire.

Merrik pushed her roughly out of the way, and Kessi fell to the floor. She saw Emiline's face then and how it had softened at the mention of Heinsvick. Kessi found herself on her hands and knees and sat up to watch the confrontation. Merrik still focused, holding Emiline at bay with his unholy symbol, although he no longer needed to. It looked to Kessi as if the vampire could be knocked over with a feather as she digested Kessi's words. Tears welled in her eyes, and she stood perfectly still, staring at Kessi.

"Get up!" Merrik ordered Kessi.

Kessi ignored him, knowing this was their chance for freedom, and said, "Emiline, help us so that we can get you home. We need your assistance!"

For her efforts, Kessi received a backhanded slap from the priest. His focus was still on Emiline, so the strike was not accurate or forceful. Still, it had Kessi falling to her hands again, leaving her cheek stinging. It reminded her briefly of when Heinsvick would hit her out of frustration, yet the priest seemed much weaker, giving her a little bravado.

"Emiline, please!" she said and scrambled away from the two.

Rage suddenly replaced the confused and sad look on the vampire's face, and she hissed once more, lunging for Merrik's symbol. The priest was ready, however, and brought the small skull symbol in line to burn Emiline's arm. There was a hiss of burning flesh, and Emiline flew back unnaturally with a great leap, holding her arm. She screamed in pain and protest, cradling her forearm, which now smoldered. She backed away into the far corner of the cell, near the door to Kessi's cell. Sabrina and the others quickly moved away from the vampire, clearly frightened by the undead creature.

Kessi took in the scene and was so focused on the injured vampire that she didn't realize the priest was beside her. He grabbed a fistful of her hair and tugged her to her feet, which elicited a yelp of surprise and pain. Once she was standing, Merrik grabbed her arm tightly and backed toward the door the servants had just exited. The two guards held the door open, their swords drawn. He dragged Kessi with him, and she could only focus on Emiline, who cowered in the corner of the cell. She was injured, not severely, but it was Kessi's fault, and guilt washed over her for being so concerned with her escape that she disregarded the vampire's safety. Merrik dragged her through the cell, and the guards quickly shut and locked the door behind them.

"One of you take these slaves back to their cells; I need to teach this troublemaker a lesson," Merrik ordered as he dragged Kessi up the hall.

Kessi looked through the cell to the far side, where Sabrina, Kimmie, Natasha, and the others stood watching the spectacle. Emiline had moved back to her coffin, wailing as she did, and Kessi knew her pain was both physical and mental. The vampire crawled inside her resting spot and slammed the lid home. With Emiline gone, her cellmates approached the bars of the cell and helplessly watched as Merrik dragged Kessi away.

MERRIK ROUGHLY GUIDED KESSI OUT OF THE CELL BLOCK. ALTHOUGH she had spent some time in the higher levels of Nesin when she first arrived, she did not recall anything outside her prison home, so the rock walls seemed foreign. She had no idea where the priest was taking her, but she knew he was angry. Her feminine wiles no longer seemed like such a powerful weapon. Kessi tried to memorize the route if they escaped the horrid place. However, they made many turns, and she quickly lost her way. Merrik took her deeper into the caves, passing several sets of guards as he did. The place was not as heavily guarded as she expected, and none of the guards carried spears. Just as she and Sabrina had suspected, the men of Gorl were nowhere to be found.

Soon, the two were standing in front of a door at the end of a tiny hallway, which appeared more like an alcove, about ten feet long. Two sconces held torches on either side of the door which burned with purple flames, giving the area a mysterious, almost peaceful feel. Merrik fished out another set of keys, unlocked the door, and pulled Kessi roughly inside. More purple flames lit the large room, and strong incense burned within, giving the place a nice ambiance despite the evil scenes that decorated the walls. Merrik shoved her into a chair and locked the door behind him. She quickly surveyed the place and discovered many simple furnishings, such as a bed, a nightstand, a dresser, a chest, a table with chairs, a fireplace, a wooden bathtub, and a cupboard. Kessi also noticed that a purple curtain hid the room's far corner. Looking at it made her uncomfortable, and she knew she wanted no part of what was behind it.

He fixed a goblet of unidentifiable liquor and pulled a chair over to sit before her. He took a long sip of it as he looked her in the eye. She suddenly felt very vulnerable and aware of her near-naked breasts. She absently tugged at her torn dress to cover herself a little better as his eyes slowly undressed her during that silent sip. She knew she was in trouble; her plan to have Emiline assist her had failed miserably, and Kessi had no choice but to proceed with the seduction she had started. However, now, the reality of that path weighed on her, crushing her resolve and stealing her courage. What was she to do, sleep with the repulsively evil man and hope he fell in love so her friends and she could escape? She did not like her chances or the awful deed that would be required to see it through.

"Explain your actions," he finally said.

"I find you—"

"Not the lies about desiring me sexually. I am referring to the nonsense you told the vampire about Heinsvick."

"I just don't want to die, and I thought I could use Emiline to help me escape," Kessi said honestly. Trying, once more, to play on his sympathy and hoping he did have some level of feelings for her.

"My name is Merrik, and I am the second-ranking priest in this place, and I assure you, I am no fool. So, stop your lying and tell me the truth."

Kessi did not know precisely how to respond. The man was not being fooled by her antics or charmed by her seduction. She had spoken truthfully, which had not fazed him as he had not believed her story thus far. As her predicament worsened, she decided the best path for her to take would be one of honesty, hoping that would somehow win the evil man over. She was taking a risk by doing so, but she feared for her safety if Merrik caught her lying.

"I am Kessi Rho, sister of Cassandra Rho, and I was sent here by Heinsvick as a trade for Emiline."

"You tell me nothing we do not already know," Merrik said, taking another long draw from his goblet, his eyes roaming her body again.

"Sorry, I just want to be honest with you. Over the last few weeks, I have watched you come and go, delivering our food and collecting our plates. I felt a connection with you during that time, and I hoped that the feeling would be mutual," Kessi said, hoping this one necessary lie would not be detected if mixed with her honesty.

He just stared hatefully for a moment, then reached up and took the torn neck of her dress and moved it below her shoulder. She did not resist until it nearly revealed her breast. She caught it before it exposed her.

"No, let it fall," he said huskily, taking another long sip.

Kessi wasn't sure what to do, but she thought this was a good sign, and perhaps her words and actions finally had the desired effect. Maybe she was seducing him and would find a way out of Nesin. She lowered her hand, and the dress continued its descent, eventually exposing her.

"Lovely," he said, licking his lips and staring at her.

She felt uncomfortable but did not want to impede the progress; her cellmates counted on her to succeed. So, she forced a smile and blushed despite herself.

"So, you are trying to save yourself, hoping I will have feelings strong enough to save you from Matilda's long, crooked blade?"

"No, I mean, yes, I want to live."

Merrik nodded, reached over, and slid the other side of her dress down her shoulder. She did not stop him this time and soon sat topless before him.

"Magnificent," he whispered.

Kessi looked down at her nakedness and blushed, wanting nothing more than to cover up and leave. Being back in her cell didn't seem like such a bad thing then. As she contemplated what would happen next, Merrik was upon her. She had no time to react as he kissed her. She was thrown back in time to the elven village not so long ago when Bart and not-Bart, two not-so-nice men, had tried to kidnap her. Fortunately, Heinsvick had saved her from that fate, but not before Bart had forced a kiss on her. It had been disgusting, genuinely awful. This kiss was similar but gentler, and she held on to hope that perhaps Merrik cared for her. She cared nothing for him romantically but would use his feelings to free her friends and herself if possible.

The kiss seemed never to end, but when he pulled back and looked her in the eye, she saw love there, not lust, and knew her ruse was working. If she could somehow get him to fall for her, they all had a chance to escape, so as unnatural as it felt, she smiled a warm, inviting smile, hoping he would do whatever he intended to do quickly. At that strange moment, she thought of her mother, Sera, and how she had made the same sacrifice for Cassandra. She had slept with Lord Ronnis and even accepted a strange and abusive relationship with the evil lord to protect Cassandra. Kessi steeled her resolve and reached for Merrik's hand, placing it on her breast.

He smiled back and caressed her and eventually touched her other breast, massaging her gently. Kessi closed her eyes and found his touch soothing. It surprised her to enjoy his hands groping her, but her nipples responded to his touch, and she moaned slightly. Soon, he kissed her again as his hands did their work. Kessi managed to kiss him back convincingly and, to her surprise, slowly became aroused. He pulled away after many moments, smiled warmly, and gently stroked her cheek with the back of his hand. She closed her eyes, thinking this sacrifice might not be so bad.

That was when he slapped her hard, knocking her from the chair. She found herself on the floor, holding her throbbing cheek. She looked at him to see him gritting his teeth, and he grabbed two fistfuls of her hair. He tugged her up forcefully, pulling out more than a few hairs. She stifled a cry, but the strike already had her eyes watering, and it was hard not to weep openly. However, she vowed not to give him the satisfaction. Once she was standing, he pulled her dress to her ankles, leaving her in just her underwear. She instinctively covered her breasts, ashamed that she had become aroused at the horrible man's touch.

"Do not cover up now, dear," he said with a wicked smile, pulling her arms away. "This is what you wanted, so I will play."

He went to work on her breasts again, but this time roughly, pulling and scratching and hurting her. She tried to pry his hands from her and step away, only to fall back in the chair. He pinned her there and continued his assault.

Through gritted teeth, he whispered in her ear, "You will regret what you have tried to do today. Don't doubt that if the circumstances were different, I would rip the virginity from your loins so forcefully that you would walk bow-legged the rest of your days. However, you have just tried to destroy everything I have worked for, my life's purpose. Never would I have imagined having the opportunity to meet my god, but that will indeed come to pass, regardless of your meddling!"

He slapped her hard again and pulled her up roughly by her arm. "And now you will suffer the consequences. You will be punished and will never set foot in that cell again. You will never eat a proper meal, never see your friends or the vampire again."

He looked her in the eyes, and a most evil smile creased his face. "And don't fret, we will sacrifice you at the altar of Marnelphion, assuming Matilda doesn't kill you upon her return. And your sister will surely die a horrible death before it is over."

He laughed and dragged Kessi out of the room and to a new one she recognized immediately. Memories came flooding back to her, memories of her few days spent at Nesin before she became a prisoner. She remembered Matilda had promised her the life of a queen, then proceeded to torture her for information, information she did not know. The metal contraption in the center of the room reminded her of the whipping Matilda had administered, and the scars on her back ached in response. It was a circular metal device, ten feet tall, with shackles for both hands and feet. It conveniently held prisoners so Matilda could torture them. Kessi had survived the thing once before, but with scars to show for it.

"No," she whispered as Merrik dragged her roughly toward the large, circular contraption.

HAILEE'S TAVERN WAS FULL THE NEXT DAY, AND AS JAMISON DID BUSIness with the king and queen that morning, Binta had the perfect opportunity to visit the tavern. Jamison was still very concerned about her well-being and told Kleve to watch her closely. Binta had assured Jamison she was fine and then easily convinced Kleve that she was going for a walk for some fresh air. He had resisted letting her go alone, but Binta convinced him otherwise and even declined the carriage always available to her. In truth, she did not want Kleve or Jamison involved in her meeting with Inuentas, assuming the creature even showed up.

As she entered the crowded tavern, her stomach was in knots, her anxiety about meeting the half-demon getting the best of her. Inuentas had hinted the previous night that he could help progress her newly found powers, and she wanted that more than anything. She mostly wanted to be able to locate Cassandra and save her from the evil that was hunting her. Perhaps with her newfound mental powers, she could do so.

She took a deep breath and entered the busy place. She vaguely heard a waitress tell her to find a seat anywhere she liked as she hurried past with a platter of dirty dishes. Binta surveyed the place. Most patrons appeared wealthy; this was the city's north side where coin was plenty. She looked through the gathered diners and quickly found what she wanted. In the back of the room, alone at a table, was Inuentas, and he raised his glass in a toast to her when she saw him. He stood out because of his appearance and the empty neighboring tables. People packed into the place, but none dared approach the strange-looking fellow. None sat close.

Binta made her way there and had to consciously tune out the mumblings around her. She had difficulty determining if they were spoken words or simply stray thoughts, but she knew enough of her strange powers that if she concentrated hard, she could tune them out. When she arrived, Inuentas pulled out a chair for her, and she accepted. He had a bottle of ale on the table and two glasses, one already in use, and a third of the bottle gone.

"I didn't think you'd show," he said.

"I had every intention of showing," she replied.

"I delayed my lunch order hoping you would. However, the tavern grows busy, so I'm not sure when we'll have an opportunity to eat."

"I'm not hungry or thirsty," Binta responded, holding up a hand to stop Inuentas from pouring her a glass.

"As you wish," he said with a shrug, filling his glass instead.

After a long draw, he put the glass down and smiled at her. Her old self would have been intimidated sitting at a table with a creature like Inuentas. Still, she felt confident with her new awareness and was sure she could protect herself if needed.

"So, tell me, then," Binta prodded.

"Just like that, no small talk? You want to know why I invited you here and nothing more?"

"Exactly."

A barmaid came over to take their order. Binta declined again, even after Inuentas offered once more for her to get something. That didn't stop the half-demon from ordering a large meal of shark steaks, kale salad, and more ale. As he spoke, Binta decided it was time to know a little about her strange companion. She attempted to read his thoughts, knowing that they usually were more accessible to read when the person was distracted, as Inuentas was at that moment. But she could read nothing the creature was thinking, as if a wall were stopping her from doing so. She tried once more and received the same empty feeling. The resistance puzzled Binta, for each time she tried looking into someone's thoughts since she had developed her newfound skills, she had always succeeded.

"Trying to figure out why your mind-reading powers didn't work on me?" Inuentas asked, breaking her from her thoughts.

She looked up to see that the barmaid had left, and the half-demon was pouring himself some more alcohol. "You knew?"

"What, that you tried to read my mind? You bet. I could feel you inside my head nosing around."

"I'm sorry, I didn't mean to—"

"Yes, you did, and that is why you need me. You don't have any idea how to control or even use your new powers, am I correct?" Inuentas said.

Binta thought about it for a moment and realized he was correct. "Yes," she said with a nod.

"First lesson: don't try to read the thoughts of those who are not human. We can sense it and don't like it. Understand?"

"Yes, of course."

"Good. Lesson two: you must read the rest of the tome."

"What? It nearly killed me; how can I read further?"

"It didn't kill you, now, did it? Huh?" Inuentas asked, pouring more ale for himself and finishing the first bottle.

"Well, no, but—"

"You are beyond that now, Binta. You have a sixth sense far greater than what a human should have. The tome has granted you a gift and a grand opportunity. The question is, will you take advantage?"

"So, what you are saying is that I should not listen to the warnings of the New Order, and I should go against their wishes and read further?" Binta asked doubtfully.

"Yes, they are ignorant about X'lor and, therefore, fear it. The little bit they think they know of him is wrong."

"But, people have died from reading it, so their concern has merit."

"If the tome were going to kill you, it would have done so already," Inuentas said.

Even without the ability to read his thoughts or understand what the strange creature was thinking, Binta believed him. But she wanted to understand what was at stake for her. "Why should I read further? I barely remember glancing at the first page; there was no writing. It was just a blank page," Binta said, her words trailing off as she recalled the mysterious tome.

"You want to find your friend?"

"Cassandra?" Binta said, making eye contact with the half-demon.

"Ah, yes, more than a friend, then," Inuentas said with a smile.

"What do you mean by that?" Binta snapped back.

"I mean, you do not need to be a mind reader to understand how you feel about her."

Binta blushed and looked away. The half-demon was bright and seemed to know what she was thinking. She'd had the same impression when Kringus spoke about him, as if Inuentas was chock-full of information, but made others uncomfortable listening to him. Binta was experiencing the uncomfortableness that Kringus had surely felt, and it seemed that Inuentas was looking right through her.

"Look, let's get something straight. You reached out to me when I left the castle last night, and I know nothing else about your motives here. Yet, you seem to know everything about me. I need us to be on equal ground if you want me to trust you."

"Very well, let's start from the beginning. You read the Tome of X'lor, that much you admit. However, you have not completed the work. I am here to tell you that you should do so for the best interest of you and your lost friend."

"Why do you care?" Binta asked.

"I care for one reason—you may be able to stop the summoning quicker and more efficiently than the New Order."

"And your prophecy did not foresee that?"

"No, I expect the prophecy does not account for a human reading the tome. Surviving and gaining from the experience makes you a rare individual."

"But how?"

"How did you survive?"

"Yes, why me?" Binta asked.

"I have a theory; I feel you were overwhelmed by an emotion. That emotion, whether it be happiness over your love of the new steward of Pelesea or grief over the loss of your friend—"

"Despair," Binta interrupted. "Deep despair."

"Despair, then. The emotion was so strong that it had a two-prong effect, in my estimation. First, the tome called to you, which is one of its innate abilities. It can sense deep emotions, and from your story, it sounds like that is what occurred. Second, an overwhelming feeling such as despair can keep the tome in check, keeping you safe from it destroying your mind. The tome knows this, so it beckoned you to read it. It wants to impart its wisdom to you."

"But I was bedridden for weeks after glimpsing the first page. What will happen when I continue reading it?"

"You have survived the initial shock; there is no more danger. Now, all that is left is learning and growing your newfound powers."

"So, what are you suggesting? Read the tome in full?" Binta asked.

"Yes."

"To what end?"

"As I said, grow your powers."

"And how will that help Cassandra?"

The barmaid returned with the food, and there was a pause in the conversation. Inuentas poured another glass of ale and unfolded a napkin onto his lap. He took several bites, letting Binta's questions hang in the air for a long while. After a few mouthfuls of salad, he continued, "It will give you the strength to find her location."

"Why can't someone else do that, like Kringus?"

"Because there is one being powerful enough in your world to give you the location. At one time, he was a god, but he was cast down amongst the mortals for crimes against his brethren. Now, he is the most powerful entity known to exist here in your world. Any attempt to contact this being will result in death unless you have obtained a higher level of consciousness, one offered in the pages of the Tome of X'lor," the half-demon explained.

"So, this being knows Cassandra's current location?"

"If anyone does, he will. But he will not help you unless you survive the mental bombardment he will throw at you. If you survive that, you may get your answers."

"And the New Order knows nothing about this being?"

"I have told them nothing because there is no need. They are powerful enough to eventually track down this Matilda person who is the orchestrator of the prophecy, but it is unclear if they will stop her. I guarantee you this: none of them could survive a meeting with the being of whom I speak."

"And how do I find him?" Binta asked curiously.

"You don't until you are ready. Then you come and see me, and I will point you in the right direction," Inuentas explained, taking a bite of his steak and savoring it. "I do so love your human food," he said with a satisfied sigh and a large gulp of ale.

"So, I must read the tome?"

"Yes, and when you complete it, you must confront the weakness that prevents your success. You must master what may hold you back against the god-like being."

"What is that?"

"You know."

Binta thought about his words momentarily, and her mind stretched out, trying to solve the riddle. She immediately knew what he referred to: her desire to serve Cass. Her weakness was sexual, a perversion that Kima had started long ago when she held Binta down, pierced, and painted her. Then Greyson fueled that fire with the promise of a perverted sexual affair with Cassandra. And finally, Cass had taken full advantage of her weakness, taking her as a sex slave. As she thought this through, she temporarily lost awareness of her surroundings. When things returned to focus, she found Inuentas smiling at her, taking another bite of his steak.

"You have figured it out?"

Binta nodded.

"Good. Read the tome, then find the source of your greatest weakness and confront it. If, and only if, you succeed, we should meet again. Do not come to me until you have successfully dispelled what ails you because I promise, this god-like being will exploit any weakness, and you will not only fail but perish."

Binta considered this and nodded absently. She suddenly did not feel confident and was unsure if she could help Cassandra. But she would try, and she would give her life for her friend if that was what it took.

"What is this being's name?"

"No one knows. He is referred to simply as The Mystic in the many circles of hell."

"The Mystic? And you know where to find him?"

"I can arrange it," Inuentas said confidently.

"Very well, I will finish the work and confront my weakness. Where do I find you when I am ready?"

"Here, of course. I am here every day at midday, enjoying this succulent food," he said, then took another bite of steak, closed his eyes, and chewed in satisfaction.

Binta stood and turned to leave but stopped and turned back to the half-demon. "And you need nothing from me? Do you have no ulterior motive?"

"Dear woman, I am here for the game, to watch the pathetic humans run around trying to stop something they probably cannot or will not. However, I am tasked with destroying the beast if it comes to pass that the New Order fails. I would rather just enjoy the fruits of this world as a messenger and not an assassin. You are my insurance policy that the humans may stop the summoning."

"So, you simply want to use me and exploit my feelings so you can sit back and eat shark steak and not get your hands dirty?"

"Oh, there are many things besides this wonderful shark steak that I'm enjoying. Sea urchin pie, dolphin soup, calamari, and your favorite—lobster."

"And how do you know so much about me, anyway? Such as my love for lobster, among many other things you have mentioned?"

"Dear woman, in your current condition, and until you complete the tome, you unwittingly broadcast your surface thoughts to beings like me. Learn to control your powers; your mind will be as challenging to read as mine.

"To answer your question, I would rather sit this battle out. I can and will destroy Marnelphion if need be, but I would much rather the humans deal with this, not me. So, become immense and return to me. I will point you toward The Mystic, and you will be well on your way to finding Cassandra Rho."

Binta nodded and said, "I'll be back soon."

Inuentas retuned the nod and took a long sip of his ale. Binta left, knowing time was of the essence. She intended to find Cassandra before the New Order even left Pelesea. She returned to Jamison's mansion with renewed confidence, her love for Cassandra spurring her on.

New Beginnings

Cerus stood over Jozerah as the barbarian continued to convulse and foam at the mouth. He had survived the snake's bite somehow, and as Ronnis walked up to stand beside him, Cerus kicked Jozerah hard in the side. The proud warrior could do nothing to defend himself, and so he curled into a fetal position as the convulsions worsened. Ronnis looked down at the poisoned man for a moment but showed no emotion. He saw Matilda and Cass approaching and walked to them to retrieve his mask from Cass. Before he could even ask for it, Cass pointed to its location in the sand. Without a word, he passed them by and made his way to the covering that he seemed to rely on more and more as the days passed. Matilda and Cass regarded him briefly before continuing to Cerus and their squirming captive.

"Why does he live?" Matilda asked.

"Antidote, most likely. Why does he live?" Cerus countered, pointing at the departing Ronnis.

Matilda turned back to the strange man and shrugged. "He has a purpose, one I recently discovered. He can shape-change into a snake, and I see many uses for that."

"I see many uses for this one," Cerus countered, nodding to Cass, who smiled seductively.

"That one is strange and does little other than eat our food and wear that stupid mask," he added, pointing his spear toward Ronnis, who was shaking the sand from his mask. "He can't even poison someone correctly."

"He wants Cassandra as much as I do and will stop at nothing to find her. Therefore, he is valuable, which is the end of the discussion, my husband," Matilda said sternly.

Cerus gritted his teeth and glanced at Cass, who only smiled and gave him a wink. His gaze drifted past her to Ronnis, now sitting on a rock, drinking his brandy from a glass as he frequently did. His mask was lying beside him, and he watched the dying battle with little interest, sipping from his glass regularly. Cerus eventually looked back to Matilda, who was glaring at him and waiting for a response. So, he nodded slightly.

"Good. Then, have your men kill the wounded savages that pepper the dune. Save this one. He will tell us the name of the barbarian king who holds Cassandra, and we will then drag him along with us. I need him alive," Matilda ordered, pointing to Jozerah.

She walked away, and Cass followed, looking over her shoulder at Cerus as she did, flashing him that mischievous smile again. Cerus gritted his teeth again and kicked Jozerah for good measure. He summoned a few of his men and ordered them to walk the battlefield and stab any barbarian still breathing. "No survivors!" he urged as the men ran off to perform the macabre task.

Matilda collected Ronnis and summoned the priests together. "We are victorious here, easily slaughtering the savages. I also feel that Cassandra is being held by their tribe. We will know soon after their leader has recovered from Ronnis's sweet bite."

All turned to regard Ronnis, who said nothing and appeared emotionless, wearing the mask again. Only his eyes sparkled from the holes in the porcelain covering, indicating he was interested in the conversation but had nothing to add.

So, they all turned back to Matilda, who continued her instructions. "We have lost few, and we will easily replenish the undead we lost." The dying scream of a barbarian far up the dune interrupted her, and they all chuckled.

"As I was saying, our victory is complete, and we will pack up camp now and move to the north to find Cassandra," Matilda said.

As the priests began to disassemble the camp, the warriors of Gorl made a line behind the undead that were now scouring the top of the dune, looking for anything to tear to shreds, any living creature to rip apart. No barbarians remained standing, and the few that remained alive were horribly killed, their pitiful screams echoing through the valley. Cerus and his men ended any barbarian still struggling to live after the wave of ravenous undead rolled over them.

Jak had been one of the archers at the top of the dune during the surprise attack from the Gorl warriors. He had suffered three stab wounds during that encounter, two minor and one that he was sure would prove fatal. The initial attack destroyed his bow, but only because he sensed the attack at the last moment and brought the weapon around to block. However, that same attack had sliced open his forearm. Another attack from the same warrior had opened a garish wound on his thigh as well before Jak had grappled the man into submission and eventually broken his neck. Unfortunately, during the confrontation, another interloper had stabbed him in the back, taking a kidney, and that was the wound he suffered now, feeling the blood draining from him.

He was lying on his back, facing the baking sun as the undead feasted nearby, the dying screams of his brethren haunting him as the zombies completed their task. Then he heard men screaming below him, lower on the great dune. Jak summoned enough energy to sit up and look beyond his boots to the line of warriors making their way slowly up the hill, taking great pleasure in stabbing their spears into the chests of the wounded and dying. He couldn't hold that position long, and he plopped down with a grunt, sending shards of pain through his back. He grimaced at the cloud of agony and focused on remaining conscious. He knew that if he drifted off, he was as good as dead. Of course, if he didn't move, he was dead anyway because if the ruthless interlopers that now approached found him, they would make quick work of him.

He looked around, trying to find a way to hide, perhaps using one of the sand pits from which the warriors had ambushed them. However, they had magically concealed themselves, he understood, and Jak knew there was no way to hide himself as proficiently as the murderous interlopers had. As his mind progressed through the possibilities, he noticed movement in his peripheral vision. He turned to see that one of the undead creatures, one of his deceased brethren from the Tribe of the Serpent, was bearing down on him, running on all fours faster than a desert lizard. His eyes widened at the atrocity, knowing the creature was most likely someone he knew. The horror of that thought became all too real when the beast was upon him.

"Vixa," he whispered.

If the creature heard him, it did not indicate it understood him. Driven by hate, it had only one focus—to kill. But he understood the nature of this one, which he knew formerly as Vixa, daughter of Zorn. She had died months earlier at the hands of Maltor, as she had been an unwitting participant in the ritual known by the barbarians as the Warrior's Heart. Her heart had been taken from her chest by the shamans and fed to Cassandra, imparting Vixa's skills in melee combat to her. In life, Vixa had fiery red hair and was quite skilled with her hand axes.

Now, the creature had only a slight resemblance to its former self. It had Vixa's face, but the flesh had rotted off or, in most places, had been picked clean by scavengers. Her scalp was mostly intact, and a line of skin ran down her right cheek and under her chin. She no longer had her bright blue eyes; deep, empty sockets stared back at him. The teeth of the creature had grown unnaturally long and were covered in blood with bits of flesh stuck in between. Aside from a few rotting patches, her chest was fleshless, showing ribs. The sternum and ribs closest to where her heart had been were broken, giving further proof that this indeed used to be Vixa. But the most telling feature was the wild red hair that still adorned the top of her crown, greedily clinging to the rotted scalp. This creature was the perversion of Vixa, and it repulsed Jak to witness it.

He didn't have long to consider whether it was Vixa or that he was surely doomed because the creature's attack was quick and powerful. It grabbed Jak's injured arm and clamped its maw around the wound, eliciting a grimace from the proud barbarian. Jak managed not to scream because he knew the interlopers would have him then. He was far enough away that perhaps they would not discover him soon, assuming he could escape from the animated corpse of Vixa. The creature dragged him along effortlessly, giving credibility to its strength. Luckily, it pulled him toward an outcropping of rocks, away from the carnage and the line of advancing spear-wielders.

The pain in Jak's arm was unbearable, but to his credit, he remained silent. He tried to find a weapon during the short trek and grabbed a discarded arrow. He wanted to stab the thing but had no idea where to attack it, for the little flesh left on its bones did not give him much of a target. How could he possibly attack the skeletal creature and succeed in hurting it? Still, he had to try something, so he summoned the energy to stab it repeatedly in the face. It had little effect, and the creature did not acknowledge the blows. The weapon broke in half, and he lost his grip after only a few stabs.

Soon, the creature pulled him into the rock outcropping, and he thought possibly that the beast that once was Vixa was trying to conceal him from the outsiders to save him. He quickly dismissed that thought when it released its grip and slashed him with its unnaturally long and sharp claws, digging gashes across his chest. He cried out in anguish but stifled it the best he could. The creature was not trying to hide him; it simply wanted to play with him. Perhaps it was a thinking creature and knew he was one of Maltor's advisors. Possibly, what little remained of Vixa in the shell of a body wanted revenge. What else could it be? She had dragged him into the concealed area so no one could witness her kill or interfere with it.

Suddenly, the creature lunged at him with a supernatural quickness. It bit deeply into his shoulder, tearing muscle and cracking bones alike. He knew then that he was doomed, so he screamed fully, joining his other dying brothers as they all sang the same song of death.

Just as he had succumbed to the fact he was going to die, the creature stopped chewing and rose slowly, blood dripping from its teeth. It stood motionless for a few moments, long enough for Jak to half crawl, half drag himself away from the beast and prop himself up against a rock. It just stood there, with its dark, empty orbs where its eyes had once been, watching him. Its wild red hair blew in the hot desert breeze, and for a brief moment, Jak thought that perhaps Vixa had somehow regained control of her dead body.

"Vixa?" he managed to whisper once more.

Still, it made no move, and Jak was at a loss. From his vantage point, he could see a thin section of the dune where the undead were swarming.

The cries of his dying brothers faded then as the creatures completed their task and began to walk calmly back down the dune and out of sight. Soon, Vixa turned and exited the rocky outcropping to join her brethren. Jak understood then that the interlopers had recalled them. Whatever devil had created the perversions was calling to them, and they were listening. He blacked out, the pain finally too much to bear.

SOMETIME LATER, JAK AWAKENED TO THE SOUND OF VOICES. HE WAS lying on his side, his shoulder and back still bleeding, which made him think he had not been unconscious for long. He crawled on his stomach, which caused excruciating pain to his battered body, so that he could see through a small opening between the rocks. The army of interlopers had gathered at the top of the dune, four on horseback. A few of the evil men bound a lone captive. Jak blinked away the weariness in his eyes and focused on the unlucky survivor. To his horror, he saw a battered Jozerah being tied to the saddle of a large man, obviously a leader of this group, by a length of rope that led to Jozerah's bound wrists. He would walk, or they would drag him, and Jak figured it would be mostly the latter.

They were preparing to leave, to head deeper into the desert, but why? Jak did not understand who these evil invaders were or what they wanted, but his answer came soon enough when the prominent witch who had perverted the dead of his tribe spoke. She was small and wore strange black clothing adorned with mysterious symbols. She wore a skull necklace around her neck, similar to how the shamans of Jak's tribe carried trinkets to help with spells or curses. There were several others dressed similarly, obviously lesser shamans. She was the only one on a horse, making him believe she was the leader of the devils.

She told the large warrior dragging poor Jozerah, "He knows where Cassandra Rho is, and we will perform a ritual to confirm it this night when our powers will be strong enough to coax that information from him."

"He will not knowingly give you information; the savage is stubborn," the man replied.

"I will break him; Marnelphion will see to it. For now, drag him a bit, lower his resistance, and make him suffer for daring to stand in my way, dear husband," the small woman said.

They laughed with the other two riders, including another female and a masked man. Soon, the caravan of interlopers was moving deeper into the desert. Jak watched in horror as the horse pulled Jozerah along after he had taken a few steps and fallen. No one slowed, and the giant warrior on the horse mercilessly dragged poor Jozerah behind. After the four riders, the shamans walked along, dressed in black and laughing gleefully at the sight of Jozerah struggling to regain his footing. Behind the evil shamans, the army of warriors, all brandishing spears, marched precisely. Jak knew from the ambush that their fighting tactics were perfect and formidable. The most unnerving sight, however, was the mass of undead creatures that brought up the rear of the marching interlopers. Hundreds remained, and the animals were supernaturally dangerous. If they were heading to his home, all was lost. Not even Maltor could hope to defeat the army of interlopers, especially with most of his men dead on the dune in front of Jak.

He dropped his head to the sand, laying a cheek flush against the hotness. He lay like that for a long time, losing energy, losing blood, and losing hope. It took a long while for the creatures to finally pass his position, and he drifted into darkness before they did. The last thought he had was of Cassandra. Was this group of invaders looking for Maltor's dead bride? Jak knew Cassandra was a witch of some kind, and the abundance of shamans in the invading group made it a distinct possibility that they were looking for her. He thought it ironic that Cassandra's corpse was one of the undead who fought for the evil witch, yet the interloper had no idea Cassandra was among them. He found that humorous for a moment. He felt cold even with the burning desert sun still high in the sky, and then the darkness took him once more.

LESS THAN SEVEN MILES AWAY, TUCKED INTO A HIDDEN HOME AMONG the rocks of the southern stretch of the Yaddaton, Cassandra dreamed. She was in the hot mountainous room where Zolmex lay on the stone table. It was the same dream Cassandra had had so many times before. Her father was there, the man she called the dark man, but he seemed less "dark" to her and clearer. She could see his face for the first time and found him quite handsome and not intimidating. His dark eyes revealed a wealth of knowledge and wisdom. He indeed seemed god-like and yet not threatening.

She knew the routine: she would reach for the artifact, and it would disappear, then the phrase "To find a king" would be scribed on the table in its place. Not this time; she willed herself to look her father in the eye and deny the routine. She used her anger and frustration to break the pattern she had lived through in her dreams over the last few years.

"I have found your king, Father, and escaped him. Yet, here I am without Zolmex. All you have given me is the phrase 'Notel X.' You have done nothing to help me."

She walked past the table and toward the two windows; the man she believed to be her father watched. He did not move or answer her, and although she found that infuriating, she was proud she had not reached for the artifact. She was altering the vision that her father fed her time and again. She did not have to follow the prophecy as the gods intended; she was tired of being a pawn in some game of power. So, she walked past the table and to the windows. Her father's gaze was piercing, and she tried hard to ignore it. It took all of her willpower not to turn back to him or the table, and her resolve began to fail until she peered out of the window to view the desert terrain. As always during this part of the dream, she felt herself whisked away and, to her relief, out of the room.

She was then on the desert floor, near the sea of dead. She turned to look behind her, and sure enough, the skull-shaped mountaintop loomed there. She was looking back to the spot where she'd stood just moments before, and as always, she could sense her father there, looking out of the skull-like windows. He was there, watching her, judging her as he always did. The vision continued to feel different; something was amiss. She looked around, but everything seemed as it always did in this part of her dream. But she knew it was different, and it slowly dawned on her how.

She suddenly lost her nerve and broke out in a cold sweat. She looked up, and the sky quickly clouded, blocking the burning desert sun. However, the heat not only remained but intensified. She wanted to wake up, she desperately needed to wake up, but she knew her father wouldn't allow it. She would not escape this vision so quickly, and she knew she would have to bring herself to turn back to the sea of death before he released her back into reality. She swallowed hard and slowly turned back to the barbarian gravesite. As she suspected, it was empty of all bodies and was nothing more than an old, dried-up riverbed, just like in the mountain she and her friends had ventured to not so long ago. She recalled the skeletal guardian of that place, and fear washed over her, especially when she looked on the other side of the riverbed.

There stood the dead, once buried in the barbarian grave. The creatures were zombie-like and unmoving, focusing on Cassandra's every move. She felt the hate and the danger emanating from that side of the ravine. She noticed that their teeth elongated as she stood there, and their hands turned to claws, razor-sharp nails sprouting from their fingertips like some perverted plant. She stood frozen with fright and could sense something awful was about to happen. The sky somehow darkened more, and the creatures, in unison, jumped to action, running straight for her, some on all fours. Panicked, she willed herself awake just before the undead creatures reached her.

The first thought she had as she came out of her long slumber was how much pain she was indeed in. Her head throbbed with a dull ache, and as she regained a few of her senses, her arms and mouth flared to life with a suffocating wave of agony. She squinted in the bright light that filled the strange room, fueling the pain in her head. As her vision became focused, she made out a beautiful woman sitting beside the comfortable bed where she lay. The bright sunlight and her blurry vision made it difficult to see any details of the woman's face. Cassandra felt that she must be in the heavens, and this was an angelic version of her mother.

"Sera? Mother?" she whispered.

"No, my name is Sitra, not Sera," the woman answered.

Cassandra closed her eyes and pinched the bridge of her nose, trying to find some relief from the immense headache. "Who?" she managed to say.

"My name is Sitra, and you are safe in my home."

"Where are we?"

"You are in the Yaddaton Desert, Cassandra."

"You know my name?" Cassandra asked in surprise, opening her eyes to regard the woman.

She was beautiful, but as Cassandra's vision came into focus, she quickly realized that she was not dead, and the woman was certainly not her mom. Sitra was blindfolded, and to Cassandra's surprise, wore her hair back in a long ponytail comprised of small, slithering snakes. She gasped and sat up, which sent a lightning bolt of pain through her head. She grimaced and brought her fingers to her temples, rubbing them lightly and shutting her eyes again.

"Easy, you are severely dehydrated," the woman said soothingly, handing her a cup of water.

Cassandra remained motionless, waiting for the waves of pain to subside, then slowly opened her eyes to find the cup presented before her. She took it and sipped slowly, eyeing the woman cautiously.

"And yes, I know your name because your fairy friend told me it," Sitra explained.

"Gophia?"

The woman nodded and smiled. "She is very protective of you and will be glad to see you are awake."

The two sat silently while Cassandra finished her water, then returned the empty cup to Sitra. When she didn't move to take it, Cassandra knew the woman truly could not see her. As she contemplated her strange caretaker and wondered why she could be blindfolded, Sitra spoke. "Finished?"

Cassandra made a confused face and said, "Yes, but how—"

"How did I know without being able to see?"

"Yes, exactly."

"I can do lots of things without my eyes. I have trained myself not to use them or rely on them. You were no longer making the all-so-subtle sound of drinking your water. I assumed you had finished."

"May I ask why you are blindfolded?"

Sitra smiled, reached for the cup, and refilled it. When she returned the cup to Cassandra, she said, "To protect those around me."

"From what?"

"I am a sleeth, a race typical to Yaddaton. Have you heard of the sleeth?"

Cassandra remembered the creatures well, having battled against them in the barbarian tournament a month earlier. A sharp pain in her side reminded her of the battle against Roxin, who had broken several of her ribs.

"Yes, I know of the sleeth."

"We are born with blessings and curses, each of us differently afflicted. My curse is my gaze, which can cause those looking into my eyes to be petrified."

"You mean like a gorgon?" Cassandra asked, remembering her brief studies at Victoria's School of Magic, where she learned of the legendary gorgons of old.

"I don't know what a gorgon is, Cassandra, but if you mean turning people to stone, then yes."

Cassandra thought about that for a moment and then asked, "And your blessing?"

Sitra shrugged and said, "I don't know; perhaps it is the same because I can defend myself well when needed."

"No, her blessing is her beauty!" came a roaring voice from outside the room.

Soon after, a large man came into view at the doorway. Cassandra immediately noticed that he had no pupils and appeared blind.

"My husband, Mateon," Sitra said with a smile.

The beautiful sleeth stood, went to her husband, and put an arm around him. He kissed her gently on the cheek, and Cassandra understood what a powerful bond they had. She also agreed with Mateon's assessment: Sitra was physically stunning.

"Our patient is awake, then?" Mateon asked.

"Yes, but far from healed," Sitra confirmed.

"I hurt all over," Cassandra said, sitting on the edge of the bed and hugging her arms to her chest.

"Stay with her. I will make her something to eat. I've gotten water down her over the few days she's been here, but no food. I will make her a light soup," Sitra said, leaving the room.

"Ah, you are in luck; my Sitra makes a mean yucca soup," Mateon said with a large, toothy grin.

Cassandra smiled, or at least began to, and a sharp pain shot through her mouth. She rubbed a finger on her swollen gums, massaging them gently.

"Sitra removed the needles there so that you will heal in time. It might take a while, though. I assume the barbarians did that to you?"

Cassandra was amazed once more that the blind man knew she was rubbing her gums. She was impressed that the couple could function so well without their vision. She also knew that Sitra was only blindfolded because

Cassandra was in their home. She imagined Sitra did not usually wear it. Cassandra looked at her aching arms, where she wore blood-stained bandages on each forearm, and the skin on the edge of the wrappings appeared darkly bruised.

"She removed them there as well," he said with a grin, pulling a yellow fruit from his pocket and biting it as one would eat an apple.

Cassandra watched in amazement as he chewed through the tough skin. He pulled a second one out and held it out to her. "Want one?"

"Is that a lemon?"

"Not any old lemon, a Yaddaton lemon!"

"As hungry as I am, I must decline," Cassandra said with a sour face.

Sitra added from the kitchen as she prepared Cassandra's meal, "No lemons, Mateon, you'll make her sick."

"Yes, dear," the large man called out, then shrugged and pocketed the extra lemon.

Soon, Sitra had Cassandra's soup and some warm, soft bread. Cassandra knew she was hungry, but once she smelled the delicious aroma of the meal, her stomach gurgled and growled uncomfortably. Sitra made sure Cassandra didn't eat too fast and was there to offer her refills of soup and bread. After the third serving, she put a stop to the feeding frenzy.

"Let this settle for a bit, Cassandra. If you want more, I have plenty, but let your body adjust to eating again but at a slower pace."

Cassandra understood the woman was right, but the food was extra tasty, and the warm soup soothed her injured gums. After sitting for a few moments, she understood the wisdom of waiting as her stomach began to cramp. She lay back down and held her midsection, letting the food digest.

"So, where is Gophia?"

"She likes to flit about in the desert during the day but always comes home as the sun sets to sleep beside her friend," Mateon said, nodding toward the wall above Cassandra.

Cassandra craned her neck to the indicated spot and saw a small bed attached to the wall above her. She smiled, thinking how loyal the little fairy had become, and she looked forward to seeing her again. Cassandra owed the creature her life, and the fairy owed Cassandra similarly. She hoped Gophia would stay with her for a while. However, her smile faded as she thought of her future. What was she to do now? She couldn't stay with Mateon and Sitra forever, or perhaps she could if they allowed it. She felt hopeless, and it did not sit well with her.

As if reading her thoughts, Sitra said, "So, where are you from, Cassandra?"

"Far across the sea, I'm afraid."

"And do you plan to return home?" Mateon added.

"I have no home, Mateon, and have no way to return," Cassandra answered, keeping her gaze locked on the tiny bed above her.

"Surely you have someone to return to. If not family, at least a friend or two?" the big man said, polishing off the lemon and smacking his mouth as he chewed on the core.

"My mother is dead, and my sister is missing."

"Missing?" Sitra asked.

"Like you? Is she with the barbarians?" Mateon added.

"I don't know where she is, and in truth, she is probably dead now. She is not with the barbarians, though. Thank goodness she has avoided that torture."

Cassandra did not feel like discussing her life or her family; it was too painful. She just wanted to sleep, heal, and eat once her stomach settled.

Luckily, Sitra decided to stop the conversation, probably sensing Cassandra's discomfort. "You should rest now, Cassandra. We can talk about your future after you heal. For now, you need your sleep."

"Thank you," Cassandra whispered, and she turned to face the wall. She heard the couple leaving, and she was thankful they did not stay long enough to hear her cry herself to sleep.

THE BUGS CONTINUED TO BITE GREYSON AND HIS FRIENDS AS THEY made their way to the outskirts of Swamp Ikma. Greyson carried his magnificent staff, gaining insight into the item's powers each morning during his prayer time. He was overwhelmed with it and didn't fully understand what it could offer, but Breeston was confident it would soon become invaluable to him.

"Why do the bugs not bite you?" Alleah asked Breeston, smacking a giant mosquito on her neck.

"Their god is my god, and they know not to hinder one of their own," the druid said with a smile.

Greyson could not tell if he spoke the truth or was covering the real reason he was able to repel the vicious bugs. He believed it had something to do with the staff, one attuned with the god of the swamp, Malebak the dragon.

"Well, this is where my journey ends," Breeston said.

The forest was thick with greenery now, and the swampy odor had subsided hours ago. This area of the woods was the edge of the swamp and, therefore, the limit of Breeston's reach.

"If you follow the river along here, it will spill into the ocean. According to your tales, that is how you first entered Ikma. However, if you'd like to stay dry on your trek to Racip, then might I suggest going north," Breeston said, turning his back to the river and pointing straight ahead.

Greyson felt sad at having to say goodbye to their new friend. They had only been in the swamp a few months, but the four of them had shared a bond, and Greyson truly felt he was leaving a good friend behind.

"We will truly miss you, Breeston," Alleah said as she hugged him.

Chloe followed suit, and then the druid turned to Greyson. "You are all welcome here anytime. Greyson, you hold the key to finding me if you ever need me."

"Me? How?"

"The crystal. We are joined spiritually because Zeva's loins birthed our crystals."

Greyson saw the shadow that passed over Alleah's face when Breeston mentioned Zeva. She had discovered that Zeva was an illusionist and was taking her form most times that she and Greyson were intimate. The true Alleah had not said it, but he knew she felt betrayed and embarrassed by it. Greyson had to apologize for his insensitive actions, and luckily, his friendship with Alleah outshined her anger. Still, he knew the wound was fresh, and the mere mention of Zeva's name would get a reaction. Her slight frown turned to a wry smile, and he knew they would be all right.

"So, the crystals are connected?" Greyson asked, turning his attention back to the druid.

"Absolutely, just as they are vessels to our respective gods. The crystals will communicate if you return to Ikma and concentrate on me through the staff. So, come back anytime, my new friends," Breeston said.

The two men clasped hands and hugged, Breeston patting Greyson on the back several times during the embrace. "We thank you for your hospitality, my new friend, and we hope to return to Ikma one day," Greyson said.

"I do hope to see you soon, all of you," Breeston added, turning to regard Greyson's companions.

"Well, I guess we venture into the unknown now," Alleah said, turning toward Racip.

The others turned in the same direction, and Breeston and Greyson walked up to stand beside the two women. The city was not visible from their vantage point, and no sound made its way through the thick vegetation. Greyson could only hear the buzzing of various bugs as summer loomed in the not-so-distant future. Entering Racip seemed like suicide to him, but he had agreed with Alleah: they owed it to her sisters in faith to at least verify they had perished. According to Chloe's stories, her experience as a captive of Cerus and his Gorl warriors was horrible. If any still survived in the custody of those cruel men these months later, Greyson wondered how much of their minds would still be intact.

"We should pray, Alleah," Chloe said with a shaky voice.

Greyson could tell that the memories of Racip, although brief, were flooding back to her, and they were not sitting well with the young priestess of Sinnis. Greyson and Alleah joined her in a moment of prayer, and even Breeston placed a hand on Greyson's shoulder as Chloe recited a prayer of hope to her god.

"Well, I guess this is where we part ways, Breeston," Greyson said after the prayer.

"Sadly so, Greyson, but I advise you not to enter Port Racip without a proper disguise."

"We have no way to disguise ourselves," Alleah said.

"No, but I do," Breeston said with a smile.

He nodded to the purple stone set on his staff, and Greyson understood that his staff's power could help them navigate the dangerous streets of the chaotic city. Greyson looked to the women, and each wore an expression of doubt. But he knew it would be wise to proceed with caution, and they should accept Breeston's help if he had a plan.

"What do you have in mind?" Greyson asked.

"The swamp remembers the invaders and can temporarily grant you the guise of the warriors who had captured Chloe. Not specifically, but in their dress and weaponry. The effect will last less than a day, so hurry to Racip, find your answers, and get out quickly."

"No," Alleah said, shaking her head. "I will not be part of this blasphemy."

"I concur," Chloe added.

"But, my friends, to enter Racip the way you look and dress is to spell certain doom. You will not become warriors of Gorl; you will only look like them for a short time," Breeston said.

Alleah and Chloe shared a knowing look and didn't even give his words a moment of consideration as they both said immediately in unison, "No!"

"Fine," Breeston said with a sigh. "I do not want you to get in harm's way, and I feel like I'm sending you into a death trap if I don't disguise you somehow."

"Find a different way," Alleah pleaded.

"I'm sorry, Alleah, but my powers of disguise are minimal, and I am at the mercy of the short memories of the swamp."

Alleah and Chloe began a heated discussion with the druid about how they would never portray Gorl warriors and that to consider such an act in light of the tortures and murders of their sisters at the hands of the evil warriors was blasphemy.

Greyson interrupted them as something came to mind. "I have an idea," he said with a smile.

An hour later, they entered the city of Racip, walking confidently along the main westerly road. Greyson now appeared as a Gorl warrior, with chainmail armor and his staff appearing as Cerus's great spear. He led Alleah and Chloe, undisguised, as prisoners. The vines that bound the women's hands and comprised the leashes tied around their necks were loose but looked sturdy through the illusion, according to Breeston.

Greyson held the ends of those leashes, and as they entered the city proper and people noticed them, he pulled hard on Chloe's leash, making her nearly fall.

"Sorry," he whispered. "I have to play the part if we are to be believable."

They both looked at him wide-eyed, but he smiled slightly to let them know he wouldn't dare take it too far. So, as they walked among the city folk, they played their parts perfectly, Greyson wearing a wicked smile and both "captives" hanging their heads. Alleah even added some sniffling for effect. Greyson would tug on their leashes occasionally and mutter curses at them. They passed a couple, and it was almost as if Greyson were looking in the mirror; the woman had her head down, walking submissively just behind the man, who smiled and nodded to Greyson as they passed. A strange-looking creature that reminded him of Zeva, just not quite as hideous, passed in front of them with a dog, which whined pitifully as the creature carried it away. Greyson thought momentarily that the animal might be a snack, not a pet. Either way, they blended well in the wicked city, and he thought they might fit right in. That was until he saw the six large guards approaching them.

"Uh-oh," he whispered. "And so, we come to the first test, my friends. Be prepared."

"You! Halt and state your business in Port Racip," the largest and meanest-looking of the group yelled to Greyson.

The man was huge, standing over six feet tall and muscle-bound. He wore a nicely polished set of chainmail armor and a longsword strapped to his hip. He sported a neatly trimmed beard matching his dark hair and darker eyes. The man's appearance was not friendly, and his scowl only worsened as he approached. The other five walked behind him, dressed similarly, indicating to Greyson that the giant man in front was the leader.

"I asked you a question," the large man said.

Greyson noticed that even the common folk who walked the city streets steered clear of the group. Greyson wanted to speak but knew he needed to act like a Gorlian warrior to fool these ruffians. If they did not believe him, they were goners.

"I care nothing for your questions, guardsman! Why do you hamper me so?" Greyson said with as much conviction as he could muster.

The man kept approaching even when the others stopped a few feet away. Greyson was worried that the man might walk through or over him, but he stopped just short, and Greyson found himself face to face with the large man—or, in this case, face to chest. Greyson had to crane his neck to look him in the face, and the hate he saw in the man's eyes was great. He could only recall one other time he'd stared into the eyes of evil: when he confronted Cerus that day in Tara.

"I asked what you are doing in our town, and I expect an answer," the man said through gritted teeth.

"I have captured these weaklings for Cerus's entertainment," Greyson said, jerking the leashes so forcefully that Chloe fell temporarily to one knee.

"Cerus the Grey?" the man asked, a shadow passing over his face at the mere mention of the man's name.

"The same," Greyson said.

The man's visage softened slightly, and his gaze went to the captives as he licked his cracked lips. "Cerus is coming here?" he asked, almost nervously now.

"No, we are just traveling through."

The man looked relieved, and a big smile spread across his face. "I am Sebastian, and we welcome you to Racip," he said, motioning with a hand to the men behind him. They all nodded and relaxed with the change in Sebastian's demeanor.

"No need to tell Cerus of this misunderstanding; we did not know you were a man of Gorl, agreed?" the large man asked.

Greyson stared hard at the man, playing the part of a Gorl warrior the best he could. He knew little of them but understood they were fearless. The vision of his friend Darian swinging from a tree, his insides spilling onto the temple yard, filled his thoughts. Sebastian's smile eventually faded, and his visage grew more sour the longer Greyson waited to respond.

"I don't have to, no," he said with a smirk.

The man nodded and looked over Greyson's captives once more. "These are for Cerus?"

"Yes, and they must remain unspoiled."

The man looked at him doubtfully, and his gaze eventually reached Greyson's staff, which appeared as a giant spear. He nodded and motioned for his men to spread out, which they did, forming a circle around the three newcomers.

"I am in charge here, and I say we visit the tavern and get to know each other a little better."

Greyson looked around, and all five other men had their eyes on the women. He did not have to be a mind reader to understand their intent. He also did not see any easy way out of this.

"And if I refuse?" was all he could say.

Sebastian laughed and placed a hard hand on his shoulder, squeezing with enough strength to make Greyson cringe slightly. "Now, how can you?" he asked, shaking him with a grip of steel.

Greyson didn't know how to take that. Did Sebastian mean it as a friendly term of endearment, or was he stating that there was no way to avoid doing precisely what Sebastian wanted them to do? He received his answer when the lead guardsman extended a hand to a nearby tavern and said, "I insist."

Greyson nodded and walked toward the bustling establishment, his mind spinning with what lay ahead for him and his friends. Sebastian's hand was still on his shoulder, and he felt like a prisoner even though he was not in binds like his friends. As they approached the door, a man stumbled out, holding a mostly empty bottle of ale, and appeared very drunk. His eyes widened when he saw Sebastian and his men, but his reflexes were far too slow in his drunken stupor to avoid the confrontation.

"Get out of our way, you drunken fool!" Sebastian said and grabbed the bottle out of the man's hand.

"Heeey!" the drunkard said, and Greyson could smell the thick aroma of alcohol on his breath.

With a flash, Sebastian smashed the bottle over the man's head, and he dropped to the porch of the tavern, blood gushing from several lacerations. Chloe gasped in surprise, and Greyson stood there gawking at the spectacle.

"Does Gorl approve?" Sebastian asked, laughing.

Greyson knew this was a test he desperately needed to pass because he felt like he was losing any upper hand he may have had by throwing Cerus's name around. So, he did the only thing he knew to do and kicked the drunk in the ribs. The man screamed and folded into a fetal position, vomiting a large amount of ale. The sight got the other guards laughing, and they all took turns kicking the poor soul as they passed. Guilt washed over Greyson, and he felt his face growing warm, knowing he had been the instigator of such an awful act. At least the heinous action kept their true identity concealed… for now.

The tavern was full and smelled of food and sex. The women in the place dressed scantily, some even topless. They were working the customers, sitting close or even on their laps. Some women led men up the stairs to waiting rooms. Greyson could only imagine what acts they performed behind those closed doors. It temporarily piqued his interest before he looked at Alleah and saw the fear in her eyes. The tavern was not a place he wanted them to be. He felt bad enough in the foul place but knew his friends were in deep trouble.

Sebastian led them to a large round table that was free of patrons. Greyson figured it was permanently reserved for the bunch of "lawmen." However, only Sebastian sat with Greyson; the others stood in a circle around the table. Alleah began to sit at the table, and Greyson thought quickly, pulling her hard to her knees.

"You sit on the floor, both of you!" he screamed and brandished his "spear" toward Alleah.

He didn't feel convincing, but he knew it sufficed when Sebastian said, "I like your style, my friend. I didn't catch your name, stranger of Gorl."

Greyson had to think quickly because he had not considered the need for a name or what it should be. So, he blurted out the first name that came to mind, a kind of mash-up of his proper moniker: "Kavin Lightbringer."

"Kavin, huh?"

Greyson nodded and placed his staff on the table near him. Sebastian shrugged and waved at a barmaid, who came over immediately. He pulled her onto his lap, and she could not resist. Sebastian took the liberty to place an order for all of them. He ordered a steak for him and his men, a tuna fillet for Greyson, and nothing for the women. The pompous guardsman also ordered drinks for the men, then whispered something into the woman's ear. She looked at Chloe and Alleah as he did, and Greyson detected a hint of sadness on the woman's face.

"Understand?" the large man said.

The woman nodded, and Sebastian let her up, smacking her on the rump as she left. He turned to Greyson, and the smile was gone. What Greyson saw in the man's eyes was pure hate. He narrowed his dark eyes, and the men around the table moved closer. Greyson anxiously eyed the "spear" that was close at hand.

"So, why are you really here, Kavin?" he said threateningly.

"I told you—"

"No, you lied to me. Now tell me why you bring such lovely creatures into my city."

Greyson's mind spun, trying to come up with an answer. He knew he was in trouble, but he was more concerned with Alleah and Chloe's fate. They were fools to have come to Racip, and he had told Alleah as much back in Ikma. Now, they would pay with their lives. Suddenly, a leather strap slipped around his neck from behind him and pulled tight, cutting off his oxygen. He reached for his staff, but Sebastian took it in the blink of an eye. Two guards wrestled the leashes out of Greyson's grasp, pulling the women away.

"You sure don't fight much like a Gorl warrior, boy," Sebastian said.

Greyson brought his hands up to try to pull the strap free so he could breathe, but the hold was tight, and his face began to flush from the lack of oxygen. He noticed that people moved away from the table, most not even looking his way, and none stopped to help. He was doomed, and so were his friends. He managed to catch a glimpse of Alleah and Chloe struggling with the guards. Alleah tried to untangle her vines but wasn't fast enough. The evil men held them tight, swords poking them in the ribs. He barely registered the fear on Alleah's face as the man behind him pulled him to a standing position, the strap digging deeper into his throat. Greyson began to swoon as the lack of oxygen took effect.

Sebastian stood with a cocky grin and said, "Hold him."

The grip on him tightened, but Greyson understood there was no need; he was losing consciousness and couldn't fight back or move much. That was when the sharp pain exploded in his mouth as Sebastian's punch connected. His lip tore open, snapping him back into reality. As the man behind him readied him for another punch, Greyson realized the man had lost hold of the leather strap, and he could breathe again. His mouth throbbed with pain, he tasted blood, and he was too disoriented to fight back. He saw the second punch from Sebastian, another hook that exploded against his left jaw. Just before it slammed home, he heard Alleah protest, but a guard abruptly stopped her. He saw stars, and everything became a blur.

The beating continued, and after a few more punches, his mouth was a wreck and bleeding profusely, and one eye swelled shut. He could not stand alone and would have been lying on the floor if the guard behind him was not still holding him up. He could barely see and lost track of his surroundings; the continued barrage to his face, the sound of Alleah's protests, and the sight of the patrons completely ignoring his beating were all lost to him.

Sebastian mercifully stopped the assault and grabbed him up by the hair so he could look him in the eye. Greyson felt blood pour down his chin and dribble all over his clothes and the floor. He could see Sebastian's angry face, blurry and up close.

"So, Kavin, I appreciate you delivering the wenches to me; I will thoroughly enjoy the exotic-looking one," Sebastian said through clenched teeth.

Greyson didn't need to see which of his companions the evil man was talking about. He knew Alleah was the most beautiful and exotic woman he had ever met, and Chloe, although stunning in her own right, did not compare.

"The priestesses of Sinnis do not willingly spread their legs, but she will do exactly that for me, I assure you," Sebastian continued.

Greyson tried to object, tried to plead with the man to let them go, but all that came out of his busted mouth was gibberish, followed by more blood.

"What is that? You want to watch?" Sebastian said dramatically and looked for a reaction from his cohorts. They laughed heartily at Greyson's expense.

When Greyson didn't answer, Sebastian dragged him by the hair over to Alleah and pulled him down to face level with her. She was kneeling on the floor, and Greyson could see her swollen cheek through his tired eyes. She was crying and reached out a hand to touch his battered face, but Sebastian smacked it away.

"Well, my new little pet, your boyfriend, Kavin, wants to watch us play. Is that all right with you?" Sebastian asked sarcastically. He took a handful of her hair, like with Greyson, and forcefully nodded.

"Good, take them all to my quarters. I'll eat my meal, then come up to claim my prize," Sebastian said with a laugh.

"You are a tough man, beating up children, Sebastian," came a sinister voice from behind them.

Sebastian immediately released Greyson, who fell face down on the floor. In Greyson's dazed and beaten state, he wasn't sure, but it sounded like a touch of fear was in Sebastian's voice when he answered.

"Vlad, what are you doing here?" Sebastian said nervously.

"Glime is not amused," Vlad responded calmly and coolly.

Greyson tried to turn to witness who or what was interrupting Sebastian's fun, but he could only lie there on the floor and bleed.

"We were just goofing around, Vlad. We're all just having fun here," Sebastian said desperately.

Greyson lost track of the remainder of the conversation as he drifted from reality. Before he passed out completely, he felt gentle hands on his face and heard Alleah chanting softly. Soon after, he felt a soothing wave of healing wash over him. Alleah was free to heal him, which meant they had a chance. At that moment, he was thankful for Vlad and very grateful for the distraction.

Binta was under scrutiny that evening as Kleve informed Jamison of her walk as soon as he arrived home. Of course, Jamison could not stay mad at her, but he was very concerned with her well-being. She assured him she felt perfectly fine, and in truth, she did. She had big plans that night and expected to take the next step with the tome, which was to follow Inuentas's advice.

"I would prefer a priest to stay with you for the next few days while I spend time at the castle," Jamison said over dinner.

"A priest?"

"Yes, to watch over you. Go where you want, take your walks, but have a priest handy."

"Jamison, have you not been listening? Victoria advised a wizard needs to be involved, not a priest."

"I know, I just don't understand how a wizard can help your well-being."

"Because this is an affliction of the mind, my love," Binta said, leaning close to the table.

Knowing how protective Jamison was of her, she reached out with her fledgling powers and probed his mind. She wasn't good at controlling her newfound skills when she didn't focus on them, but if Binta concentrated, she found them formidable.

"You have disposed of the tome?" she asked.

His eyes seemed to gloss over, and guilt washed over her. How could she take advantage of this incredible man who had given her a new lease on life and loved her unconditionally? She put the thought out of her mind; this was for Cassandra.

"Not yet. I will have it delivered to Victoria tomorrow."

She saw a flash of an image when he said that. She saw the tome, which was locked in a case in the study where she found it. The door to the study was locked as well, but she could get around that. She ceased the intrusion into her lover's mind and finished her dinner. He never even knew that she had probed around his thoughts and taken advantage of him.

"Good," she finally said with an inviting smile.

"Will you consider staying at Victoria's school for a while, or even better, come to the castle with me tomorrow? Stay there where Victoria can look after you herself," Jamison pleaded.

"I will consider it, but I assure you, I feel fine; never better, actually," Binta insisted.

Jamison smiled and let it go at that. She knew he wanted her to be safe, but she was determined to complete the reading. She felt the creature, Inuentas, was telling her the truth, and she needed to take the next step to fully understand what was going on in her brain.

She found herself incredibly excited, not just over the inevitable meeting she would have with the tome that night, but she felt sexually charged. She easily seduced Jamison over their post-meal fig and lemon tea and didn't even need to use her powers to do so. She took her lover to bed and drained him thoroughly. The sex was amazing, like always, and left her very satisfied afterward. But she wanted to tire him out and instigated a whole evening of lovemaking.

She never slept, though, and patiently waited until Jamison breathed heavily, indicating he had found a deep slumber. She quietly got out of bed, donned her robe, and padded out of the room. Before Binta had taken a dozen steps, she felt the connection with the tome; it knew she was coming. She quietly went to the kitchen and recalled the first time she'd discovered the book, when the raven guided her. She didn't need that now; she knew what she wanted, and the old book did not need to trick or guide her. She also knew not to go directly to the study, for it was locked. Instead, she made her way to Kleve's room. Guilt washed over Binta again as she knew she would have to manipulate someone she cared for to get what she wanted. She noted how bad it felt and promised herself not to do it when rescuing

Cassandra was complete. However, now were desperate times, which called for desperate measures.

Kleve was fast asleep in his wool pajamas and sleeping cap. He snored, which Binta found endearing. She truly liked the man, and again, the guilt weighed heavily on her as she gently shook him awake.

"What? Who is there?" he said, sitting up with a snort.

"It is me, Kleve."

"Oh, my lady, whatever is the matter? Are you feeling all right?" he said, trying to shake the cobwebs of sleep and gain his bearings.

"Yes, yes, I am fine. I'm sorry to bother you, but I need the key to the study," Binta answered, and quickly she found herself in his thoughts, persuading him to be helpful.

She knew he would know the location of the key and that she could make this little interaction seem like it never happened. Manipulating Jamison and Kleve, two people she had grown to care for deeply, felt wrong. Her feelings for them grew with each passing day, and she vowed again that this would be the only time she would do this to a friend.

"The study?"

"Yes, remember, I need the key."

He sat still for a moment and blinked a couple of times as if trying to remember something; then, a slight smile came to his face. "Oh yes, I almost forgot; here you go," he said, reaching into the breast pocket of his pajamas and producing the key.

"Thank you, Kleve. You go back to sleep, and I'll return it later."

"Yes, my lady. Goodnight."

"Goodnight, Kleve," she said with a smile and slipped out of the room.

Soon, she found herself before the study, and the door was most certainly locked this time. She used the key and entered quietly, locking the door behind her. She assumed Jamison had another key, but she wanted to make it as hard as possible for someone to interrupt her. She needed to take the time to read the entire work. She remembered nothing about her glance at the magnificent book except for the first blank page.

The room was dark, and there was no fire or other light source. Binta felt foolish not thinking of this before. She felt her way blindly to the bookcase, close to where she remembered it. She finally felt it but could not budge the secret door. She cursed herself for not thinking her excursion through better. She had no idea how to open the hidden door. She was about to leave and scour Jamison's mind for an answer when there was a loud caw from a nearby bird.

The sudden noise made her jump and let out a little scream. She sat in the dark for a moment, holding a hand over her heart, unable to see the creature but knowing it was there.

"X'lor?" she whispered in the dark.

Another caw from the bird had her jumping, but not as severely because she knew it was there to help her, sent from the tome like the last time. She gingerly reached out a hand where she last heard the caw, searching for a loose book or something else that might open the secret passage. She fumbled around unsuccessfully before her fingers latched on to a decorative carving protruding from the bookshelf. It felt to her as if it were the head of a bird, possibly a raven. She tried to turn it or move it, but finally, it pressed inward just a bit, triggering the mechanism to unlatch the secret door.

It was just as heavy to move as she remembered, and when she finally pushed it open enough to walk through, she searched for the lantern. The first time it hung on the wall with a lighting stick. She gently felt along the wall until she found both. Unfortunately, there was no fire in the fireplace to ignite the stick and light the lantern as there had been the last time she'd visited the room. She made her way out of the passage and to the fireplace, knowing there had to be flint and steel to light a fire. It took her quite some time to find it, but eventually, she had a small fire going and easily lit the lantern. Finally, it was time to find what she came for.

She returned to the passage and, holding the small lantern before her, made her way down the small hall. The Tome of X'lor was in the same spot as before but encased in the metal box that she had glimpsed in Jamison's thoughts. It was a steel box with a padlock. She sighed in frustration as the process of even reaching the tome grew more complicated at every turn. She did not know how long it would take her to complete her reading, but she knew her chance waned as it was past midnight, and she still had not started.

Another startling caw had her nearly dropping the lantern. She jumped, and her anger boiled. "Enough!" she yelled instinctively, turning to see a raven perched on the top of a bookcase filled with scrolls and other tomes.

For a moment, the bird stretched its wings and looked to take flight, but her voice stopped and shattered it as it burst into a hundred tiny pieces of light that danced in the air for a few moments and then faded to nothingness. She looked at the tome, understanding that the raven was a manifestation of the artifact.

"Thank you, but enough with the birds," she said.

She walked calmly to the bookcase where the bird had perched and held up her lantern to examine the area. Nothing was obvious, so she reached to feel the top of it and found a key. The tome was guiding her, but she also knew the dangers the old book posed. She had to start winning the mental battle before peering into the work's depths again. She took the key, which fit perfectly into the lock. Soon after, she removed the magnificent book from its protective shell.

She could feel the power resonating within the old book and sense it probing her mind. She adjusted quickly, and the feeling became more of a synergy than an intrusion. Without thinking much, she took another book from one of the shelves and put it in the protective case. She kept the key, slipping it into a pocket of her robe. She then returned to the fireplace where she could sit in the comfortable chair and peruse the book. She put the tome in her lap and closed her eyes, reaching out to it, feeling the book's raw power. She finally took a deep breath and opened the cover.

Like last time, she immediately went into a strange trance. However, this time, she did not lose consciousness but fell deep within herself. She knew she was reading the tome, and could feel herself turning the brittle pages, but it seemed to her as if she were watching it unfold instead of living it. She did not know what she read, nor could she make out the many strange symbols scribed across the pages. Instead, she could feel her mind opening, becoming more aware of everything around her. She understood there were one hundred and fourteen books on the bookshelf that opened to the secret passage and that the wood burning in the fireplace was oak and would easily burn for another three hours.

She could recall details about her life that she had forgotten or never even remembered, just like the first time. The tome opened her mind so far that it brought forth the memory of her first hunger pain and the first time her leg fell asleep because she was lying on it awkwardly: both *in utero*. Her life played out before her just like it did during the first reading, but instead of dreaming glimpses of memories, she relived them. She wasn't aware of her actions, but she flipped the pages quickly, absorbing the words.

The tome fed off her memories, making her mind strong with them and powering her emotions. She felt more alive than ever, knowing this was a unique experience. She sensed the book's power and understood that not everyone could do what she was doing, and their minds would melt from the level of awareness she was obtaining. It was a surreal feeling, and the more she read, the faster she flipped the pages, and the more powerful she felt.

Then, the book showed her minor flaws, such as being an outcast most of her life or a mediocre wizard. It pointed to one glaring weakness that had a feeling of dread wash over her. She knew immediately that the tome was warning her that this flaw would be her downfall. She saw an image of Cass, and her heart raced. She felt anger and hate at first, but a tingling in her stomach that quickly made its way to her crotch replaced those harsh feelings. She became aroused, and as the image of her enemy came further into focus, she smelled the pheromones. She discovered that Cass was not human and had used those pheromones to manipulate her. And still, her excitement grew.

She remembered being used by Cass and Malikai and how good it had felt to give in to those submissive desires. Her despair at losing her friend made it so easy to fall into that role of sex slave, yet even now, knowing that Cassandra lived, Binta wanted to serve Cass. She wished she were there now so Binta could pleasure her. The tome showed her the demon milk that Cass had made her consume. It was the catalyst for Binta's obedience. Mixed with Cass's pheromones, it was the perfect mixture for her to become submissive to the woman for eternity. It was the only true weakness that the tome showed her.

She opened her eyes sometime later after entirely consuming the book, her memories fully restored and the weakness carefully cataloged in the recesses of her mind. As her vision adjusted to the dim lighting offered by the low-burning fire, she found that she still sat in the comfortable chair but viewed the room differently. The view was from higher up, as if she were standing, and she realized the chair was floating about three feet off the floor. She was levitating! She concentrated on that fact and slowly brought the chair down to rest on the floor. She looked wide-eyed at the tome and understood her powers now. As in the words of Inuentas, she had indeed become immense. When she left the cozy little study a few moments later, with the Tome of X'lor tucked under her arm, she was one of the most powerful beings in Pelesea.

THE NEXT DAY, SHE AWAKENED WITH A GREAT SENSE OF PURPOSE. HER thoughts were calm and focused. The sun spilled into the room, and the breeze from the open window gently blew the curtains. She sat up and stretched, letting the warm, late-spring breeze wash over her. She recalled the previous night, and like the last time, she could not remember turning one page. She felt mentally and physically fine but could not recall what was on the pages, even with her new extra-sensory perception. She sat there for some time, contemplating the great book and how it had granted her powers that could genuinely injure others, protect herself, and indeed find her lost friend. Jamison entered the room during her daydreaming with a smile on his face.

"You are awake, I see!" he said, beaming.

"Yes, and someone is happy this morning," she said, snapping out of her trance.

"Well, it is nearly noon, my love, hardly morning."

"Just the same, I am glad to see you in such a fine mood," Binta said, throwing aside the covers and tucking her feet into the slippers at the side of her bed.

She thought it ironic that the slippers had become her routine in such a short time. She couldn't imagine life without them now or why she had never had a pair before. As she contemplated the simple question, Jamison said, "How can I not be in a good mood after last night?"

He took her hand and kissed it, then helped her to a standing position. He looked her up and down in her sheer nightgown, and she knew he could see all her curves through it. He didn't look at her like most men; his staring was appreciative, and she could still feel his love through his lustful gaze.

"Also, the tome is gone," he added.

"Gone?" she repeated, trying to act non-interested.

"Yes, I delivered it myself to Victoria's tower this morning. She met me there and was still very concerned for your health."

"What did you tell her?"

"Well, first, I agreed that I was also concerned, but then I understood that you are an amazing woman and seem to be handling the effects perfectly. We were lucky it did not hurt you, my love, but I am excited to have it out of the house. Now, I can relax and not fret over you so much."

"I am glad, Jamison, and I, too, am happy you removed it," she said, playing along.

"Well, I am off to the castle once more. I may be there a few days before returning. Would you care to join me?"

"How about breakfast first?" she asked, fetching a robe from her closet.

"I have already eaten, but I can have the carriage take you to the castle after you eat."

"That would be splendid," she said with a smile.

He beamed, his smile nearly engulfing his face. "Very well, then. I am off and will see you soon. Enjoy your breakfast, my dear. Be sure to pack enough clothes for a few days; the king is nearing his public announcement of the pending New Order journey, and we will spend a few days within the castle walls."

She nodded and smiled, and that seemed to make him happy. He kissed her gently on the lips and took his leave. She watched the door shut softly behind him, then strolled to the window where the breeze blew her hair. She closed her eyes and relished the feel of the warm sunlight and soft breeze. She felt guilty that she would not see Jamison again before she began her journey to see The Mystic, but he would never let her leave if he knew her true intentions. She felt guilty until she remembered this was for Cassandra, then she steeled her resolve.

She went to the closet and began laying out clothes for her trip. Fancy dresses and high-heeled shoes, everything a proper lady would wear to live in a large city's castle. However, she did not intend to wear these; they were simply for show. Sure enough, Kleve came in shortly after, sent by Jamison, she knew.

"My lady, I trust that you slept well?"

"I did, Kleve, how about you?" she asked, recalling that she had awakened him for the key.

A puzzled look washed over his face, and he scrunched his brow as if thinking. Then, he said, "I slept well but seem to have dreamed something I cannot recall."

"I've done that, and I find it maddening," she said.

"Yes—maddening! That is exactly the word for it, my lady."

He stopped and scratched his head, his eyes going to a place far away as if he was thinking hard about the night before. She just smiled and continued to lay out her dresses on the bed. He eventually snapped out of it and said, "Leave those, my lady. Jamison wants you to be at the castle as quickly as possible. I'll have Rose finish the packing for you."

"That would be nice, Kleve. I am famished," she said with a smile.

They made their way to the kitchen table, and Kleve quickly took her order and made her brunch while she drank her tea. He chatted as he worked, and she smiled politely. She would miss him, Rose, and the carriage driver and stable caretaker, Tumins. She knew Jamison had a gardener, a maid, and several other servants, but she had not met them. The people in this house were amazing, no less so than Jamison, and she made a vow once more to never use her powers on people she cared for; it felt wrong.

An hour later, Binta had eaten her fill, dressed, and packed. Rose had done a marvelous job gathering her things, and her pack lay on the bed, neatly filled with all the expensive clothes she would need.

As she lingered in her room, Tumins waited for her at the front of the mansion. She opened her pack and smiled, took the clothes out, shoes included, and stuffed them under the bed. She then replaced them with her stash of old clothes she owned before moving into the mansion, including the outfit she wore on her quest with Cassandra. Her role as a lady of Pelesea would have to wait. She took the Tome of X'lor from its hiding place under the mattress, recalling that she had taken it from the study and replaced it with another magical book. The tome now tucked away in Victoria's tower was nothing more than a decoy. She left the key for the metal box that had held the decoy under the mattress. She rubbed her hand across the leather cover and smiled, the power of the ancient book pulsating under her fingers. She quickly tucked it under her clothes and sealed the pack.

The last order of business was to take out the crisply folded letter she had penned to Jamison the previous night and lay it on his pillow. She stared at it and understood it would hurt Jamison when he read it. It was an unavoidable evil if she intended to find Cassandra. A light rap on the door broke her from her contemplation.

"Yes?" she called.

Kleve poked his head in. "Are you ready, my lady?"

She smiled and said, "Yes, I am off to the castle, Kleve, and I am so excited!"

Her joyous response made Kleve so distracted and happy that he never noticed the letter when he picked up her bag from the bed and carried it to the carriage. Nor did he suspect he was holding her old clothes and the mighty tome. Rose was there talking to Tumins when they arrived. The sweet woman lit up when she saw Binta and made her way over to hug her tightly.

Binta laughed and said, "Easy, Rose, I just ate!"

"My goodness, please accept my apologies, my lady," she said with a curtsey.

"I will miss both of you, Rose. Take care of Kleve for me," she said, pointing her thumb over her shoulder to the older man who was handing the pack to Tumins to put in the storage compartment of the carriage.

"We will miss you, as well, but my lady, you will only be gone a few days," Rose said with a smile.

Binta felt sad, knowing she would be gone for more than a few days. She didn't know where she was going, but she knew she was going on an adventure, and this time, it would take months to complete, maybe longer.

She hugged them both again, and they shared their goodbyes. Binta waved to them from the carriage as it pulled away. She hoped she would return and that her life could be made in Pelesea, living with Jamison and Cassandra together in perfect harmony. There were lots of doubts in her mind and plenty of obstacles in the way before that could happen. She smiled as the bouncy ride jostled her slightly, and she held up the diamond ring Jamison had offered her. She belonged to him and wore the ring to remind her how much she owed the kind man. She took a steadying breath—the day was about to get interesting.

ςTEELY RESOLVE

THE WHIP CRACKED ONCE MORE, AND KESSI FELT THE EXCRUCI-ating pain as it dug into her back. She screamed out between sobs, but she had little energy left to even cringe with each stinging hit. Merrik had stripped her naked and had whipped her mercilessly. She did not know how many lashes she had taken because, after the second one, the pain was so intense they all ran together. All she knew was that her back felt shredded, and her blood trickled down her legs and dripped off her feet. Her head hung limply, and she vaguely noticed the pool of blood beneath her.

Eventually, the whipping stopped as she struggled to remain conscious. Her back flared with a constant sting that permeated through her body, and her wrists ached from the pull of her binds. She was barely aware of the boots that now stood in the pool of blood. The tips were visible, peeking out from under the black robe of Marnelphion. Merrik was before her, but she couldn't summon the energy to lift her head. She was afraid to try, fearing that any movement would have her back flaring in pain. So, all she did was weep silently. She felt the whip, wet with her blood, rub against her bare crotch, and she lifted her head slightly to find Merrik sneering as he rubbed her with the coiled weapon.

"There, is this what you wanted? You wanted to seduce me, to break my pact with Marnelphion. You wanted to destroy everything we have worked for, didn't you?"

Kessi could not answer and hung her head, resting her chin on her chest. She had thought the man was corruptible, that her charms could seduce him. How could she believe that when she wasn't the least bit interested in him and had no idea how to seduce anyone? She felt the fool and had doomed all her cellmates with her carelessness.

"Don't feel like answering? Well, I'll leave you alone so you can think about what you've done. I'll be back tomorrow for your daily beating," Merrik spat.

That warning crushed Kessi. She could not handle more whipping; her back could not take any more, and she cried all the more thinking of it. She was in such a delirium she did not hear him softly chanting, casting a protective ward upon her. Nor did she hear him instruct the one guard he left at the open door that he was not to touch or defile her in any way. Merrik extinguished the torches before he left, leaving her in total darkness save the little bit of light coming through the open doorway.

She could feel something in that horrible room with her, an otherworldly evil that reminded her of the encounter with Vasheba. She knew without seeing it that a demon or devil was watching her. All seemed lost, and she finally passed out, the pain getting the best of her.

She slipped in and out of consciousness. Her dreams were troubled, filled with visions of horrific creatures murdering innocent people or of tortured children crying for their parents. And as she hung there, her arms and legs spread wide by the metal whipping contraption, alone in the dark and very afraid, she dreamed of home. Sera and Cassandra filled her mind, and she focused on that to distract her from the evil visions that fluttered through her mind. She was in her room, brushing Cassandra's hair again, their mother watching with a smile. Sera's beautiful smile helped her remember there was good in the world. She missed her mother desperately and ignored the whispers in the dark that hinted at Sera's death. She hoped she would see her mother and sister again one day, but the voices in her head said otherwise. Her hope quickly faded. That room contained no hope, so Kessi struggled to maintain it.

Merrik stood before the cell, looking in with a smirk, the coiled whip still red with Kessi's blood. The cell's occupants huddled in the far corner like frightened children. Sabrina stood before them, ready to protect them the best she could. None of them knew what had happened to Kessi, but it was obvious that it had not been a successful ploy.

"Who wants to volunteer to accept the punishment for your friend's crime of seduction?" Merrik spat.

There was a long silence. After many moments, he pointed to Kimmie and said, "You, come here."

Kimmie shook her head and backed further into the corner. Merrik's smile faded, and he gritted his teeth, fishing in his pocket for the key to the cell.

"It looks like you've punished Kessi enough, so leave us alone," Sabrina said.

He looked at her with those horrible grey eyes, and all expression left his face. "She got a taste of what I wanted to do to her. I had to remove myself, or I would have killed her. Therefore, one of you will receive the rest of my wrath."

"I'll do it," Sabrina said as he slid the key into the door and unlocked it.

He opened the door and walked up to her, and she stood, unblinking, eye to eye with him. He leaned close and whispered, "I remember you; you were first to arrive here. I guess that makes you the fearless leader of this group of miserable losers then, doesn't it?"

"I guess," Sabrina whispered, and she swallowed hard despite her best efforts not to.

He backhanded her across the face with blinding speed, knocking her to the ground. As Sabrina shook away the cobwebs, he walked briskly to Kimmie and pulled her from the grasp of several young women who tried to hold her tight. The unrolling of the whip had them letting go and scattering further into the cell. He dragged Kimmie out of the cell before Sabrina ever found her feet. He slammed the door shut and locked it again, a frightened Kimmie at his side.

"Kimmie!" Sabrina cried, finally gaining her feet and going to the bars.

"Don't worry, I'll be brave," Kimmie whispered, nearing tears.

"Will you? Truly?" Merrik teased.

He pushed Kimmie toward Emiline's coffin, where she fell to her knees. "Awaken, Emiline, I have a feast for you!" Merrik cried.

Kimmie looked on with horror as the coffin lid slowly opened.

"No," Sabrina whispered and backed away.

Emiline emerged and stood there, looking down at Kimmie, who was shaking with fright. Emiline turned her head sideways as if trying to figure out why the woman was so afraid.

"Feed on her, but do not kill her," Merrik ordered.

"Feed?" Emiline asked in confusion.

"Yes, you fool, drink her blood, taste her."

"But she is one of the chosen, one I must protect. Matilda demands it."

"You take orders from me, and I command you to do this," Merrik said with more conviction, presenting his unholy, skull-shaped symbol to the vampire.

Emiline seemed not to flinch at first, but it was quickly apparent that the symbol of Marnelphion compelled her to listen to the priest. Kimmie finally snapped out of her daze as she watched the vampire's eyes grow wild and her gentle smile turn into a snarl. The young woman was up quickly, running back to the cell. Emiline was faster, though, and caught Kimmie well before she reached the door, grabbing her from behind and pulling her head back roughly. The vampire hissed and bared her fangs, her mouth only inches away from the petrified Kimmie's neck.

"Excellent! Now feed!" Merrik ordered.

"No!" Sabrina protested, reaching an arm through the bars and trying to get to her friend.

Emiline growled and bit hard into Kimmie's soft neck. Kimmie let out a yelp, but it was cut short by the immense pain, her face contorted into one of abject horror. Her mouth moved slightly, but no words came forth. The sickening sound of Emiline sucking the lifeblood from the poor girl only added to the horrific scene. All but Sabrina fell back, most gently sobbing at the spectacle. A line of blood poured forth from the wound and ran down Kimmie's blouse.

Merrik turned toward Sabrina with a confident smirk and said, "So, let this be a lesson. If any of you try something like Kessi did, this will be your punishment."

He leaned in further and whispered, "And if you think this is bad, wait until Matilda learns of your treason. It is too late for Kessi, but you still have hope. Keep your cellmates under control, and Matilda won't learn that all of you played a part in Kessi's failed attempt to seduce me."

"Please make her stop," Sabrina said, her voice quivering and her eyes locked on Emiline.

Merrik turned to find Kimmie very pale as Emiline continued to drink her blood. The vampire's eyes were wild with blood lust, and she was close to killing the young woman.

"Enough!" Merrik demanded, presenting his unholy symbol once more.

Emiline growled and backed toward her coffin, dragging Kimmie as a wolf might drag the carcass of a fresh kill.

"I order you to stop, vampire filth!"

Emiline dropped her meal, and Kimmie fell unconscious to the floor. "Back to your hole, Emiline."

The vampire's wild look slowly faded, and she looked like an innocent elf once more, but with blood smeared around her lips and running down her chin. She whimpered and went back to her coffin, gently shutting the lid.

"You will not eat this night, none of you!" Merrik growled. "And if you rebel again, I will cast all of you out of this comfortable cell, and there will be no more fresh meals as you sleep with the stinking slaves. Do you understand me?"

Sabrina nodded, and Merrik went to Kimmie and kicked her in the side. Her moan indicated she was still alive, so he gave one last evil smile toward Sabrina and left. He conversed with the guards on the far side of Emiline's cell, ordering them to put Kimmie back in her cell. They didn't seem thrilled about entering Emiline's lair; they had not entered it since Matilda had left weeks earlier. They were afraid of Emiline, and with good reason. Reluctantly, they entered and quickly moved Kimmie back into her cell, dragging her roughly, all the while keeping an eye on the coffin. As they left and hurried through Emiline's cell and back to their post in the hall, Sabrina looked over Kimmie.

"Is she all right?" Sara asked, wiping away her tears.

"I don't know, Sara. She looks pale as death, but she is breathing."

"Barely," Natasha added.

Sabrina locked eyes with Natasha, and they shared a silent communication that neither was confident Kimmie would survive the attack. Then Natasha shrieked, and her eyes grew wide. Something behind Sabrina took her breath away. Sabrina's cellmates reacted the same way as they took in the sight. Sabrina slowly stood, and it took her a very long time to turn around and see what everyone was upset about. She had a feeling before she even turned what she would find there, but seeing the vampire standing at the bars, blood staining her pale chin, made the hairs stand on her neck.

"Emiline," Sabrina managed to whisper.

"She is dead?" Emiline asked, pointing to Kimmie's still form.

"No, not yet."

"I did not mean …" Emiline began, but she bowed her head as her words trailed off.

Sabrina inched to the bars and whispered, "It is not your fault, Emiline. That awful man made you."

The vampire looked up, and fresh tears streaked her face. Her gentle façade gave the other women courage, and they came to stand behind Sabrina.

"He was in my head. I did not mean to hurt her," Emiline said, and her shoulders began to bob up and down as she sobbed quietly, hanging her head once more.

"Help us, Emiline, so that we can help you. You are not a monster and are as much of a prisoner here as we are. We are all doomed unless we help each other. Will you assist us?" Sabrina asked.

"Yes, help us, Emiline, and we can escape this horrid place," Natasha added, moving to stand beside Sabrina.

"I cannot; the evil man will make me do bad things," Emiline said, then looked over her shoulder to the guards outside her cell, whispering and oblivious to the fact that the vampire was out of her coffin. She turned back and softly added, "And the one named Cerus hates me. He beats me when Matilda is away."

Sabrina and Natasha shared a concerned look, and Sabrina said, "All the more reason to get you out of here before he returns."

"I cannot," Emiline said, shaking her head and wiping her tears. "I am afraid."

"We all are, Emiline, but if we work together, we can save Kessi and leave this place," Natasha said.

"Kessi?"

"Yes, the one that evil man took from here earlier today. Remember her?" Natasha said.

Emiline cocked her head, a look of confusion plastered across her face as she tried to recall the events.

"She knows Heinsvick," Sara added from behind.

"Heinsvick?" Emiline said, her eyes growing wide.

"That's right. Heinsvick. She knows him, Emiline, and he sent her here to bring you home. She can lead you back to him," Sabrina added excitedly.

"Heinsvick doesn't want me anymore," Emiline said, nearing tears again.

"That's what Matilda has told you, but I have a feeling that is far from the truth. We need to find Kessi before they kill her. If she dies, we'll never know," Sabrina said.

"How?" Emiline asked doubtfully.

"We need a key to open this door," Sabrina said.

"A key?"

"Yes, if we can unlock this door, I have a plan."

Emiline pulled on the door, and with a loud, metallic screech, it opened, her unnatural strength breaking the locking mechanism. The sound gained the guards' attention, and one yelled into the cell, "Keep it down, or we'll fetch Merrik!"

"By the gods, that thing is out!" the other guard said, noticing Emiline.

They both walked backward down the hall, far enough away from the volatile vampire to feel a little safer, but still close enough to keep any eye on the prisoners. They were mercenaries hired by Cerus and had little experience with the undead, especially those as powerful and dangerous as vampires.

"Emiline, you can escape these cells?" Sabrina asked in amazement.

"You could have escaped long ago," Natasha added.

Emiline shrugged, and Natasha stood there at a loss for words. A smile crept across Sabrina's face, and she said, "I have a plan."

THE FOLLOWING DAY, MERRIK ENTERED EMILINE'S CELL ALONG WITH two slaves carrying sacks of food over their backs. It was a familiar procession. The emaciated slaves, living on crusts of bread and little water, barely had the energy to carry the food. Sabrina's cellmates had grown to three dozen, so the amount of food had gradually increased, adding to their burden. All of the cellmates felt guilty over this arrangement, and Kessi had started the ritual of giving the poor men pieces of their food when the guards weren't looking. They all felt guilty at the sight of the men staggering under the weight of the foodstuffs, and the look in their eyes when they received food meant everything to Sabrina and the other virgins.

Merrik walked behind them, his coiled whip at the ready. All seemed normal. The women were huddled at the back of their cell as they had been trained, eager for food after having none the evening before. The slaves were struggling, but neither dared to stop or drop their sacks for fear of death. And so it was with great surprise that Merrik noticed Emiline inside the virgins' cell as he fumbled for his keys.

"What are you doing in there, Emiline?" he asked.

Her eyes were wild, and she stood deep within the cell like a shadow. Merrik tried to blink away the vision as if he did not believe what he saw. He never heard Sabrina move out of the coffin where she had rested through the night, a large rock in her hand. The stones were plentiful because when Matilda was about, she forced the slaves to dig regularly to expand the cell that Sabrina and the others called home. The guards carefully removed all debris after such digs, but sometimes, they forgot a few pieces. The one in Sabrina's hand was the size of an apple, a more significant piece than she hoped for and a perfect weapon for bashing skulls.

The slaves saw her coming and moved slightly out of the way, their eyes wide with hope. Merrik presented his unholy symbol and ordered Emiline out of the cell. That was when he discovered he no longer needed a key, as the cell door was slightly open.

"What?" he managed to squeak before turning suddenly to face Sabrina.

It was too late; the attack was already coming. The stone cracked Merrik on the forehead, knocking him off balance enough to fall against the bars of the cell. The strike wasn't perfect, and Sabrina knew she needed to hit him again quickly before he could use any of his god-given powers against her. She raised her hand for another strike but stopped when she realized Emiline had grabbed Merrik from behind the bars, pulling him tight.

He tried to present his symbol, a desperate move to ward off the vicious vampire, but he fumbled with it, and the delay cost him dearly. Blood ran in his eyes from Sabrina's strike, making the situation even more desperate. Finally, he grasped the tiny skull symbol, but before he could use it against either Sabrina or Emiline, the vampire grabbed both sides of his head and turned it hard, snapping his neck. His eyes were wide, and he tried to speak, his mouth quivering but with no words coming. Eventually, he fell to the floor, dead well before landing in a crumpled heap.

Sabrina turned to regard the slaves, who had dropped the sacks of food and quickly stepped away as if trying not to gain Emiline's attention. Sabrina began to speak but was cut off by one of the guards on the far side of Emiline's cell. "What's going on in there?"

The two guards noticed Merrik and whispered something to each other. Soon, one ran off. The other one drew his sword and backed away in the same direction like a frightened child. It seemed like a slight breeze would startle him enough to run in fear.

"Emiline, you must stop them. If they alert the rest of the complex, we're doomed," Sabrina pleaded.

Emiline busted through the broken cell door and ran to the other side of the cell so quickly that she appeared a blur to all who witnessed it. One of the slaves let out a yelp and threw up his arm, falling on the seat of his pants. But Emiline was not interested in anything but stopping the two guards, so she hardly noticed him. When she reached the far side of the cell, she slammed it open, pieces of the broken lock flying away.

The remaining guard had already turned, yelled for the other guard to hurry, and ran as fast as possible. He still had his sword drawn but did not attempt to use it, the fear of the vampire keeping him running as quickly as his legs could carry him. It wasn't fast enough as Emiline pounced on his back and bit deep into his neck. He screamed and stabbed his sword over his shoulder. The desperate guard would have impaled her in the face if she had not quickly grabbed the blade. He sawed at her hand, the pain and fear making his attack desperate and ineffective. Still, the blade cut deep grooves in Emiline's palm, so she did the only thing she could and ripped his neck open. She pulled muscle and tendons and severed an artery.

The guard fell to the ground, dropping his sword and bringing his hands to his torn neck. He squirmed and cried and bled. Emiline froze at the sight of it, and if her hand had not ached and dripped with her blood, she would most likely have fed on the dying man. Instead, she brought her wounded hand to her face and stared at it, tilting her head sideways as always when she couldn't quite remember something. Then, the vampire recalled the other guard. With a growl, she ran on with her supernatural speed. Even with her quickness, she could not catch the man before he reached the next door that led out of the prison area. Luck was with Emiline, though, as that door was locked and unguarded. If Cerus's men had been in Nesin, there never would have been a chance of such an important portal being unguarded. As it was, the mercenaries had left it unattended.

The man desperately yelled for help, peeking over his shoulder at her as he did. He exuded fear, and Emiline grew tired of it and his obnoxious screaming. So, she killed him before anyone heard his cries. Emiline was not dumb and knew enough to return both bodies to her cell. When she arrived, the two starving slaves ate hungrily from the sacks they had carried as Sabrina unlocked their shackles with the key she had liberated from Merrik's corpse.

"Emiline, you did well!" Natasha said.

The two slaves, as hungry as they were, both stopped eating and watched intently for Emiline's next move.

"Emiline, this is Fredor and Mensh. They know the layout of this place because they have worked in various locations within the complex. They can help us," Sabrina explained.

"Uhh, nice to meet you," Fredor said, then swallowed hard, choking slightly on the biscuit he had just devoured.

Emiline stood there, expressionless, holding the two corpses up by their collars. The pale faces and torn necks unnerved them all, and it took the vampire a few moments to understand that.

"Emiline, you may put them down now," Sabrina said.

Emiline looked at the two dead men in her hands and tossed them aside. She then turned on Fredor and Mensh just as Sabrina unlocked the shackles on their feet. They both dropped their food and staggered backward, fear evident on their faces. Emiline, with an unnatural quickness, reached behind her back and pulled forth the dead guards' swords, which she had tucked in her belt. She offered the men the swords. They stared blankly at them, not understanding the gesture and indeed not trusting the vampire.

Sabrina smiled and said, "She is offering you the weapons. Do either of you have a skill set for using them?"

A few moments passed before Fredor reached up and took one. Mensh followed suit and said, "I can use one."

"Good, then eat quickly, and let's go. Today, we leave Nesin!" Sabrina said.

There was a small but muted cheer from the three dozen girls who had become like family. They were armed with two swords, a vampire, and keys to take them anywhere in the fortress. They dared not hope, but they were all starting to believe they had a chance at freedom, the first time they had felt that since coming to the mountain fortress. Even Kimmie, in her weakened state, seemed to come alive with the possibility, but she still kept a safe distance from Emiline. The vampire was dangerous but powerful, and there was hope if Emiline remained an ally. None knew how long that allegiance would last, especially without Kessi.

"Now let's find Kessi and go home," Sabrina said after they shared a speedy breakfast. The group finally left their cell a short time later, hoping to do just that.

Cassandra awakened to the dull sound of wood striking wood. In her grogginess, she could not remember where she was. With the strange sound and the heat of the desert sweltering in the room, she briefly thought she was in the barbarian training pit. The sticks sounded very familiar to her, and she was sure she heard wooden practice weapons smacking together nearby. When she finally gained her bearings, she remembered where she was, and she recalled her gracious hosts, Sitra and Mateon. She was safe for now, but how long would it last? She sat at the edge of her bed, feeling weak and shaky. She looked at her blackened forearms and thought that perhaps the swelling and the bruising had diminished slightly. She ran her tongue over her gums, and for the first time in a long while, they seemed less painful.

"Cassandra, my friend!" came a small cry above her.

Cassandra looked up, which hurt her head slightly, to find Gophia peering over her makeshift bed on the wall above her. Cassandra was unaccustomed to the smile on the fairy's face, and she realized then that she had never seen the creature smile. She recalled that the entire time she had known the little fairy, Gophia had been a prisoner and did not have much to smile about. Now, her smile engulfed her tiny face. She flew down to Cassandra, her butterfly wings quickly taking her to Cassandra's shoulder, where she landed. She hugged the side of Cassandra's face and made a noise that sounded to Cassandra like a cat purring.

"Gophia, also my friend," Cassandra said, relishing the tiny hug.

"You live, and Gophia is so happy," the fairy said.

She flitted around the room in her excitement, laughing all the while. Cassandra could not help but smile, having never seen her new friend act this way. If she listened closely enough, she could hear a sound similar to tiny bells ringing every time Gophia giggled.

After many moments, Gophia landed on her shoulder again and tangled herself in Cassandra's hair. Cassandra loved the bond she shared with the fairy, and it was evident that the fairy felt the same way. Both would be dead or, at the very least, prisoners to the barbarians if they had not helped each other, and their bond was strong because of it.

Cassandra summoned the strength to stand and nearly toppled over. She pitched forward so hard that Gophia had to take flight once more. As Cassandra steadied herself and waited for the dizziness to pass, the little fairy flew around her face, a concerned expression now plastered there.

"Do not be so concerned, my friend; I am just weak. I haven't been on my feet for quite a while. My strength will return, do not doubt. I'm on my way to recovering, thanks to you."

Cassandra brushed her hair from her shoulder and tapped it lightly with her hand. "Come, let's find out what this racket is that woke me from my deep slumber."

Gophia's smile returned quickly, and she took her spot on Cassandra's right shoulder. Cassandra felt her bury herself in her hair as if she were hiding. Perhaps that is what culiem fairies did; Cassandra didn't know. But she liked it and felt somehow protected with the hidden creature close to her.

The whacking of stick weapons seemed to come from outside, and as Cassandra made her way to the open door, the desert sun poured into the stone structure. The house was not large; the ceiling was only a few feet above her head, and the room she had slept in for weeks, maybe months, was quaint and cozy. The room she found herself in now was very decorative. Many plants hung near the windows, and the painted walls reflected greens, yellows, and reds. Woven rugs and tapestries adorned the floor and walls; beautiful furniture filled every corner. For something so simple, Cassandra found the room quite breathtaking. She walked gingerly to the open door on the far side that led into the desert.

She made her way into the marvelous evening sun, squinting away the brightness the best she could. Despite her efforts, she was temporarily blinded, the intense desert sun overpowering her from having not been outside in so many weeks. The cadence of the sound intensified, and she knew it was near. She could see two blurry figures dancing in the sand about twenty yards from where she stood. As her vision slowly became focused, she discovered Mateon and Sitra were having a sparring match: Mateon and his staff and Sitra with a wooden practice sword. They struck, dodged, and moved in perfect rhythm. The sound she had followed was the banging of their weapons with each successful parry.

Mateon was blind, and Sitra was blindfolded, fighting equally without sight as her husband. However, their moves were as graceful and coordinated as any warrior she had witnessed. The scene took her back to her months living with the barbarians, who were more about brute strength. The two warriors before her were disciplined and proficient. She watched in amazed silence as the two battled, sensing openings without using their eyes, sensing attacks before they ever came. Cassandra now had a vast knowledge of melee weapons, but she had never seen a show like the one before her.

"Amazing," she whispered.

Both warriors stopped, stuck in a parry, and remained perfectly still. They broke the parry at the same time and turned in Cassandra's direction.

"You're awake!" Mateon exclaimed.

"Yes, but how—"

"How did we know you were there?" Sitra asked for her.

"Yes, I mean, well, yes."

Sitra smiled, and both husband and wife made their way to stand before her. Sweat poured from both, and it looked like they had been at it for quite a while. Mateon's knuckles were bloody, but other than that, neither fighter showed a wound.

"We use senses other than our eyes. I have done this for so long that I have become proficient at blind fighting," Sitra explained.

"I can vouch for her," Mateon added, holding his injured hand.

"That was a lucky hit; you fell," Sitra said, blowing off the compliment.

"Still, if that had been a real sword you wielded, I would have lost my fingers."

"Well, that means I won this evening's contest, and you are cooking dinner."

With a sigh, Mateon nodded. "I believe you are correct. If you ladies will excuse me, I need to start cooking and will do so after a nice bath," he said, kissing Sitra on the cheek and taking his leave.

"How do you feel?" Sitra asked after Mateon was inside the tiny house.

"Weak, but much better," Cassandra said.

"Come, sit over here," Sitra said, motioning to several large rocks. "This is one of my favorite spots. I love to sit here, think, and feel the warm sun on my face."

They sat silently before Sitra said, "I see Gophia is happy with you finally awake." Gophia's tiny laugh followed, and Cassandra felt her move slightly on her shoulder.

"How did you know Gophia was with me?"

"Because I can hear her breathe and sometimes make that purring sound when she is pleased."

"That is truly amazing; I wish I could do that," Cassandra said.

"I can show you how."

"How to what?"

"Fight without using your eyes. To use all of your senses when engaged, not just your vision. I can teach you to fight blindly."

"To what end?" Cassandra said, a cloud moving over her face, one that Sitra could not see but surely noticed.

"What troubles you?" Sitra asked, taking the ribbon from her hair and shaking her tiny strands of snake hair loose.

Cassandra was taken aback by the vision, forgetting that skinny snakes comprised Sitra's hair. They slithered in unison, giving the illusion her hair was blowing in a gentle breeze. Cassandra studied Sitra for the first time since becoming her guest and quickly developed an appreciation for how beautiful the woman indeed was. By all accounts, she was stunning, but with the slight physical manifestation of having snakes for hair. But that wasn't enough to detract from her beauty.

"You have a story to tell, and I hope you share it in time. For now, I say we focus on making you whole," Sitra said, making Cassandra look away.

"I feel much better," Cassandra said honestly. "Thanks to you and Mateon," she added.

"And Gophia," said the tiny voice from her shoulder, somewhere within her hair.

"And Gophia," Cassandra agreed, and they all laughed.

"You need water, food, and most of all, a bath," Sitra said after the laughter finally died.

"Excuse me?"

"You have been a guest in my home for many weeks. I have fed, watered, and healed you but not bathed you. I am sweaty, but you are the one who stinks, Cassandra."

Cassandra was about to lash out at the insult, to say something degrading about Sitra, but her anger melted away as quickly as it came. Sitra smiled and patted Cassandra's leg, and she understood that this place was different. Cassandra was safe, and these were good people. There was no need to defend herself as she always had in the past; there were no insults or threats here.

"Then let's bathe and then eat. I am starving!" Cassandra said with a smile.

"Come with me. I will take you to the springs," Sitra offered, and she held out her hand for Cassandra to take.

Again, Cassandra had to tell herself she was safe with Sitra. She didn't know the lovely couple, and she didn't know exactly how far away she was from the barbarian tribe; she wondered if she was truly out of harm's way. She kept her guard up because she had trusted people before; she thought of Boz, Cass, Greyson, and others she had erroneously trusted. They had all let her down, so she kept her guard, even if minimally. After all, she had been here for weeks, and they had not harmed her but had healed and watched over her. Cassandra liked Mateon and Sitra and owed it to them to trust them. She only recalled bits and pieces of the events leading up to being a guest in their home. Cassandra then remembered the symbol of

Gella, which she had found in the tangle of dead bodies. She instinctively reached up to feel it around her neck, but it was gone.

With her hand still extended, Sitra asked, "Is everything all right?"

"My things. Where are they?"

"Your things? You hardly had any possessions when you arrived."

"I had a necklace, maybe not around my neck, but perhaps in my hand. Did you see a necklace?" Cassandra asked, nearing a panic.

"Come with me," Sitra said, beckoning Cassandra to take her hand.

Cassandra did, and Sitra led her back inside and to her room. There, Gophia flew out of Cassandra's hair and landed on her tiny bed, exhaustion overtaking her. Gophia fell asleep almost immediately, and Cassandra smiled at how fast her new friend fell unconscious. Perhaps it was a fairy trait, and her smile grew as she knew she would learn the different characteristics her new friend possessed in the coming weeks. Sitra went to a wicker basket and removed the lid. Inside was a change of clothes and Gella's medallion. Cassandra knelt and took the medallion in her hand, holding it to the light by the thin chain.

"The chain was broken, so Mateon took the liberty to repair it for you. I hope that is all right."

Cassandra slipped the chain over her head and grasped the symbol tightly. She could feel the positive energy it exuded running through her hand, nearly making her weep. She felt very close to her goddess then, knowing she could fully trust her hosts.

"Yes, it is perfect. The two of you have been so kind to me."

"Would you expect anything different?" Sitra asked, puzzled.

"Yes, I would," Cassandra admitted sadly.

"Ah, yes, I hope you will share your story with us."

"It's not a tale I'm anxious to share."

"In your own time, then."

"Yes, perhaps," Cassandra said. Then she added, "Also, these clothes are beautiful, both what I am wearing and those in the basket, but they are not mine."

"I know, they are mine. You look about the same size as me, so I dressed you in some of my most comfortable clothes," Sitra said with a kind smile.

Cassandra's eyes widened at the thought of someone dressing her, but Sitra seemed to read her mind and added, "Don't worry, Mateon was out with Grog when I dressed you, and he hasn't seen you nude. He is blind, remember?"

"Grog?" Cassandra asked to change the subject.

"Yes, our closest neighbor. You will meet him soon enough. But first, please, to the baths."

Cassandra laughed. "Yes, I could use a good soak, please."

"Come along," Sitra said, taking Cassandra's hand. "Grab that change of clothes, if you will."

Cassandra did, and soon they were in a small storage room at the back of the house. This was the only room that Cassandra didn't find inviting. There were no windows, and it was dark, with no furnishings other than some racks for storing supplies such as food, blankets, and clothing. There were also some chests neatly arranged on one side, all locked. A large rug adorned the center of the room, but nothing else seemed cozy about the little area.

"Why are we here?" Cassandra asked.

"I'm about to show you our real home."

"What?"

Sitra released Cassandra's hand and walked to one of the nearby storage racks. Once there, she reached behind a blanket on the second shelf and pulled a lever. There was a click, and then the floor under the rug popped up, showing a trap door underneath, the same size as the rug.

"The door will seal again in but a moment, so hurry," Sitra said, grabbing the edge of the door and holding it up for Cassandra.

The rug never moved, obviously attached to the door. Underneath the door, light and wonderful smells rushed into the small, unadorned room. Cassandra could see a ladder, and after Sitra's reassuring nod, Cassandra climbed down. Sitra followed closely behind, the trap door shutting quickly behind them.

The ladder took them about twenty feet into a natural cavern, and the air was warm, with many pleasant scents assaulting them. Cassandra could smell a solid citrusy aroma mixed with vegetables. A vine that ran along the ceilings and walls lit the place, its leaves glowing purple and blue. The hallway led in one direction but looked to branch off in several areas. It eventually spilled into a large room about fifty yards away, where Cassandra could see many large containers holding leafy plants. Some of those plants sprouted lemons or other fruits, and Cassandra recalled Mateon's affinity for lemons.

"What is this place?" Cassandra asked.

"Paradise," Sitra answered with a smile, and she retook Cassandra's hand, leading her on.

They passed a few rooms that seemed to be fully furnished bedrooms, the strange vines giving each one they walked by a continuous happy glow. Two hallways branched away from the main corridor, one to the left and one to the right. Sitra told her that the one to the right would take them to the natural spring, where they would bathe. However, Mateon was still there, so they had to wait. That was evident by the man's awful singing, which echoed up the hall from that direction. They shared another laugh and moved on.

The hallway to the left spilled into a massive living area with plush furnishings. Bookshelves holding hundreds of books lined the far wall. Cassandra reasoned that if she weren't there, Sitra would not be wearing the blindfold, and she must enjoy reading. The large room had many lovely furnishings and even a plush bed of pillows. The vines were thick in this room, making it bright and cheery.

Next, Sitra took her back to the corridor and continued to the large room housing the produce, Mateon's singing still resonating from the passage leading to the spring. The room was several hundred yards long, and many plants hung from containers tethered to the ceiling. There was no soil, and the roots wrapped around the metal contraptions that suspended them in the air and eventually ran into a water basin. The heart of the glowing vines spread across the ceiling and flowered in many locations, the flowers shining beams of purple and blue in many different directions. Water from the natural spring ran along pipes in the ceiling and dripped down into the plant holders. The various scents were intoxicating, reminding Cassandra she had not eaten real food in many days.

"Hydrofarming. No soil is required, and we can grow things that naturally do not grow in the desert. Also, the plant, called a falinca vine, gives off enough light to replicate the effects of the sun, but in a gentler way," Sitra said, pointing to the magnificent plant adorning the ceiling.

"How did you even put this together? Does anyone else know about this?" Cassandra asked in awe.

"No, just the four of us."

"You trust Gophia and me with this amazing secret, even though you do not know us?"

"Yes, we know people and trust you, Cassandra Rho."

"Where did this glowing plant come from, and how did you engineer such an amazing farm?"

"The plant is natural to the area, and when Mateon and I stumbled across these caves years ago, it was already here, thriving. Mateon's parents were farmers and had already invented the hydrofarming process, so he implemented it easily enough. Mateon installed the pipes to route water from the spring to this room. We gathered seeds from various places and began the process of planting and growing. You must remember that everything you see before you has taken decades to build and with nurturing hands."

Cassandra was left speechless, and Sitra showed her the many rows of plants, identifying each one. Some Cassandra knew, others she did not, but one thing was sure—it was indeed an underground paradise. Mateon came out of the bath area shortly after and grabbed one of the many baskets near the entrance to the unique garden. He began picking fruits and vegetables for dinner, and Cassandra and Sitra made their way to the spring.

The bath was so relaxing for Cassandra, and in that blissful moment, she realized she was experiencing something that had been missing her entire life—happiness. She was happy here and could see a life for her in the desert with her new friends. She had some thinking to do, and as she closed her eyes and meditated on those things in the nice, warm bath, Sitra once again amazed her.

"You don't have to tell us, but we would appreciate knowing your story. Where you came from, how you came to be at our house, and where you plan to go next," Sitra said.

Cassandra cracked an eye open and looked toward Sitra, who similarly held her head back against the edge of the spring, meditating and enjoying the feel of the warm water. She smiled and closed her eyes. How could this woman, obviously blindfolded, know when she had something on her mind?

"No pressure, but it would be nice to know," Sitra added.

Cassandra never answered, but she understood she had some soul-searching to do. She decided that this was the perfect place to do that. They did not speak again until they were clean and ready for supper. As they returned to the house, Cassandra decided she owed it to them to tell them everything.

She did not feel up to the task but Sitra had asked multiple times, so she would be honest.

The dinner was incredible, as Mateon had made a lemon steak out of wild antelope plentiful in that part of the Yaddaton Desert. The food was unlike anything Cassandra had tried before, and she ate her fill. After the main course, Mateon served them a yam pie, which was better than Cassandra thought it would be. They sat around the table, all full and relaxed, except for Gophia, who was still nibbling on some pie. Cassandra decided to tell her story.

"So, you want to know about me, and I think that is fair. I appreciate what you have done for me. You saved me, and I am eternally grateful," Cassandra began.

"And Gophia!" the little fairy said, yam pie smeared across her tiny face.

"And you, Gophia; I am especially grateful for you," Cassandra added with a smile. That appeased the fairy, and she smiled and returned to her work on the dessert.

Cassandra took a deep breath and proceeded. "I was born an orphan nearly twenty years ago and grew up in a small town called Oldorburg, across the Nepress Sea. My only fond memories of that place are times spent with my sister and my mothers."

"Mothers?" Mateon asked.

"Yes, orphanage workers are assigned to the orphans. They essentially become mothers, at least the closest things we have to them. Kessi, my sister, and I were assigned two because the first one was killed by wolves when we were five years old."

"I'm sorry, Cassandra," Sitra said.

Cassandra's eyes welled with tears, and she took a moment to hold them back. She suddenly realized how tragic her life story would sound as she sorted out the details. After a few moments spent collecting herself, she continued, "I learned from an early age that I can summon and control ravens."

"Ravens?" Sitra asked.

"Yes, large black birds. They are brilliant, and I have a kinship with them. I don't know how or why. Also, I can see magic symbols floating in the air when I focus on them. I can manipulate and use them to cast spells."

"Symbols?" Mateon asked.

"Yes, they are strange, geometrically shaped symbols that give all spells their structure."

"You are a wizard, then?" Sitra asked. "That is why the barbarians inserted the cactus needles into your arms and gums?"

"No, and yes. I'm not a wizard in the traditional sense. I can cast spells without using clumsy components or a spellbook. Some people have called me a witch, and I guess that description fits as well as any. As you suggested, the barbarians used the needles because of my affinity for magic."

There were a few moments of silence as Sitra thoughtfully processed the information.

"Gophia here is a great source of arcane symbols; they float all about her. That is the reason I was able to escape."

Gophia looked up from eating at the mention of her name and patted her belly. She let out a tiny burp, which again sounded like little bells ringing. She then flew up to Cassandra's shoulder and found her hiding spot within her hair.

Cassandra smiled and found the strength to continue. "To make a long story short, my powers were deemed unlawful by the sheriff of Oldorburg, which set off a sequence of events that included two arrests, two near rapes, two kidnappings, and finally captivity by the barbarians."

"That is an amazing story," Sitra whispered.

"Well, that's not everything. I have also discovered that I am the center of some evil prophecy set in motion by the gods themselves."

"Oh?" both asked in unison.

A smile creased their faces, and they found each other's hand, their love evident. Cassandra longed for that, making her sad to think she might never experience it.

"Yes, supposedly I am a sacrifice that will bring back the demon lord Marnelphion. Oddly enough, the prophecy suggests that I will use my birthright to smite the beast and send it back to hell."

"But how can you do that if you are dead?" Mateon asked.

"Exactly. I have no answers for that one, but I assure you as the days pass, I become more convinced it's real. I have had a recurring dream over the last few years, one that shows my birthright and where to find it. I believe it is near to where we sit at this very moment."

Cassandra noticed how their hands tightened at the news, their grasp strong as if the act would generate enough love between them to ward off an evil prophecy.

"So, what is your next move?" Sitra asked.

"I simply don't know. I am tired of the games and all the bad stuff that seems to follow me. I have no family now, a casualty to this prophecy."

"Your mother and sister?" Sitra asked.

"Yes, my second mother was a beautiful woman both inside and out. I did not give her a chance for many years because I did not want to be hurt again," Cassandra explained. That finally started the flow of tears, and she had to take a few moments to compose herself.

"Now she is dead because of me, and I wish I had not wasted so many years when I had her there beside me."

They sat silently for a long time before Mateon finally said, "And your sister?"

Cassandra shrugged and said, "I do not know. I have no proof that she is dead, but if Ronnis has any say in the matter, I'm sure she is gone as well."

"Ronnis?" Sitra asked.

"Yes, the administrator of the Oldorburg Orphanage. He hates me, and the feeling is mutual. I tried to kill him because of the way he treated my mother and because he kept pushing me. I wish I'd succeeded, because he will stop at nothing to find me and kill me. He is the one responsible for killing my second mother. I flee from him as much as I do the prophecy."

"When will this prophecy occur? I mean to say, when are you to be sacrificed?" Sitra asked.

"What season is it?"

"What?" Mateon asked.

"The season? I have not been well, and there have been no seasons in the desert since coming here, so I have difficulty telling the time of year. I believe it was spring when I finally escaped the barbarians."

"We are in the first days of summer," Mateon said.

"It will be next fall, near my 21st birthday."

"So, what are your plans now?" Sitra asked.

Cassandra shrugged again, saying, "I have none other than to stay here as long as you allow me to."

"But you said you are close to your birthright?"

"Yes, I am, Sitra, because my father guides me to it."

"Your father? I thought you were an orphan?" Mateon said.

"I have recently discovered that my father is a self-made god who is using me like a pawn to fight the prophecy."

"So, you are a demi-god?" Mateon asked with amazement.

"Well, I haven't thought of it that way, but yes, I guess I am."

"But you are tired of the game," Sitra reasoned.

"Yes, very much. I have lost everything because of this stupid game the gods are playing with my life. I grow weary."

There was a long silence, and the cool desert night air started filtering into the cozy house. Mateon excused himself so he could shut the door and shutters. It grew cold in the desert at night, even in the summer.

Cassandra suddenly felt very tired and wanted to go to bed. "So, that's it," she said.

She watched Sitra's reaction and understood the woman was unhappy with the lack of details but let it go. The two sat there quietly as Mateon completed his chore.

Finally, Sitra spoke. "And your sister?"

"Like I said, she is lost."

"But you just said you do not know for certain."

"No, I don't, but I have little energy to play this game. I don't know where or how to begin if I want to find Kessi."

"I understand that, Cassandra, but your love for your sister should spur you to find her. And surely there are others?"

"Other what?"

"Friends or loved ones back home. Surely you want to be reunited?"

Cassandra thought of Binta then, and the tears flowed quickly. She broke down into a sob, which made Gophia flutter out of her hiding spot and land on the table, watching her friend's distress with great concern. The crying only grew stronger as Cassandra finally released the pent-up pain and frustration from a lifetime of abuse. Sitra was there and hugged her tight. Cassandra wasn't necessarily the hugging type, but she accepted the embrace and cried on Sitra's shoulder. She just let it out and cleared her mind of Binta, Kessi, Sera, and any other memories that brought her grief. She focused only on the tiny serpent tongues that flicked against her neck and face, the many tongues of Sitra's snake-like hair.

THE CARRIAGE STOPPED AT THE CASTLE GATES, AND FOUR ARMED MEN came to greet it. Binta stepped out as Tumins was chatting with the castle guards.

"I present to you Miss Mulay, the first lady of the new steward," Tumins said from atop the carriage.

"Lady," the lead guard said and bowed.

"Tell Jamison to send for me if there is anything you need or anywhere you'd like to go, my lady," Tumins said.

"I will, thank you," Binta said, waving.

The guard took the one pack she had brought along. A strange look passed over his face as he studied it.

"What is it, master guardsman?"

"Oh, nothing, except this pack seems well-traveled and lightly packed. I figured the steward's lady would need room for all her outfits."

"Let's just say I don't plan on staying long," Binta said with a smile.

"Very well. Jamison has been expecting you, so if you'll follow me," the guard said and started through the gate.

"Shut and lock the gate after we are through, and do not open it until I return," he said as they passed the other three guards.

"Yes, sir," one confirmed.

The gate clanged shut behind them, and Binta could hear the carriage leaving simultaneously. She heard many things, primarily thoughts from the four men in her immediate vicinity, but elected not to listen. The thoughts were theirs, and she had no business intruding. She could control her powers much better now and intended not to take advantage of other people's secrets unless it helped the greater good. As they approached the grand castle that towered before her, her attention turned toward the thick, lush garden. Bees and hummingbirds fluttered about, and the smell of odiferous plants was thick.

"Master guardsman, may I ask you a question?" Binta said, stopping.

The guard turned to her and said, "Of course, my lady."

"First, what is your name?"

"I am Jespen, captain of the castle guard, at your service," he said, his smile beaming.

"Oh, what an honor to have the captain escort me to the castle."

"It's my privilege to do so," he said with a bow.

"Jespen, before we proceed inside the magnificent castle, I wish to visit Daro's cottage."

Jespen turned to the apple orchard and looked precisely toward the cottage. They could not see it from their vantage point because of the thick tree canopy, but he knew where it was. "I'm sorry, my lady, but the castle is on high alert right now, and we must not stray from the path."

Binta knew the rejection was coming before he spoke it, so she focused her new powers and planted a friendly persuasion in his thoughts. "I used to stay there. Would you care to escort me?" she asked.

He stared blankly at her for several moments, then said, "Yes, of course, I remember. Right this way, my lady," and started toward the orchard.

It was too easy, and Binta's guilt raised its ugly head once more. She had to tell herself Cassandra was in danger, and Binta needed to find her now. Because of that, there was no time for niceties, even with friends. However, she did not like manipulating people and vowed once more to stop the nasty habit of doing just that once she found Cassandra. It felt wrong, every time.

So, she followed the young guard, and eventually, the tangle of trees gave way to a small field with a pond straight ahead and the cottage to the left. Jespen was walking for the house, but that was not Binta's intention.

"Jespen?" she said.

"Yes, my lady?"

"Please put down my pack and return to your guard. I shall be there shortly."

"Of course," Jespen said, laying her pack gently on the ground and leaving as if under a spell.

Binta found the ease with which she could now manipulate people startling. It was strange to have this much power over other human beings. She appreciated the phrase Inuentas used before, about becoming immense, because she felt that way. She picked up her belongings and headed to the pond. She sat on the bench she had sat upon not long ago when life was different. Since then, her life had changed for the better. The days of despair were forever behind her now. The only weakness she could feel within herself was the one that would present a difficult challenge. Sex was her stimulant, her addiction, made worse by Cass and now controlled by her as well. Binta didn't foresee any problems as long as she stayed away from temptations, especially if Cass Ruben orchestrated them.

She closed her eyes and took in a deep breath. The late morning sun shone brightly and warmed her as she meditated. She called out telepathically, which was a strange sensation and one she was trying to become familiar with. Her call focused on one individual—Baxter Von Glord. She didn't think the call would go far, and it certainly wouldn't reach anyone she didn't know very well. She knew Baxter was in the castle, close enough for him to hear her. She reached out and beckoned him to join her at the pond. She felt his presence vaguely but could not determine if he heard her.

When she opened her eyes, she spotted the rock at the pond's edge. She grabbed her pack and went to it. Behind it was the log and packed dirt underneath, still unspoiled and remaining as she had left them. She dropped her bag, moved the log, and began to dig. She remembered it not being very deep, but it took her more digging than she cared to endure before she reached the metal box and then even longer to dig out each edge. Finally, she extracted the box and opened it quickly. There, she found the tiny dress Cass had used to parade her around Poppy's Inn that first night of servitude. Also in the box were the tiny underwear and the most essential items—the leash and chain.

She removed them, placed them gently in her pack, refilled the hole quickly, and replaced the log. She had just finished when she saw Baxter walking briskly toward her. She smiled on the inside—her telepathy worked! It was a fantastic skill that she had complete control over now. She found it refreshing and empowering. She stood and smacked the dirt from her hands, a warm smile creasing her face as Baxter wore a troubled expression.

"Binta!" he said as he got closer. "What happened?"

"I called to you."

"Yes, I heard you inside my head, but how?"

"I finished the tome, Baxter," Binta said, and she slipped the pack over one of her shoulders.

"The Tome of X'lor?"

"The one and only."

"Jamison delivered it to the school; Victoria now has possession of the work."

"Yes, but not before I finished reading it."

The news put Baxter back on his heels, and Binta thought the look on his face was comical. It was a mix of fear and confusion, but she knew he cared for her. After all, he had answered her call. After a long silence during which his eyes looked her up and down, trying to find some indication that she was not well, he spoke. "So, what now?"

"I'm glad you asked, and I called to you because I need you."

"Binta, we must tell Victoria what has happened; you could be in danger."

Binta ignored the comment and stated, "You love her, don't you?"

"Victoria?"

"Cassandra," Binta replied and studied his reaction.

It was as if she had punched him in the stomach. He stammered over his words, and his face turned red. Binta knew at that moment that he indeed loved Cassandra. "I care for Miss Rho very much," he finally said.

"Then help me."

"Help you do what?"

"Save her."

"You know where she is?" Baxter asked excitedly.

"Not yet, but I will soon, and I can't do it without you."

Baxter put his hands on her shoulders, a worried expression on his face. "Binta, you must not do anything irrational. We need to speak with Victoria and make sure you are well. Also, the New Order will find Cassandra."

Binta gave him a sour look, and he took his arms off her shoulders. "I need the carpet, Baxter. I need you to take me somewhere very quickly, and the carpet is the fastest way I know to travel."

He wrinkled his brow in confusion and said, "Where are you going?"

"I don't know, but I will find out tonight."

He stood there looking at her; his expression hinted that he thought she might be ill.

"So?" Binta asked.

"So, what?" Baxter asked in confusion.

"The carpet. Can you take me?"

"You are in luck. The carpet is here; Professor Xavier just returned it. He took it to deliver the message to Nessor that Von and Lenore should return to Pelesea immediately. He arrived this morning, and the flying carpet is in Victoria's tower."

"So, you will take me?"

"Not until I know more about where you are going, Miss Mulay."

"Can't you act more like a friend than a professor?" Binta asked with a sigh.

Baxter couldn't help but smile at the comment, but that did not break his resolve. "Not when your life is potentially in danger."

"Cassandra's life is in danger, Baxter, not mine."

"As I told you before, the New Order will handle it. We leave in a few months."

"That is the problem; the New Order is waiting too long to take action. I don't want to blame Kringus, but he seems to never be in a hurry when haste is required."

"Binta! Kringus is a great man and—"

"A great leader," Binta interrupted. "I agree, and I owe him and the queen my life. However, if he was in such a hurry, why didn't he have Professor Xavier bring one of the elves home, then turn around and fetch the other? You could then be leaving on your journey in days from now, not months."

Baxter's puzzled expression spoke volumes, but he recovered quickly and said, "True enough, but we still couldn't leave right away; there is too much involved in transitioning Pelesea to the care of our steward. Your man, Jamison, is of the highest character but knows nothing about ruling thousands of people. Kringus and Penelope will not be willing to leave until they are comfortable with his ability to rule in their absence."

"So, in the meantime, Cassandra could die, and the world would be in serious trouble?"

Baxter shook his head and sighed. "You are right, Binta. I have shared your anxiousness the last few months as we prepare to leave. I care for Cassandra, so I feel the same as you."

"Then take me where I need to go. I'll find Cassandra and have her back here before the New Order ever leaves."

"Binta," Baxter said, shaking his head. "I'll do it if you let me go with you. We could take some members of the New Order and help bring Cassandra home if you know where she is."

It was Binta's turn to shake her head. "That's impossible. Only two can sit atop the carpet, and no one can venture where I'm going."

"And where might that be? You said you don't know your destination yet."

"I don't, but I know what awaits me at the end of it. I know that anyone other than a powerful telepath could not hope to survive the ordeal."

"And you think you can?"

"I read the Tome of X'lor, remember?"

"Yes, but—"

"But, nothing! The tome is powerful enough to frighten Victoria, yet I mastered it."

They stood silently for a bit, and Binta decided to take the opening while Baxter pondered her words. She handed Baxter the dirty metal box she had exhumed and said, "Please give this to Daro; I borrowed it and failed to put it back when I moved out of his cottage. Also, meet me at Victoria's tower this night, near midnight. Have the carpet ready."

"Binta, I—"

"For the love of Cassandra," Binta said, using a play on words to make Baxter think she was referring to his love for Cassandra, but secretly she also meant her love. She was confident Baxter had no idea how she felt about Cassandra.

He finally nodded, and she hurried toward the castle gates, leaving him holding the dirt-caked metal box. She felt nervous but exhilarated as everything had worked out precisely as she needed. If the rest of the day went as smoothly, she would soon see Cassandra again. She knew it in her heart and, more importantly, in her mind.

Hitching a ride to the southern part of Pelesea was not too difficult either. After Jespen freely allowed her to exit the castle grounds, she walked past the enormous temple. Her memories warmed her as she passed it: memories of her and Cassandra spending that one night alone and naked, battling the temptation of lust and love while waiting for Greyson, who never showed. After the grand structure of the temple, the docks came into view. She turned briefly to regard the balcony Greyson and she had stood on while watching Cassandra confront Kringus at the docks.

Soon, she found herself amid many wagons with dockhands loading them with goods from the recently docked ships. Big, sweaty, dirty men unloaded the boats and loaded the wagons with their goods. All of them stopped and stared at her as she passed. She intentionally tuned out their thoughts. She did not need to read their minds to understand their vulgarness. She discovered quickly that a nicely dressed lady of Pelesea could easily find transportation with the wagon drivers.

The driver's name was Samuel, and he was heading to the southern part of Pelesea, where no woman dressed like Binta should be going. He was an older man in desperate need of a bath. He didn't seem to notice the stench his filthy body produced. Binta would have waited for another driver, but Samuel was packed and ready before the others. So, she climbed aboard the coach, Samuel offering his hand to assist her, which she took. She wasn't in the comfortable carriage she was used to now, but she enjoyed the slight breeze and the warm sun as they rode.

It took nearly an hour to get from one side of Pelesea to the other because the markets were busy on the streets, and the crowds milled about, hampering progress. Samuel occasionally spit curses at those city folk who did not move quickly enough, or when they came to a complete stop as the road would become clogged with wagons delivering goods.

"I hate ship docking days when there are three of the damned vessels. It's just too much product to deliver!" Samuel said.

Binta only smiled and closed her eyes, soaking up the warm sun. She could peripherally see him looking her up and down. What he was thinking was apparent as well. She realized then that if she couldn't conquer her weakness for sex, she could probably sleep with half the men in the city just by dressing up and walking along the city proper. She was beginning to understand why she loved Cassandra so much. Men were stupid and weak.

"So, where'd you say you're headin'?" Samuel asked.

She cracked her eyes, regarded him, closed them, and turned back to the front. After a pause, she said, "Poppy's Inn."

"Poppy's Inn, on the southern tip of the city?"

"The same."

"Now, why would a woman like you want to venture to a seedy place like Poppy's?"

"I used to work there."

"You did?" Samuel asked with surprise.

"Yes."

"As a barmaid?"

Binta turned to him fully, her dark eyes wide and sparkling, and said, "Not even close."

He just stared at her with his mouth agape and nearly ran over a pedestrian. He mumbled a few curse words but did not ask her more questions. Binta tuned into his head, receiving his thoughts loud and clear. One did not have to be a mind reader to understand his thoughts, but she had no idea he was that vulgar! Whispers floated in his head of how attractive he found her, what her legs might look like under her fancy dress, what she would taste like if he kissed her, what she would taste like elsewhere.

As they approached the inn, his thoughts became darker and more threatening. He wondered how many drinks it would take to get her to loosen up enough to get her dress off. The thoughts only got worse from there, so she decided to part ways with the stinky driver when they finally stopped a few buildings away from Poppy's Inn a short time later. Sure enough, as he helped her down from the wagon, he offered to buy her a drink after he unloaded. She declined, and as he mumbled a few curse words under his breath, she quickly planted a helpful seed in his mind. Samuel never noticed the slight tickle in his brain, which was Binta's suggestion. She paid him a silver piece and walked away. He held the coin to the sunlight and studied it but immediately forgot about Binta.

When he lowered the coin, Binta was still in sight and walking toward Poppy's. For reasons unknown to Samuel, he did not even notice her and instead became enamored with his horse. He suddenly realized how breathtaking his horse indeed was. A few months later, he would be jailed by the new steward of Pelesea because bestiality was frowned upon in his city.

Binta walked toward Poppy's but did not enter. Instead, she made her way to the back of the building and as she passed through the alley, she noticed the dirty window of her old room. She thought of all the naughty things she had done in that room, and that familiar tingling in her lower stomach returned at once, especially when she thought of the things Cass made her do. Of course, that was why she had come. The tome was clear: she had to defeat this weakness to gain complete control of her new powers.

She found a secluded place among the rickety crates and garbage. The smell was terrible, but she welcomed it; she was lowering her standards, and the stench was reasonable for what she had planned. She took off her pack and removed the small dress, tiny underwear, and collar that she had taken from Daro's metal box near the pond. She then undressed, removing the expensive and delicate clothing that contradicted the tiny dress she was about to wear. She could hear the second shipyard nearby, the source of most of her clientele when she worked as a prostitute months earlier. Binta suddenly wondered why Samuel had a delivery down at this end of the city if a second shipyard was so close. She realized then that he might have been lying to her all along. Was it possible that she could still be fooled even with her newfound awareness? She pondered that for a moment, then shrugged and finished changing.

The petite dress was shorter than she remembered, perhaps because she was used to wearing a lady's clothing now. Either way, she pulled it down as far as it would go, which was just barely enough to cover her butt. The last item she added was the collar. It felt familiar around her neck, and just putting it on made her weak in the knees. Wearing it again made her feel naughty and submissive, precisely as she knew it would. Now the moment of truth. She stuffed her pack in one of the old crates and closed her eyes. She had to get her mind right for this, so with a deep breath and intense focus, she opened her eyes and made her way to the front of the inn, exaggerating the sway in her hips.

She walked through the front door, and the familiar smell of food, alcohol, and sex filled her nose. The place wasn't as packed as it would get after the sun went down, but there was a large lunch crowd there. She stopped just inside the door and stared at the stairs on the far side of the room, the ones Cass had led her down that first night to show her off to the many patrons. They were also the stairs that led to the second floor and ultimately to her old room. The memories flooded back and assaulted her. It took her many moments to realize the place had quieted, and everyone was staring at her.

Large men, most of them dirty and unkempt, sat silently, their eyes wide, their mouths agape, taking in the sexy sight of Binta Mulay. Five women were in the room as well, some sitting with the male patrons or standing nearby, and they all wore the same heavy layer of makeup and tight-fitting clothing. Whores, Binta understood. All of them were the ones who had come after Binta was rescued, and when Kringus forced Cass to stop her illegal activities. Prostitution was difficult to control and impossible to eliminate. Remove one set of prostitutes, and eventually another set replaces them. The women stared at her with similar dumbfounded expressions but with a hint of jealousy plastered across their faces. The looks made Binta want to work the men, to lure them upstairs, all of them, and let them do to her whatever they desired.

"Well, well," one of the closest patrons said.

He sat at a table near her and looked her up and down like she was a tasty morsel and he was about to partake. He was enormous around the midsection, filthy, and not attractive in the least. He repulsed her. He was not the one to test her. She walked up to the table and stood before him. He scooted his chair out a bit and patted his thigh. "Come sit that sexy little ass on my knee, girl," he said.

She reached out mentally and gave him an answer in a way he did not expect. The man suddenly stood and made a fist, his eyes wide and unbelieving as he watched his hand move without consent. Binta moved to the next table, walking into the crowd of people.

"I seek someone to please me. Anyone care to try?" Binta asked.

Behind her, the man who was staring at his fist just moments ago howled in pain as he punched himself between the legs. The strike had him buckle over, and the second and third hits had him on the floor. The last one connected solidly and had him losing the lunch he had consumed just moments ago. Binta ignored him and continued to walk through the patrons. Most of them were busy watching the man beat himself between the legs, but others watched her closely. A man nearby licked his lips and dared to reach out and grab her arm.

"I'll take real good care of you, darlin'," he said.

The alcohol from his breath repulsed her; he would not do. His plate of food suddenly flew up and smashed him across the face, spraying bits of food and plate around the immediate vicinity. He crumpled to the floor, out cold. People stood and moved away from him, and one of the women screamed in surprise, a large gob of potatoes sticking in her hair. One man fell over his chair and landed on the floor with a grunt. People scattered, giving Binta room as she walked into the midst of them. She held her arms out to her sides, which made her already too-short dress rise and reveal her underwear. Her leash dangled from her collar, beckoning someone to take control of her, to dominate her.

"Is there no one here worthy of pleasuring me?" she asked.

She began to levitate, and anyone who might have been interested in trying to tame her suddenly lost interest. She rose three feet off the ground, her mind easily lifting her with little effort or concentration. It was as if the power were an extension of her, almost like her heart beating or her lungs taking in air. And still, her thoughts reached out, scouring the crowd, searching for someone to challenge her sexually. She touched down lightly on a table and stood above them all, her arms still stretched like a beacon, hoping to find a worthy mate.

"Any man or woman here worth my time? I seek a skilled and thorough lover, someone to take my leash and make me do nasty things. No simpleton or fool will do."

She turned to observe the crowd and reached out with her mind, absorbing the patrons' thoughts. The women mostly felt hate, except for one who was in awe of the spectacle. Binta made a mental note of her, a quiet redheaded woman at the bar. The other women wanted nothing to do with her; she was quietly a threat to the rest of them. The challenge before her rested with the men, at least twenty of them. She could not stop them all, and that old feeling of wanting to be dominated started to churn in her lower belly exactly as she needed it to. The thought of these men taking her excited her greatly and took her back in time to when she serviced men like this every night. All their thoughts were lustful, and they wanted to take her and hurt her.

"Yes," she whispered and closed her eyes.

She could feel each man's movements and thoughts more vividly. They gained courage with her closing her eyes, appearing vulnerable. Four from behind her whispered to each other and approached her carefully in a coordinated effort. Just before one of them reached and took her leash, the chair nearest to her flew at them, knocking them back and cracking the reaching man across the chest. He fell to the ground, several ribs broken and a tooth missing. The other three made their way to the exit, and the rest began to back away, understanding she was beyond them.

She rose a foot off the table and craned her neck to the ceiling, her eyes closed in meditation. "No one here is worthy of bedding? Are there no real men in this place?" she asked, her voice louder than one would expect from a person of her stature.

Other tables began to float in the air, chairs as well, just a foot or two above the ground. She found it easy to perform the task, and to her surprise and delight, it did not tax her. Soon, every table and chair floated lazily in the air, as well as goblets of ale, plates of food, and utensils. Even some food and drink floated without a plate or chalice to hold it. A handful of peas and a half-eaten steak with a knife still stuck in it hovered above one table. She was becoming lost in her mental ecstasy, quickly snuffing out the tiny bit of sexual excitement that had begun to build between her legs. These people were not challenging enough, and she indeed needed that challenge; she needed to know if she could control her sexual urges. Without that knowledge, she knew she could not stand against the powerful Mystic of which Inuentas had spoken.

She sensed him before he ever spoke, and she turned to the bar to regard him as he moved through the floating food and furniture toward her. He was a large, tall, broad man with a scowl. He was not overly handsome, but she found him more attractive than any other man in the room. More importantly, he feared walking into her storm of floating debris. His desire to dominate her, to overpower her, and even hurt her was overruling his sense of danger. He wanted to be her master so he could do bad things to her and have her do the things her submissive side longed to do. This man was her test.

He tried to appear unafraid, but she knew better. As he approached, she recognized him as the barkeep from when she called the place home. She closed her eyes and let him come unhindered. She sensed him standing before her and waited for him to speak. Eventually, he did. "I am worthy of your time, Binta Mulay."

She opened her eyes and regarded him. His frown was more pronounced, and he held her leash. The patrons were near the door, watching but wary of getting too close to her. The women were now upstairs, peering over the railing, except the redhead she had sensed earlier near the bar. She was still there, watching intently.

Binta said, "And you are the barkeep, Barlow, if I recall correctly?"

"You remember me? Then you will also remember that I do not tolerate things that are bad for business. You are scaring my patrons and making a mess of the place. That is bad for business."

"Careful, Barlow. I am not the same person that was forced into prostitution those months ago. That is the only warning I will give."

"You look the same to me, and you have come to seek a job once more. I will let you pay for this mess on your back. If I feel you are worthy, I will deem your debt fulfilled."

"I can do things none of those other women would even think about doing, and I assure you, you will find me worthy."

"Very well, then, you have come here dressed like a whore, and have promised things only a whore would promise, and so I take your leash and claim you as my property. Is that what you want?"

His words ignited an excitement between her legs so strong she could only gasp. She felt her lips part as she closed her eyes once more and tried unsuccessfully to stop the building excitement that was easily winning the battle of wit and sex. She felt her nipples harden and squeezed her legs together to thwart the growing urges she felt there.

"That is what I thought," he whispered, running a hand along her upper thigh, his doubts of subduing her now gone.

She gasped and let his hand roam freely. When he reached her crotch, she shuddered, and her levitation suddenly ended. Binta landed lightly on the table, and all the levitating items in the room dropped immediately. It rained wood and metal briefly as the debris fell all around them. Barlow had her leash still in his hand and rubbed the fingers of his other hand together, the ones he extracted from her crotch.

He smiled and said, "Wet."

Binta's mind raced as she quickly lost the battle. She had the power to stop this fool, to drop him where he stood. Yet, she wanted to be submissive, and he would take advantage of that. It reminded her of being in Cass's presence, but not nearly as sexually overwhelming. Since Cass was not here, the barkeep would do.

"Once a whore, always a whore, I guess," he said, then tugged her leash hard enough to make her almost fall off the table.

She did not need him to tell her what to do; she knew exactly what he wanted and the heat in her loins was burning like a wildfire. She fought to maintain control, but Inuentas was right; she had a weakness inside her and could not hope to defeat it. All she wanted at that moment was to serve this man and let him do bad things to her. She could not believe he had dominated her so easily. Perhaps she was not worthy to stand against The Mystic and find Cassandra. A life of pleasing this man suddenly seemed an acceptable alternative.

She obediently stepped off the table and stood before him. He towered over Binta, which only made her feel more submissive. She bowed her head, looking at her feet, trying to find an answer to the predicament. She had come to Poppy's Inn for this moment, yet she had not thought she would fail this miserably. Barlow grabbed her chin tightly and lifted her gaze to meet his. His lust-filled eyes and devious grin only made her more excited and willing.

"You have come here willingly, and now I claim you as my property. I predict that your sexy little body will generate more coins for me than the five whores I already own."

She wanted to fight back, and that was the challenge she faced. She could easily dispose of the idiot or let him take her as his newest addition to his female workers—no, not workers, but property, as he had just said. She decided to fight back, but only enough to entice and lure him into the challenge. She would not use her powers on him but would fight back with her tongue.

"Don't call me that," she breathed through clenched teeth.

"Call you what?"

"I am not a whore, and you do not own me."

Barlow laughed and grabbed a handful of her hair. "You are sadly mistaken, woman. You come in here and flaunt yourself and make this display in front of my patrons," Barlow said, looking around the place, trying to find words for what she had done. "Now, I will take you upstairs where you belong and teach you a valuable lesson, understand?"

Binta stubbornly did not answer, and she could feel both the lust and the anger building inside of her. He tightened his grip on her hair and nearly lifted her from the floor.

"Yes!" she screamed, and he released her hair, only to roughly grab her chin once more.

"What do you call me?"

Binta stared hard at him, but the look he gave her, the one of complete confidence and control, made her wilt. So, her submissive side won out, and she squeaked a reply: "Master."

"Good. I remember you, Binta Mulay, and I have longed to replace you as a source of revenue. No whore has come close since the fool king eradicated you from this place. Now that you have returned, my business will flourish, especially without that Cass creature hoarding all the profits."

Binta had nothing to say, so she bowed her head again, thinking of the next step. He would take her upstairs, and there she would have to defeat the lust or forever fall victim to it. The danger was real, and she was not as confident now as when she'd first entered. She had a bad feeling she would lose this fight.

"Lift your dress and show everyone the goods," Barlow demanded.

Binta stubbornly held still, disobeying him and provoking his wrath. He backhanded her, and she fell to the floor, narrowly missing a knife that had dropped there. As she regained her senses, she focused on the knife, understanding she could easily demand it to slice into Barlow's neck. Before she could gather her thoughts and do anything in retaliation, he pulled her hard by the leash, bringing her to her knees as her hand instinctively went to the collar. She did not expect this turn of events. Cass had never been this rough; the buffoon who now held the other end of the leash was not a gentle or kind person. He grabbed her by the hair and hoisted her to a standing position.

Her eyes watered, and her cheek throbbed. He brushed the hair out of her face with a smile and gently touched her swollen cheek, his touch soft but still threatening. He smiled calmly and evilly. She instinctively grimaced and recoiled, but the hit had extinguished the fire in her loins enough that she was gaining control of her wits.

The demand came again. "Pull up your dress and show everyone your goods. And if you sit there without doing exactly what I say, you will receive a long overdue beating. Now do it."

Binta did not hesitate and took the edges of her tiny dress and pulled them up so that her skirt bunched around her waist, showing off her little underwear. He smiled and pulled her along toward the stairs. He stopped at the gathered patrons, who continued to watch in amazement.

"Take a look, gentlemen. This whore is Binta Mulay, my latest offering. She is five silver pieces for an hourglass of time."

"Five silver?" One man spoke up with an edge of disbelief. "The other whores are only one."

"And the others are not as pretty as this one, nor can they do the nasty stuff this one can. Trust me, Billy, she is worth your coin," Barlow said.

No one said anything, but Binta could hear a murmuring in the crowd. She knew Barlow was right; she was utterly submissive to Cass and did everything she asked. Given the chance, she would do it for Barlow as well.

"I get the first go at her, and when I return, I will accept the coins from the next man in line. Also, she likes to take several at a time, up to three. Talk amongst yourselves while we are gone, and decide who would like to try the goods."

Barlow led Binta toward the stairs leading to the second floor. The other women were coming down then, nervously, and as they passed, he barked orders for them to clean the place up before he returned. They scampered away. Binta felt that old sensation between her legs as she walked up the stairs, holding her dress up so everyone could see her. She could feel every eye on her, which excited her immensely. They did not go to her old room, which she found a bit disappointing, but instead went to the one at the end of the hall. The room was furnished poorly, just like all the others, but it was bigger.

"This will be your new room for turning tricks. It will allow more men at a time. I think you can do better than three. The more we cram in here, the more money I can make each night," Barlow said, crossing his massive arms over his chest and smiling at the thought. She did not have to read his mind; she knew this man well enough to understand everything he had planned.

"Get on the bed," he ordered, releasing her leash.

She followed his directions and sat on the bed, hugging her knees to her chest. She wanted Cassandra or Jamison with her; even Baxter or Greyson would suffice. She needed someone to give her the strength to stand up to this man. As each moment passed, she became more his servant. He took off his shirt and tossed it on the floor. The sight of his hairy chest started her juices flowing again. She could not help it; this man was not that attractive, but the thought of him naked and taking her excited Binta. His boots and pants followed, and then he was nude before her. He was not as well-endowed as Greyson but wasn't small, either. She bit her lower lip despite herself.

He climbed on the bed and pushed her down forcefully so she was on her back, and at the same time, he pulled her knees apart. Was she truly going to let this happen? She had to fight the urges as they had peaked. This was the moment of truth: was her mind strong enough to resist her sexual urges and submissive nature?

He fell on top of her, bringing his full weight upon her. He kissed her hard, his tongue exploring her mouth. She did not like the taste, and he was not a good kisser, but she kissed him back anyway, yet another defeat in her battle for control. She felt him pull her underwear aside and play with her. She moaned into his mouth and lost another step. Before she knew it, he entered her, thrusting fully into her in one swift motion. Her eyes widened, and she tried to speak, but his tongue prevented that. The pain was only a flash, and pleasant sensations soon replaced it.

He grunted and slammed into her forcefully like an ungraceful animal. He was as bad at lovemaking as he was at kissing, and yet she was reaching her first climax already. She closed her eyes and fell within herself. If she did not stop this now, she would not only give up on her quest and never see Cassandra again, but she would willingly become a permanent fixture there. She would indeed become Barlow's property. She thought of herself in front of The Mystic and how powerful he would be, not taking her physically, but mentally. She had to fight the urges, or Barlow would win, The Mystic would win, and worse, Cassandra would lose.

As her orgasm neared, she could sense the demon milk boiling in her gut. Cass had made her drink it, had made her into this submissive sexual deviant. She would not let that woman control her any longer. As the slapping of their bodies became a rhythm and she became more aware of how awful this man was, she found more and more footing. He was no longer kissing her, and he towered above her, now, sweat forming on his brow. She somehow managed to calm herself, pushing the orgasm back, finding peace as she did. She suddenly felt sick to her stomach that she had allowed a bullying fool such as Barlow to be taking her as he was. She would stop it now.

"Stop," she said calmly.

And he did stop for a moment, a drop of sweat falling from his brow and landing on her bruised cheek. "What did you say, my little whore?"

"I said stop."

He laughed and began his mundane lovemaking again, thrusting hard into her as if he were trying to hurt her. He pulled the top of her dress roughly, exposing her left breast, and suckled it hard. She closed her eyes and focused. He never saw his shirt floating in the air until the sleeves suddenly wrapped forcefully around his neck. His eyes widened, and he gained his knees to pull on the tightening sleeves. His face quickly became red as Binta continued to tighten the grip. Then the shirt floated higher, pulling Barlow off her and into the air.

She calmly got off the bed and watched as he kicked his tree-trunk legs helplessly. He tried to speak, but the shirt was wrapped too tight, and his head looked like it would pop. Binta watched with a peaceful expression plastered across her face. She even managed a slight smile. The approaching orgasm had subsided, and she felt no sexual urges at all. She had defeated her weakness and resisted the temptation when it was most potent. She looked up and noticed Barlow had gone limp, yet his shirt tightened. As much as she wanted to kill him, she would not do it this way.

She commanded the shirt to lower him to the bed. She did not want to touch him, to feel him for a pulse, so she just stood there waiting for some indication he was alive. When he finally coughed and sucked in a breath, she closed her eyes and commanded the shirt to once again go to work for her. Soon, it had his hands tied to the headboard tightly, so much so that they began to redden.

He finally opened his eyes, and once he saw his predicament and Binta standing beside him, he struggled mightily to free himself. When she saw the binds would not give, she smiled and walked out the door, fixing her top to cover her breast. She could hear him threatening her as she left, but the words hardly registered. He called her names again and told her she would be back and he would beat her to within an inch of her life when she did return. This time, his words did not affect her; she was in complete control.

She pulled her dress down, straightened the creases, and walked to the stairs. There, she found most of the patrons waiting for Barlow. The men gathered anxiously at the steps while the five women cleaned the overturned furniture, spilled drinks, and dropped food. They all looked puzzled as Binta, not Barlow, appeared at the top of the stairs.

"Where's Barlow?" one man asked, trying to be brave.

"Who is first?" she asked.

The men looked at each other, panic on most of their faces.

"We three," one of them said finally, pointing a finger at himself and the two beside him.

One she recognized as the first man who had tried to touch her when she had entered the inn, the man whom she had easily made hit himself continuously in the crotch, and he did not look too happy with her. She descended the stairs, and all the men moved back except those three. Together, they found courage. After all, Binta was a tiny woman who did not look threatening now.

Once she arrived at the bottom step, she reached out her hand and said, "Your coins."

"Why are we paying you and not Barlow?" one man asked.

"Oh, don't worry, Barlow will get exactly what's coming to him. Now give me your coins." She added a little persuasive thinking with her last command, and the three men quickly handed her fifteen silver pieces. She smiled and said, "He is in the last room, and you have all night. Enjoy."

She made her last comment laced with a powerful suggestion, which the three men had no hope of defeating. They looked at each other briefly and then to the top of the stairs, lust ravaging their thoughts. A large smile appeared on one man's face, and another licked his lips in anticipation. They quickly proceeded up the steps and down the hall.

When they were out of sight, Binta found the redheaded woman picking up broken dishes. As she walked across the room, the other patrons moved out of her way.

She gave the silver to the woman and said, "Find another life; you are worth more than this."

She did not enter the woman's mind, although she easily could have. She did not want to use her powers of persuasion on the good people she encountered. The woman was shocked by the gift and at a loss for words. So, Binta left it at that and with a warm smile, exited the inn and made her way to the back of the building. She dug her pack out of the crate and changed. Several times during her quick change of clothes, she heard Barlow's screams of pain and subsequent cursing coming from the second floor. She had to stop and listen each time, which only made her smile. Binta could only imagine Barlow's fun with his three new friends.

PRELUDE TO DOOM

INTA AND INUENTAS SAT ONCE MORE AT A TABLE IN HAILEE'S Tavern. Inuentas dined on a fired seahorse with red potatoes, washing it down with a strong ale. Binta watched. She was neither hungry nor amused as her dining companion had insisted on ordering food before discussing business. So, as he chewed, savoring each bite with closed eyes and a satisfied hum, Binta sat impatiently. The sun had set long ago, and she wondered how long Baxter would wait for her at Victoria's tower. Her time was precious, and Inuentas was milking the meeting to no benefit of hers.

Inuentas opened his eyes and saw her dissatisfied expression. He wiped his mouth with his napkin, chased down his last bite with drink, and then sat back from the table, studying her. "Why so impatient, my dear Binta?" he asked with a smile.

"You know why."

"And you believe you are ready and have somehow overcome your weakness?"

"I am, and I have," Binta answered, unamused.

"You stink of sex. Are you so sure that you are no longer a whore of Pelesea?"

Binta shifted in her chair and could feel her face turning red. She had come straight from Poppy's to Hailee's, and so Inuentas was probably correct; she most likely did smell of sex. She knew he was toying with her and had little time for his arrogant behavior.

"I am not a whore, and I have met the challenge and defeated it. I need Cassandra's location, and if you will help me, please do so now."

"Ah, your impatience is driven by your desire to find your friend."

"Of course. I feel Cassandra is in serious trouble, and I need to find her quickly."

"She is probably already dead, you know," the half-demon said, taking another bite of seahorse. "Mmm, you should try this." Inuentas stabbed a piece of food with his fork and held it out to her.

She took the fork from his hand and gave him a hateful look before dropping the utensil onto the tray of a passing barmaid.

"Hey, you just wasted a bite," Inuentas said.

He gave her a dubious look, and when she stared blankly at him, he got up with a sigh. He went to the closest table with patrons and took the fork off a young man's plate. "You're done with this, right? Good," Inuentas answered before the man could respond.

Inuentas retook his seat and began eating with the newly acquired utensil. He looked at the man and smiled as he chewed on the seahorse. The man looked away quickly, obviously taken aback by the half-demon's appearance. For effect, Inuentas wagged his tail. Binta did not have to read his mind to know that the tail was all for show. Still, she tried to reach into the man's thoughts and retrieve what she needed. Her patience grew thin, and Inuentas seemed happy to toy with her.

He suddenly gave her a stern look and tapped his temple with a finger. "I told you that won't work on me," he said, smiling.

"Inuentas, can't we move on from this silly game?" Binta asked. "I need something you've got, and you obviously want to help me find Cassandra, so why the delay?"

The half-demon wiped his mouth and pulled back from the table again to study her. After a few silent moments, he shrugged and said, "You misinterpret my assistance for caring. Trust me when I say I care little for this Cassandra Rho person. I am willing to assist you because I believe you can succeed, making my time here in your world much more enjoyable."

"I know, we've been through this already. I find Cassandra and stop the sacrifice, and you don't have to get your hands dirty if the New Order fails."

"Naturally, it makes good business sense. However, I still feel you're not ready and that this excursion will be the death of you."

"I am as ready as I'm going to be. Now tell me where to find Cassandra," Binta growled.

"Very well, but payment first," Inuentas said, standing.

"You know I have access to wealth. Name your price—coins, jewels, gems?"

"You," the half-demon said, then rose from his seat and walked toward the stairs. He casually tossed the fork back to the owner. The man blanched and was so shaken by the interaction that the fork hit him in the chest and bounced to the floor.

"I am not a whore," Binta said, standing.

She said it a little louder than she intended and received some amused looks from the patrons closest to her. She blushed and hurried to catch up to Inuentas, who was starting up the stairs. She noted that Hailee's was laid out very similarly to Poppy's, the only difference being the higher quality structure and upgraded clientele.

"Didn't I just leave this party?" she asked as she walked up the stairs next to Inuentas.

"Perhaps, but I think you can afford one more test of your submissive nature. After all, your friend is worth it, right?" He stopped at the top of the landing and looked at Binta with an all-too-familiar lustful gaze.

"Really?" she said, crossing her arms over her bosom with a sigh.

"You cannot deny the logic, Binta; it makes sense. Give me the desired payment, and you will have the necessary information. Within a few hours, you could be on your way to see The Mystic."

"A few hours!" she shouted, again making some patrons notice the couple with great interest.

Inuentas started walking again, and after a bit of a delay, Binta sighed once more and followed. He took her to a room and produced a key from his pocket. The scene was too familiar, and she felt repulsed by the thought of being with the half-demon. She did not feel the familiar ache between her legs at the idea of being forced into a sexual situation. She truly believed she had beaten her submissive nature. She was glad because she knew this Mystic creature would be formidable. She could have no weakness.

Inuentas ushered her into his room and locked the door behind him. Binta was pleasantly surprised at the stark difference between this room and the one she had just been in on the city's far end. The decorated room included silk sheets and matching curtains, flapping in the early summer breeze, and a large mirror set atop a sturdy oaken dresser. Many pillows lay across the bed. It looked more like a comfortable home than a rented room above a tavern.

"What is this place?" she breathed.

"It is everything that hell is not. It is the life I would want if I were but a free person."

Binta turned to the half-demon, and her feelings toward him changed at that moment. Sure, he was arrogant and annoying, but he was just another poor soul trapped in his existence. He was merely a pawn in a game waged by demons and gods. He was not free to be himself, and she empathized with him then. He no longer repulsed her, and in a way, she was happy to give him some pleasure. And so, she tossed her pack to the floor and untied the expensive dress that Jamison had purchased for her. It crumpled to the floor, and she stood before him in just her underwear.

"A true lady of Pelesea," he said, closing to stand before her, his face just inches from hers.

"After this one last act, yes. I will not willingly cheat on Jamison again. Those days are behind me."

"So, I will make the most of it then," he said and, with one quick motion, picked her up.

Binta was not a big person; she was short in stature and always considered a runt as a kid. But the ease at which Inuentas cradled her in his arms was a testament to his strength. He carried her to the bed and gently lay her down, pillows cascading out of the way as he did. He kissed her, not on the mouth, but everywhere else. He started with her hands, then her fingers, ears, toes, and armpits. By the time he finished, he had kissed every inch of her body, which tingled in anticipation. He was not quite as well-endowed as Greyson and she was relieved at that. His lovemaking was loveless but passionate. He was thorough, and her multiple orgasms left her satisfied.

As the moon reached its zenith several hours later, Binta was wrapped comfortably in his arms in a half-sleeping state. Inuentas's breathing was shallow, and she wanted to sleep and stay with him until morning. However, she knew what she had to face and suddenly remembered Baxter was waiting for her. She sat up, and Inuentas was immediately awake, which was another clue as to his life in hell, and how he could never fully relax. He quickly gained his bearings and calmed at the sight of her nakedness. A smile crept across his face.

"As good as advertised," he said.

Binta rose and began to dress. He propped himself up on an elbow and watched with a lustful gaze. She let him look, not caring at that moment, changing her focus to the task at hand.

"Tell me of The Mystic and how I can find him," she said, pulling her dress back on.

"I wish you would stay. The Mystic will kill you."

"It is my choice. I must try."

"Very well. The Mystic is a god, or at least used to be. He was banished from the heavens, imprisoned in a forest called Vasym."

"Vasym? I've never heard of it," Binta said with a confused expression.

"Yes, few have because it is in an untamed part of the world. The Mystic was once the god of plants, and he can sense them wherever they grow in your world. They connect with him, and his soul is a part of their existence. He can transport you to any place a plant grows, which, as you know, is pretty much anywhere in your world."

"He will know where Cassandra is?"

"I believe he will. And if you beat him at his mind games, I feel he will send you there."

She sat on the bed and pulled on her tiny boots, absorbing the information. With a frown, she finally said, "Mind games?"

"Yes, he is a powerful telepath. If you want to know where Cassandra is, you'll need to give him something for that information, and you'll need to resist his mind-controlling abilities."

Binta absently nodded and had a bad feeling this would not end well.

"Stay. Forget your friend; let the New Order chase her. I feel that if you leave, you are as good as dead," he said, taking her hand and kissing it.

A tingle ran through her arm and shot straight to her stomach. "No, I have no more time for that," she said, taking her hand away and standing.

"As you wish, but I will treasure our short time together, Binta Mulay. You are quite a specimen."

Binta smiled despite herself and said, "Just tell me where this Vasym is."

He lay back and crossed his arms behind his head, staring up at the ceiling. "It is past Godhomme, to the east."

"Godhomme, the stronghold of goblin hunters?"

"The same. It is far past that, even beyond Lake Elfkind and the giant and goblinoid lands. It lies six hundred miles past the lake and into the wilderness so unpopulated that even the elves won't go near it."

"Sounds fun. How will I find The Mystic?"

"If you find the heart of Vasym, which is simply a large, lonely wood, you will find him. Although if you enter his woods at any spot, I'm sure you'll garner his attention."

"How do I find the center?"

"Easy. If you live long enough to see it, the center is obvious because of a perpetual raincloud, a cloud darker than night, with unending rain covering it. It is a curse similar to the one Marnelphion left on Novafontera, but this one is a curse from the gods. The Mystic is trapped within the radius of the raincloud, never able to leave it."

"But he can send me to Cassandra."

"In theory, as long as you can withstand his mental intrusions."

"Anything else I need to know?"

Inuentas looked her up and down as she put her backpack on. She could see it in his eyes; he believed she was as good as dead, that she would not return. She gave him a half-hearted smile and turned for the door when he offered no words.

"Binta?" he said as she reached for the knob.

She turned to regard him. "Yes?"

"Be careful. You are special, and I'd love to see you again."

She smiled slightly and said, "This will never happen again," pointing a finger at herself first, then to Inuentas. "I have exorcised that demon."

Inuentas laughed at the pun, but she could tell he was disappointed. Binta did not mind; it was time to take care of business. She opened the door and left Inuentas behind, her thoughts now solely on Cassandra.

Baxter was waiting anxiously at the base of the tower when Binta arrived. He rushed up to her when he saw her and said, "I have been out here for hours! I thought you weren't coming."

"I am glad you did not leave, Instructor Baxter, for I desperately need you."

They sat there momentarily, and she could feel Baxter studying her. She was different to him now, and she thought he was unsure of carrying out her request. She smiled and said, "The adventure we are about to undertake could change the world. More importantly, it could save Cassandra. She needs us, Baxter."

That seemed to ease his mind, and she was glad of it. She needed him with her on this, or the mission would fail. He was a good person; she knew without a doubt that he would be suitable for Cassandra if the two ended up together. But she could not deny the pang of jealousy she felt at the thought of it. "Let's be off immediately," she said.

"Of course. I didn't know how long we would be gone. I packed some clothes and food, but for a week's trip only," Baxter said, collecting his pack against the tower.

"It will be enough. You are only my ride there, and you may return immediately."

"Without you?" he asked doubtfully.

"Yes, I will find my way back."

Baxter looked at her curiously and said, "Are you sure we should not get the New Order involved?"

"Only if you wish Cassandra to die while they sit and discuss politics."

"Binta—"

"I know, I know, Kringus and Penelope are good people. I agree, Baxter, they are good people, just not good at rescuing people who are in trouble."

He shook his head doubtfully and said, "For Cassandra, then."

"For Cassandra," she agreed with a smile.

He turned toward the tower and whispered a command. Shortly after, a door appeared on the tower wall before him. He retrieved the neatly rolled carpet that leaned just inside. He unrolled it and spoke another command word, and it hovered about two feet off the ground.

"You know, this amazing item has saved Cassandra twice already. It will always remind me of her."

"It's almost as if that is its sole purpose. Let's hope it has a third rescue mission embedded in its magical weaving," Binta said.

Baxter nodded and managed a weak smile, then held out his hand. She took it, and he helped her get atop the floating rug. Binta felt that she might fall, as if the item were unstable. After a moment, she got her bearings, especially when Baxter climbed on behind her.

"Where to?" Baxter asked after he was in place.

Binta looked around her—the school to her right and the castle and temple to her left. She suddenly had a bad feeling she would never see Pelesea again. Her heart raced, and she second-guessed her decision to pursue the crazy quest. But eventually, her heart made up her mind: she was going, and nothing had better stand in her way!

"Do you know of Vasym?" she asked him.

"Vasym? No, where is that?"

"Far to the east, past Lake Elfkind."

"It will take half a day to reach the lake. How far past that?"

"Far," she said.

"Then let us go," he said, spurring the carpet higher.

Soon, they were flying quickly, and they promptly left Pelesea behind. The ride was exhilarating for Binta, and the warm night air on her face made her close her eyes and smile. She loved the sensation and the speed at which they traveled, which gave her hope that they could reach the desolate forest of Vasym in a few days. She thought of Cassandra and how she must have loved the sensation as well. She smiled, knowing she was experiencing the same thing Cassandra had on multiple occasions while atop the magical rug. She desperately missed her friend and couldn't wait to discuss the carpet ride with her once this mess was over.

As the sun began to crest in the eastern sky, Baxter pointed out God-homme to her. "You will not remember the place, but those people took you in after your injuries in Kane's Mountain," he said.

He was right; she did not recall it, and her mind drifted to the adventure in that horrible mountain. They were close to the landmark, and she was sure of that, but the thought of it gave her chills. She took a deep breath and steeled her resolve. It would not be the last time she would do that over the next few days.

"We should stop at Godhomme for food and maybe a few hours of sleep," Baxter suggested.

"I'd rather not stop, Baxter. I can keep going if you can."

"Well, this will be the last settlement I know we can stop at. If Vasym is as far away as you think, this will be our last chance to get a warm bed and some good food. We can also bathe and restock supplies. Gabriel and Adam are generous hosts."

For a moment, she wondered if she stank. After all, Inuentas had smelled sex on her, and that was before they had made love multiple times. That was the deciding factor for her as she readily agreed and they put down in front of the gate. The guards of Godhomme quickly welcomed them in, and Baxter was right: Gabriel and Adam made great hosts.

MALTOR WAS NOT HAPPY. HE LAY ON THE PILE OF PILLOWS IN THE large tent with a frown. He was naked, sweat glistening on his chest, his hair wet from fornicating with his new wives. All four lay around him, also naked and sweaty. He had made love to each of them several times that morning, and all he could focus on was Cassandra. The new mast that replaced the one he had chopped down now stood in place, a pillar of strength and a stark reminder that Cassandra was gone. Also, the cage that had held the fairy, the creature that had ultimately taken Cassandra from him, lay on its side in the corner of the tent, the door missing.

None of his new wives compared to Cassandra. He had wanted her as his queen and had helped her achieve that goal. He had given her the warrior's heart, but Cassandra had been the one to win the Queen's Tournament. She had been worthy of the title, and Maltor's sexual desire for her perfect body had overwhelmed his senses by the time of their marriage. And yet, he had been robbed of the pleasure.

With a growl, he pulled Benala by the hair and had her on all fours. He mounted her quickly and thrust hatefully into her. He did not hate her, but she was not Cassandra. He would gladly give all four of his wives up for Cassandra; if there were a way to do it, he would have already done so. She whimpered as he stabbed her with his manhood, intent on spending himself until he could take no more and drift off to a welcomed sleep. He plowed into her hard enough for a sheen of new sweat to appear on his chest and to drip from the ends of his long hair.

The tent was empty, and no guards were required to keep an eye on his prized bride. Jak and the others he kept close were gone on their mission to eradicate the interlopers gathered at the burial grounds. They were well past due now, and that began to bother him. He focused his visage on the new mast next to the pile of pillows and it reminded him of Cassandra. He thrust harder into Benala, eliciting squeals of both pleasure and pain. He pulled her hair roughly, making her look straight up to the ceiling. Thoughts of killing her with his bare hands flashed through his mind as he grew closer to orgasm. He let out a yell and emptied into her, then pushed her away as he plopped back down on the pillows.

Benala crawled away to curl up at the edge of the pillow mound. She was crying, and that made him feel a little better. He lay his head back and closed his eyes, breathing heavily and waiting to regain his stamina. Teena would be next, and when he took her, he might very well kill her if she didn't perform better than the last two times. His patience was wearing thin. As he considered these things, the scout, Slorin, entered the tent.

"My king, are you busy?"

"Do I look busy?" Maltor asked as he lay on the pillows naked and his legs spread lazily over the soft mound.

When the scout didn't reply and seemed to be at a loss, Maltor said, "Enter. Tell me what news you have. It will make my day lively to hear that Jozerah is victorious and brings new slaves to the procreation tent."

Slorin's reaction told Maltor all he needed to know as the young warrior looked at him nervously. The king rose and strolled over to the scout without a shred of modesty. The man had difficulty looking Maltor in the eyes, and the king knew something was terribly wrong.

"Where is Jozerah?" Maltor asked.

"It is not good, my king. He may be dead."

"What did you say?" Maltor said with a growl.

"They might all be dead now—" Slorin said before Maltor grabbed him roughly by the throat.

"I sent one thousand men and my two captains to deal with the outlanders, and you're telling me they failed?"

The young man didn't want to respond, but he nodded the best he could through Maltor's death grip, his face quickly turning red. Maltor gritted his teeth and considered strangling the fool. However, he was providing important information that the king needed. His anger melted away, and he released Slorin, who doubled over into a coughing fit.

When he had composed himself, Maltor calmly asked, "Where are the interlopers?"

"Marching here, less than a few hours away," came a voice from the tent's entryway.

Maltor looked over to see Bolin, one of his highest-ranking warriors within the tribe, sweat-covered with dried blood caked to his hip and leg.

"How?" Maltor asked in disbelief.

"They had a hidden army, my king," Bolin said, wincing in pain as he entered the shade of the tent, his torn hip screaming with each step.

"A hidden army?"

"Yes, and you're not going to like it."

"Tell me," Maltor growled.

Slorin took the opportunity to move away from the volatile king and take a position at the door, rubbing his sore throat but knowing better than to leave.

"They are using devil magic to make our dead into warriors."

Maltor had been king for a long time and had seen many things, including devil magic; after all, Cassandra, his chosen bride, dabbled in the weakling art. But he had never heard anything like this before. A terrible thought came to mind, and his eyes widened. "Cassandra?" he whispered.

"My king?" Bolin asked.

"They are not using Cassandra to fight my men?"

"I cannot say, but I did witness the burial ground after they departed."

"And?"

"It is empty; not one dead body remains."

Maltor trembled with anger, but he was at a loss. It was one of the few times in his life he had felt that way. But with two-thirds of his men gone and possibly dead, and a mysterious group of outsiders closing in, he did not feel confident in a fight against the weaklings. More importantly, he could not allow them to desecrate the graves, especially of his beloved Cassandra.

He turned to Slorin and said, "Fetch the five highest-ranking warriors left in the tribe and summon Grink and the rest of the shamans."

"My king," Slorin said with a bow.

"Now!" Maltor roared, which startled his brides and had the scout running out of the tent.

He turned to face his wives, who were huddled together and clearly afraid of him. He didn't even register them at that moment. He focused on how his life had changed for the worse since Cassandra had died. How could this have happened to him? He had no answers, but he would prepare like he always did. Strenna be damned if he was going to let interlopers conquer his tribe. He would color the sand of Yaddaton with their blood.

THE VOICES WERE CONSTANTLY GNAWING AT HER BRAIN, SUGGESTING awful things and giving her glimpses of things to come. Kessi struggled against the barrage, understanding she was not alone in the dark room. She still hung limply by her wrists, which had grown so numb she could no longer feel her hands. Her back throbbed with every heartbeat, but at least the blood dripping from those wounds had slowed. Merrik had left her in the dark, but not alone, as he had summoned something evil to keep her company. She could not be sure whether that being was just a figment of her imagination or if a demon shared the room with her. All she knew was that there was more than one voice poking around in her mind.

They had taunted her about Unis and Sera, assuring her that they were both deep in the bowels of hell, their souls forever locked in agony and torture. She didn't want to believe that Sera was dead, and she indeed denied the claims that both now called hell their home. She understood that demons were masters of lying, and so she hoped most of the images they imparted to her were to torture her and weren't based on facts. Either way, she had an awful feeling that Sera was gone. The demons knew of her death or were forecasting it, and it broke her heart.

They suggested that Cassandra would join Unis and Sera very soon. She caught glimpses of their evil plan to capture, torture, and ultimately kill her.

They showed her visions of Cassandra's dead body lying on a cold stone altar, her eyes wide and lifeless and her throat cut ear to ear. Through those images, Kessi discovered what Matilda and Cerus were plotting. And if they succeeded, she saw how the world would become—overrun with demons who slaughtered people for food or just for the sport of it. It would become an evil world with no hope for humanity. She understood that Cassandra was the key to it all. Without her sacrifice, it wouldn't happen. They knew who she was now, and Matilda had left Nesin to find her. It all made perfect sense in the worst possible way. Kessi could only cry, for all hope seemed lost.

But she also fought the best she could, ignoring the voices and horrific images. She reached out to her god, trying to find hope when there seemed to be none. A tiny white dot of light found its way among the images of carnage and death flittering in her brain. It was her god, Adlesk, she was sure. She focused on the light and tried to tune out the distractions. For her sanity, she would need to do so.

She whispered a prayer in the dark: "Adlesk, please give me the strength to foil this plan, to save my sister and, ultimately, the world."

An evil giggling infiltrated her mind, snuffing out her prayer like a strong wind blowing out a flame. She lost focus of the light, and the horrific images of rape, death, and torture began to fill her mind again until she thought she'd go mad. She growled away the intrusion and refocused her effort on her god. As the hours passed, she would sometimes succeed in holding off the mental attacks, and sometimes she would suffer them.

In the dark and alone, she fought to maintain her sanity. She did not register time and did not hold on to much hope, but she fought, nonetheless. She knew she could not escape the room without convincing Merrik to set her free, but she had to try. For the sake of Cassandra, Sabrina, and the rest of the virgins herded together in the prison cell, and for all the goodly races of the world, she had to fight. She believed she now had important information that she could use to hinder Matilda. She now felt powerful and yet helpless. And every time she made progress focusing on her inner light, the demons would laugh at her and break her mental barriers. She was more alone in that battle than she cared to admit, but Kessi never gave up on the love her god shared. It was the only thing she could focus on; she would surely go mad without it.

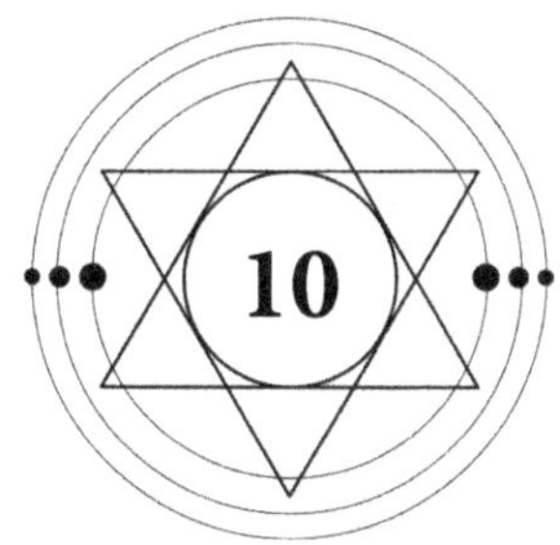

10

GARDEN OF SINNIS

REYSON KNEW SOMEONE WAS DRAGGING HIM BUT COULDN'T find the energy to open his eyes. Two strong hands held him halfway up under his arms, and his feet dragged behind him. His eyes wouldn't work for a while, but eventually, one groggy eyelid popped open. His left eye would not heed his call and remained shut. His entire face and head throbbed from the beating Sebastian had administered. He was in a long hallway, lit sporadically every fifteen yards or so by a weak lantern hanging on the wall. The floor was carpeted, and the walls were made of stone. He had no idea where he was or how he had gotten there. The last thing he recalled was Alleah's reddened cheek where the snake man had struck her.

The thought gave him courage. He glanced up to the man on his right to see a creature there that reminded him a little of Breeston's wife, Zeva. His skin was slightly green, and his pupils seemed snake-like. His nose was small, almost like a little nub on his face, and he was scaly. Greyson couldn't see well, but it looked like the man had the tongue of a snake, too. Greyson mumbled a greeting from his torn mouth, but the man didn't respond, nor did he even look down to address him. Greyson decided it was best not to struggle, so he let them drag him along.

He was eventually dragged through two large oaken doors, and he noted as they passed that two more snake-men guarded them. Inside, a large room was lit brightly with braziers, and many scents invaded Greyson's bloodied nose. He smelled food, alcohol, and perfume, all mixed with a spicy smoke that hung thick in the air. Many people were in the room, eating at tables or lying on plush couches, sharing a drink. None were human, and all seemed to be snake-like in appearance, similar to the men who had "escorted" him there. There was music playing in a back section of the large room, and Greyson noticed a band with unusual instruments while scantily dressed women danced around the tables near that section.

A large man sat on an even bigger chair, similar to Kringus's throne. The man was not human; his skin was dark green and his eyes yellow and snake-like. He wore a white silk shirt, and his muscles bulged against the fabric. The man appeared hairless, his head and face void of it. When he saw the men dragging Greyson to him, his face developed a most unpleasing smile.

His escorts tossed Greyson before the large man to land face down at his feet. When he looked up, he saw that the man held a staff very similar to the one Greyson owned. The tree used to carve the staff looked suspiciously similar to the wood from Ikma. The setting for the stone at the top had crooked wooden fingers, just like Greyson's. The only real difference was the color of the gem—grey, whereas Greyson's was green. Greyson was about to speak when he noticed another snake man standing next to the throne and holding his staff. His good eye widened at the sight, and he worked hard to stand.

As soon as he accomplished the difficult task, a swift kick on the back of his knees caused him to fall hard to a kneeling position. "Do not stand, human; you are not worthy," the snake man behind him hissed.

Greyson turned to address the assailant, one of the men who had carried him into the large room, but he froze when he saw Alleah and Chloe being escorted through the large doors by more snake men. The creatures led them to either side of Greyson and forced them to kneel.

"You look horrible," Alleah whispered to him.

A backhanded slap that knocked her to all fours met her words. "No speaking," her attacker said, standing over her.

Greyson moved to stand. He was not able to do much, but he was not about to let this man hit one of his friends, especially if that friend was a woman. Before he could even stand, Alleah's attacker was before him brandishing a knife, its sparkling blade inches from Greyson's face. Greyson had not even seen him move; it was as if he were a blur. The man tilted the blade back and forth in front of him with a wicked smile. Greyson noticed then that the man had six fingers.

"Don't even think about it, hero," the snake man said.

"Enough!" the large man on the throne said.

The knife disappeared and the guards slid behind the three captives again quicker than Greyson's mind could register. Greyson looked to Alleah, who stubbornly refused to rub her reddening cheek. He wanted to punch the man who had struck her, but he knew there was nothing he could do. He glanced Chloe's way as well, and she gave him a slight nod as if to say she was fine. He offered a smile, then regarded the man on the throne.

"You would be wise not to upset my men; they are snevols, quick to temper, faster than the wind, and impossible to beat in a confrontation… if you are human." The man chuckled.

"Especially when they are beating defenseless women," Greyson added before he could stop himself.

"Silence, you fool!" the man on the throne said. "You realize you are in a predicament here, Kavin Lightbringer, right?"

"I don't even know where I am, actually, Your Highness," Greyson mockingly answered.

"Careful. Disrespecting me could be disastrous for you and your friends. After all, you were ignorant enough to stroll into Racip with these beauties. Foolish, at best."

Greyson and Alleah shared a glance, but eventually, Greyson only nodded.

"Good; now if you can keep your bravado in check, we'll get on to business. My name is Glime, and I rule this place beneath Racip. I am not a friend to you, but I am certainly not an enemy yet.

"This is my second in command," Glime said, holding a hand to the man standing next to him, carrying Greyson's staff. "His name is Vlad, and he is the one who rescued the three of you from the idiot Sebastian."

Greyson's face ached at the mention of the violent man who had beaten him. He gave an appreciative nod to Vlad, but if the man even noticed, he did not respond. Greyson needed to get the staff back, and if he managed to do so, he would never let it fall into the hands of an enemy again. He was thankful Glime had retrieved it from Sebastian but doubted Glime had good intentions for him and his friends.

"Now you know our names, and I certainly understand yours is not Kavin Lightbringer. So, do you care to come clean and tell me your true name and why you are here in the city of chaos?"

Greyson swallowed hard and glanced nervously at Alleah. Given the circumstances, he decided the truth would be better than any alternatives. "I am Greyson Kavince, and these are my friends, Alleah Mansuell and Chloe Fraland. We have come to Racip to find the rest of our party," Greyson said, nodding to each of his companions as he introduced them.

"Interesting. You were on the vessel Cerus the Grey tried to capture during the storm a few months back?" Glime asked.

"Yes."

"Then you know already that the rest of your crew are dead?"

"We want to see their bodies just the same," Alleah blurted out.

The snevol behind her flinched as if to hit her again, but Glime waved him off.

"So, you walk into our city to find the bodies of your lost friends, even if that means getting yourselves into a world of trouble, which is exactly what you have done?" Glime chuckled.

"You might not understand it, but it was the right thing to do, Glime," Greyson said, sticking up for Alleah.

"Doing the right thing in this part of the world will get you killed, foolish one. Nevertheless, I can appreciate your courage. And I will see that you find the remains of your friends."

Chloe, having witnessed the murder of some and the raping of others, let out a pitiful sob and soon lost control, crying freely. Alleah stood boldly and went to her, ignoring the bristling guards behind her. When Glime nodded for them to allow her movement, Greyson stood as well.

"Why are you helping us?" he asked.

"I am not helping you; I am paying off a debt to Breeston of Ikma, that is all."

"You know Breeston?" Alleah asked as she comforted Chloe.

"Isn't it obvious, woman, that Greyson and I are familiar with Breeston's insatiable wife, Zeva?" Glime asked, holding his staff up to accentuate the point. Alleah glanced at Greyson, who shifted uncomfortably and refused to make eye contact with her. The mention of Zeva made Greyson nervous because it was now a sensitive subject to Alleah.

"I knew you were coming well before you arrived because Breeston let me know."

"How?" Greyson asked.

"I'm a telepath and a bearer of a Zeva stone. Breeston can send messages to me through his stone since Ikma is nearby. And, of course, I could sense you before he called to me because you carry a similar stone."

Glime nodded to Vlad, who offered Greyson his staff. Greyson tentatively took it and immediately felt Plath's power coursing through it. He felt complete once more with the powerful weapon in his hand.

"Your religious symbols are safe, and you will get them back shortly," Glime added.

"You're a telepath? Then why ask us any questions at all?" Alleah asked.

"Being a telepath is not something I expect a human to understand. The human mind is not cut out for it. I could have plucked the thoughts from your minds as easily as if I were reading a child's book. But I chose to let you speak."

"You would know if we lied. It was a test," Greyson added.

Glime shrugged and said, "Again, we are not enemies, but to lie to me, steal from me, or cheat me would be unwise."

"So, we passed your test. Now what?"

"Now, I give you what you want. I will have you escorted to where the remainder of your friends are. Then you will leave the city. Once you leave, my debt to Breeston will be fulfilled, and I will no longer protect you. Any run-ins with Sebastian and his cronies after that are your problem, not mine."

"Great. Well, we do appreciate your help," Alleah said as Chloe finally gained control of her senses and pulled away, wiping her reddened face.

"And now, you will be offered a bath, because each of you stinks of swamp, and a fine meal, rations for the road, armor, and weapons. Then I will have my scout send you to this Tara place you seek."

"I never mentioned Tara," Greyson said.

"You don't have to," Glime said with a smile, tapping his forehead.

Guards escorted them separately to their rooms, still treating them a little roughly. But true to Glime's word, they were offered a nice bath, in which they all partook. When each returned to their designated rooms, they found fine clothing, traveling gear, and belongings intact, with their holy symbols even polished to a shine. Shortly after, the guards reunited them in a large banquet room where Glime and Vlad sat with many other sleeth at a large table.

When Greyson saw Alleah walk in right behind him, he had to stop. She was breathtaking, and he realized it was the first time he had seen her cleaned up in quite a while. He found Chloe very attractive as well, as she stood beside Alleah. But she was no match for Alleah's rare beauty, and Greyson's thoughts suddenly dwelled on the many encounters he'd had with Zeva, disguised as Alleah—the look on Zeva-turned-Alleah's face while in sexual ecstasy had him growing flush.

"What is wrong with you, Greyson? You look like you've seen a ghost," Alleah asked, suddenly before him.

"Yeah, what's wrong with you?" Chloe added, coming to stand beside Alleah.

Greyson could only smile and felt his face growing warm. He was at a loss for words, and only his staff gave him enough strength not to melt onto the floor like hot wax.

"Come, let us eat," Glime announced loudly, waving the three friends to the table.

The snevols helped them on their way with a little nudge. Greyson made eye contact with the snevol who had hit Alleah earlier, and the smirk on his face let Greyson know there was an open invitation if he wanted to challenge the arrogant guard. He bit back his pride and made his way to the table. The snevols sat him on one side and Alleah and Chloe on the other, a few seats further down.

The food was strange but surprisingly good, and the mead was better than anything they had tasted before. Most of the diners at the table were higher-ups in Glime's ranks, but Greyson cared little for the titles of the various men and women and so only politely nodded as Glime introduced the closest ones. Vlad sat next to Greyson, directly between him and Glime.

Greyson thought the other sleeth were rather nice, but he could not hold much conversation as his eyes continuously ravaged Alleah.

As the dinner neared its end, Glime spoke softly to Greyson. "She will decide in time, young Kavince."

Greyson, who had been staring at Alleah as she spoke with several sleeth who sat near her, nearly spit out his mead. "What?" he managed to ask, narrowly avoiding a coughing fit.

"Your little crush over there," Glime said, nodding to Alleah. "If you want it to happen, she will eventually have to choose between you and her faith."

"That's ridiculous, I would never—"

"Yes, you would! You have thought about it this entire meal," Glime interrupted.

"She would never lose her faith, and if she did, I wouldn't want it to be because of me."

"Of course, of course," Glime agreed. "But when the time comes, can you truly resist what you so greedily crave?"

"What do you know?"

"Nothing. Only Alleah's surface thoughts. She is not as unreachable as you might think," Glime said, taking a long draw of his mead.

Greyson watched her interact with the others around her, and he could not help but admit his desire for her. She was perfection, and flashes of her sweat-covered face, her wet hair matted to her forehead, and her face holding an expression of ecstasy made his primal urges more prevalent. Had Zeva's depiction of Alleah's nakedness and sexual depravation been accurate? He sorely wanted to know.

"And would this Binta creature who dwells at the forefront of your thoughts approve of your desires?"

"Stay out of my head, Glime," Greyson said, suddenly feeling guilty at the mention of Binta.

"I'm sure she has taken up the faith that you pressed onto her, and she would not too terribly mind if you frolicked with this one."

Greyson fixed him with a cold stare and gritted his teeth. He could then feel the sleeth prodding ever so lightly at his thoughts. He hadn't noticed it before because it was slight, almost a soft breeze blowing on his skin. To combat it, he changed the subject. "So, I know that all sleeth are born with a blessing. I assume yours is being a telepath? I also know that all sleeth are born with a curse. So, what is yours?"

Vlad tensed, and Greyson held tight to his staff that leaned against his chair in case the sleeth warrior tried something. The silent showdown lasted but a moment as Glime gently touched Vlad's shoulder to calm him.

"Fair enough. My weakness? My curse? I hate the sunlight; it makes me ill to be in it."

"That is why you stay here and let Sebastian rule the top?"

"Sebastian is an idiot, and I can have him removed anytime. Remember, I'm not too fond of the sunlight, but that doesn't mean I can't walk amongst the surface-dwellers. Besides, Vlad and the other sleeth of my community can come and go as they wish. If I want Sebastian, trust me, I'll have Sebastian."

Greyson nodded, and the two shared a moment of silence. They measured each other, finding mutual respect. As Glime had already announced, they weren't friends but were not enemies.

"Come, let's get you and your friends some nice armor and weapons," Glime said, standing.

Vlad stood as well, and before Greyson, Alleah, or Chloe could stand, their snevol escorts were beside them. Their movements were nearly a blur, and Greyson wanted to be done with this business and be far away from the nasty creatures.

They visited a different part of the underground lair, and in the first room they found many well-made suits of armor. They searched the armor racks, and after a lengthy discussion, all three decided to wear something light that would allow them to move freely and cast their spells when needed. The armorers measured them and adjusted their hand-selected pieces: three suits of leather armor with metal studding enforcing the protection but not adding too much weight. As they waited for their armor to be adjusted to fit, Glime and Vlad escorted them to the armory, where they were overwhelmed by the weapon selection. Thousands of weapons lined the walls.

"These are snevol-made weapons, some of the best in the land," Glime said.

"There are so many," Alleah breathed, taking in the magnificent sight.

"One can only expect trouble in Racip, my lady, and so we prepare for it," Glime explained.

It did not take them long to find what they needed. Greyson had never used anything but a mace as a weapon. He recalled his journey into the priesthood in the caves of Plath. The mace he used during that trial had saved his life. The one he picked out from Glime's supply was similar: light, yet powerful. Alleah and Chloe were each comfortable with that type of weapon, and soon, all three carried a silver mace.

"Of all the weapons I have, the three of you have selected the most boring and possibly insignificant of all," Glime said. "What will you do for long-range attacks if they are needed?"

"We have spells," Chloe said.

"And my staff," Greyson added.

Glime shook his head and said, "Priests. I hope you don't encounter any seasoned warriors, because you won't survive the encounter."

Greyson shared a nervous glance with the other two, and they all knew Glime spoke the truth. Fortunately, the sleethian blacksmith broke the silence by summoning them to try on their armor. The leather armor fit snugly but comfortably, and soon, they donned marvelous armor and weapons. Glime had their packs filled with food and supplies, and they were finally ready to venture back to the surface.

"And now comes the time where we part ways," Glime said with a hint of disappointment.

"We appreciate what you have done for us," Greyson said, extending his hand.

Glime didn't take it and instead smiled. "I didn't do it for you. And we are not friends, so we do not shake."

Greyson let his arm fall to his side and nodded, understanding.

"And now to our sisters," Alleah reminded.

"Yes, of course," Glime said, then turned to Vlad. "Is Lud ready?"

"Yes, my lord," Vlad said with a bow, then snapped his fingers.

A strange-looking creature entered the room, and Greyson knew what it was as soon as he saw it. He had to fight the urge to flog the thing as horrifying memories of the goblin ambush on his journey with Cassandra, Binta, and Cass came flooding back. Lud was small, only about four feet in height, with dark green skin and long pointed ears. His eyes were too large for his head, and his grin showed many teeth, some very sharp and most yellow or black.

"Goblin," Greyson breathed as Lud sidled up beside Glime.

"Correction! Not just any goblin; Lud is the best goblin scout I have! He can find your Tara quickly enough," Glime said.

"Hello, ugly humans," Lud said with a bow.

They just stood there momentarily, looking each other up and down. Finally, Glime leaned and whispered something in Lud's ear. The little goblin's eyes widened, and a panicked look crossed his face.

"Lud is sorry. He meant to say 'hello,' only because Master Glime beats poor Lud if he offends."

"That is better, Lud. And what else?" Glime asked.

"Oh, Lud almost forgot!"

The goblin scout then made a fist and said, "Bad Lud!" and punched himself in the face.

Chloe let out a little scream at the spectacle, but none of the three friends knew what to do. Lud was holding his swollen eye and cursing under his breath.

"No thanks, Glime; we can find our way without this creature," Greyson said.

"Nonsense. Lud is a little unusual, even for a goblin, but he is an excellent scout. He knows the back trails and the ways around trouble. He is also very familiar with this wild land. He will know if there are signs of danger. You should take him; he is my final gift to you, and my debt to Breeston is fulfilled whether you take him or not."

Greyson looked to his friends, and they slowly agreed that the little goblin would be handy to have around, so they eventually took the sleeth up on his offer. Soon after, the snevol escorted them to the large double doors that led to the surface world.

Before opening them, Glime said, "Remember, find your friends quickly, and be on your way soon. You are protected while in Racip, but once you leave, you are on your own, even if you return later. Our association ends now. Word will quickly spread that you have returned to the surface, so do not delay."

"And what of Lud?" Alleah asked.

"He will complete his task faithfully, then find his way home."

The door opened, and Glime recoiled slightly from the dim sunlight the long tunnel to the surface let in. Greyson nodded to Glime in appreciation and started to follow his three travel companions out the massive doors. Glime grabbed his arm, stopping him before he had taken his first step.

"You should know that he lives," the sleeth whispered.

"Who?"

"You know."

Greyson thought for a moment, and then his eyes widened. "No," he breathed. "We saw him against the dragon; the beast breathed on him. Cerus is dead!"

"No," Glime insisted with a shake of his head. "He survived and staggered into Racip a few months ago, nearly dead. Matilda eventually showed up and healed him."

Astonished, Greyson couldn't speak for a long while. He swallowed hard, suddenly breaking out into a cold chill. "Where is he?"

Glime shrugged and said, "I would guess his fortress home of Nesin. It isn't too far from here, so I warn you. He could return anytime, and I imagine your name will circulate quickly here over the next few days. You and your friends should be long gone before he returns."

"Thank you," Greyson said as the hairs on his neck stood on end.

Glime nodded, turned, and walked away. Greyson watched him go, unable to move. Eventually, his legs responded, and he moved to catch up with the others. He wanted out of Racip more desperately now than before but wouldn't rush his friends. He knew the next step was a dire but essential part of their journey, and they couldn't hurry through it. He decided not to tell Alleah and Chloe the news about Cerus just yet.

They soon found themselves in the surface world where the sun was just past its zenith. They had lost track of time, and no one had realized how long their stay with Glime had been.

"This is good timing, I think," Greyson said.

"How so?" Alleah asked.

"We can find your sisters, say our goodbyes, and pray over them. Then we can leave under the cover of night," Greyson answered.

"Then let's get this over with," Chloe said. She had personally witnessed most of the ordeal and knew roughly where the bodies should be. She would have to hold strong as the barrage of terrible memories would surely haunt her.

"First, we fix this," Alleah said, standing before Greyson with her symbol of Sinnis.

She closed her eyes and whispered a few words while gently touching Greyson's face. He felt the soothing healing of her goddess wash over him, relieving some of the pain there. When she opened her eyes once more, he was smiling at her.

She returned the smile and asked, "Better?"

"Much. Thank you," Greyson answered, his heart aflutter.

Glime's words echoed in his head, predicting that he could have Alleah if he wanted her. He considered the cost of that possibility and thought it could be worth it. After all, she could always become a follower of Plath if she lost favor with Sinnis. They could build the temple in Pelesea: he, Binta, and Alleah.

"Then let us be off," Alleah said. "Lud, lead the way."

She looked around, and the goblin was nowhere to be seen. Greyson looked to Chloe, who stood with her arms crossed and with a look of disgust. "What is it, Chloe?" Greyson asked.

She pointed to a little alleyway nearby. There, he saw horses tied to a post, obviously the mounts of weary travelers who partook in the libations of the adjoining tavern. Crouched in the alleyway, Lud was eating fresh horse pies. The stuff was all over his face, and he was sucking a finger clean as they looked on in horror.

"I don't think I can travel with him," Alleah said.

"I agree. We'll let him show us the bodies of your sisters and lay them to rest. We'll then part ways," Greyson said with a nod.

"Well, one of you must fetch him because I'll be sick if I have to," Chloe said.

Greyson nodded and went to the goblin quickly and as inconspicuously as possible. "Lud, what are you doing?"

Lud stood up quickly and said, "Just snacking, ugly human."

Then he laid his head in his hand and shook it. "Oh no, Lud repeated a bad word!"

The goblin balled up a fist, and before Greyson could stop him, he started punching himself in the face again. Many passersby took notice, and Greyson knew their time in Racip would be short, given all the attention the goblin was sure to draw. He eventually got Lud to stop, but not before he was bleeding profusely from his nose.

Greyson calmed him down and said, "Lud, you don't have to hit yourself like this. We aren't offended by your words, all right?" He summoned the power of his god and let the energy flow freely from his staff through his hand and onto the goblin, healing his damaged face.

"There, does that feel better?"

Lud's eyes went wide, and he said, "Yes!" He started feeling around his face, amazed at the effect.

Greyson almost lost his dinner from the stench of the goblin's breath, and he stood quickly, leading Lud back to his companions.

"Can you show us where our friends are?" Alleah asked, holding her nose from the stench the little goblin now reeked of.

"Lud can take you there." He nodded, his large ears flapping with the effort.

Soon, Lud was leading them to their friends' gravesite. All three felt a great sense of dread at the prospect. But this was why they had returned to Racip and they meant to see it through. Greyson knew it would be tough for Alleah, especially since she'd led the expedition, and Chloe's ordeal from her time spent with Cerus had scarred her. Greyson didn't look forward to the coming discovery, but nothing prepared him for what he saw.

They came into a small forested area a few hundred feet from the docks, near the water's edge. The area was thick with trees and was the intended landing spot for the sisters of Sinnis. It was simply a clump of wilderness that sat perfectly out of the way and provided concealment for their landing. Instead, Jessica, the ship's captain, had set a trap and had Cerus and his men prepared and waiting when the sisters of Sinnis emerged from the water.

When they walked into the clump of trees, Chloe began sobbing, and Alleah fell to her knees. Greyson stopped in his tracks, unable to move. Distant but vivid memories flooded him, and he nearly broke down as well. There, in the trees, were the decayed bodies of the missing priestesses. Scavengers had already picked over them, and anything of value was missing, including their holy symbols, weapons, and other belongings. A fleeting thought of how thieves had taken the armor from the corpses crossed his mind before he realized with horror that the women were probably nude by the time Cerus and his men hanged them.

Greyson imagined that Cerus gutted them before hanging them, but none of that remained as scavengers had grown fat the last few months cleaning up the mess of innards. In most cases, the only thing that remained of the women was their hair, long strands clinging stubbornly to the skeletal remains. It was a horrible sight, and Greyson couldn't breathe for a long time, recalling the murder of his family and friends performed in the same way. Alleah and Chloe cuddled in the entrance to the macabre scene, leaning on each other and crying for their lost friends.

Greyson moved to stand beside them and put a hand on Alleah's shoulder. She didn't look up but put her hand over his. He let them stay that way for many moments, crying it out. They had known this was what they would find, but the reality was finally setting in. Meanwhile, Lud sat on a nearby log, studying a map. A passing thought occurred to Greyson that perhaps the goblin would guide them well. It passed quickly when the creature started picking his nose.

"I knew it would be bad," Alleah said, standing and pulling Chloe up.

"But not this bad?" Greyson added.

She nodded, and the tears nearly started again. She held it together, and Greyson understood her struggle. He had never had the chance to grieve his friends and family, and if they did make it to Tara, this would be the same scene he would encounter there.

"I remember it like it just happened," Chloe squeaked.

"Chloe, don't," Alleah said, wrapping an arm around her.

"Those men did horrible things. Things that I cannot even speak of." Chloe nearly lost it then as she recalled the vivid memories, but instead, she wiped away the tears and continued. "Afterward, they hanged them, and Cerus took this awful, wicked-looking blade and stabbed them. He twisted it and jerked it out, and their insides just poured out of them. I watched them all die!"

She nearly collapsed, but Alleah stubbornly held her up. The tears formed in Greyson's eyes as well because he had seen that technique of Cerus's firsthand, used on his dying friend, Darian. He vowed that if he ever saw Cerus again, he would use every ounce of power his staff would offer to obliterate the evil man.

"Greyson, we will pray and then cut them all down. Are you willing to help? It will take a long while to bury them properly," Alleah asked.

He smiled at her, took her by the shoulders, and said, "Of course. We're stuck in this part of the world, and there's no reason to hurry along other than to simply get out of Port Racip. But this is important. So, pray to Sinnis, and I'll ask for Plath's blessing. Once you're ready, we fix this together."

Alleah hugged him tight, and Chloe followed, all three locked in an embrace of pain, sympathy, and friendship. None of it seemed to matter to Lud, who was now eating whatever he found in his nostrils. Greyson wanted to usher the repulsive creature away but didn't want to make a scene during that tender moment with Alleah, so he just watched the goblin as he hugged his friends.

And so, the two remaining sisters of Sinnis prayed for their lost friends and sisters in faith. Greyson prayed separately and could feel the warmth of his staff as he did. Plath was with them, watching over their dead friends; Greyson could feel it. After a long prayer, he stood and walked to the water's edge. Alleah and Chloe continued their prayer, and one or the other would start sniffling occasionally, but he let them deal with the pain the best they could. Finding strength in their god was probably the only way to accept this.

He looked up to regard the closest dangling corpse. It was smaller than the others, and he surmised it was probably Masie, the youngest of the group. She could have been no more than fifteen. He remembered her; she was pleasant, very cute, and would have made a great priestess one day. Now, she would never get the chance. He noticed then that one of her boots was missing. Had thieves taken it, or had she lost it in her struggle? It didn't matter; her pale, bony foot no longer needed it, which weighed heavily on his heart.

His thoughts were interrupted by Lud snorting loudly, burping obnoxiously, and then turning over to settle once more into his goblin slumber. Lud's manners and his total disregard for their dead friends repulsed Greyson. The scout cared nothing at all for them.

Greyson looked to the ocean where the *Lady of Faith*, their boat, had been anchored near the docks. There was no sign of it now, although many ships docked at Racip. He truly felt trapped in Varish at that moment. He hoped that after they finished their business here, they could do the same for his people in Tara, and then they would go to a different city to find passage back to Pelesea. They would never return to Racip; there was too much death associated with the place and too many bad memories linked with the journey to the evil city. With a sigh, he turned back to the woods to find Alleah and Chloe standing near him.

"We are ready," Alleah said with a smile.

Her face was puffy, and her eyes red. Chloe looked worse, as if a feather could knock her over. He kissed them both on the forehead and smiled. Then Greyson saw the intruders over Alleah's shoulder, entering the small, wooded area. His smile melted away, and he pulled both women back and stood between them and the men who had now moved in closer.

Alleah turned to follow Greyson's stern gaze and whispered, "Sebastian."

"Oh no," Chloe moaned.

Greyson looked back at them and nodded to the water. "We swim back to Ikma if we have to."

"In this armor?" Alleah asked.

"Only if things turn dour. Only if we're desperate," he said with a frown. "All right?"

Alleah and Chloe looked at each other and nodded their agreement. "Agreed," Alleah finally said.

Greyson could see at least twenty men, but he felt there were more in the trees, waiting and watching things unfold. It was a desperate situation, and his face suddenly throbbed as he recalled the beating Sebastian had recently administered. He closed his eyes for a moment and whispered a quick prayer. Vibrations coursed through his arm from the staff. He opened his eyes in astonishment and remembered the power he now carried with him.

He turned back to the approaching men just in time to see one of them gently kick the sleeping Lud. The little goblin yelped in surprise and sprang up, shaking his head to orient himself from his dream and struggling to understand what was before him. He watched with his mouth hanging open as Sebastian and the men moved past him toward Greyson.

Greyson found the courage to move his legs and walked confidently toward the intruders, already considering what he could do with his staff. He thought at first to call a blinding light so they could escape, but he wasn't sure he could blind all of them. He thought to summon another storm, one he knew would be much more potent than the first one he had formed at Racip's docks months earlier, but that would take too long. Ultimately, he decided to do something that could benefit them the most. With a devious smile, he strode forward, quickly closing the last twenty yards. Soon, he was toe to toe with his newest rival.

With a snort of derision and a shake of his head, Sebastian looked Greyson up and down before gazing at his two female friends. "Well, well, Lightbringer, you three clean up real nice now, don't you?"

"Yes, we do, Sebastian, and I wish I could say the same for you."

Sebastian's face reddened, and he gritted his teeth. Greyson felt the same exhilaration that had coursed through his body in his waning moments in Tara when he had stood up to Cerus. It took all his willpower to stand there after the insult, a simple smile plastered across his face.

Sebastian stepped closer, only inches from Greyson, and whispered, "You will pay for that, Lightbringer. You will pay dearly for every stupid word that comes out of your mouth."

Before Greyson could respond, Lud pushed him back as he wedged himself between the two men. "Hey ug—I mean, nice humans, these people are under the master's protection," Lud squealed, shaking a little finger at Sebastian.

Racip's evil guardian looked down in disgust and held out his hand. "Randin!"

"Yes, sir," one of the men said, coming forth.

"Bring me a large rock."

"Yes, sir," Randin said, looking around the area for the perfect rock for his boss.

"You can't touch me or them," Lud said, pointing fingers at Greyson and his friends. "Master is watching."

Sebastian stood there with his hand outstretched, awaiting the rock's delivery. Lud watched as Randin finally found one and had to kick and claw at the half-buried rock before it came loose. Once he had it, he ran over to Sebastian, wiping off the dirt. Lud gulped audibly as Sebastian now held the rock, Randin backing away, pleased with his successful mission.

"Here," Sebastian said, offering the rock to Lud.

Lud looked stupidly at Sebastian, then the rock, and back to Sebastian again.

"Go on, take it," Sebastian coaxed with a smile.

"Leave it, Lud," Greyson said.

Sebastian turned a hateful glance Greyson's way and said, "Stay out of this, Lightbringer; I'll deal with you next." He turned back to the goblin and shook the rock before him, tantalizing the little scout.

Lud reached for it, and Greyson expected Sebastian to smack Lud with it at the last moment. To his pleasant surprise, he gave the rock to Lud. The goblin looked on, obviously expecting the same thing, and when Sebastian just smiled in response, Lud gained confidence. He started tossing the rock up and catching it in his hands, almost like a child, easily distracted and playing a new game.

"Now, what did you call us?" Sebastian asked suddenly.

"Ugly," Lud responded without thinking.

The terrified goblin looked up to Sebastian and said, "Uh-oh."

Sebastian nodded and said, "Uh-oh is right. You know what you must do."

"Stupid Lud!" the goblin said before smashing the rock to his forehead.

Greyson saw what would happen just before it transpired, as if caught in a dream and moving too slow to stop it from happening. The rock hit the goblin, who staggered for a moment and dropped face first into the dirt, out cold.

The men laughed at the sight, and Alleah ran to his aid. She knelt and turned the little goblin over, blood gushing from a cut on his forehead. "Why did you do that?" she asked as she prepared a healing spell.

"I didn't do anything, woman; he did it to himself. We all saw it," Sebastian said.

"Enough, Sebastian; playtime is over," Greyson growled.

The men stopped laughing as Sebastian returned to Greyson, saying, "I have a good mind to whoop you, little boy, to finish what I started."

"But you can't, Sebastian, because Vlad is probably watching you right now, right?" Greyson said, standing his ground against the bully.

Sebastian looked around, as did many of the gathered hooligans. When he found no sign of Vlad, he turned back to Greyson with an evil smile. "That's right, Lightbringer, the three of you are safe for now. You fail to see that the overgrown toad, Glime, will only protect you until you leave. Once you set one foot outside of Racip, that pact dies, and so do you."

"Then we'll stay," Chloe said, standing beside Greyson.

"Oh yes, we prefer it if you do, don't we, fellas?"

The other men nodded eagerly, and some whistled, making Chloe take a few steps back. Alleah stood, done with her healing on the still unconscious goblin, taking up a battle stance to protect her remaining sister.

"Especially you, my exotic creature," Sebastian said to Alleah. He looked her up and down and licked his lips. The men crowded a little closer, making both women put their hands on the hilts of their maces and stopping the advance at least momentarily.

Sebastian turned back to Greyson with a wicked smile and said, "Besides, we have all the time in the world. The three of you can stay as long as you want because I've sent word to Cerus, and I'm sure he'll be quite curious to see what an idiot like yourself is doing impersonating a Gorl warrior. And I'm sure he'd like to meet a few more sisters of Sinnis." Sebastian laughed and held his arms up to the trees where the priestesses of Sinnis blew in the breeze like skeletal windchimes.

"Cerus is dead," Alleah said before Greyson could intervene.

Many of Sebastian's men laughed at that remark, and Sebastian said, "I don't think so, my lady. You see, Cerus is immortal; you can't kill him."

"We saw him; he fell to the dragon of Ikma."

"Perhaps in your dreams, darling, for I saw him here in this city just a few months ago."

"You lie," Alleah said, shaking her head.

"I do lie, but not about this. Cerus is alive and well and in his mountain fortress, not even twenty miles from here."

"No," Chloe said, the memories finding her once more. Her legs buckled, and she plopped onto the ground. Alleah knelt to comfort her.

"Sebastian," Greyson called.

"What?" he said, tearing his attention from the women.

"Why don't we start over? After all, we got off on the wrong foot with me lying to you. Let me make amends."

Sebastian spit on the ground right at Greyson's feet. "Too late for that, Kavin Lightbringer. You are going down, one way or another."

"I understand your anger is great, but you remember, I'm an ally of Glime, right?" Greyson said, pointing to his staff, one very similar to the one Glime carried.

Sebastian began a rebuttal, but his glance at the glowing green gem stopped him in his tracks. He stood there, mesmerized, as did all the men close enough to witness the marvelous staff.

"I propose we work together for mutual gain. If you and your men can help us cut down these bodies gently from the trees and give them a proper burial, I'm sure these two ladies would show their appreciation," Greyson said, waving a hand to Alleah and Chloe, who still huddled on the ground.

Alleah rose when she heard Greyson's words, and a crease on her forehead showed she was not supportive of his plan at first. But she caught Greyson's wink and nodded slightly, understanding the ruse. Sebastian looked at her like she was a juicy steak, his mouth watering, and he even smacked his lips before looking back to Greyson and, more specifically, the gem atop his staff.

"So, why don't you boys get to work? After all, the sooner we get this done, the sooner we can have some fun," Greyson said with a nice smile.

Sebastian smiled and nodded, a tear running down his cheek as he could not force himself away from the sight of the staff, not even long enough to blink. The glowing gem subsided, and Sebastian shook his head, as did most of the men behind him who had witnessed the exchange as if they were trying to regain their bearings. Greyson knew that was exactly what they were doing, and he was confident they were thoroughly charmed. The waves of power that had washed over the men were far more potent than the charm he had used on Cassandra, and that one had nearly worked perfectly.

"You heard him, men. Randin, you take Jake and ten others back to the mercantile; bring back shovels and some nice cloth to wrap these bodies in," Sebastian ordered.

"Yes, sir," Randin said, and he and half the party journeyed back into the city proper.

Sebastian smacked Greyson on the shoulder and said with a genuine smile, "You're all right, Lightbringer. After our frolic time with these two, I'll buy some nice ale, and we can share our stories. I'm sure you've got plenty to tell."

"Absolutely, Sebastian; you're a good friend."

Sebastian laughed, saying, "We'll cut the ropes and gently lower the bodies while the three of you catch them and ease them down."

"That sounds good, Sebastian," Greyson said, then added, "Also, the gentler you are with them, the more fun these two will be." Greyson pointed a finger over his shoulder to Alleah and Chloe. Sebastian looked at them lustfully again and nodded slowly before turning back to Greyson and smiling again. With another pat on Greyson's shoulder and a wink, the self-proclaimed ruler of Racip organized his men efficiently and effectively for the task.

Soon, the other men returned with supplies, and they got to work. The men were cautious with the bodies, gently cutting them down and wrapping them. Chloe and Alleah prayed over each body one more time before they were eased into shallow graves and appropriately buried. It took most of the day, but they finished just before nightfall. The men stood around, sweating profusely and wiping the sweat from their brows.

"Well, that's it, we're done. Time for payment!" Sebastian said, suddenly grabbing Alleah and pulling her close.

"Wait, Sebastian!" Greyson said before Alleah could draw her mace.

"What?" he said as Alleah stayed her hand long enough to hear what Greyson would say.

"Not here; this is a sacred place now."

"Oh?" Sebastian said, releasing Alleah.

"Yes, from this day forward, this area of Port Racip is called 'The Garden of Sinnis,' and it is holy ground, blessed by the gods."

Sebastian and the others, including Lud, who now wore a bandage around his head, looked around in awe. The trees seemed fuller now, not with bodies, but with chirping birds as the setting sun glowed warmly behind them at the entrance to the area.

As everyone took in the sight, Greyson called forth powerful magic from his staff and felt a new sensation, a new spell appropriate for the moment. He closed his eyes and waved his staff all around. He heard the gasps and smiled, not daring to look or break his concentration until he completed the spell. Once finished, he opened his eyes and stood straight. All the fresh graves now sprouted flowers, beautiful and fragrant, with many hues of blues, greens, yellows, and reds. It was stunning and the most they could have hoped for, given Racip's hostile environment and the horrible ending all their sisters had faced. Alleah and Chloe were there beside him then, each crying and with an arm wrapped around him. Tears found their way to Greyson's eyes, too, as he became overwhelmed with the power of his god.

"It's beautiful, Greyson. Thank you," Alleah whispered.

He smiled at her and then noticed the men were watching them closely. He needed to keep them engaged and hopefully keep the charm intact. "Now go, Sebastian," he said.

"Go?"

"Yes, go and bathe, get cleaned up because these women are now in your debt, and you should all be clean for such a rare occasion. For the worshippers of Sinnis are chaste and do not indulge in sexual relations. However, the work of you and your men is worthy of such an exception. So, go and bathe and meet us at Glime's lair within the hour. There, you will collect your prize. Alleah and Chloe will meet you there, freshly washed and eager to please."

"Glime? Are you sure he'll allow us there?" Sebastian asked.

Greyson pointed to his staff again and said, "Yes, remember, we can communicate through our twin stones. He's looking forward to making peace and may have a few lady sleeths if any of your men have a taste for the exotic creatures."

Sebastian walked up to Greyson and shook his hand. "Within the hour, then, Lightbringer."

Greyson smiled, thinking that Sebastian would be on his way. But the will of evil men is hard to break, and the lust rose to the top of Sebastian's thoughts. He grabbed Alleah and pulled her close. Alleah looked desperately to Greyson for answers.

"What are you doing, Sebastian? I just told you—"

"I'm not leaving without a kiss," he grumbled.

Greyson knew what happened next would determine whether the charm continued or failed. They were close to freedom and he needed Alleah to play along just a bit longer. He nodded to Sebastian. "Of course. One kiss as a promise of the delights to come."

Alleah's eyes widened, and she was about to object when Sebastian forced a kiss on her, thrusting his tongue into her mouth. Greyson assumed it was her first time kissing a man, and she did well seeing it through. After what seemed like an eternity to Greyson, the man finally broke the kiss and pulled Alleah back to arms' length, looking her up and down.

"I'll see you soon, little lady," he said, playing with her hair.

She smiled and allowed it, but her reddening face told Greyson she was either embarrassed or furious, and most likely both. Finally, Sebastian let her go and smacked Greyson on the shoulder again. "All right, men, to the bathhouse. Time is of the essence!"

The men cheered, gathered the tools, and soon left the Garden of Sinnis, full of flowers, birds, and bees. It was the most beautiful spot in the city, and Greyson viewed it proudly. He was responsible for creating it and felt a sense of pride. Plath had used him as a conduit to change the cursed land into a place of peace and beauty. He smiled and took it all in as the last of Sebastian's men left.

"Not you, Lud!" Alleah said, suddenly walking past him and breaking his moment of peace.

He realized that Lud had been following the men out of the garden, obviously just as charmed as the others. He watched Alleah collect the goblin and examine his head. She glanced at Greyson, and he saw anger there.

"What?" he said.

"Pig," Chloe added as she walked past and scowled at him.

"What? Look at what I did," he said, holding his arms out to the magnificent garden.

His words fell on deaf ears, and the women ignored him, gathering their packs for the road. He knew he was in trouble, but they would get over it. After all, he had orchestrated their escape, buried their friends, and created a holy garden. How could they stay mad?

They left Racip, heading north toward Tara as the sun slipped below the horizon. Their goblin scout had them far away from Port Racip, long before a freshly bathed and eager group of men, led by Sebastian, showed up at the doorstep of a powerful and annoyed sleeth. As the rain of angry snevol fists pounded Sebastian and his men, they finally realized the deception. By then, Greyson and his friends were far out of the city.

MALTOR'S STAND

"SHE LEFT WITH BAXTER? TO GO WHERE?" AN IRATE JAMISON asked Victoria.

"He didn't specify in his message, Jamison. He said they were going somewhere hoping to find Cassandra," Victoria answered.

Jamison sat back with a huff in the giant, comfortable chair in the king's study. The New Order was only days away from making their public announcement to the citizens of Pelesea for their plans to venture to Varish. That would officially notify all that Jamison would be the steward while the king and queen were absent. If that weren't stressful enough, Victoria had just told him of Binta's new adventure.

"She should have come to me. She lied; she said she was coming to the castle. Then she runs off on some crazy adventure?" Jamison said, running his hands through his hair.

"She is not herself, Jamison. The Tome of X'lor has poisoned her mind. When she returns, I will do all I can to alleviate her burden," Victoria said.

"It's all my fault, Lady Victoria. I purchased the tome, but I didn't understand the evil found within its pages. My love is flying around the world on a magical carpet, deranged and needing care. Why did Baxter support her decision?" Jamison asked, suddenly looking very annoyed.

"Trust in Baxter, my friend. I have known him for a long time, and I respect his judgment. He would not help her unless he thought there was a real chance for them to make a difference," Victoria answered.

Jamison nodded and said nothing more, but he was obviously not comforted by her words.

Kringus and Penelope, who sat nearby in the study, listened intently to the conversation. "We must not let the distraction deter you from your responsibility," Kringus said. "You are our choice for steward of Pelesea, but I do not want your mind preoccupied while in charge of our city."

"I understand, my king, and I vow to be mentally prepared to take the helm when the New Order journeys forth," Jamison assured him.

Kringus studied him for a moment and eventually nodded his approval, then took a draw from his flagon.

"Then it is settled; we'll get some rest and sleep soundly knowing that Baxter is with Binta and watching over her," Penelope said.

All was silent for a few moments until Jamison finally said, "Very well. If it meets your approval, I think I'll turn in. I'll be ready tomorrow morning to continue my grooming to be your steward. Binta's actions will not be a distraction."

"Very well, my friend. Rest easy, and we will see you at breakfast," Kringus said with a toast of his drink.

Jamison forced a smile and nodded, then left the three friends, closing the door gently behind him. They didn't have to say a word; all three understood what the others were thinking: Binta was in serious trouble.

"What can we do?" Penelope asked when they were alone.

"Trust in Baxter," Victoria said with a sigh.

"But you're worried?" Kringus asked, reading Victoria's expression.

"Of course. Binta is unwell and may be leading them into danger. I assure you that Baxter is no novice wizard, and he is smart enough not to do anything unreasonable," Victoria said.

"Are you convincing us or yourself?" Kringus asked.

"Both," Victoria and Penelope said in unison.

There was a knock on the door, and Kringus said, "Enter."

Arrin opened the door slightly and said, "May I enter, Kringus?"

"Of course, my friend, come join us," Kringus said, waving a hand to his companions.

Arrin entered and shut the door. "I hope I'm not disturbing you. By the looks on your faces, you're discussing something important."

"Just the usual," Penelope said with a tired smile.

"Here, grab a flagon of elvish lager, my friend," Kringus offered, nodding to the small table where an opened cask stood surrounded by several empty bottles.

"From Nessor?" Arrin asked hopefully.

"None other," Kringus said with a smile.

Arrin fixed a drink for all of them and gave Kringus a refill before taking a seat where Jamison had sat moments earlier.

"So, what brings you to my little study tonight, Arrin?" Kringus finally asked.

"I just spoke with the captain of the guard who met with Binta this morning."

"And, what did Jespen say?" Penelope asked before Kringus could. Her husband gave her a look, but she ignored him, other than to playfully slap his leg. But her focus was on Arrin.

"He remembers taking her to Daro's cottage. He knew he wasn't supposed to, but Jespen said he felt like it was appropriate at the time and didn't think twice about it."

"And did Binta meet with Daro?" Kringus asked.

"No, Daro never saw anyone, and the guard couldn't remember where he left her. No one is sure what to make of it."

"Victoria?" Kringus asked.

All turned their attention to the great wizard, and she shook her head. "As we said earlier, Binta is in danger. However, if she has obtained even an inkling of the powers promised by the Tome of X'lor, she is powerful."

"And dangerous as well?" Penelope asked.

"I would think so. I've never examined someone who survived reading the work. My guess is Binta is unstable and definitely not herself. I worry for her, but now I worry for my friend as well."

"But you said Baxter is powerful just moments ago, Victoria. Now you worry about him?" Kringus asked.

"That was before we heard Arrin's report. If she has mastered the tome, and can control people's thoughts, then this is beyond me and certainly beyond Baxter."

The four of them sat there for a long time before they spoke again. Each contemplated the possibilities and envisioned the many ways the excursion could end in tragedy.

THE LONG WOODEN STICKS FELT AWKWARD IN CASSANDRA'S HANDS. They were similar to the weight and size of scimitars, slender swords with curved blades that were standard to the Yaddaton Desert, but they were entirely too long for her to be comfortable with. She wanted to throw them like a hand axe, but that would be ridiculous. She desired the feel of hand axes, but her hosts didn't have replicas with which to spar. Sitra had suggested the scimitars but hadn't yet convinced Cassandra that they were a good alternative. She had no training with weapons, and the sticks should have felt awkward in her hands, but the knowledge of weaponry that Vixa had unwittingly imparted to her was real. She could wield various weapons proficiently, including the practice scimitars, all thanks to Vixa's sacrifice.

"You've told us about the spectacular procedure the barbarians put you through to become a grand warrior. Let's put those skills to the test," Sitra said.

They stood outside the little dwelling that Mateon and Sitra called home. It was one of the best places Cassandra had ever known, and she never wanted to leave it or her new friends. She had been there for over two months and felt she could stay forever. If there weren't the little matter of a particular prophecy that had her looking over her shoulder every waking moment, she would consider herself happy for the first time. Of course, missing Binta and Kessi didn't help ease her mind, either.

It was nearing mid-summer, and the hot desert air was thick that evening. The orange sun was setting behind Sitra, coloring the sky a bright, flaming red. Sitra wore a light garment that allowed her to move swiftly, and the wondrous material didn't cling to her when she perspired; she was sweating profusely now as she and Mateon had just finished their sparring. As usual, Sitra had won that challenge. Now Mateon sat on a large rock, one of his favorites, near the door to their home and ate a lemon. He loved his lemons, and Cassandra loved how he ate them, peel and all!

Cassandra had watched the two fight many evenings; their love for the sport was only exceeded by their love for each other. They were very evenly matched, Mateon blind and Sitra wearing her blindfold. But Sitra won most matches, and Cassandra knew she was the best fighter. Sitra had asked her several days ago to take a turn. Cassandra was not interested at first, but as she watched the dance of the two lovers at play, something in her slowly awakened, something that longed to feel weapons in her hands once more.

She knew those desires weren't her own, but memories of the exotic Vixa, whom Maltor had somehow meshed with her in the awful ritual known as the Warrior's Heart, were overwhelming. As she tested the weapons, a smirk came upon her face. They weren't her favorite weapons, but she could use them. She didn't know how, but she let the muscle memory take over and started to twirl them simultaneously, testing the weight.

"You approve of the scimitars?" Sitra asked, somehow sensing Cassandra's smirk.

"They are not hand axes, but they will do. Are you sure you want to do this?"

"Of course. Mateon and I would love to see your skill level after the barbarian procedure. If what you say is true and you have no formal training, then I should be able to take you down in a few moments. But if the ritual worked, you should be formidable."

"I've watched you over the last few weeks; I know your moves and will easily predict them," Cassandra said, moving closer, bringing her weapons ready. "After all, I'm not blind, and I did win the Queen's Tournament."

She immediately regretted those words and glanced at Mateon, who seemed not to notice. He wore a pleasant smile as he devoured his fruit. "I am sorry, Mateon; I meant no offense," she offered.

"None taken, young lady, but you should know that being blind is an advantage, not a disadvantage. Sitra will beat you."

His words weren't arrogant, and she knew he believed them. However, that didn't convince her. She turned back to Sitra and said, "I am ready."

Sitra had a six-foot wooden staff, and she used it well, Cassandra knew. She held it before her and started twirling it, and it picked up speed quickly. Soon, the weapon was a blur, and Sitra closed the ground. Cassandra was amazed at the weapon's speed and how Sitra made a straight line toward her. Watching the sleeth warrior hone in on her without using her vision was amazing. Sitra had her snake hair pulled back in a ponytail, and as she approached, the little serpents that comprised her magnificent hair began to writhe excitedly.

Cassandra moved a few steps as quietly as possible, but Sitra followed. So, Cassandra tried a different tactic and went on the offensive. Sitra was ready and blocked both thrusting swords quickly, batting them aside and stabbing with her staff. Cassandra nearly took a hit and quickly regrouped. She found her focus, summoning Vixa's combat skills. She easily discerned the sleeth's fighting rhythm, having watched her for the last few days. Cassandra knew when she would attack high or low and could tell if it would be a thrust or a sweeping attack, depending on how she bent her knees.

She quickly realized that none of that mattered because she was measuring her opponent and learning her techniques, but her delay in doing so was giving Sitra the advantage. Using her eyes when Sitra couldn't was becoming a handicap. Frustrated with the realization, Cassandra pressed the attack and had Sitra retreating a bit from her blurring scimitars. No hit could get through the expertly wielded staff, though, and that frustrated Cassandra more than she thought it would.

The dance continued for quite a while, and neither fighter gained an advantage for long. One of Sitra's attacks had grazed Cassandra's thigh, and she was surprised at the pain the dull weapon inflicted. On another occasion, when Cassandra rushed Sitra with a blur of swinging blades, she nicked one of Sitra's fingers, drawing blood. Neither stopped, both so attuned with the fighting that the sight of blood did nothing to stop their sparring. After Sitra suffered the minor wound, they separated momentarily and began circling each other with such intensity that even Mateon noticed, sitting up on his rock to listen. Both were sweating, and Cassandra could feel her wounds flaring from the exertion. Her labored breathing reminded her that not so long ago, she was at death's door. Her forearms flared with each swing of her weapons, and even her gums throbbed. They were about to reengage when Cassandra stopped and looked over Sitra's shoulder. Something big was coming, its form blotting out a good piece of the setting sun.

"What is it?" Sitra asked, sensing Cassandra's change.

"I'm not sure. Something big and moving fast toward us."

"Grog?" Mateon asked.

Cassandra relaxed at the mention of their large lizard neighbor. She squinted into the sun and used her hand to shade her eyes. It was soon apparent that Grog was moving quickly toward them. "Yes, it is the lizard," Cassandra confirmed.

"Then he has brought us a surprise," Mateon said, coming to stand beside the women.

"What do you mean?" Cassandra asked.

"Well, he gets excited when he finds something in the desert. It will either be a dead animal or …" Mateon trailed off.

"Or what?" Cassandra asked nervously as the giant lizard was almost upon them.

"A human," Sitra finished.

"What?"

"He will bring back a human from time to time. Most of the time, they're dead, but sometimes—" Sitra began.

"Sometimes they aren't entirely dead," Mateon finished.

They both looked Cassandra's way, though both were blind, and she knew they were referring to her. She swallowed hard, remembering her ordeal from a few months earlier. She was still amazed at how she had escaped the barbarians with her life. She glanced down at her wooden sparring sticks and shook her head. They felt so comfortable in her hands, yet she had no formal training with any weapon. The barbarians had inadvertently given her a great gift, and yet, she despised them. They were savages who did not tolerate women or magic. She put the thoughts out of her mind as Mateon and Sitra moved to meet the lizard's approach.

The magnificent beast had saved her life because of her new friends' training. They had taught the lizard not to eat humans so it would fetch and bring them home. Her heart raced at the thought of Grog bringing another person to Mateon, who was clearly Grog's trainer. When it came within range, she was relieved to see it wasn't dragging a dead or dying person behind it. That relief was short-lived as it spit out a man gently at Mateon's feet, and was rewarded with a handful of lemons.

"Cassandra, eyes shut; I'm taking off my blindfold!" Sitra said, quickly discarding her eye covering and kneeling beside the man.

Cassandra quickly closed her eyes but refused to take a step toward them. She was petrified and hardly able to breathe. She had caught a glimpse of the man; whether he was dead or badly injured, she couldn't tell. But she knew the person and had mixed feelings about his well-being. She didn't wish death upon anyone, except maybe Cass and Ronnis, but if this person was alive, her time with Sitra and Mateon was over.

"Bad man," Gophia whispered as she landed lightly on Cassandra's shoulder and tucked herself into her hair.

"No, Gophia, not a bad man. He is not our enemy," Cassandra said, steadying her breathing and waiting anxiously for Sitra's evaluation.

Gophia flew back into the house, obviously not too happy with Cassandra's sweaty hair, and as she left, imparted a reminder to Cassandra telepathically: "*Eyes shut.*"

"Mateon, he is alive, but barely. Please bring him inside. Cassandra, do not look; I am turning your way," Sitra said.

Cassandra nodded and stood perfectly still. She heard Sitra move quickly past her, and she knew Mateon had knelt and picked up the injured man. Cassandra was sensing things without using her eyes, just as her friends could. A fleeting glimpse of that spectacle almost brought a smile to her face until she heard Mateon, struggling to carry the large man, move past her.

Soon, they were both inside, and Cassandra slowly opened her eyes. She still had her back to the tiny house and was facing the sunset. She saw Grog's long tail slipping into the small cave he called home a few hundred feet away. The sun set, and the sky darkened. She was still unable to move, and panic gripped her. She had hidden there with Sitra and Mateon to heal and run from her destiny. Now, she would have to leave. And where would she go? Pelesea was on the other side of the world, and she couldn't get back there even if she wanted to.

She knew her birthright was close, though, and she had an idea her father had sent this man to flush her out and get her back on the trail of Zolmex. Of all the barbarians she had met, she only thought highly of two. One was Vixa, whose death Cassandra could not help but feel responsible for, and the other was Jak, the only one in Maltor's tribe who seemed to care for her. Now Jak was in the care of Sitra and Mateon and, from the sound of it, wasn't doing well. She glanced down at the holy symbol of Gella hanging around her neck; the wand and trailing stars spoke to her as always. She knew what she had to do, so, with a determined sigh, she walked over and picked up Sitra's discarded blindfold and put it on. She went inside with some help, using her weapons as walking sticks.

KESSI VAGUELY FELT HERSELF LOWERED FROM THE CONTRAPTION, HER besieged mind barely registering the relief in her arms and wrists. She could not focus on the reprieve; she had to maintain her mental barriers against the barrage of evil thoughts and images that had plagued her for so very long. She had lost track of time and had no idea how long she had hung there by herself, but she was sure now that a new torture was in store for her. Merrik was mad, and he would exact a new punishment soon. The voices in her mind diminished, and that was all that mattered to her. She welcomed any new torture if it meant the demons could no longer whisper to her.

Her eyes fluttered open as the voices gradually faded. She expected to see Merrik's face, full of hate, but instead, she saw Sabrina, her friend. Sabrina scrunched her face with worry and spoke to her, though Kessi could not hear at first. Slowly, her words became audible, and Kessi smiled. She hugged Sabrina tight and was nearing tears; she was so glad to see her friend. She didn't let go for a long time for fear that Sabrina was an illusion.

"Kessi, are you all right?" Sabrina asked, trying to pull away from her so she could look her in the face.

Kessi held tight, though, not wanting the illusion to end. "Sabrina, tell me it's you and not a trick."

Sabrina relented and hugged her tight, careful not to touch her wounded back. "Yes, it is me, Kessi. We're leaving."

Kessi sat back so she could see Sabrina's face. Her muddled mind had been under attack for the time she spent hanging from Matilda's torture device, and now she found it challenging to determine lies from the truth. But looking at Sabrina's face, she knew it was her; she was safe from the evil that had dwelled in her thoughts for the last several days. She looked around, taking in her surroundings, and found all her cellmates crowded around, along with a few malnourished men whom she recognized as Matilda's slaves. She was sitting outside the pentagram from which the torture device loomed, and her eyes widened at the thought of what evil lurked there.

"Don't go in there!" she said, pointing at the pentagram.

Sabrina glanced that way and said, "We won't; you're safe. But you are hurt. Can you walk?"

Kessi couldn't feel her arms more than a tingling sensation, and her back had hurt for so long that she had grown used to the immense discomfort. But when Sabrina asked, and she focused on the pain, she realized how badly Merrik had beaten her. She had no answer for her friend because she wasn't sure if she could walk. So, she shook her head slowly and whispered, "I don't know."

"Fredor, Mensh, free your people and bring them back here. Also, bring clothing for Kessi if you find any," Sabrina said, tossing one of the men a set of keys.

The man nodded once and nudged the other. They left quickly with their swords ready. Kessi realized her nakedness then but couldn't find the strength in her arms to cover herself. Sabrina saw her discomfort and smiled.

"We will have clothes for you soon, Kessi. Just relax," she said.

The slaves were free and armed, and her friends had freed her from the device and the constant torture she experienced within the pentagram. They were free from their cells, something none of them had ever hoped for. Now it was a reality. "How?" Kessi asked, still trying to put all the pieces together.

"Because of her," Natasha said.

Kessi turned to regard Natasha's pointing finger and followed it to find Emiline standing nearby, her hand wounded and dripping blood. Kessi's mind raced at the thought of it. Emiline had helped them escape! Kessi had suspected that the vampire would help them and that she wasn't the monster the others thought. Her memories of Heinsvick came flooding back, and Kessi knew she could relate to Emiline. The vampire would be a tremendous ally, which was clear to all of them.

"Help me stand," Kessi pleaded, reaching a shaking arm to Sabrina.

"But you're injured; you should rest," Sabrina argued.

"We don't have the time unless you're certain Nesin is vacant of all its evil inhabitants. The way our new friends just cautiously left to free the others makes me believe that's not the case."

Sabrina locked stares with Natasha and, after a moment, took Kessi's arm to help her up. Natasha took the other, and with great effort, they finally had her standing. The pain made her swoon, and she felt nauseous from the effort. It took her a few moments to steady herself before the dizziness subsided and she could focus on Emiline.

"You're hurt, Emiline," she said, nodding to the vampire's hand.

Emiline looked at her hand as if she were unaware of the injury. She said nothing but brought her hand up to her mouth and sucked the blood from the wound. The act made the girls nervous, and some shifted from foot to foot while others backed away. Kessi didn't understand much about vampires, but she had dealt with Heinsvick enough to understand her behavior.

Kessi, still leaning heavily on Sabrina, reached out her arm toward Emiline, turning her wrist to display the bite marks that Heinsvick had left. "I know Heinsvick; I can take you to him."

Emiline stopped her sucking, and her eyes widened. She walked over and took Kessi's arm to examine it. Kessi felt Sabrina and Natasha tense with the vampire that close, but Kessi only smiled. She also pointed to the puncture wounds on her neck that had healed over and were barely visible now. But Emiline saw them and rubbed her cool fingers over Kessi's wrist and neck, mesmerized at the sight.

"I'm sorry I didn't tell you earlier. Matilda and Cerus did something to erase my memories, and I couldn't recall you or Heinsvick. But trust me, Heinsvick sent me here so that you could be released," Kessi said.

"You are like me?" Emiline asked, looking intently at Kessi's mouth for a sign of elongated canines.

"No, I'm not a vampire, Emiline, but Heinsvick did bite me. I know him, and he wants you back. Matilda tricked him, and that's why you're still here."

"Heinsvick wants me?"

"Yes, more than anything. Matilda tried to kill him, but I feel that he escaped her trap, though I don't recall completely how."

Emiline nodded and smiled, and the two connected as sisters might. The vampire's reaction was sincere, and Kessi knew Emiline would trust her from that point forward. "We must leave this place, Emiline. Do you know the way out?" Kessi asked.

Emiline shook her head.

"Can you get us to Matilda's room? I believe I was there at first, and she has my things. If I can find my holy symbol, I may be able to summon some of my powers as a priestess," Kessi explained.

"I have been there, but I am afraid I do not know the way," Emiline said.

"I do," came a male voice from the room entrance.

All turned to find Fredor there. "Well, at least my wife does. She cleans their room, among other things," he added, lowering his gaze in shame as he spoke the last part.

A pretty woman appeared beside him then, and Fredor draped an arm around her. She was attractive, and Kessi quickly surmised what other activities the woman might be performing for the evil couple.

"I am Patricka, and I will show you the way," she said, then smiled at her husband, who lovingly returned the gesture.

"But I'm afraid our friends are panicked and will not linger. They want out of this prison and won't journey with you to find this room. And my advice is that if you do this, do it quickly, for time is against us," Fredor said.

"We think the caves are mostly deserted. Matilda, Cerus, and the priests are gone," Sabrina added.

"They have left to find Cassandra. They must know where she is," Kessi said sadly.

"Your sister?" Natasha asked.

"Yes. It is the only explanation for leaving us unattended."

"There are men here still, the ones left behind by Matilda," Sabrina said.

"Yes, but they aren't loyal. They may let us go if we outnumber them. Where is Merrik? He is our biggest threat."

"We disposed of him," Sabrina said with a sudden fire in her eyes.

Kessi had never seen that look from her usually gentle friend before, but she understood the girl's desire to live, to be free of the godforsaken place they had all called home for far too long. She also understood that Merrik was dead, and she could not have been more thankful. The last few days had been the worst of her life, and she was eternally grateful for her friends rescuing her from that hell.

Suddenly, Patricka was there, gently placing an old, filthy shirt on her shoulders. "This is all we have, but it will cover you," she said.

Sabrina and Natasha helped Kessi ease her arms into the thin garment. At the same time, a bustling outside the room had them all turning to see hundreds of men, women, and children gathered outside, with panic and hope in their eyes. Mensh led the procession and entered the room, still brandishing the sword, which now dripped with blood.

"There are still some evil varmints about. Be careful," he said.

"Everyone all right?" Fredor asked, noticing the sword.

Mensh shook his head and said, "No, three ambushed us. We managed to overpower them but lost some good friends in the process."

"Who?" Patricka asked nervously.

Mensh lowered his eyes and whispered, "Roi and Dallen."

Patricka gasped, and Fredor held her tight, both visibly upset by the news. Kessi understood these people were just like Sabrina, Natasha, and the others she had come to know but had been treated much worse. Some had been worked to death and had eaten very little, whereas Kessi and her cellmates always had plenty of food. Their journey differed from Kessi's, but she understood their desperation to leave. So, when Mensh bid his farewell and led the large group of escapees away and hopefully to freedom, it didn't surprise Kessi.

"Kessi, we're going with them," Kimmie said, speaking for six of her cellmates.

Kessi smiled and said, "None of us will think less of you for leaving now. Go and find your way to safety."

"Be mindful of that one. I have felt the vampire's bite, and she is vicious," Kimmie whispered, nodding toward Emiline, who seemed not to notice.

"What? When?"

"I'll explain later," Sabrina said.

They shared hugs, shed a few tears, and said their goodbyes. The strength of the bond of being held captive together for so long made the parting difficult. Kessi had a bad feeling she would never see Kimmie or the others again.

"Where will you go?" Kessi asked before Kimmie and the others departed.

"Mensh is leading us to a place called Ikma, not far from here. A kind spirit-druid guards it, so he says. We will be safe there, and Matilda and Cerus won't follow."

Kessi saw Fredor and Patricka's glance at the mention of Ikma and made a mental note to ask them about it later. For the time being, she gave Kimmie one last hug and promised to meet her there if possible. After the departure of Kimmie and the small group of cellmates Kessi had come to know as family, only Kessi, Sabrina, Natasha, Emiline, Fredor, Patricka, and two dozen young virgins, including Sara, the youngest, remained.

"We will not go to Ikma," Sabrina said.

"What is Ikma?" Kessi asked.

"It is a swamp just south of here, and some legends say that the druid there is not good and that he can turn into a dragon and eat you!"

"And you let them go?" Kessi asked, now alarmed.

"It's safer than being here, and it is true, Matilda would probably not follow."

"We should go to Attins instead," Fredor said.

"Where is that?" Kessi asked.

"To the north. Most of us are from there and would like to return home."

"Let's get out of here, and then we'll decide," Kessi said.

Just then, a scream, followed by shouting and a scuffling, erupted in the direction Mensh was leading the escapees. They all listened intently, and it seemed that the skirmish was short-lived, so they put it out of their minds, hoping their friends had once again overwhelmed the enemy.

"I don't know how many mercenaries still guard this place, but we must leave now if we're to have any hope of escaping," Kessi said.

Patricka led them quietly and stealthily deeper into the caves and away from the passage that led to freedom. It was hard for them not to flee with the rest of their friends, but Kessi needed to check on her belongings. She couldn't remember but thought she'd had her holy symbol when Heinsvick handed her over to Matilda. He would have allowed her to have it to maybe give her an edge against the evil she would face at the hands of the evil priestess. However, it was taken from her when she first arrived, along with her clothes. There had been maidens who had undressed her then redressed her in Matilda's desired outfit. As she gingerly walked to whatever waited for them in Matilda's room, she struggled to pull down the shirt Patricka had given her. She was naked underneath and very self-conscious about it. She needed her clothing and holy symbol to heal her damaged back. She hoped they would find them in Matilda's lair and prayed that her little detour wouldn't cost them their freedom.

MALTOR WATCHED FROM ATOP THE WALL OF THE TRAINING GROUNDS, the very ones Cassandra had occupied months prior; his warriors, those that remained, lined the walls, along with the shamans. He had sent most of the female and elderly members of his tribe to the Culiem Tribe to seek sanctuary and plead for reinforcements. He knew the reinforcements wouldn't arrive, but he hoped the neighboring tribe would not deny his people entrance. If they did, it was better than the fate that would befall them if they stayed. Others in the training compound included a handful of artisans, cooks, and even a few breeding slaves from the procreation tent. Most of the outlanders in the tent were left there, Maltor having no time to herd them somewhere safe. If the invaders captured or killed them, so be it.

Maltor was a seasoned warrior, a king of the Yaddaton Desert, and had led many raids into foreign lands to rape and pillage. The many battles and excursions he had participated in did little to prepare him for the vision that was Matilda. She led her army through the tents that comprised Maltor's homeland. The sun was high in the sky when he first spotted her, but that did not deter her minions of death. As Bolin had claimed, a swarm of zombies, undead creatures comprised of the people who once roamed Maltor's land and called it home, accompanied her.

The creatures were swift and attacked anything in their path; whether a small animal, a cactus, or even a tent, they tore it to shreds. Maltor estimated that between five hundred and one thousand creatures were coming forth, like ants invading a deserted plate of food. He watched in horror as they came straight for the training compound, where he would make his stand if need be. He didn't have Jak, but he had many archers at his disposal, and they prepared their bows to rain death upon the invaders. Maltor needed only to give the order. His shamans, six in total and led by the powerful shaman Grink, stood nearby.

"These creatures were once our people?" Maltor asked Bolin, who watched the spectacle beside him.

"Yes, my king," Bolin said, bowing his head.

That fact repulsed Maltor. He could fight an enemy to the death and gut them proudly on the field of battle. However, fighting against his own people, reanimated with dark magic, offended him greatly. To make matters worse, they weren't his people as he remembered them. The weaklings responsible for the perversion had given them sharp talons with teeth to match and an unnatural agility. Once they spotted Maltor standing proudly on the wall, they rushed toward him at a speed equal to a camel's.

"Grink!" Maltor yelled, never taking his eyes off the coming swarm of creatures.

"Yes, my king," Grink said, standing nearby.

"Prepare the holy spell of Strenna now—first defensive spell, as we discussed."

"Yes, my king," Grink said, then rushed off to the designated spot at the front of the wall, the other five shamans quickly following.

Once they reached the spot and looked out to the swarm of undead quickly approaching, they began their joined chant. Grink dug out a flask of sand and a dropper of water. One of the other shamans took the dropper as Grink uncorked the bottle of sand. They added several drops of water to the flask and followed that with a tar-like substance. They continued their chant, and the water began to bubble. Once all three components mixed, Grink heaved it toward the coming swarm. It landed about fifty feet in front of the wall. The shamans' chant grew in pitch and cadence as the bottle spilled.

Matilda stood back behind the rushing mob of undead, understanding now that the barbarian king had locked himself and probably Cassandra in the small fortified structure at the center of the tribe. All the other structures were tents, and her undead army tore through them quickly, but this was different. She would have to be smart to breach the walls of the small barbarian fortress.

"He hides; he cannot be formidable," Cerus said, standing beside his wife.

"He is dangerous by all accounts, my husband, and should be treated as such. I will negotiate with the savage to obtain Cassandra. She is all that matters."

"Your creatures will destroy them all," Ronnis spoke from behind his mask.

"No, Lord Ronnis, they will only surround the place; they are perfectly under my control and will kill no one unless I demand it," Matilda answered.

"I cannot wait to have some fun with her; I owe her tremendously," Cass added from behind Ronnis, absently rubbing her chest where the wound caused by Cassandra's attack during their adventure had nearly killed her.

"First, we must obtain our subject, then you will have fun with her," Matilda said.

"How much fun are we allowed?" Ronnis asked.

Matilda looked at him, and her visage left little doubt about what she meant. "You and Cass are going to be my chief tormentors for Cassandra Rho, but you may not kill her. That is why I will monitor your actions."

"We have no desire to kill her if that is your plan for her anyway. We merely want to exact some revenge," Ronnis said.

"And we have a whole year to do it in," Cass added with a childlike giggle.

"Sir," one of Cerus's men said, running up to stand before his leader.

"What is it, soldier?" Cerus said.

"We have scoured the tents and have found a few supplies but no barbarians to speak of. However, there is a large tent full of women and a few children. The women seem to be captives, chained to their beds. They don't seem native to the desert."

"Beds?" Cerus asked curiously.

"Yes, they appear to be part of a brothel."

"More subjects for the great sacrifice," Matilda said excitedly. "You may pick a couple to your liking, Lord Ronnis, to play with after this business with the barbarians is over."

Ronnis looked at her curiously, and Matilda added, "You may take out your sexual frustrations on them; I don't want your inappropriate desires to spill over into your tortures of Cassandra."

"Very well," Ronnis whispered his approval.

"So, the whole place is deserted, except for a tent full of prisoners? This is too convenient, but I won't question our good fortune," Matilda said with an evil smile. Then she added, "Cass, why don't you and Ronnis go and look over the new prisoners? Ronnis, you may take claim to two. More importantly, look for Cassandra. If she is there, then we can reasonably assume she lost her virginity to the savages. If so, I'll have the barbarian king's head on a stick."

"With pleasure," Cass said, and she grabbed Ronnis's arm and pulled him along.

"Send some men with them, Cerus. I do not trust those two alone with Cassandra, and if they find her, I want to know immediately."

"Very well," Cerus said, and he nodded to the man who had delivered the news. "Take three men and send word if she is found."

"Yes, sir," the man said and ran off.

Cerus turned back just in time to see the ground before the fortress suddenly transform into a murky swamp-like liquid. The first wave of undead creatures rushed headlong into the trap, where the wet sand began to suck them down.

"Quicksand!" Matilda yelled out in horror as she immediately lost hundreds of her creatures. "Quickly, call them back!" she yelled to the priests.

In unison, they began calling to the undead, and the unthinking creatures started to retreat. They watched as the quagmire swallowed them. The spectacle didn't last long, and when it was over, the sand dried up again. All the undead caught in that temporary fiasco were gone, gobbled up by the earth.

"He will pay for that, Cerus," Matilda hissed. "Bring me the prisoner."

"The outlanders are no match for the powers of Strenna, my king," Grink said with a smirk.

Maltor smiled and nodded, understanding their enemy had suffered a tremendous blow. That was when Bolin whispered, "By the gods!"

Maltor turned to regard his commander, who seemed crestfallen, staring at their enemies. Maltor's smile melted, and he turned to take in whatever horror Bolin was witnessing. The small woman, obviously the leader, accompanied by a huge man, one large enough to be a barbarian, stepped out from the rest and approached the stronghold. Behind them, dragged by a horse, was one of Maltor's men. He was on his back, unconscious, with one leg tied to the horse's saddle. His arms were above his head, trailing behind his lifeless body. It appeared as if the outlanders had dragged him across Yaddaton, and little of his skin remained. He was a bloody pulp, and he left a trail of red behind him.

"Who is that?" Maltor asked Bolin as Grink slunk away, no longer in the mood to brag.

"Jozerah," Bolin said softly.

"Impossible! Jozerah is smarter than that. He would never …" Maltor's words died off as the truth set in. The bloody mess that remained of their captive was Jozerah, the general of his army.

The procession stopped about fifty yards from the wall where Maltor stood. Then there was silence; only the blowing wind echoing through the training center provided sound, along with the occasional wisp of sand it churned.

Finally, the woman spoke. "Honorable King of the Serpent Tribe, I come to barter with you."

Maltor crossed his arms over his large chest and made no sound. The stare he fixed on the woman promised revenge, and Bolin took a step away from the volatile king.

"I have one of your generals here," she continued with an arm extended toward Jozerah's remains. "I will gladly hand him over for healing, and I require only one thing to make this trade."

Maltor remained silent, and his elevated breathing told Bolin and anyone who knew the proud barbarian that he would destroy the foolish woman.

"All I ask in return for this man's freedom is one member of your tribe. Well, she is not a member, just an outsider like me. I am here to take her back where she belongs. I ask that you hand over Cassandra Rho, and I will exchange this man's life for hers."

At the mention of Cassandra's name, all around Maltor witnessed his muscles flex and tense, and a low, feral growl emanated from deep within the proud warrior. "Keep your magics ready," Maltor whispered to Grink, then turned to Bolin and added, "Have the archers ready. If they try anything funny or break our rules, destroy them all."

"But my king, what is your plan?" Bolin asked.

"To save Jozerah."

"But how?"

Maltor only smirked, then rushed down from the wall and ordered the gate open. Two guards hurried to comply, barely opening the giant door before the king trampled them and burst through the portal. He walked out to meet the outsiders, and the doors quickly sealed behind him. The Serpent Tribe crowded around the front of the wall to witness what their king had in mind. He limped, which stemmed from the injury suffered during his fight with King Boskel a few weeks earlier. He eventually stood within ten feet of the woman and her giant ally.

He eyed the woman suspiciously, understanding her to be deeply rooted in dark magic but confident he could break her neck if he could get his hands on her. She seemed unfazed by his hard stare, which was uncommon for an outsider, much less a weakling female practicing dark magic. He eventually shifted his gaze to his motionless general behind the couple.

The man standing near the small woman snorted and smirked as he followed Maltor's gaze. "You think he's dead, barbarian?" the large man said.

He walked to Jozerah's still form and picked up a limp arm. He snapped the general's pinky finger with a quick flick. Jozerah screamed out in pain and thrashed around for a bit, seemingly unaware of his surroundings. The large man dropped Jozerah's arm and stood beside the woman.

"He is alive. For a bit longer, at least," the man said with an evil smile.

"Cerus, we do not need to insult the great king. He is wise enough to understand the value of his general's life compared to an outsider's. What do you say, King? Cassandra does not belong here; let me take her from you."

Maltor's rage welled inside him as the fools continued to discuss Cassandra. He had avenged his queen's death by destroying Boskel, and now these interlopers dared to ask for her? Did they honestly not know her fate, or was this just a game to them? It was no game to Maltor, and they were about to find out the hard way.

He unsheathed his massive sword and said, "Here, in my land, we settle disputes honorably. Since you trespass on this land, my home, I am not required to offer you the chance, but I will grant you one attempt at honor."

With the tip of his blade, he began to etch a circle into the Yaddaton sand, similar to the one he had drawn for his battle with Boskel. Maltor didn't use a toe as he did then, for the pain in his injured hip would give away a weakness he knew he couldn't afford against the large interloper standing before him. Once he completed the circle, he stabbed his sword in the middle and crossed his massive arms over his chest.

"I challenge the fool to a fight to the death," the barbarian king said, nodding toward Cerus.

Cerus smiled and started for the circle, but Matilda reached out an arm to stop him. "What are the terms of this challenge, good king? We want to respect your honorable ways, but we also want to understand what awaits the victor," she said.

"If I win, you hand over Jozerah; if you win, you get what you came for."

A wide smile crept across Matilda's face and she whispered excitedly, "You *do* have her!" She stepped toward Maltor, nearly unable to contain her excitement, and asked, "Tell me, good king, is she still pure?"

Maltor gnashed his teeth and fought the urge to reach out and strangle the ignorant woman. He didn't want to disclose the fact that Cassandra was dead, for he was confident he would beat the challenger, and then his men would overwhelm the woman and her meek followers. But her continued discussion of his beloved dead queen made it difficult for him to stay in control and keep that little secret hidden.

When he didn't respond, the large man added, "Did you spoil her with your impotent seed, King of Nothing?"

Maltor grabbed his weapon and beckoned Cerus to enter the circle, pointing his finger at the large adversary. "Come and taste the bite of my sword. Your time in my home has ended, interloper!"

He ended the rebuttal with several quick swings of his blade, cutting the air around him and finally bringing it up to a ready position, assuming a battle stance. Matilda still held her small hand on Cerus's chest, trying to get an answer to the critical question concerning Cassandra's virginity. When Maltor said nothing, she moved her hand, and Cerus stepped quickly into the circle.

"Very well, King, you fight my champion, Cerus the Grey by name. The winner receives the spoils we have agreed to," Matilda said.

Cerus and Maltor circled each other for several moments, feeling each other out, studying the other's movements. Maltor did well to hide the limp he had sustained from his fight against Boskel. Cerus was slightly taller, but both were muscled and seasoned combat veterans. However, the sand was Maltor's friend, and he was advantaged here. He started to advance on Cerus, studying the large spear the man carried. He was confident that the weapon was inferior to his great sword.

Maltor briefly noticed the gates of the training center were open, and a contingent of barbarians came out to stand on Maltor's side of the circle. Cerus's men did the same and stood on the other side, flanking Matilda as the priests kept a distance, holding back the small army of undead they controlled. Likewise, the shamans of the Serpent Tribe, who remained on the wall with Bolin, readied their spells to combat any magic they detected on the battlefield below. A mass of barbarian warriors waited anxiously at the gate. On Bolin's signal, they would rush out and into battle if it came to it. Archers also lined the wall, watching Matilda's priests intently.

"If they break any of the rules, or if the fools breach the circle, unleash your wrath," Bolin instructed the shamans, then relayed the same message to the archers.

The next few moments were tense as both armies wanted nothing more than to tear into each other. But they remained in control of their battle lust and watched as their leaders circled each other in the designated battle area. Finally, Maltor let fly a guttural scream and charged in.

He didn't expect to score a hit with his initial attack but wanted to evaluate how the big man handled himself. As expected, the metal shaft of the great spear intercepted his attack, and the counterthrust surprised Maltor, who had to maneuver quickly to dodge the attack.

Cerus smiled and took advantage of Maltor's off-balance stance. He came at him with several stabs of the spear, which Maltor managed to knock aside with his blade. Then he quickly changed tactics, bringing the spear horizontally to the ground and punching the shaft toward Maltor's face. Maltor got his sword up at the last moment to block, and Cerus kicked him hard in his injured hip. There was a flash of pain in that strike, and Maltor nearly lost his balance as the wounded hip threatened to give out. He had underestimated his opponent, who obviously knew of the injury all along.

Cerus smiled and said, "Do you need to sit and rest a bit, old king? I'm sure that lump of bloody flesh you call a general can make it a while longer before he fades into the afterworld. He doesn't look in need of immediate healing at all."

Maltor charged in swinging again and was equally frustrated the second time, unable to penetrate Cerus's defenses. He was more knowledgeable now of the large man's tactics and easily parried any counterattacks. So, the two fought for a long while, weapons flashing for strikes and parries, and each warrior breaking into a sweat in the beating sun of Yaddaton. Neither was able to score a hit or gain an advantage, and eventually they broke their attacks, each breathing heavily and Maltor limping badly.

"You're wearing down, old man," Cerus taunted as the two began to circle again.

Maltor snorted and said, "You are the outsider who wilts under Yaddaton's sun, not me."

"You will die today, barbarian king, do not doubt. You fight well for a cripple, but your time of ruling these savages is over. I am the new law now," Cerus said and smiled.

Maltor could not resist the taunt, and although he knew Cerus was toying with his emotions, he would no longer listen to the ignorant words spewing from the interloper's mouth. It was time for Cerus to die! He rushed in with another primal yell, sword slicing and slashing in a blur. Cerus was immediately overwhelmed as Maltor gained the offensive. Cerus retreated the best he could while remaining in the circle, but Maltor had him on his heels, and it was time to finish off the loud-mouthed fool.

Cerus fell to one knee, exhaustion getting the best of him, and Maltor took the opportunity for a lethal attack. After one near miss due to a desperate parry, Maltor kicked out, and although Cerus was fast enough to dodge most of the surprise attack, Maltor's boot struck him in the arm, dislodging the spear. Cerus fell on his back, his eyes wide in disbelief. Maltor understood by that look that no one had bested the man in combat before. But Cerus had never fought Maltor, King of the Serpent Tribe of Yaddaton!

Maltor was quick to pounce atop the prone warrior and bring his sword stabbing in a downward thrust aimed at Cerus's throat. Cerus threw a handful of sand as Maltor attacked, but the barbarian king had seen that ploy many times, having called the desert his home all his life. He closed his eyes tight for a moment as the sand pelted him, then reopened them to find Cerus desperately bringing his hands up to grasp the sword. To his credit, Cerus was strong enough to stop the powerful thrust, but it cost him deep gashes on the palms of his hands. Blood flowed freely down his forearms, and the sword slowly sank closer to Cerus's throat.

Somewhere behind him, Maltor heard the female leader say, "Get up, Cerus! We cannot lose Cassandra!"

Maltor smiled as he put all his weight on the sword hilt, slicing through Cerus's hands and inching closer to the kill. The large outlander finally understood his doom, the shock of his pending defeat plastered on his sweat-covered face. Maltor would win this challenge, then take the woman as a fifth wife, not because they had agreed to it, but because he was Maltor, King of Yaddaton, and could do whatever he wanted!

The barbarians watched intently, looking for any possible interference. Their king would be victorious here, and if the interlopers breached the circle, they would swarm in for the kill. Bolin and Grink stood ready on the training compound's wall, Bolin prepared to signal the archers, Grink and the other shamans ready with their spells. The doors to the training pit were unlocked and ready to fly open to pour forth the rest of the concealed barbarians. Everyone in the Serpent Tribe was prepared to do their part to defend their king and their home if the outsiders interfered in any way.

The warriors of Gorl and the priests of Marnelphion looked on in disbelief as the sword tip inched closer to Cerus's throat. None had seen their leader defeated, and they stood in shock, especially Matilda, who was caught off guard by the change of events. Her general was defeated, but more importantly, her husband was about to die.

All focused on the imminent defeat of Cerus the Grey and no one saw the strange zombie with flaming red hair running on all fours from the group of undead massed behind the priests. She was Vixa, daughter of Zorn, and this was the moment of her glory. A few priests saw her at the last moment, just before she leaped over the line of Gorl warriors, watching their leader slowly lose the match. Those priests were dumbfounded, as were the few others who witnessed the rogue, self-acting zombie enter the circle. None had commanded her to action.

Those who witnessed the dexterous creature were far too slow to react, and nothing hampered the beast as it closed in on its unsuspecting prey. Maltor grinned as his sword sliced through Cerus's palms, and the tip continued its descent, slightly piercing Cerus's throat.

Then, something slammed into Maltor, knocking him off his victim. The strike was unexpected and powerful, dislodging the sword in the process. Maltor managed to stand and not fall under the weight of the new assailant. The first thought that rushed through his mind was that the interlopers had broken the challenge's rules, and they would pay dearly. But then the pain in the side of his head demanded all of his attention as his attacker remained lodged on his back and bit hard into the side of his head. Unnaturally sharp teeth raked his scalp, and his right ear was torn from his head, bitten off by the red-haired zombie.

Maltor staggered around the circle. Blood poured from his injured scalp, and the creature clung to his back. He yelled in defiance and slammed a fist blindly into the zombie's face, shattering teeth and lodging several of the sharper ones into his fist. A second fist followed, and a third broke the jawbone, dropping the unnatural beast from his back. Maltor held the spot where his ear used to be and looked down at the creature in disbelief, blood gushing from the wound and running down his neck and chest.

He looked at the wounded creature and whispered in disbelief, "Vixa?"

He knew right away that the creature was once Vixa, trainer of his female warriors, and the unwitting sacrifice to help Cassandra win the Queen's Tournament. He brought a foot up to crush its face, to stomp out what devil magic coursed through the corpse to give it animation. Maltor saw what looked like a smile as he did so. Even with her broken jaw and missing teeth, he registered a smile on her distorted face. He stomped down with all his might, his anger behind the wicked attack. The creature perished, unmoving and once again at peace. That was when Maltor felt the biting tip of Cerus's spear enter his back.

DISCOVERIES

"There is nothing I can do," Sitra said with a sigh, sitting back and surrendering to the inevitable.

She had worked on Jak for several hours, applying her limited healing knowledge to his broken body. She was not a healer by trade and had little ability aside from the menial skills she possessed with herbs and cactus milk that could heal minor injuries.

"I am sorry, his injuries are too severe, and he has lost a lot of blood. I was lucky to have saved Cassandra, but this one is too far gone and in worse shape than Cassandra was when we found her. All we can do is make him comfortable for the short time he has left in this world," she continued.

Sitra and Mateon both loved all living things, and the loss of a human life weighed heavily on their shoulders. Sitra stood and turned to Cassandra, who, although still blindfolded, sensed the action. Cassandra closed her eyes behind the mask, then removed it, handing it to Sitra.

She felt Sitra take it, and then she breathed in her ear, "After we bury this stranger, we should train you in the art of blind fighting. You sensed I needed my mask without the use of your vision. You are a natural. Open your eyes, my friend; it is safe."

Cassandra did, and Sitra stood before her, now the one blindfolded. Cassandra had to adjust her vision to the lamplight, blinking away the temporary blindness. When her vision came to, she looked upon Sitra's face and saw exhaustion mixed with sadness. Sitra forced a smile, patted Cassandra's hand, then turned and walked out of the room.

Mateon pulled the blanket over Jak's still form, tucking it at the man's chin, a feeble attempt at making the dying man comfortable. He turned to Cassandra and said, "Come, let's have some tea with lemons; that always makes us feel a little better during troubling times."

"I will be along shortly," Cassandra said.

Mateon smiled weakly and nodded, then turned and exited the small room. Cassandra could hear the couple rummaging for a pot in the kitchen to make the tea. She closed her eyes, listened, and picked up small bits of the conversation. She knew that Sitra felt guilty about failing to help Jak, and she heard her discussing it with Mateon. In turn, he consoled her.

She opened her eyes just as Gophia entered the room and landed on her usual perch on Cassandra's shoulder. When the little fairy saw Jak, she squealed and hid in Cassandra's hair. "*Barbarian!*" the little fairy imparted telepathically to her.

"Yes, but a friend, Gophia. Don't be frightened."

"Friend?" Gophia said and stuck her tiny head through Cassandra's hair.

"Yes, and he won't harm you. He's dying."

"Maltor killed?"

"I don't know, but I wouldn't think so. Jak was a good man and I wish I knew his story."

Cassandra closed her eyes again, this time not to listen to the conversation in the next room, but instead she called to her goddess. She grasped the holy symbol and knelt beside Jak. She had forged a new bond with her goddess during her time with Mateon and Sitra. Gella had saved her from the barbarian burial ground, had saved her from Yaddaton itself. She felt close to Gella, and the power of her goddess found her heart, pulsing good feelings and hope with each beat. She opened her eyes and lowered the blanket that covered Jak. She removed the rudimentary dressings that Sitra had applied, the stench of herbs and rotting flesh wafting in the air.

"*Yuck!*" Gophia imparted to Cassandra, then fell back into her hiding spot in Cassandra's hair.

Cassandra paid her little friend no heed—the sight before her took her hope. Not even Gella could fix the broken man. He had a nasty gash on his forearm and several across his chest, all three deep and infected. A sword wound on his thigh had turned an ugly purple, and his upper thigh swelled from it. More significantly, he had a wound to his back that was deep and fatal, as dark blood still leaked slowly from it. Cassandra brought an arm around to feel the scar on her own back where Cass had stabbed her. She remembered how that felt, and she knew Jak's wound was far worse than the one she'd suffered. Her heart went out to the barbarian.

The worst-looking wound, though, was his right shoulder, which looked crushed as bone and muscle protruded from deep tears. His arm hung limply, and the darkening flesh around that wound indicated that rotting had set in. Sitra was right; the man was beyond repair and as good as dead. How he still drew those shallow breaths was a testament to the hardiness of the Yaddaton barbarians.

When she'd first seen Jak drop from the lizard's mouth, she'd wondered if Maltor had taken out his frustrations on him, something Cassandra had not considered during her daring escape. Now, after examining his wounds, she knew Maltor had not done this. The cuts were a mix of short blades and vicious animal-like attacks. The stab wound in his back was not deep enough to be a sword but was a blade similar to the one Cass used to stab Cassandra in the caves of Kane. She didn't know how she knew this but understood it was probably Vixa's wisdom at work. All she knew was that Maltor's great sword had not made that wound.

"I'm sorry, my friend," she whispered, touching his clammy forehead.

He moaned at the touch, the slight indication he still lived. He had been good to Cassandra when she was Maltor's prisoner, and she had to try something. She closed her eyes and opened her heart, like when she first received Gella back in the temple at Pelesea. She focused only on her goddess and grasped her holy symbol tightly.

Finally, she prayed. "Gella, goddess of magic and giver of life, please use me here. I am not a priestess or even an acolyte, and I am surely not worthy of this prayer. However, this is a good man, and I believe in you. I owe you my life, and I will gladly give it to save his if you deem it necessary. Use me as a conduit to save him. Heal his broken body if you find us worthy."

She felt her goddess in her heart but felt no change. She opened her eyes, and Jak remained very still, clinging to what little life remained in him. She looked over the symbol she held, disappointed but not surprised that Gella denied her. With a heavy sigh, she stood, prepared to leave him in peace to die alone. She paused and grasped her holy symbol and felt the energy pulsing within. Gella was listening, but Cassandra wasn't doing her part. She didn't believe in herself, and so she failed.

She knelt beside Jak once more and gently touched his shredded shoulder. Even that slight contact had him screaming out in pain. She paid no mind to his reaction, cleared her head, and focused on her goddess. She took up her symbol with her other hand, kissed it, and held it tight.

"Gella, I ask once more in faith and servitude, use me to heal this man. You are great, and I believe you can funnel your power through me to do this."

Her symbol grew warm, as did the hand that touched Jak. She dared not open her eyes as her hope grew that the healing might work. At that moment, she saw things differently. When she first learned to see the arcane symbols at a young age, most prominently in the spellbook in Ronnis's office, she had always commanded them to create spells. Gella's blessing was different; this was faith. She had no symbols to command and relied solely on her goddess to make the healing spell.

"Gella, use me to heal. I believe in you, and as your priestess, I believe in me!"

Her heart filled with the power of Gella, and just as the water in Kane's deep cavern, she felt it flow through her, from her holy symbol, through her body, to her hand, and into Jak. She felt the energy flow true and strong. After many moments, it dissipated, and Cassandra felt cold and slightly sad as if her goddess had suddenly left her.

Expecting the worst and fully ready to be disappointed at what she would find, she slowly opened her eyes. Jak's shoulder was fully healed, and the mangled mess that was there before was now gone. She examined his other wounds but found no sign of them. Her spell had fully healed him! She was overwhelmed by the experience, and tears slowly fell from her unusually bright blue eyes. Jak opened his eyes slightly and smiled weakly, and she broke down, sobbing, hugging him. It had worked, and it was not a minor healing. She had brought this man back from death's door. At that moment, she was indeed a priestess of Gella.

TRUE TO HER WORD, PATRICKA LED KESSI AND HER FRIENDS TO MATILda's chambers. The place was deserted, but Kessi sensed a presence there like she did during her time hanging from the torture rack. It was as if something evil watched over the place.

"This place is unpure; we need to be quick," Kessi said.

Kessi stood at the room's threshold, afraid to enter because of the evil she might find within. Her eyes scanned the room, where a dull purple, unnatural light seemed to glow all around. Kessi couldn't find the source of that light, and she guessed that it was magical as the dark pool in the center of the room seemed to glow the brightest, as well as the many tapestries hanging in the room, depicting demonic orgies and sacrifices.

The light was enough to illuminate the room, so the giant, soft bed Matilda and Cerus shared was easily visible, along with two dressers, a large table, several chests, and an extra bed that Kessi recalled. Her memories flashed through her mind, and then she remembered being tethered to the wall during her brief stay with the evil couple. She had to squint to see it, but the collar and chain were lying on the bed, the end of the chain bolted to the wall. Her back ached as she remembered trying to rest on that bed with her freshly whipped back throbbing so much she thought she'd die.

There wasn't much else in the decorative room, so she surmised that her belongings, including her holy symbol, were hopefully in one of the chests. Again, the feeling of something watching over the room began to creep into her thoughts. She needed to be quick, and they all needed to flee just like the rest of the prisoners had.

"Stay here. I don't think it's safe inside," Kessi said as she stepped into the room.

"It is unsafe there, but I know what safeguards they use. I will accompany you," Patricka said, gently grabbing Kessi's arm.

"And if she goes, I go," added Fredor.

Kessi looked each of them in the eye and knew she would not deter them; they knew the dangers. She also needed guidance, so she nodded and said, "Let's go then and be quick about it."

As Kessi entered the unholy place, a chill ran down her spine. She felt a presence, and whatever it was immediately bombarded her with impure thoughts and wicked images. She imagined herself prone on the bed, wearing the collar, Fredor on top of her, thrusting his manhood deep inside. The thoughts were overwhelming, and she turned to Fredor to see the lust in his eyes. He took her by the hand and led her to the bed. He picked up the collar and moved to fasten it around her slender neck. Kessi pulled her hair up to give him access. She licked her lips in anticipation and wondered why she had never done this before. Why had she maintained her virginity? At that moment, she wanted to be anything but pure. Sex was her objective, and sex she would have.

Fredor clasped the collar around her neck, although there was no key to secure it. Both knew that Kessi would not attempt to remove the device. They moved to kiss, but before their lips touched, the feeling of wanton lust quickly faded, and they both paused and shook the thoughts away. Embarrassed, Fredor moved away, a look of fright on his face. He was a man now accustomed to beatings for wrongdoings, and he looked around nervously, expecting just that.

"I am sorry, Kessi, I do not—" he began.

"Don't apologize. I felt it, too," Kessi said, quickly unfastening the collar and throwing it on the bed.

"The statuette gave you the thought," Patricka interrupted.

Both turned to regard Fredor's wife. The look on her face offered no judgment, even though Fredor's guilt was evident by his body language. He was sorry for his actions, and Kessi could tell he greatly loved Patricka.

"Patricka, my lovely wife, I have betrayed you," he said, hanging his head in shame.

She approached him, tilted his head to meet her gaze, and kissed him lovingly. "You did no such thing. The statue of Marnelphion, Matilda's guardian, gave you the feelings. They were not your thoughts," she said. "Nor yours, Kessi," she added, turning with a forgiving smile.

"Thank you, Patricka," Kessi said, feeling her cheeks redden.

"It is out of sight; I threw it in the pool. If it cannot see you, it cannot suggest," the beautiful woman added.

"But why were you not affected?" Kessi asked, suddenly curious.

"That statuette and I have done many bad things together. I am somewhat immune to its call," she said. It was her turn to hang her head in shame.

Fredor lifted her chin gently and said, "Those days are behind us, and similarly, those were not your thoughts. There is no need to feel ashamed, my love."

"Kessi, hurry, we heard more fighting in the passages!" Sabrina called from the doorway.

That got all three moving quickly. Kessi made for the chests, but Patricka stopped her. "No, they're trapped! I know where your belongings are stored. Follow me."

Kessi looked to Fredor, who could only shrug at his wife's knowledge of the place. They watched as she made her way to the bed Matilda and Cerus shared. Kessi could sense the woman's discomfort as she felt along the wall behind the massive headboard. She could only imagine what acts Matilda and Cerus had forced Patricka to perform on that very bed.

"Here it is!" Patricka said excitedly and withdrew her hand, now holding a key.

She walked briskly to the far wall and looked for a secret door. "Cerus made the mistake of showing me this room. He would take me here at nights and—" She glanced shamefully at Fredor, who smiled and nodded his understanding, though Kessi could tell the words stung him.

"Anyway, he did it without Matilda's knowledge and only when she was away from Nesin. I think this is the place where the sacrifices were supposed to occur."

Kessi and Fredor shared a knowing look and suddenly felt more hesitant about entering the room.

"Here!" Patricka exclaimed.

She had found a keyhole, and even with her finger holding the place, Kessi couldn't see it. The rock wall looked nondescript, and Kessi saw no entrance until Patricka slid the key in and turned it. Part of the wall protruded, revealing the hidden door. Patricka struggled to open the portal, and it took Kessi and Fredor to help before it slowly opened outward. Nothing prepared Kessi for what they found inside.

A large stone slab sat at the right, large enough for one person to lie atop. Leather straps adorned the corners, obviously to hold the subject. Strange symbols adorned the cave wall above the slab. A large pentagram loomed on the floor to the left of it. Above the pentagram, protruding from the wall about ten feet above the floor, was a sculpture of a demon, its torso and upper body sculpted from the stone, its legs disappearing into the cave wall. The creature had hideous, giant bat-like wings protruding from its back and a barbed tail waving. The beast's face was skeletal, with large ram-like horns adorning its forehead. It held two female humans, one in each hand, naked with their faces twisted in terror.

The sculpture was realistic enough that Kessi thought she saw it move when they entered. She froze in fear at the sight of the beast. She waited and intently watched for it to move again. It took her some time to tear her eyes away from the sculpture, and when she did, she took in the rest of the room, which was quite large, with a giant open space on the floor between the sculpture and the slab.

"Cerus told me that area is for the bodies of those sacrificed at the time of summoning," Patricka said, pointing to the open floor space. "And your belongings are underneath the sculpture."

Kessi looked under the statue to find several drawers at the base.

"They're locked," Patricka said, handing the key to Kessi.

Kessi nodded as she broke out in a cold sweat at the thought of approaching the statue. She made her way reluctantly to the cubbies and avoided the pentagram as she did. Once there, she noticed six drawers, each about two feet in diameter, comprised of a strange black, polished metal. Each contained a keyhole and several bas-relief images of demons and tortured souls.

She knelt below the statue, looking up occasionally, expecting it to move. When she finally took her eyes off it, she fumbled to put the key into the first lock. She swallowed hard and turned the key. She heard the click of the lock, and the door opened slightly. An awful odor assaulted her, and she had to bring her hand to her face to block the stench. It took all her willpower to pry the door open the rest of the way. Inside was dark, and she couldn't see, but the smell overwhelmed her, and she hurried back to the entrance where Patricka and Fredor stood.

She breathed a little easier there and said, "I can't see anything in there. What is behind those drawers?"

"I don't know, I'm sorry," Patricka said.

"And we have no light source," Fredor added.

"Perhaps we should just go. We're wasting valuable time," Kessi said dejectedly.

That was when Kessi saw the macabre decorations above the door they had entered. She was now facing the wall where human skeletons were nailed to it, naked and staked through the hands and feet—six in total hung above the door. In the middle of the six skeletons a bucket was nailed to the wall with several trails of dried blood running down it. A large spike was about a foot above the bucket; hanging from the spike were multiple chains, each the size of a necklace, extending down into the bucket. Kessi knew that one of those chains was hers, and at the end of it was her holy symbol, soaking in whatever evil the bucket contained.

"We need Emiline," Kessi said.

She quickly made her way back to the entrance to the room, where she found Sabrina nervously waiting for her. "Did you find your belongings?" she asked when she saw Kessi.

"I believe so, but I need Emiline's help to retrieve my holy symbol."

The crowd behind Sabrina parted as Emiline made her way to Kessi. Even though Emiline assisted them in their escape, none trusted the vampire, and all feared her. Not Kessi—she had dealt with Heinsvick and knew Emiline was less powerful than her master.

"Emiline, please follow me," Kessi said.

When Emiline entered the room, a cloud crossed her face as she looked hatefully at the pool, obviously remembering some unhappy event. Kessi didn't ask and instead focused on accomplishing their task. She led the vampire quickly to the secret room. Emiline was hesitant to enter, perhaps sensing the danger within.

Once inside, Kessi pointed to the skeletons, specifically the bucket. "Emiline, can you bring down the contents of that bucket?"

Emiline wasn't listening and wasn't even facing the bucket. Instead, she was observing the sculpture, tilting her head to the side as she tried to comprehend what she saw.

"Emiline?"

Eventually, the vampire turned, and Kessi could tell she was out of sorts. And Kessi wanted nothing more than to leave the room and Nesin altogether. No one, not even the vampire, was comfortable in the awful place.

"Emiline, can you reach the bucket? I feel the medallion of my goddess is there," Kessi asked.

Emiline stared at the strange scene for a long while, seeming confused. Eventually, she turned to Kessi and said, "It is evil. Your necklace is tainted."

"I understand, Emiline, but I cannot leave it like it is. We must remove it from the bucket. Please help me."

Emiline looked back to the bucket and walked under it, never taking her eyes off the strange object. Once underneath it, she began to float toward it. Kessi and her two friends watched in amazement as the vampire easily levitated the thirty feet to the bucket and took up all the chains in one hand. She lifted them up and out of the bucket, spilling coagulated blood. Kessi and the other two stepped aside as the blood sloshed on the floor with a sickening splat. Emiline paid it no heed; even the sight of the blood did not change her demeanor. Usually, the sight and smell of it would rile her, but she wanted no part of the blood found in the bucket.

She lowered herself to the floor with the fistful of necklaces. There were six or seven of them, and Kessi assumed they were all holy symbols, probably from various goodly gods, desecrated by Matilda. She couldn't make out any shapes as the thick, dark blood clung to them and slowly ran to the floor in a long string of semi-solid vileness.

Emiline presented the bloody mess to Kessi, who stepped back to keep from being soiled by the foul-looking blood. "No, Emiline, we need to clean these. Can you take them to the pool and wash them?"

"Matilda's pool?" Emiline asked, cocking her head to the side.

"Yes, Matilda's pool. Don't fret; she can no longer hurt you, Emiline."

"Hurt me?" the confused vampire asked.

"Yes, we're leaving, so she cannot punish you for soiling her pool."

"Emiline is leaving?"

"Yes, you're coming with us; I will not leave you here."

"How?" Emiline asked and again tilted her head as she always did when she did not fully understand what was said to her.

It dawned on Kessi then precisely what the vampire was confused about. Emiline couldn't travel in the sun. There was no way she could leave with them. Kessi shook the troubling thought away and said, "I will figure it out, Emiline. For now, please go wash those off," pointing to the bloody mess in the vampire's hand. Emiline nodded and quickly went to Matilda's cherished pool, leaving a trail of blood behind her.

"The creature doesn't seem affected by the blood like I thought she would be. The stories I've heard about vampires and the things I've seen this one do made me believe she would go into a feeding frenzy at the sight of so much blood," Fredor said nervously.

"The blood is spoiled," Patricka said. "Not even the vampire desires it."

"Let us take our leave," Kessi said, glancing again at the giant looming demon statue.

Fredor and Patricka made their way out of the room. Kessi stopped to assist Emiline in cleaning the necklaces. The blood stuck to them stubbornly, and it took a long while, but eventually, they found Kessi's teardrop-shaped symbol of the god Adlesk.

"Thank you, Emiline!" Kessi said, taking the necklace and splashing it in the water again to wash off the remaining evil taint.

"And what of these?" Emiline asked, holding up the others in one fist.

"They are clean now. You have washed them of the perversion that is Marnelphion. We will take them with us and free them from the caves."

"Everyone will be free but me. I'll never see Heinsvick again."

"Listen, Emiline. You have helped us and given us a chance to escape. You are one of us now, and we will not leave you behind. Understand?"

Emiline nodded slightly, but she teared up. Kessi's heart went out to her. She knew that Emiline wasn't an evil creature, and she had to find a way to take her with them. She couldn't travel in the sunlight, and they certainly couldn't carry the casket in which Emiline slept. Kessi would have to figure out something quickly because their time in Nesin grew short.

Once she had thoroughly cleaned the symbol of her god, she placed the necklace around her neck, and the familiar feel of it made her somewhat whole again. She and Emiline left the room and joined their friends in the passageway.

"Who here is hurt?" Kessi asked, holding her symbol ready.

The group looked around and realized none were. Sabrina smiled and said, "Just you, Kessi. Can you heal the wounds to your back?"

"I will try," Kessi replied, unsure if her god would answer her call through the befouled symbol.

He did, and Kessi felt relief from her damaged back for the first time in days. As she administered the healing spell, she silently asked for guidance from Adlesk concerning Emiline. Kessi needed an answer quickly.

"Emiline, let me see your wounded hand," Kessi said after the throbbing in her back subsided.

The vampire looked confused by the demand but slowly lifted her cut hand. Kessi examined it; it was a very deep laceration. Also, it looked like Emiline had sucked most of the blood from it. She gently held it and prayed to Adlesk. Her healing energy coursed through her and into Emiline. The vampire gasped slightly, and after Kessi finished her work, she held her hand in amazement before her eyes.

"You are a healer?" Emiline asked.

"No, my god is. I am just a conduit."

Emiline cocked her head and tried to absorb Kessi's words. Kessi smiled and was about to explain more about her god when Fredor interrupted them. "We need food before we leave," he said. "Mensh said he saved us some in the store room. We can stop by on the way out."

"How do we carry it?" Kessi asked.

"Hopefully, there will be sacks," he said.

That gave Kessi an idea, perhaps a way they could get Emiline to travel with them. Fredor led the way, knowing the path to the kitchen all too well since he delivered meals daily to Kessi and her friends. Emiline took up the rear, watching for any trouble from behind.

They arrived shortly after, and their find was even better than Kessi had hoped for—plenty of dried meats, loaves of bread, and fresh water. There were ten large sacks, as Fredor had suggested, and they stuffed them full of food. Across the passageway was another storage area where they found clothing and other traveling supplies. Kessi was relieved to wear pants again and found a nice pair of high leather boots that fit her tiny feet.

Once fully clothed, she went back into the food stores, looking for a container as the others gathered the remains of the food. It took her quite a while, and the group was ready to leave before she found what she was looking for. She held up a glass jar that once contained some dried meat. The escapees had emptied and discarded it when they transferred the contents to the sacks. She wasn't sure it would do, but it was large enough to hold her intended cargo.

"What is that for?" Sabrina asked.

"Emiline."

"What? I don't understand."

"I know, but hopefully, this vessel will allow us to carry her safely in the daylight."

"How?" Sabrina asked.

"Where is Emiline? Hopefully, we'll have our answer once I speak to her."

"She scouted ahead to see if evil men still roamed the passageways. We may have to fight our way out of here yet," Fredor said, holding up the sword Emiline had given him during their escape from the dungeon.

Soon, the vampire returned from their intended passage and said, "There may be no one left behind us, but there is activity ahead."

"Then let us leave the godforsaken place while we can," Fredor said, taking the lead.

No one argued, and they quickly fell in line behind him. As they formed up, Emiline lingered behind, separate from the others. Kessi and Sabrina made their way back to join her.

"Why are you back here, Emiline?" Kessi asked.

"Yeah, I thought you said no one was behind us," Sabrina said.

"The others shun me. I am a monster."

"You must not think like that," Kessi said.

"You're one of us now, Emiline," Sabrina added.

"One of you?" Emiline asked, stopping and turning her head to study the young women. "I can smell your blood, and I think about feeding on you all the time. I am afflicted and am not like either of you." Kessi and Sabrina shared a glance, but neither could deny her words. Emiline added meekly, "I was once like you until Heinsvick found me."

"Listen to me, Emiline, you are afflicted with undeath. We know this, and it makes you dangerous at times. But we believe in you and know what is in your heart. You *are* one of us."

Emiline nodded, but her expression told Kessi she didn't believe her words.

"We're closer alike than you care to think, remember?" Kessi added, showing the white scars on her wrist where Heinsvick had bitten her.

Emiline studied her arm and smiled slightly. "But I'm stuck here because I'm truly not like you," she said.

"I have a plan for that," Kessi said.

Before she could explain, several screams and swords clanging echoed down the passage ahead. The three realized they had been so engrossed in their discussion that they'd lost sight of their friends. Kessi and Sabrina looked at each other nervously and ran off to investigate.

Their cellmates huddled in a corner of the passage with six armed men blocking their way. Each carried a sword at the ready, and a large man at the center of the blockade held a sack in one hand and his bloodied sword in the other. Kessi noticed Fredor lying limply in Patricka's arms, his chest bloodied, and his eyes staring blankly at the ceiling. Patricka sat before the man with the sack, rocked back and forth, and wept uncontrollably.

"Now, unless the rest of you cell rats want to taste my sword, you'll turn and march back down to the cells where you belong," the man with the sack said. "Get them moving, Renson."

The other five moved in front of the man and made their way toward their huddled and frightened friends, swords pointed straight ahead as if prodding livestock. Kessi's cellmates backed away, some crying now, their spirits broken at being so close to freedom.

"Leave the grieving widow; she'll need someone to keep her warm tonight, and I'm up for the task," the leader said, pointing to Patricka.

She didn't seem to hear, lost in her world of grief, and didn't seem to notice the men as they walked past her. Kessi's friends all made their way deeper into the cave, passing Kessi and Sabrina, who stood their ground. Soon, only they stood in the way of the approaching men.

"Stand your ground, my friends! We're not going back!" Kessi shouted.

And they did. As frightened as they were, they all stopped scampering and stood behind their leaders, Kessi and Sabrina. All the cellmates had looked to them for guidance during their long stay in the bowels of Nesin, and now they summoned their courage to make a final stand.

"We'll run you through," Renson said with a smirk, now only a few feet away.

"We're not going back, and we outnumber you, five to one. You cannot beat us," Kessi shot back.

"We have swords, and you are unarmed," he said, but he stopped his advance, and the others followed his lead.

"You will kill some of us, but you cannot hope to beat us all; we will overwhelm you, and you will die," Kessi said.

"Or you can get out of our way and live to see another day," Sabrina added.

"Well, well, don't this beat all," their giant leader said, coming to stand beside Renson.

He moved past Patricka, paying her no mind as she continued to sob and cradle Fredor's still form. "You will move back to your cells now, or I will hang you back on the apparatus that Merrik strapped you to. And if you think the whipping Merrik gave you was harsh, wait until I get my hands on you," the man said with an evil smile.

"Herd them back to their cells, and if they resist, stab them. Keep as many alive as possible so they can all feel the sting of my whip!" the mercenary added.

The men began to move forward, but none of the women moved, finding their resolve in Kessi and Sabrina's bravado. Before the men could take two steps, Emiline appeared from the shadows, moving to stand beside Kessi. The men blanched and backpedaled.

"That thing is back!" Renson warned.

Even their leader was at a loss for words at the sight of the vampire. He sheathed his sword and backed up with the rest of the men, never taking his eyes off her. He brought the sack in front of him and began untying it.

"Are we supposed to do that?" Renson asked.

"Matilda said only if all else fails. I'm not fighting that thing," the leader said.

The giant of a man stiffened, and his grip on the sack slowly loosened as it fell to the floor, flat as if empty. The leader of the mercenaries looked down at his chest and at the bloody blade that protruded from it. It withdrew, and the man collapsed face down near the sack. Behind him stood Patricka, Fredor's sword in her hand, and a determined, vengeful look splayed across her pretty face.

"Now, Emiline!" Kessi screamed.

The vampire flew into action, attacking the closest mercenary with blinding speed. The man was half turned toward Patricka and unprepared for the vicious attack. Even Kessi was surprised by the vampire's brutality.

With one quick lunge, she tore the man's throat out with one deep bite. Blood sprayed anyone close to the man, including Emiline, who relented the attack almost immediately. When she turned back, Kessi saw that blood stained her pretty face and poured from her mouth. The guard's sword clanged to the floor, and he held his torn throat, blood squirting between his fingers with each pump of his dying heart.

The other four men retreated, scampering down the hallway, wanting nothing more to do with the volatile vampire. One was brave enough, or perhaps terrified enough, to swing wildly at Emiline, cutting a slight gash in her arm as he fled. The vampire caught him and threw him against the cave wall, where he staggered back to her, dazed and swinging his sword wildly.

Emiline grabbed his wrist and squeezed. Tendons popped and bones cracked as the man dropped his weapon and fell to his knees, screaming in agony. Emiline bared her teeth and hissed, seeming more creature than elf in that heated moment. She prepared to fall atop the man, but Kessi was there to thwart her attack.

"Emiline, release him. He's hurt and won't hamper us. He doesn't need to die," she said.

"Please, listen to her! I don't want to die!" the man said.

Emiline seemed torn. Her pupils dilated, and the blood stains on her face gave her an eerie appearance. The group of prisoners, the young women from Kessi's cell, moved away, terror splayed across their faces.

"Emiline, release him. You're not a murderer," Kessi repeated.

Eventually, Emiline's demeanor changed, and the animal-like visage faded, leaving a confused Emiline holding the man's crushed wrist. He squirmed and grimaced, his free hand unsuccessfully trying to pry open her vice-like grasp. When she realized she was hurting him, she released him. The man scampered away, holding his wounded arm to his chest. When he finally made his feet, he sprinted up the passageway where the other guards had gone. Soon, he was out of sight, and everything was quiet.

"Are you all right?" Kessi asked Patricka.

The woman seemed in shock and dropped the sword, bringing her hands to her face, sobbing once more. Kessi went to Fredor's still form as Sabrina hugged Patricka, trying to console her. Kessi examined Fredor, hoping she would find a little life left in the man, but she didn't; his eyes were wide and lifeless. She closed them gently and shook her head, whispering a prayer.

Everyone was so focused on Emiline, Kessi, and the distraught Patricka that they didn't see the leader, the large man Patricka had stabbed, slowly reaching for the empty sack lying beside him. He was still face down, and much blood had pooled around him, but he found the strength to move. When he finally grasped the sack, he turned over to his back with a groan, and the group finally noticed him. He smiled, revealing his red-stained teeth as blood leaked from his mouth.

He untied the sack but held it closed on his chest. He half laughed and half gurgled as more blood poured forth. He pointed to Emiline and said, "A gift for you, vampire, for all of you!"

His laughing increased, and he opened the bag. None of them knew what the crazed man intended, for the sack appeared limp and empty, turning red from the dying man's blood. When a small creature the size of a large bat flew out and landed on the man's face, his laughing turned to screams.

To Kessi's horror, she discovered that the creature was not a bat but a beast she had never seen before. It had the wings of a bat, but its tiny body was human-like, its hands and feet ending in claws. Its face was almost monkey-like, with hateful red eyes. The most horrific part was the tail that had a barbed stinger. The creature clung to the man's cheek as its tail repeatedly stung him in the throat. Soon, greenish-white foam seeped from his mouth, and he fell still, quite dead. The creature hissed and flew straight for Patricka. She shrieked and fell away, but the thing wasn't interested in her. Instead, it flew straight up the passageway behind the fleeing mercenaries.

"What was that?" Sabrina asked, helping Patricka off the floor.

Before she could answer, two more of the things flew from the bag, one getting tangled in Sara's hair, the other flying straight for Emiline. Kessi looked on in horror as the one in Sara's hair began to pull the girl in all directions, leading her by her locks. Sara screamed and held her hair, the creature tearing more than a few strands from her scalp. The second one was too quick for Emiline, and it stabbed her in the chest with its tail, then flew out of reach, only to come back around and stab her in the back. Emiline grew frustrated, hissing and swatting, but she could never catch the strange creature.

"Kessi, we have to close that bag," Sabrina said, picking up Fredor's sword and moving toward it.

Before she reached it, a third one flew out into the mass of screaming women. As the strange bat-like creature swooped into the gathering, they ducked and flailed their arms. Its tail stabbed Vera in the abdomen as it passed, making her shriek in pain. The scream was short-lived as her hands went to her injured midriff, and foam poured from her mouth. She quickly fell face first to the stone floor and was silent.

"They're poisonous. I have to stop them!" Kessi yelled at Sabrina over the chaos and screaming.

Kessi grabbed her holy symbol and began praying. She didn't know what the creatures were, but she hoped Adlesk would bless her with something to save her friends. Her praying was short-lived, however, as she witnessed the creature pulling Sara about, slamming her face first into the wall with a sickening crunch. The girl fell limp, but the beast was strong enough to hold her upright momentarily. Eventually, her hair began to rip from her head, so the creature released her, and she crumbled to the floor.

Kessi ran toward her, no longer concentrating on summoning a spell but focused on her friend. Sara was the youngest among them, only sixteen years of age, shy, and very pretty. She had a long life ahead of her, and Kessi wanted to make sure she had a chance to live it. The creature landed on Sara's chest, and a smile creased its face.

"*Toss away your holy device, priestess,*" it hissed in her mind.

Kessi froze. The thing was not just some animal; it could think, and the voice reminded her of the voices she heard while she hung from the contraption. As she came to terms with what this thing could be, it waved its stinger tail near Sara's face, bringing Kessi back to the moment. She quickly tossed her holy symbol aside, hoping she could negotiate with the thing. She felt the connection to her god diminish immediately.

Sabrina reached the bag just as a fourth creature flew out. She screamed and awkwardly slashed the sword at it. Her attack missed badly, and the thing flew around, striking at her with its tail. Somehow, Sabrina fought it off with her sword. She wasn't proficient with the weapon, and the creature seemed to know this. Soon, it began to taunt her, coming in lazily only to move at the last second as Sabrina swung wildly at it. In response, it would scratch her arm or neck, letting Sabrina's fear of dying seep in.

The creature fighting Emiline had scored more than a dozen stings on her. The vampire bled profusely now, and her unnatural dexterity didn't match the creature's. Emiline finally began to slow down and stagger, and the creature smiled. The venom was doing its work. It left Emiline there to die and joined its brethren, flying into the crowd of screaming women.

Kessi said, "There, I tossed it aside. Please leave her be now."

The creature said nothing and simply stabbed its tail into Sara's chest. Sara jolted slightly from the sting, then greenish foam began bubbling from her mouth.

"No! Sara!" Kessi screamed and ran for her holy symbol.

The creature was much faster and landed atop the symbol just before Kessi reached it.

"*You are defeated, priestess. Your weakling god has no authority here,*" it hissed in her mind.

It smiled, and its eyes turned to look over her shoulder. Kessi was afraid to look; she was aware of the chaos that had erupted in the passageway, and she knew in her heart that Sara was dead. She hadn't kept up with the others, but their screams were prevalent. She slowly turned to see three creatures similar to the one before her.

One toyed with Sabrina, whose arms, face, and neck had been raked and were bleeding. She swung her sword awkwardly, and the creature dodged it easily. It was toying with her; she was as good as dead. Two others chased the women about the passage, pulling hair, scratching deep grooves into soft skin, and occasionally stabbing with their stingers. More than half a dozen young women lay strewn about the passageway, most likely dead. Patricka brandished the leader's sword and fought well, but Kessi knew they were no match for these hellish creatures.

Kessi's heart broke when she saw Emiline staggering her way, spitting foam and trying to stay conscious. Her gown was stained crimson with blood from many wounds. Kessi had thought nothing could defeat the vampire, but these creatures had done so handily. She turned back to the beast to see that it had urinated on her holy symbol, which hissed in protest.

"*And now sweet death comes for you all,*" the creature said, spreading its wings to hover above her befouled holy symbol, which still smoked and hissed.

Kessi eyed the symbol. The creature had defiled it with urine just after she had cleansed it from the unholy blood. Even if she could reach it, would she be able to commune with her god through it? Emiline was there, then, and placed something in her hand. Kessi looked down to see a cheaply made replica of her god's symbol. It was made of copper and contained a reddish hue.

Kessi looked confusedly at Emiline, who said, "One of the necklaces bathed in blood. I kept them all."

The vampire held out her trembling hand, holding at least six other holy symbols of various gods, each from the same vat where they'd found Kessi's necklace. Kessi didn't question her good fortune. She was not a high-level priest, but she had been a faithful servant to Adlesk for the last seven years. If her god could help them, he would see it done, using her to perform his bidding. She began praying, searching for some power that could help them.

She turned in time to see the creature flying straight toward her, a look of hate splayed across its face. Its beady red eyes promised death as it flew for her face, barbed tail leading. Kessi knew she had no hope to stop the attack, she had but moments before that awful stinger impaled her. She could feel her god with her and understood he was there in that passage. She had never felt closer to him, and time seemed to freeze. There was a welling deep inside her, and she felt Adlesk move through her. It was the most amazing feeling!

Kessi wasn't sure what she was doing or what spell she could possibly put together, but she didn't have to—her god was doing it for her. The creatures were a perversion straight from hell, and her god would not tolerate them in the human world. Adlesk needed Kessi's faith, which was pure and potent, and a lesser priestess would have failed. Not Kessi; she opened her heart and welcomed the power her god offered.

A bright light suddenly bathed her. A warmth washed over her, and light and energy pulsed through and away from her in all directions. The immediate area of the passageway grew as bright as day, and the evil creatures all seemed to move more slowly and eventually froze. Kessi was aware of this but could do nothing else. She relaxed and let the spell remain intact for as long as possible. If she moved, it would end, so she closed her eyes and basked in the glory.

All four creatures hung in the air, caught in the light. They didn't fall to the ground when their wings stopped beating; they just froze in midair, suspended by the light. Emiline was the first to react, the vicious killer within her surfacing again. She took the creature in flight toward Kessi and ripped its head off, tossing the head one way and the body the other. She then collapsed on the ground at Kessi's feet.

Sabrina slashed her sword at the one in front of her. She wasn't proficient with the weapon, but even a novice could hit a still target. The creature's head fell away, and the body dropped to the floor soon after. She quickly took the sack and retied it before any other evil beings could spew forth. She collected herself and moved toward the two other frozen creatures. She helped Patricka untangled those two from their friends' hair and made quick work of them, using their swords to hack them to pieces. Natasha found the third sword and soon assisted in their furious attack. Once they disbursed the creatures, Sabrina, Natasha, and Patricka stood before Kessi, mesmerized at what they saw.

A soothing white light bathed Kessi, seeming to generate from somewhere within her. Her eyes were closed, and she had a blissful visage. Her hair seemed to flow as if caught in a gentle breeze, and it appeared just as white as her clothes, which seemed to exude the light. They could all faintly hear music, beautiful and pure but very faint, but none heard it as clearly as Kessi who smiled at the angelic sound. As they stood in her vicinity, Kessi willed an invisible wave of pulsating energy toward them. As it washed over them, their wounds healed. Sabrina, the most injured from the clawing and raking of the teasing creature, was healed fully. Even with her eyes closed, Kessi could sense her relief.

The three friends basked in the glory of Kessi's song as their physical and emotional wounds healed instantly. Emiline could not hear the music, and Kessi could sense that her powerful spell was not helping her vampire friend.

"Kessi, can you hear me?" Sabrina asked.

Kessi immediately opened her eyes and smiled but was still in the throes of the spell. The energy still pulsed, and the light shone brightly.

"The creatures are dead, and it's time to leave," Sabrina said

The spell began to wane, and the light diminished gradually. The dark passageway seemed all the colder without it. Kessi looked around to gain her bearings, seeing several of her friends lying still and lifeless. She looked to Sabrina, who embraced her in a giant hug.

"You saved us, Kessi," Sabrina said, squeezing her friend tight.

Soon, Natasha and even Patricka joined in the hug. Slowly, all the women in the group joined the loving embrace. They were the survivors, and their love for each other was strong because of what they had been through. Even Patricka shared a kinship with the others. She was not imprisoned as a virgin to sacrifice, but her life had been much more demanding in a lot of ways. They all shared the ordeal, and at that moment, they were one, joined in the cause and shared experiences.

There were no dry eyes when the group broke and gathered themselves. Kessi surveyed the area and counted six friends lying motionless on the cold floor, including Fredor, whom she considered a hero for their cause. Her heart broke for them all. They had been close to freedom, and their deaths were a tragedy. Kessi understood that Matilda had given the mercenaries the bag to use in the unlikely event that something like this happened. The bag that housed the creatures was a fail-safe to keep anyone from escaping. The woman was so evil she would rather see them all dead than have anyone escape.

Kessi visited each person, confirming they were gone. Fredor she had already examined and knew he had passed. Next, she went to Sara, and the tears started again. The young girl was barely beginning to live her life when Matilda imprisoned her in Nesin. Kessi liked her a lot, and her heart broke when she witnessed her cold, lifeless form.

The other four dead included Vera, who was one of Kessi's good friends; a young woman named Simrin, whom Kessi found pleasant; a girl almost as young as Sara named Laina; and an older woman, nearing her mid-twenties named Ana, who had always been a bit of a loner, even in the crowded cell they'd shared. Kessi had no healing powers left after the spell she had just summoned and nothing in her repertoire that could bring someone back from the dead. The venom in the creatures had been the most lethal Kessi had ever seen. The sting of those hellish creatures seemed to kill within moments.

Once she had confirmed that they could save none of their injured friends, Kessi turned to Emiline, who sat propped against a wall by herself. The vampire looked horrible, much paler than usual, yet she would survive the venom. She had inadvertently saved lives by distracting the deadly creature for so long. Kessi could only guess how many others would be dead if Emiline hadn't battled the one creature as she had.

"Can you travel, Emiline?" Kessi asked, kneeling.

"No, I will stay here. I cannot venture forth without my coffin. This is where we part ways, my sister of Heinsvick," the vampire said. She took Kessi's hand and turned it over to observe the old bite marks on her wrist. She gently ran her cold fingers over them, seemingly amazed at the scar.

"Emiline, you don't need your coffin," Kessi said with a smile. The vampire looked at her questioningly as if the words were foreign.

"Only vampire lords like Heinsvick need a coffin. They tend to put their burial soil in it, which sustains and even heals them. But you were never buried. Heinsvick bit you, and you became a creature of the night. Therefore, you can live without your coffin if you need to," Kessi said.

"How do you know this?"

"From Heinsvick. We discussed many things, and I'm certain of this."

"Even so, I cannot venture into the sun," Emiline said.

"We'll travel as much as possible at night until we reach Attins. However, I was hoping you could help me make our journey easier for you. If we must travel during the day, I need you to be able to do so. If these evil men come after us, or worse, Matilda and Cerus, we may have to run during the day," Kessi said.

"I do not understand."

"Heinsvick could shape-change. He said he could assume the form of a large bat, and I witnessed him change into a gaseous cloud. Could you do that, Emiline?"

Emiline looked puzzled at the request, and after thinking about it, she slowly shook her head. "I don't think so."

"I may be able to help coax you into the gaseous form," Kessi said, then looked around the room for her sack. When she spotted Sabrina speaking quietly with Patricka near Fredor's lifeless body, she called to her friend. "Sabrina, please bring me that sack," she said, pointing.

Sabrina did so, and Kessi rummaged through it, looking for the glass container she had taken from the storage.

"We need to leave, Kessi," Sabrina said.

"I agree. We will take our fallen friends and bury them outside of this place."

"How? Those men may still be about, and at least one of those creatures got away."

"We'll carry them and take our time doing so. I won't leave them in this place. We'll bury them far from here. The men are no longer a threat."

"How do you know?" Sabrina asked.

"I just do," Kessi said with a smile. "We are nearly free of this place, and nothing will stop us now."

Sabrina returned the smile and gave Kessi another hug. "Thank you for saving us; that display of power was amazing. I had no idea you could do something like that."

Once their embrace ended, Kessi said, "Neither did I for a while. Once I recovered my memories and found this, things changed." Kessi held up her holy symbol, or at least the replacement that Emiline had given her. The copper medallion had changed and was now a stark white. Kessi looked it over, mesmerized by the change in color.

"Well, you gave us the courage to do this. You're our leader, and we will follow you wherever you go," Sabrina said. Others gathered, nodding in agreement.

"Good, because it's time for us to leave this place. I need to speak with Emiline for a moment. In the meantime, gather the swords at our disposal and determine how we will carry our friends out of here."

"Gladly," Sabrina said and turned to carry out those demands.

Kessi found her container and presented it before Emiline. "If we can get you to transform to a gaseous state and keep you here, I can carry you in my sack during the daylight hours."

"I would fit in there?"

"Yes, and you would have to keep that form for maybe twelve hours at a time."

"How?"

"My god frees the suppressed, helps those less fortunate. At the same time, he condemns perversions of life," Kessi explained, then hesitated to watch the vampire's reaction to her following statement. "Like undead."

"I am a perversion?" Emiline asked, cocking her head to the side.

"Yes, I can control lesser undead, perhaps creatures such as zombies or skeletons, but never a vampire. That is beyond me."

"Then how can you help?"

"I can help if you are willing. Perhaps together, we can transform you into a temporary state of gas. I can then release you each time we set up camp at night. Then put you back before the dawn. Do you think we can work together to make that happen?"

"I can try, my sister."

Kessi smiled and helped the vampire to her feet. After taking stock of their situation, Sabrina determined they now had four swords, though none knew how to use them well. Sabrina, Patricka, Natasha, and Kessi volunteered to carry them. That left nineteen others to bring their dead friends. Emiline typically could have taken one herself but was too injured.

And so, they marched toward freedom. Not far ahead, they found another dead guard, face down in the passage and poisoned, an apparent stinger wound in the middle of his back. They took his sword as well, giving them five such weapons. The redheaded, fair-skinned Lila, now the youngest of the group, asked to carry the fifth sword, and Patricka gave it to her with a nod. Then Patricka led them through the few turns left in the passageway, as she knew her way around the complex and assured them they were close to freedom.

They passed an area that contained six more dead: three slaves that Patricka recognized and three more of the mercenaries. Their weapons were missing, and the party reasoned that the surviving slaves had taken them. Although the sight broke her heart, Kessi was glad to see that neither Kimmie nor any of her other cellmates were among the dead. They gathered the three bodies, determined to find a proper resting place for all their allies.

Shortly after, they found the exit to Nesin; there was no sign of any of the mercenaries or the remaining creature. Bright sunlight bathed the entranceway to the cavern fortress, indicating it was probably midday. They all had to take time for their vision to adjust to the incredible brightness. As they rested briefly and blinked away the sun, Kessi turned to Emiline.

"It is day outside; you must help me transform you. We are this close to freedom, Emiline, but we are not leaving without you."

The vampire thought about it for a few moments, then nodded slowly.

"Good. I want you to focus on changing into a gaseous state and allowing me to help you accomplish the task and control you as Matilda did." Emiline bristled at the notion, but Kessi only smiled. "Not to harm you, Emiline, like Matilda would do, but to help you flee this awful place with us. We must leave, and we are taking you with us."

Emiline seemed to understand, so Kessi concentrated on her now-white holy symbol. She had never done anything like this before, but she knew her god was with her and he would help her. She spent a long while praying and in deep concentration, but nothing happened. She did this for several hours with their freedom a mere fifty yards away. Some women became restless, being so close to escaping, but none proceeded, refusing to leave without Emiline.

Finally, Kessi felt a little tremble in Emiline's life force. She could feel it like a tangible part of her own body. She connected to the vampire and saw Emiline also recognize it. Emiline began to speak, but her face distorted slightly, then turned insubstantial, as did the rest of her body. Soon, she was a ball of white gas, and Kessi easily controlled it, so she slowly moved it into the glass vessel. Once Emiline was safely inside, she stoppered the top and placed the jar gently in her sack.

When she looked up, all the others were watching anxiously. Sabrina spoke the words they all wanted to ask: "Are we ready?"

"Let's go," Kessi said with a smile.

They gently gathered their dead and marched into bright daylight, brandishing their swords in case any mercenaries remained in the area. They weren't hampered and soon basked in the warmth of the mid-afternoon sun and the gentle summer breeze. It was invigorating for Kessi, and she knew her sisters experienced the same emotions. Soon, they left Nesin far behind, finally free of the horrible place.

WHEN MALTOR FELL AT THE END OF CERUS'S SPEAR, THE BARBARIANS erupted, letting fly guttural screams, the war cries of the Yaddaton warriors. The barbarians around the challenge circle attacked, the closest ones centering their anger on Cerus. The gate to the training compound flew open, and more angry barbarians rushed out. A wave of arrows washed over Matilda's gathered priests, and the shamans began to chant, formulating a powerful incantation to attack the undead huddled together near Matilda.

Matilda had not ordered the red-haired zombie to attack Maltor. She knew it was a breach of etiquette to enter the circle, that much was clear, and the zombie appeared to have done it of its own accord. The priestess could not dwell on that event, as it took all her concentration not to lose Cerus in those early moments of the battle. She believed Boscoe would lead her priests and summon the undead into action as she defended her husband.

Cerus quickly turned and defended himself against the enraged barbarians, but he took several minor stabs from the proficient fighters before Matilda could summon a spell to hold them at bay. She held the first few where they stood, their muscles locked and unresponsive. Cerus moved to cut them down, but Matilda yelled for him to grab Maltor and pull him back. It was one of the few times that Cerus listened to his wife and did not delay. As he dragged Maltor's dying form to the back of the line to join Matilda, his men slaughtered the frozen barbarians.

As trained and formidable as Cerus's men were, the barbarians were equally proficient and just as eager for a fight. The battle raged for many moments, and Matilda's forces lost several priests and most of their undead to the shamans' sneaky destruction spells before the battle was fully engaged.

The priests of Marnelphion were no fools nor novices to battles. They used the same tactic Matilda had used with Garyn when they had attacked the priests of Tara, dousing him with oil and setting him ablaze. This time, Boscoe doused Erran, another devout priest, and lit his drenched robes. He immediately caught fire and was quickly consumed. Boscoe and the remaining priests joined in casting a spell to control the wind. This had a two-pronged effect: first the flames engulfing Erran roared to life and secondly, they used that pocket of wind to escort the priest to the wall, ready to repel any arrows the barbarians threw his way. Erran was protected from the bite of the flames, just as Garyn had been months prior. There was no ring to protect him this time but a spell from Marnelphion. It wouldn't last long, and Erran knew he would perish in the attack.

The fanatical priest ran straight for the training compound, a large jug of oil in each hand, trailing smoke as he ran. Five of Cerus's best warriors escorted Erran in case any barbarians became brave enough to intercept the human torch. As expected, arrows rained down upon the priest, and Boscoe and the other priests responded, moving the strong wind to blow them harmlessly aside. The few barbarians engaged in battle who understood the tactic and tried to stop the approaching priest couldn't hope to get too close because of the immense heat. Erran had a clear shot to the compound's wall.

The barbarians left inside, which included the shamans, Maltor's four new wives, fifty warriors, primarily archers, and the elderly and non-warrior females of the tribe, as well as Bolin, saw the attack and quickly locked the gates. Bolin tried to get the shamans to focus on the strange, burning man, but they were occupied dealing with the vicious undead. There was no way to stop the attack. Bolin watched helplessly as the man smashed the two jugs of oil into the wall, engulfing the wood with hot flames.

Erran's initial attack was devastating, and the wood caught fire quickly, the hungry flames covering it in moments. He moved along the wall, setting it ablaze in many locations. The archers were finally able to put several arrows in him, as Boscoe's control of the wind ended and he fell at the base in a heap. Moments later, the spell of his brethren failed, and the fire began to consume him. But it was too late, as Erran had succeeded in driving out the remaining barbarians. Bolin had to order the gates open because of the thick, deadly smoke.

And so, the battle raged, men on both sides died, and Matilda lost two more priests, leaving her with only nine, which would not be enough to animate and control more undead. As the fighting continued, Matilda, Cass, and Ronnis met in a large tent. Ironically, it was Maltor's living quarters, the one Cassandra had stayed in not long ago. Cerus dragged Maltor into the tent and immediately kicked the barbarian king in the ribs. Two more warriors dragged Jozerah's lifeless form behind him and dropped him to the ground near his king.

"Have your fun, my wife, for I go to make Gorl proud!" Cerus yelled, raising his massive spear in the air.

The two warriors followed suit, raising their spears and shouting in unison, "For Gorl!"

Matilda kissed her husband deeply, then said, "Go and play with the barbarians. Make your father and me proud. I will obtain our answers from the barbarian king soon enough."

Cerus nodded and turned to run into battle, but Matilda added, "Watch for a golden-haired woman; it may be Cassandra. Make sure she's unharmed."

Cerus stopped briefly and turned to his wife with a wicked smile. Then, he nodded again and ran out of the tent, the two men close behind.

"The compound burns. Will Cassandra be unharmed?" Lord Ronnis asked.

Matilda turned to the man in the porcelain mask and nodded. "She will be unharmed; my priests, Cerus, and the Gorl warriors are watching for her. However, I need to find her exact location, and these two fools will give it to me," she said, pointing to Maltor and Jozerah. "Help me prepare them."

Shortly after, and with great effort, they had Maltor tied to the center tent pole, which ironically replaced the one he had chopped down in anger a few months earlier. They managed to move him into a sitting position, which, given the size of the barbarian, wasn't easy. Matilda was a tiny woman, and Ronnis was not precisely a stout man. Still, Cass surprised them both with her strength, effortlessly manipulating the unconscious barbarian into position.

Once he was in place, Matilda performed a minor healing spell, one to keep him alive. Cerus's spear had caused the wound in his back and, therefore, a mortal injury. But she could keep him alive long enough to gain her answers. After the bleeding had slowly subsided, Matilda retrieved her alchemy kit and mixed oils and powders. It took a long while to get it right, and the sounds of battle seemed to retreat as if Cerus and his men were driving back the savages.

Once the mixture was perfect, she retrieved her knife and tongs, the same ones she had used when making Glenna a similar concoction back in Pelesea. She made fast work of Jozerah's tongue, cutting the tender muscle from his mouth. He threw a bit of a fit and screamed in agony for a moment, then lay perfectly still forever. Matilda smiled and dropped the tongue into the potion, which bubbled and popped.

"What are you doing?" Cass asked, holding her nose to stave off the stench.

"A potion of truth. Even a barbarian king cannot resist the effects, especially in his condition," Matilda said.

She recited the spell and waved her hand over the hissing container. After a bit, the potion was complete. "Now, if you could pry his mouth open, we'll get this down him and find out where Cassandra is," Matilda said with a wicked smile.

Ronnis knelt and pried open Maltor's mouth. Even though the barbarian king was unconscious, he still put up a fight, and it took all three of them to hold him still while Matilda forced the putrid drink down his throat. He coughed and gagged and fought the best he could against the invading liquid.

Ultimately, he swallowed enough for Matilda to begin her interrogation. Once his coughing settled down, she healed him again with enough warm, healing energy to allow him to gain consciousness. Blood still matted the side of his head where the self-thinking zombie had mauled him. Only a little nub remained of his ear, but that wasn't the serious wound. Matilda knew the gash in his back would reopen and eventually kill the savage, but she didn't need him to live much longer. Matilda knelt in front of Maltor as his eyes fluttered open. He seemed not to notice his surroundings but just stared straight ahead, precisely as Matilda intended.

She leaned in and whispered, "Great barbarian king of Yaddaton, can you hear me?"

His eyes shifted slightly, only to stare blankly at a different location. He didn't seem to see Matilda. "Yes, interloper," he eventually answered.

"Tell me, what is your name?"

"Maltor, Killer of Outlanders, Lord of Yaddaton, King of the Serpent Tribe, Slayer of—"

"Enough," Matilda said, holding up a hand. "I have questions concerning Cassandra Rho, and I want you to answer them truthfully. Do you understand, great king?"

"Yes, Cassandra, my queen."

Matilda gasped and nearly lost her balance, not expecting more information than she'd asked for and surely not realizing the savages of this tribe would have taken Cassandra as their queen. They hated outsiders, and Matilda was confused by the statement.

"Queen?" she asked.

Maltor didn't answer, but his jaw clenched as if the memory brought him discomfort.

"Tell me this, Maltor, did you spoil Cassandra with your seed?" Matilda asked, waiting with bated breath for the answer.

It took the great king a while before he finally answered, "No, she died before we could be married."

Upon hearing the shocking proclamation of Cassandra's death, Matilda smacked him hard across the face before. His head turned with the strike, then slowly returned to its original state, his eyes still spacy and unseeing. Matilda's mind rushed with many thoughts, surprised by the revelation.

"It cannot be, Maltor. You cannot lie to me; the serum will not allow it. Tell me once more, where is Cassandra Rho?"

"Dead," he answered immediately, tears welling in his eyes.

Matilda stood and felt as if she might pass out. Cass and Ronnis stared at her, equally lost for words. She pulled her hair and screamed suddenly, the cries of the dying just outside their door muted by her primal rage.

She turned to her associates and said, "This cannot be. Marnelphion would have told me and given me some sign. She is alive, I can feel it!"

She directed her next statement to Cass. "The amulet, let me have it."

"It no longer works," Cass said.

"Give it to me then, and let me determine if it contains worth."

Cass glanced at Ronnis, who remained motionless. When he made no move to intervene, Cass sighed and produced the medallion from her pocket. She reluctantly handed it to Matilda, who placed it around her neck. Cass had been an invaluable ally to Matilda when they first gained the trail of Cassandra because of the magical item. It could sense her life force, locate her, and it had led them here. But the magic failed and no longer answered Cass's call.

Matilda had briefly revived the power of the device recently by using Kessi's blood. Unfortunately, she had left Kessi Rho behind at Nesin, and her blood was no longer an option. She tightly grabbed the medallion in both hands, conjuring its power the best she could, desperately calling to the dead artifact. She sensed a faint answer to her call, just an inkling that the device might still be usable.

She opened her eyes excitedly, knowing she had just a tiny opportunity to summon information from it. By all accounts, it was useless, but Marnelphion was helping her. She could sense it. She held up her hand, suddenly feeling the black tar from Novafontera that had seeped into her and given her new life and profound powers over a year ago. She looked at her hand in amazement as her fingers tingled. Then she regarded the barbarian king, who still appeared catatonic.

"I told you it no longer works," Cass said.

Matilda vaguely heard the stupid girl, her mind spinning with a possible solution. Maltor was still under her control and was obviously in love with Cassandra. He had been one of the last people to see her, and what better way to find Cassandra than through his aching heart? Matilda quickly knelt once more and placed the medallion around Maltor's neck.

"What are you doing? He can't use it!" Cass said.

If Matilda had more time, she would have probably shut the stupid girl up once and for all, but time was of the essence, and she ignored her comments.

"Maltor, great king, can you hear me?" Matilda asked excitedly.

"Yes, interloper," he whispered.

"Do you love Cassandra Rho?"

"I did, very much. I still do," the king answered, nearing tears.

Matilda looked back to Ronnis and Cass with a broad smile. Ronnis shrugged, and Cass put her hands on her hips to determine what Matilda could be up to. Matilda turned back and said, "I think she tricked you, barbarian king, and she is alive. Would you like to find her?"

Maltor's eyes focused briefly on Matilda's face. She was momentarily afraid that the potion's effects were waning, but he stared off into space again, indicating she was still in control. "Yes," he answered.

"Good. I gave you a powerful device from your shamans. It is around your neck, and you can find her. Do you feel it?"

"Yes."

"Good, then focus on it. Find her!"

The king was quiet for a few moments, and Matilda didn't know if he had understood her instructions. She was about to elaborate when he finally spoke again. "She is south of the burial grounds."

"The tracks," Matilda whispered, her eyes widening.

She stood and said, "I must find Cerus. She isn't here. She isn't dead! She tricked these fools into thinking she had died. She lives!" Matilda screamed. She ran outside the tent and into the fray that was not so far away.

CASS RETRIEVED HER MEDALLION AND LOOKED CURIOUSLY AT THE barbarian king. She put the necklace on and focused on it, but it was dead and did not heed her call.

Ronnis said, "She is alive. This is good."

Cass looked at him and smiled. It *was* good. They both exited the tent to find Matilda in the chaos of battle, both anxious to leave the barbarians and be on the trail once more to find Cassandra, their hatred of her driving them.

13

The Mystic

Baxter and Binta had flown on the carpet for days without finding the storm clouds that Binta sought. They had flown from Godhomme and far past Lake Elfkind two days prior and had nothing to show for their efforts. Baxter knew they were hundreds of miles past the lake, which spilled out into the wild country of Torlia. The terrain was heavily wooded, with no civilization in sight. Almost immediately after passing the lake, it had become untamed. The last bit of civilization they had seen was the road past Lake Elfkind, which snaked north toward Whitewood and Nessor.

The terrain was thick with vegetation, and Baxter only lowered the carpet during the day so they could rest and stretch their legs. They traveled at night, assuming the untamed wilds beneath them came alive with predators at that time. As darkness waned and the sun began to stir on the third night past the lake, Baxter lowered the carpet, spotting a knoll above the thick vegetation. No trees were near it, and thorny vines covered the base and stretched in many directions, covering the ground between the knoll and the closest trees. They hovered about ten feet above the area as Baxter cast a spell to detect magical traps. He found none.

"What's wrong?" Binta asked.

"Nothing seems out of sorts, but this feels like a trap. It's too convenient."

"How many miles would you guess we've traveled from Lake Elfkind?" Binta asked, looking around nervously.

"I estimate we're five hundred miles east of Pelesea."

It was true; something felt wrong with the place. Binta studied the vines, remembering Inuentas's words that The Mystic was once the god of plants, and if that was true, he might already know they were there.

"Then we're close. Should we continue our journey through the day? If Inuentas is correct, we could reach our destination before nightfall," Binta said.

"The carpet is taxed, and we need the rest. We must stop here and continue again when it gets dark. I guess this knoll must do, but keep your ears and eyes open."

Baxter lowered the carpet so that Binta could step down onto the knoll. She hopped off, dropped her pack to the ground, and stretched her legs, working the stiffness from them. The top of the hill had plenty of space for them to sleep for a few hours. Everything appeared safe, but that was the problem. Binta knew this wasn't right. The other places they had set down during their journey were amid heavily wooded areas with abundant signs of wildlife. The knoll had no signs of life other than the vines stretching all over the area. Binta looked up and searched the sky for birds and found none. Her sixth sense was screaming at her to flee. That was when she noticed the vines were slowly creeping toward the knoll.

"Baxter, it's time for you to go," she said, raising a hand as he was about to dismount.

"What?"

"The Mystic has found us. You should leave." Even as the words left her mouth, the grass below her feet suddenly shot up and wrapped around her feet and lower legs, rendering her immobile. Baxter saw this and extended his hand from atop the carpet.

Binta smiled and shook her head. "No, Baxter, this is what I came for."

"What are you talking about, Binta? This place is dangerous. Now give me your hand!"

Binta didn't move other than to close her eyes and reach out with her new, powerful mind. "He is here. I feel him all around us. You have little time to leave. Please, go."

"I'm not leaving you, Binta. You will die!"

Again, Binta smiled and said, "This is what I came for. You have done your part, now let me do mine."

Baxter looked on nervously as the vines crept up the knoll and shot toward Binta like a dangerous snake striking at its prey. The vines wrapped tightly around her wrists, and she grimaced as the thorns dug deep into her skin. The vines pulled her arms out straight beside her. She continued to smile reassuringly at Baxter.

He raised the carpet out of reach of the vines and began casting a spell. As if sensing his intent, they raised at the base of the knoll and whipped themselves at him, sending waves of thorns his way. Several stuck in his arm, disrupting his spell, and more embedded in the carpet. Binta noticed a dark form walking through the vines. The figure appeared human and most decidedly female from the sway of her walk. Baxter saw her, too, and both witnessed the vines move so the woman had an unencumbered path to Binta and then close quickly behind her.

"Binta, someone is coming!" Baxter said, pointing in the direction of the quickly approaching woman.

"Instructor Baxter, look at me," Binta said calmly.

He did, pulling his eyes from the spectacle to see Binta standing calmly, still smiling. Her lower legs were wrapped in the suddenly tall grass, and her arms were stretched out to her sides, her wrists bleeding from the thorns. She could tell Baxter was panicking. Binta had discussed this very event with him at length so that he could prepare for it, but now that it was here, he wasn't handling it well. They both knew that the meeting with The Mystic wouldn't be pleasant.

"For Cassandra, remember?" she said.

He looked at her, dumbfounded, and she said again, "This is what we came for, to help Cassandra. Now go."

"I can't leave you like this," he said, glancing at the approaching woman.

Binta turned to regard her and saw why Baxter panicked. The woman was only about fifty yards away and closing fast. She was close enough that Binta could make out some of her features. She was tall and lithe, and her hair was as black as coal. She wore a revealing black dress with a low-cut V-neck that extended to her navel. There were slits on both sides of her dress, showing most of her long legs as she walked. Even from this distance, Binta could tell she was breathtaking.

"Go, and don't land until you clear the lake. The Mystic knows you now—I can feel it through these vines. If you land in his woods, he will kill you."

Baxter looked at her once more and nodded. He was sad to have to leave her; she could tell by the look on his face. Baxter leaving her was the unavoidable ending to their adventure, and they both knew it when they had set out from Pelesea.

"Are you sure this is The Mystic you seek?" Baxter asked, nodding toward the woman.

"Not her," Binta said with a shake of her head. "The one I seek is in these vines. I can feel him."

"You are sure?"

"Yes, there is something familiar about him. I feel the woman is his doorkeeper; she will take me to him."

"For Cassandra," he whispered.

"For Cassandra," Binta repeated and smiled.

Their conversation was interrupted by a blinding flash of light and a loud crackling sound. A line of sizzling white lightning flashed between them, nearly hitting Baxter and scorching the carpet. They both turned to regard the woman holding one hand out toward them, the palm smoking. She was only thirty yards away now, and they could make out the smirk on her face.

"Leave her, fool. Save yourself before it is too late," she said to Baxter.

With one last glance and a nod to Binta, Baxter willed the carpet high and around, flying fast toward Pelesea. Binta watched as he went and knew his conscience was getting the best of him. She hoped he wouldn't turn around—it would mean certain death for him. Binta knew right away that The Mystic and his cohorts were powerful indeed.

Binta watched as Baxter climbed higher and farther away and soon was just a tiny spot in the sky. By then, the woman was on the knoll with her, suddenly stepping in front of her and blocking her view of her friend. Binta hoped it wouldn't be the last time she saw him. She shifted her gaze to the woman's face and felt physically weak in her presence. She was more beautiful than Binta had first realized; her perfume was familiar and intoxicating. It took all of Binta's willpower not to be overcome with naughty desires just being in the exotic woman's presence. She reminded her of Cass, and she knew that would be trouble.

She soon discovered the woman wasn't entirely human. She possessed many of the characteristics that Inuentas had, including little black horns protruding from her forehead and solid-black eyes with no pupils evident. Then, with a slight twitch of her shoulders, a pair of large, black, bat-like wings erupted from her back. She smiled, and her teeth were perfectly white, with elongated canines.

"You want him to live?" she asked in a sultry voice.

"Yes," Binta whispered.

"You know I can pursue and easily kill him, don't you?"

"Yes," Binta said, realizing the woman could back up the claim.

"Then you will cooperate fully and not cause me any trouble?" the woman said with a smile, grabbing her gently by the chin.

Binta nearly swooned from the touch and managed to look into those dark, charming eyes. Her mouth was suddenly dry, whether from fear or excitement, she couldn't tell. She knew for Baxter's sake that she should do as the woman asked, at least at first.

"Yes, I will cooperate," she said meekly.

"My, aren't you precious? We will get along just fine, then," the woman said, stroking Binta's hair gently while glancing over her shoulder in Baxter's direction.

When she turned back, she said, "My name is Illa, and I will take you to the one you seek. But you must understand that no human that seeks him ever leaves this place. But of course, you already know that, don't you?"

Binta nodded.

"Then let us not delay the inevitable," Illa said, closing her eyes as if in meditation.

Binta could hear a faint call and almost sense the vines communicating back to the beautiful woman. Then she felt the vines pulling her in many different directions. Illa opened her eyes with a smile and picked up Binta's backpack. The world around Binta seemed to be stretched and distorted, just like the sensation coursing through her body. Illa remained in focus, and so Binta concentrated on her beautiful face to keep her bearings. She was being pulled toward The Mystic, similar to what she imagined a teleportation spell would feel like. Vasym awaited her, as did The Mystic.

Sitra held her staff to Cassandra's throat, who knelt before her, both of her weapons dislodged. She wore a blindfold similar to Sitra's and she rubbed her hand, a welt already forming where Sitra had smacked her with her staff.

"I failed," Cassandra said, removing her blindfold.

"Nonsense," Sitra said, offering her a hand. "You fought very well for your first time blind fighting. You are a natural, Cassandra!"

Cassandra took the offered hand and was soon standing. Mateon collected her dislodged weapons and offered them back with a smile. "You have nothing to be ashamed of. No one beats Sitra at blind fighting."

Cassandra smiled and nodded. "Thank you, Mateon." She sheathed her weapons and walked over to the water canteen on a nearby rock.

Sitra followed her, saying, "You fought well, and the fake thrust almost scored a hit. It would have been devastating for me if these had been real weapons."

"How did you know I faked a thrust?" Cassandra asked, sitting on the rock and taking a long drag from the canteen.

"The same way I know that you are predominately right-handed. Subtle differences that you will learn if you continue down this path."

"I could feel something. I don't know if it was a skill I inherited from Vixa or simply a sixth sense from not relying on my eyes, but I felt at peace with the blindfold on."

"You took a small step down a long path that will make you a much better fighter, Cassandra. Too bad you will not be staying much longer so that I could teach you more," Sitra said.

Cassandra stood, shocked at the statement. "What do you mean, Sitra? Are you and Mateon kicking me out of your home?"

"Of course not, but your life will be in danger once the barbarian is ready to leave. It would be unwise to remain here with us, right under the barbarians' noses."

Cassandra thought about it momentarily and understood Sitra's words were valid. She had healed Jak two days ago and he had rested soundly since then. What had happened to him and what he would do now that he knew her location troubled her. She knew he would be obligated to report to Maltor his findings. In that case, Sitra was correct; she would need to leave.

"Let us eat, ladies. The evening grows long," Mateon said, taking Sitra's hand and leading her toward the house.

"I'll be there shortly," Cassandra said, retaking her seat.

She had enjoyed living with the hospitable couple over the last few months, but she could sense the end was near. She couldn't help but wonder how much of a part her father played in leading Jak to her door. She glanced to the southwest to the extensive line of mountains. She knew what lay in wait somewhere within them. She could sense it keenly while she sparred with Sitra, blindfolded and reliant on her other senses. Zolmex was near, and she could almost feel it with the blindfold on. She was close to finding it and becoming legendary, as Cedric had once called her. She had no intention of entering another mountain of her father's creation, especially not alone. A chill ran down her spine at the challenges found within the last one.

She had decided to stay with Mateon and Sitra instead of continuing her quest, and she was delighted with that decision. She had healed, and her new friends had accepted her with open arms. She missed Binta. Always. She often wondered where Kessi might be. But she had taken time to heal with these good people, physically and mentally. She was content. And then Jak showed up.

She laughed derisively and shook her head. "I'm not your plaything, Father."

She made her way inside and checked on Jak. He continued to rest comfortably, his muscular chest rising and falling in a deep sleep. A sense of peace washed over her, knowing that her faith in Gella had healed the man fully and he would awaken soon. She looked forward to that moment and dreaded it just the same. With a sigh, she went to the kitchen and assisted her hosts with dinner.

They ate a wonderful meal. Cassandra absently listened to their discussion, but her mind was elsewhere. She was happy to be there with her friends and knew this might be one of her last meals with them. It made her sad to think of it, and she couldn't help but focus on one question as they ate: what could Notel X possibly mean? That was the phrase she had found scribbled on an old scroll on her last adventure, and she was sure it came directly from her father. Still, it had no meaning to her, but she suddenly felt the urgency of solving that riddle.

WHEN THE WORLD COMPLETED SPINNING, BINTA FOUND HERSELF UNDER a canopy of vines and leaves.

The strange growth of plants formed a small cubby about ten feet in diameter, with Binta standing in the center of it. The side she faced was open, spilling in a dull, grey light. It was much dimmer than the sunlit knoll they had just come from. Just outside the opening was a meadow surrounded by thick vegetation. Illa stood inside the enclosure, facing her and watching as Binta gained her bearings and took in her surroundings.

She noticed that it was snowing, or that was what she first thought. She could hear the flakes gently land on the roof of the canopy, and the little meadow was several feet deep with the stuff. Although it was powdery, it wasn't white nor was it snow. It appeared to be ash. Then Binta realized dozens of people walked along the meadow, shoveling ash into buckets and carrying them away. Each of them seemed to be in a trance, their eyes wide and tears making tracks down their ash-covered faces.

"Vasym," she whispered.

"That is right, mortal. Your new home," Illa answered with a wide grin.

"I heard that it rained here nonstop."

"Then you heard wrong. Perhaps you are not as bright as we first thought."

Binta rubbed her torn wrists where the vines had dug deeply and removed a few thorns she found there. She noticed that the canopy's vines were tight, not allowing one flake of ash to enter. The vines continuously moved like a nest of snakes all around her.

"He comes," Illa said, then turned to watch for The Mystic's arrival.

Binta felt better not under the woman's constant gaze, and she took the opportunity to admire her incredible figure. She was attracted to Illa, and her resolve slightly quivered in her presence. She quickly fell into a lustful trance, gazing upon the woman, and she had to shake her head and shut her eyes to break that spell. She had just undergone an exercise in Pelesea to defeat such desires in preparation to confront The Mystic, and she had to refocus, or she would lose everything.

She opened her eyes and concentrated, her attention now on the slithering vines in the ashy meadow, not Illa. They came from all directions of the surrounding woods and converged a few feet in front of the small cubby where she and Illa stood. They wrapped together and slowly became a humanoid, roughly eight feet tall, comprised entirely of the ever-moving vines. The openings on the face resulted in two holes resembling eyes and a third, larger opening resembling a mouth. It reminded Binta of a strange jack-o'-lantern.

When the vines completed the humanoid construction, it spoke. "Binta Mulay of Pelesea, how nice of you to visit."

"She carried only this, no weapons, spellbooks, or components," Illa said, tossing the plant-man her pack.

Before the pack made it to the creature, obviously The Mystic, several vines shot from the ground and intercepted it. The vines tightened around it momentarily, and the creature seemed to smile. "Ah, just the essentials, Miss Mulay," it said.

Binta realized that he could sense what was inside the pack without opening it. His power was raw and overwhelming, and she suddenly understood that she could not stand up to this god-like being. She regretted her decision to come, but thoughts of finding Cassandra overrode her fears. She had to find a way to focus, so she closed her eyes and delved deep into her mind, locking out the distractions and blocking his mental intrusions that had already begun. She could feel him poking around in her mind, searching for answers and her weaknesses. He had already gleaned her name from her forethoughts, but she had to stop it there. And so she fell deep inside herself and lost connection with her surroundings.

THE BATTLE WAS DYING DOWN, AND THE SURVIVING ELDERLY AND female members of the Serpent Tribe were herded into one area, surrounded by the men of Gorl. Matilda looked on with mixed emotions. They were victorious here, but the many bodies of Gorl warriors that littered the reddening sand of Yaddaton indicated it was not without a high cost. Priests slowly began to come to her like a beacon in the carnage. Boscoe was one of only six priests that Matilda counted, and the look on his face indicated that perhaps that was all that remained.

Finally, Cerus approached the gathering allies, covered in sweat and blood. Most of it was barbarian blood, but not all of it, Matilda understood from the nasty gash on his right forearm and a deep cut on his neck. He carried his massive spear on his back and two other items: the head of a barbarian in one hand and an unconscious and bloodied barbarian in the other. He was exhausted by all accounts, but Cerus wore a wicked smile. Once he reached Matilda, he tossed the head at her feet and released the body, kicking it for good measure. When it moaned, Cerus kicked it again.

"The last remaining warrior, a leader from what I can tell," Cerus said, pointing to Bolin, the moaning and gravely injured warrior. "And the head of the lead shaman," he continued, pointing to Grink's severed head.

"There are no warriors even left to fight?" Matilda asked.

Cerus shook his head, and the smile nearly engulfed his face. "None. The barbarians are stubborn fools and very loyal to their king."

Matilda looked around and quickly counted only a few dozen Gorl warriors around her. She surmised that the prisoners totaled in the hundreds, which was not a comfortable ratio.

"Tell me where we stand in numbers, my husband," Matilda said as she began casting a healing spell for his neck wound.

"We number less than one hundred men. Our prisoners, counting the whores in the large tent, total at least six hundred." He moved closer and added in a whisper, "If these savages decided to rebel, they may be able to overwhelm us by sheer numbers. They are barbarians, after all."

He closed his eyes as Matilda's soothing spell washed over him. The wounds closed quickly, and Matilda was relieved to see the energy restored to her husband.

"We have an important task at hand. The chase for Cassandra Rho continues," Matilda said.

That finally melted the smile from his face. "Look around, Matilda. The chase for her has cost us."

"But this is what you wanted, to fight and to spill the blood of your enemies. The offspring of Kane is fueling your desires."

"I want you to stop taking us on these wild chases to catch the wench. Marnelphion has not delivered the seed of Kane to you despite the powers he has blessed you with. How certain are you of this next step in the chase? The battle depleted my men, Matilda."

"They are still one hundred strong and warriors of Gorl, the most powerful and well-trained in the world," Matilda answered. The puffery worked as pride washed over her husband. "Cassandra's trail is still hot. Do you recall the footsteps you followed from the barbarian burial ground?" Matilda continued excitedly.

"Yes, they ended in a confrontation with a larger beast. If that was Cassandra, she met her end."

"I can't believe that, Cerus. She fooled a whole tribe of barbarians into believing she was dead. I must follow this lead and know for sure she is gone. Otherwise, I will have her. I promise, if she is alive, the last thing I will do is have her."

Cerus sighed and waved an arm at the gathering mass of prisoners. "If we are to take up the chase once more, we will need to kill these prisoners."

"No, I need them for the sacrifice."

"These men, although in their eighth or ninth decade of life, used to be warriors. They know how to fight and could potentially cause trouble. I would rather slaughter them now than lose men to such a dishonorable foe."

Matilda smiled and said, "I will have reinforcements for your men by morning. At that time, you, me, Ronnis, and Cass will go to find Cassandra."

"What kind of reinforcements could you possibly have at your disposal?"

"Let's just say that Marnelphion will provide, as you have doubted, oh husband of little faith."

Matilda kissed him gently and turned to find Cass and Ronnis behind her. "Drag that fool to the tent with Maltor and secure him. Stand guard over those two; they both hold value for us. I will meet you in the morning when we hastily move back to the burial grounds. Our goal is before us, I can feel it."

Ronnis and Cass shared a smile, and Cass grabbed Bolin by the arm and pulled him along. Ronnis, Matilda, and the gathered priests looked on, astonished at the young woman's incredible strength. Ronnis eventually followed Cass back to the tent.

When they were gone, Matilda turned to Boscoe and said, "It is time."

"Tonight, then?" Boscoe asked.

"Yes, at midnight. Prepare yourselves." Matilda backed away from Boscoe and addressed the six priests more loudly. "Tonight, you give yourselves fully to Marnelphion. Tonight, you reach your maximum potential!"

JAK WAS UP BEFORE ANYONE ELSE THE FOLLOWING DAY, RUMMAGING through the kitchen and gleaning any food he could find. The commotion he caused awakened Cassandra, who went to the kitchen to investigate. On her way, she checked on Jak and saw the empty bed. She knew then that there was no intruder, but she still entered the room with great trepidation, unaware of Jak's motives. Had Maltor sent him to track Cassandra and bring her back? The thought frightened her more than a little. That was why she took her wooden practice scimitars with her.

Jak stopped when he saw her, his mouth full of food and in the act of stuffing a pack. He looked strong and healthy, not the broken man that Grog dropped at their door. It warmed Cassandra's heart to know she had been a part of his miracle recovery.

"So, you are leaving?" Cassandra asked.

A growl came from Gophia, hidden from sight, deep in Cassandra's hair. Jak stood straight and looked her over, confused by the source of the slight growl. His eyes then looked to her weapons. He dropped the pack on the table and swallowed his mouthful. He stepped away from the table and into plain sight. He held his arms out to the side, showing no weapons.

"Cassandra Rho, the Deceiver, what dark magic has your hair growling?"

Cassandra recalled how powerful this man was and how gentle he always seemed to be. She smiled and propped her wooden weapons in the corner. "First, I deceived to live. You know that Maltor held me prisoner, right?"

He nodded, and she continued, "And there is no dark magic, just a friend who also remembers Maltor's knack for being inhospitable and cruel."

Gophia stuck her head out of the tangle of hair and growled once more before ducking back into the safety of Cassandra's nape.

Jak smiled, and Cassandra understood it was one of the few times she had seen any of the barbarians wear a genuine smile.

"So, you have come for me?" Cassandra dared to ask.

Jak looked puzzled for a moment, then shook his head and started packing again. "No, I don't even know how I got here."

Cassandra was puzzled at the answer but believed him. She made her way over and sat at the table. Mateon had a never-ending bowl of lemonade, and she poured herself a glass.

"Lemonade?" she asked, holding a second cup for Jak.

"Lemon what?"

Cassandra shook her head and said, "I'd never heard of it either, but it's quite good. Here, try just a bit."

She poured him a taste, and he sat across from her, dropping the stuffed backpack to the floor. He took the cup and sniffed it curiously, then made eye contact with her and gulped it down quickly. She had to stifle a smile at the sour expression on his face, and after smacking his mouth, his eyes lit up. He liked it. He motioned for more, and this time, Cassandra filled it up.

"So, what are you doing?" she asked.

"Leaving."

"To go where?"

"Home, if home exists."

"What do you mean?" Cassandra asked, suddenly confused.

"Interlopers attacked us. Maltor and the tribe are in danger. I must go and do what I can."

"Maltor? In danger? I doubt that," Cassandra said with a snort.

The serious look on Jak's face spoke volumes. The proud barbarian was not exaggerating; something had come to the tribe that made Jak nervous. He stood and grabbed the pack. "I'm leaving to find my tribe, or what remains of it. Thank you for using your magic, as dark as it is, to heal my broken body."

Cassandra stood, and the man loomed over her. She didn't feel intimidated by him. She never really had when she'd been a prisoner of the tribe, and she surely didn't now. "My healing is not dark magic, Jak, but a gift from Gella. Please don't insult it with your silly barbarian beliefs."

Jak bristled slightly at the comment but nodded, smiled slightly, then moved to walk past her. Cassandra moved to stand in his way and put a gentle hand on his arm. He looked down at her hand, which seemed so small on his massive bicep. He made eye contact with her, and she understood that a part of him, the savage within, wanted to rip her arm out of its socket for touching him, but the gentle person that he was became curious about her actions.

"Two things before you go, Jak. First, thank you for being so kind to me when I was Maltor's prisoner. You have a good heart, and I'll never forget you for that."

He nodded and smiled that genuine smile once more. "And the second?" he asked impatiently.

"I'm going with you."

"What? Back to Maltor? I told you I haven't come to fetch you home. You're free, and Maltor is unaware that you live. I don't know how you cheated death, and I don't want to know."

"No, I'm not returning to Maltor and never will. However, I need you to take me back to the burial ground if it's on your way."

A dark cloud crossed his face, and he shook his head. When he spoke again, the fire in his eyes sent a tingle up Cassandra's spine. "There is no burial ground."

There was a pause as his eyes scanned the floor as if remembering some horrific event. He eventually looked Cassandra in the eye and said, "But that is exactly where I'm going first. Why do you wish to come?"

"Well, now to find meaning in your cryptic words that no burial ground exists. Also, I have other reasons for being there. Just finding landmarks, to be honest," Cassandra said, remembering the skull-shaped mountain from her dreams that she could always see from the sea of dead, the one she now understood to be a simple barbarian burial ground.

"Fine, I accept your company to the burial ground. Should you awaken your friends? They should know you're leaving and that I'm stealing their food. I will return with barter for this once my tribe is safe," he said, holding up the pack.

"No need to tell them anything. They understand and willingly give the food; they require no barter," came a voice behind Jak.

Jak and Cassandra both turned to see Sitra leaning on the doorframe to the kitchen, blindfolded and with a smile on her face.

"Come, I have weapons for both of you, and you are going to need them if the four of us are going on an adventure," Sitra added, turning and walking to the storage room.

Jak looked to Cassandra, who smiled and shrugged. They both followed Sitra, who offered the barbarian a massive broadsword and Cassandra two scimitars to replace her practice ones. Cassandra took them hesitantly, but they felt familiar and comfortable once she had them sheathed on her belt. They were much lighter than the wooden weapons, and although they were still entirely too long for her liking, she could see a future where they could become a good fit for her.

As the sun rose, the five companions, Jak, Cassandra, Sitra, Mateon, and Gophia, who still managed to peek her head out from Cassandra's hair and growl at the barbarian from time to time, made their way toward the Serpent Tribe burial grounds.

BINTA WAS SO FOCUSED ON KEEPING THE MYSTIC OUT OF HER MIND that she didn't notice the change in her surroundings at first. Eventually, though, she felt the sun warming her face. She slowly opened her eyes to find she was in the same meadow, but the ash was gone, and the sun shone brightly. Flowers bloomed in various colors, and butterflies were abundant. She was lying on the ground, and she slowly sat up. She noticed many people dressed in colorful robes and going about their business as they picked flowers, stacking them in baskets that they carried.

"Good day, Mystic," one young woman said as she passed near Binta.

Binta stood and followed the direction of the woman's greeting to see a distinguished man with a grey beard and a fanciful robe walking toward her. He smiled and offered a return greeting to the woman, who carried on with her collecting. He walked right up to Binta and smiled.

"So, you're now in my home. Few come here, and fewer do I even allow a glimpse at such a wonderous place," he said, holding his arms out wide to encompass the entire meadow and its occupants.

Binta could easily see through the illusion and was slightly insulted at the fact this man thought he could fool her with such a simple lie. "No, Mystic, this is the same ash-covered meadow, and these people are slaves gathering and removing the ash."

He frowned for a moment and sighed. "You're a spectacular specimen, Binta Mulay. How in the multiverse did you manage to read the Tome of X'lor and live to tell about it, much less master the work?"

"I have no answer for that. I've come because I need a favor and know you can help me."

"Walk with me, Binta, so that we may be alone in our discussions," he said, holding his hand toward a path in the woods.

"Are we really walking, or am I still in the vine cubby with Illa?"

"Does it matter?" he answered with a smile as they began a leisurely pace down the path.

"It matters to me. I don't have time for games or deceptions."

"Let's get something straight, Miss Mulay. I am a god, and you are in my home. We play by my rules, and if I choose to play with your simple mind, I shall do so."

"You know why I have come?"

He looked at her, and his gaze seemed to see through her as if he were looking through a pane of glass. She sensed him in her mind briefly, but the sensation was over before she understood what was happening.

He smiled and nodded. "Yes, yes, I know why you have come, and it's quite troubling that I can easily garner what I need from your tiny brain. I thought you would be more formidable."

Binta shook her head and refocused. His words were true enough—he could quickly enter her mind. She just needed to find a way to keep him out of the parts where she kept her most significant secrets. As she pondered this, she heard a sound from the trees to the left of the path. It was a soft moan from a familiar source.

Her eyes narrowed, and she looked at The Mystic. "Don't," she whispered.

"Too late, Miss Mulay. I know the reason you've come," he said, holding an arm out to the trees where the moan had originated.

She took a deep breath and walked into the cluster. In the center of the trees was a small clearing with a thick blanket tossed on the ground. Atop the blanket were Greyson and Cassandra, finally locked in the kiss that had eluded them previously. The sight aroused Binta, and she instinctively bit her lip in anticipation. Greyson ripped open Cassandra's shirt and began to feast on her breasts. Cassandra moaned loudly and tilted her head back in pure ecstasy.

"You see, Binta, not only do I know about your obsession with Cassandra, but a glance into your mind showed me that you are a nymphomaniac."

"Nonsense," Binta whispered without taking her eyes off the scene before her.

"Oh yes, the demon milk has much to do with it, but it has only awakened what was deep inside you all along."

The Mystic moved close, but Binta couldn't pull her eyes from Cassandra as Greyson removed her pants and underwear. The Mystic ran his fingers through Binta's hair, and his touch was electrifying, sending shock waves through her body and straight into her loins.

"Remember when Kima and her friends held you down and pierced you in places that made you blush?"

"Yes," Binta whispered as she closed her legs together tightly in a failed attempt to ease the pressure forming between them.

"Remember when Freland took your virginity, just as Greyson is doing now with Cassandra?" The Mystic teasingly whispered in her ear.

"Yes," she said again, now entirely in his trance.

She watched as Greyson mounted her friend, and Cassandra's screams of pain and pleasure brought Binta so very close to orgasm. She wasn't touching herself, but the image was so powerful she was nearing a sexual release.

"That's it. Find your release, and you may join your friends in their fun."

That somewhat broke Binta of the spell, and she turned to him and focused once more. "Why are you doing this?" she asked.

"Because I am a god and love toying with simple humans."

"But I have something I can exchange for finding Cassandra, not this illusion," Binta replied, waving her hand at the couple in the clearing, and they faded away, Cassandra's moans remaining a few moments after the visual effect had failed.

The Mystic frowned and said, "What can you possibly offer?"

"The Tome of X'lor. I know that the tome enslaves your prisoners, and I suspect all of them have crossed paths with it, which makes it valuable to you."

"I have searched your pack; it isn't there."

"So, you *have* searched for it, proving that it is valuable to you," Binta said, catching the god-being off guard.

"Enough of this! You are a simple whore! Give in to your lust and give me the tome," The Mystic growled, Cassandra suddenly appearing from behind him.

Her face was a vision of beauty, and Binta remembered just how gorgeous Cassandra was. Every detail of the illusion was immaculate; The Mystic knew of her and could find her if desired. Binta looked knowingly at her dear friend, and her bare shoulder indicated that Cassandra was naked. She smiled and licked The Mystic's ear while keeping her eyes focused on Binta. Binta quickly became aroused and felt the familiar tingling in her lower abdomen, and she squeezed her legs together reflexively.

She quickly stopped the illusion and redirected the feelings. As Cassandra faded from view again, Binta said, "Not this time. It's my turn."

As quickly as Cassandra faded away, the forest began to fade with her. The Mystic looked on as the world around him, his world, changed. Binta used every ounce of her newfound mental awareness to stop his attack and change the scenery around them, not of her making, but of his. She dove into his mind as a retaliation, which he was obviously unprepared for.

A courtroom with rows of seating made from polished marble replaced the forest. A beautiful woman and two handsome men sat on a small balcony above the courtroom. They were middle-aged and attractive beyond human standards. Her sexual itch flared quickly at the sight of them, and Binta knew they were gods, given The Mystic's origin.

Equally attractive and perfect specimens filled the rows of marbled seats. A room full of gods and goddesses, she surmised. Two small tables sat facing the three apparent judges sitting on the small balcony. The most beautiful woman Binta had ever seen sat at one of the tables. Her eyes were bluer than the sky, and her hair appeared to be made of gold strands. Her white dress hugged her perfectly, and her incredible body promised delights that mortal men dreamed of. At the other table sat The Mystic, wearing a green robe. He was younger, but it was him, no doubt.

Binta watched in awe as the memory unfolded, and she could walk around it without being noticed as if she weren't there. In truth, she knew she wasn't. She had stumbled on a vivid memory and wouldn't let it go. She could feel The Mystic trying to pull her out of the vision, and he attacked her sexual nature as he did. He enticed her to orgasm, and she unwittingly did as told, nearing her orgasm once more. The vision nearly failed because of the distraction. Binta put it out of her mind and focused on the events before her.

The god on the balcony sitting in the middle chair spoke. "And so, God of Plants, we banish you from the heavens to live amongst the mortals. Your sin of adultery with my daughter," the god said, motioning with a hand toward the woman at the other table, "will not be forgiven by me or your peers."

"But I love her!" The Mystic cried out, standing suddenly and moving toward the woman. Chains appeared from thin air and draped him, their weight having him sit hard again.

"And your punishment of banishment will be sealed with the life essence of my daughter, making it quite permanent."

"No!" The Mystic cried, struggling to stand.

"Father," his beautiful daughter said, standing, "please don't do this. Our love is real, and we will marry. I will make you proud. This is temporary, and the gods will long forget this dishonor in time."

"No, my daughter, your actions will never be forgotten or forgiven. And the baby you carry in you will always remind us of your failings."

The woman cried gently, touching her stomach and retaking her seat. Binta couldn't believe what she was seeing. She felt ill at the spectacle, and her heart went to the young woman. She turned to face the judges as they rose from their seats. The female judge produced a large book and handed it to the speaker. He took it and released it to float down between the two guilty parties. Binta backed away, understanding the power that gathered there. Her building orgasm also subsided as the memory triggered deep feelings in The Mystic. With that distraction out of the way, she focused on the sentencing unfolding before her.

"We sentence you to life on the mortal world, X'lor, God of Plants," the judge said. "My daughter's life force will be trapped in this book, which will split into one hundred pieces and scatter amongst the mortals."

"Don't do this!" The Mystic shouted.

"Silence! Our judgment is final, and now the punishment begins."

He turned to his daughter and said, "I have loved you more than any being could. You captured my heart when you were born, but your crime here is unforgivable, Amphoria."

"My only crime is to love, and I plead guilty to that with all my heart!" Amphoria said, looking longingly at X'lor.

"No, my daughter, you have sinned by having sex with this man, a lesser god of plants, against your husband, whose heart breaks at the acknowledgment of such an act."

Amphoria hung her head and sobbed all the more, the weight of her father's words overcoming her. X'lor, known as The Mystic, struggled against his chains but couldn't move. He closed his eyes and focused, and a red rose appeared before Amphoria. She looked up, plucked it from the air, and mouthed, "Goodbye."

"I love you!" X'lor shouted just as the book pulled Amphoria's life force into it.

"No!" X'lor cried and began sobbing as Amphoria's lifeless body hit the floor, the rose falling from her grasp and turning brown.

The book glowed brightly with her energy, and Binta felt the place might explode. Instead, the book exploded into one hundred pieces and flew haphazardly around the courtroom. The pieces never hit the floor, however, vanishing before they did.

As X'lor sobbed, the judge spoke again. "You have shamed the heavens with your actions and have cost me a daughter. You will live out your remaining years with the mortals as a monster, growing old and eventually dying. The humans will hate you, and they will shun you. They will find the many pieces of the Tome of X'lor, which will render them daft, a curse from you. As a curse personally from me, for you taking my daughter, I will have ash rain upon you for the remainder of your existence. Now goodbye, X'lor the Betrayer."

The female judge added, "Although you are cursed, if you can gather all one hundred pieces of the tome, we will allow your essence to join Amphoria's in death so that you may be reunited. Be thankful for the mercy of this court to allow such a perversion."

The vision faded, and Binta found herself on the path again with The Mystic. There was a tear in his eye as she left his thoughts. "No one has ever read my mind before, and I would never expect that from a human," he said.

"Amphoria showed me the memory, X'lor. You couldn't stop it."

The woods faded around her, and she was in the cubby again. The plant creature was outside, looking in, and the ash fell in heavy waves. Many vines tangled Binta and held her bent at the waist, unable to move. They squeezed her breasts and spread her legs. To her horror, she realized they had sexually invaded her. The vines, or more specifically, X'lor, pumped into her causing the sexual stimulation she continued to battle. This was the reason she had struggled to maintain control during her meeting with the god-being. It took all her willpower not to reach the orgasm that X'lor desired.

As her current surroundings came into focus, she also realized her mouth was at work, greedily suckling Illa's right breast. She could feel the milk running down her chin and saturating her insides, making the fight against the climax unbearable. Illa held her head tight against her bosom, her eyes closed and her head thrown back in ecstasy. She gasped and moaned as Binta unwittingly sucked the demon milk into her, poisoning her body in the process.

She stopped suckling and instinctively began coughing up the milk. With a surprised gasp, Illa released her and stepped away. The vines untangled and withdrew from her, and she fell to her knees without their support. Binta felt weak and couldn't stand, the milk inside of her making any movement a trigger for a possible orgasm. She shivered, coughed, and threw up some milk, but she dared not move otherwise. She noticed then that she wore her short, sexy dress that she had stuffed in her pack when leaving Poppy's Inn. Her fancy dress from Jamison's wardrobe was casually discarded and was now mostly covered in ash. She looked up to see Illa smiling, covering her breast once more by pulling the strap of her dress over her shoulder.

"You have what you need?" Illa asked the plant creature that Binta knew to be X'lor.

"No, she has proven her worth. She conceals the tome from me, but she will barter for it. Draw the milk from her before she perishes. She deserves that for which she came," X'lor hissed.

Binta vomited again, and as awful as that movement was, it nearly made her orgasm. The milk would dominate her or kill her, and so when Illa approached and knelt in front of her, she complied. The demon brought her face toward Binta's and held her chin tight. When the demon kissed her hard, she orgasmed. But she didn't feel X'lor in her mind. He could have taken what he needed from her, the location of the tome, but he didn't. The climax lasted a long time, and when it finally subsided, the demoness took the kiss further, sticking an elongated tongue down Binta's throat, triggering her gag reflex, and making her vomit into Illa's mouth. The demon broke the kiss and spit the vile milk on the ground, then repeated the process.

Binta couldn't tell how long it went on like that, but Illa had her constantly vomiting the milk, and eventually, she felt more in control. The demoness still kissed her deeply between retching and seemed to garner a great deal of pleasure from the procedure. Eventually, Binta gained control of her sexual desires, and Illa broke the embrace. Binta fell to the ground, breathing hard, lying on her stomach. Without shame, she reached between her legs and masturbated to another orgasm, hoping that X'lor wouldn't exploit her mind as she lost control again. She played for a long time and realized at some point that Illa sat and watched, masturbating as well. Binta had never felt so repulsed and yet so sexually charged at the same time. It took a long time to get it out of her system and beat the effects of the nepalin milk.

THE PARTY OF FRIENDS HAD LEFT AT DAWN AND REACHED THE BAR-barian burial ground when the sun hung low in the western sky, bathing it in the usual Yaddaton red. Mateon knew the way, having visited the site several times before on his hunting expeditions. The burial site was still there but devoid of any bodies or birds. Instead, the dune beyond the burial ravine was littered with hundreds of bodies and at least two dozen birds that feasted on what little meat remained on the bones of the dead. Jak saw them and dashed, shooing the birds away. Cassandra watched the barbarian chase them and then scour the bodies, collecting weapons and supplies from his former friends and neighbors.

"We'll set up camp if you want to go see about your friend," Sitra said.

"Camp?"

"Yes, there's no need to travel the desert at night; we'll stay and travel home in the morning. You better say goodbye to your friend," Sitra said with a smile.

"Why is he leaving?"

"I feel he doesn't need to stay. His loyalty to his king and to his people drives him."

Cassandra hugged her arms across her chest and peered south, catching Sitra's meaning. She could barely make out the outline of the mountain ridge. She would have to wait until morning to see if she could locate the skull-like cave as it was in her dreams. Sitra kissed her cheek and went to help Mateon, who was unfolding the tents from his pack.

Cassandra loved Sitra and, at that moment, realized she had been selfish. Cassandra had given up her life hiding in the couple's home. She had given up on her sister, Binta, and everyone who cared about her. She had played the victim, and Sitra had let her. Now the sleeth was allowing her to begin her life anew, to follow her dreams. Her only desire prior to meeting the couple had been to become powerful and protect her family. She glanced at the ominous mountain range again and thought maybe Zolmex was there.

She fought the tears that threatened to come, turned and walked through the ravine where the dead had been not so long ago, making her way toward Jak. She couldn't see very well and stopped to summon light. She hadn't mastered that spell as it was priestly magic, but she prayed to Gella, hoping her goddess would bless her with the power since she had given her the extraordinary ability to heal Jak. She prayed, holding her symbol as a conduit, and she could feel her goddess with her. When she finished the prayer and opened her eyes, light glowed around her, centered on the holy symbol.

She smiled and said, "Take that, Greyson," remembering his uncanny power to produce light.

She walked toward Jak as he searched the dead to give him some light. She looked at the dead bodies as she passed; most were skeletal but still had their weapons, including swords and knives. Some even had bows and arrows. Mixed with the barbarian bodies were the corpses of some strange creatures, human but with enormous mouths and elongated teeth. She approached Jak, who was now examining a bow he had taken from one of the bodies.

"What happened here, Jak?"

"Interlopers were searching for …" He trailed off and stood, temporarily forgetting his scavenging.

"What? Tell me," Cassandra pleaded.

"Dark magic?" he asked, pointing to her bright symbol.

"No, the same magic that healed you. Not dark, like Maltor thinks. Powerful and dangerous, yes, but only to my enemies."

He stared at her for a while, then slowly nodded, accepting her explanation. "I heard the leader speaking after the massacre of my people," he said, waving a hand at the litter of bodies. "She was a small woman dressed in a black robe. She was looking for you."

Cassandra's heart raced, and she found it hard to breathe. Jak noticed her discomfort and asked, "What is it, my queen?"

"Don't call me that," was all she managed to say.

She thought of Kane's prophecy, and it made sense. Someone evil was searching for her, and she felt it related to the prophecy. She looked back to Mateon and Sitra on the other side of the burial ravine. She had been selfish; she was putting her friends in danger.

"Cassandra, what's wrong?" Jak asked, grabbing her arm gently.

His touch startled her, bringing her reeling mind back into focus. "Your tribe is in danger," she said in a whisper.

"Yes, I know. That's why I'm going back," Jak said, picking up a quiver of arrows and strapping them on his back.

Cassandra peered into the darkness beyond Mateon and Sitra to where the mountains were. The reason she had come in the first place. Cassandra couldn't see them, but she knew what she would find when the morning sun revealed the ridge: a skull-shaped outcropping would be like the one in her dreams. Her heart raced, and she felt lost. All Cassandra wanted to do was flee, whether to the mountains and ultimately to Zolmex or home. She just wanted as far away as possible from the evil people who were looking for her in the godforsaken desert.

She turned to Jak and said, "I am the cause of all this. I was born for the sole purpose of those people hunting me down and sacrificing me to some demon-god that they worship. All of these people died because of me." She looked around helplessly at all the dead, mixed with those strange abominations that were obviously risen undead. All of the death and destruction was because of her.

Jak broke her desperate train of thought as tears filled her eyes. "This is *not* because of you. I know you better than anyone in the tribe knows you, even better than Maltor. I was assigned to watch over you and protect you. You are a good person, and I knew that when I first saw you. I understand what my king loves about you. It's not just your beauty but your soul. You are the incarnation of Strenna, of beauty inside and out. You are *not* responsible for any of this."

He walked up to her and took her hands in his. "I go now to help Maltor. I don't know what I'll find, but if Maltor lives, I will be obligated to tell him you live. You saved my life, and I owe you this secret, but Maltor is my king and his heart aches at the thought of you dead. You will always be my queen, no matter where you go or how far you run from the Yaddaton. Even if you don't acknowledge it."

"Jak, don't go; they will kill you," Cassandra said, tears now streaking her cheeks.

"I have my destiny, and you have yours. Flee. Don't let the evil interloper catch you. If it is Strenna's will, we will meet again."

He bent and kissed her gently on the cheek and wiped away her tears. She looked up and saw a smile there. It was a rare barbarian expression that she could get used to. She returned it the best she could. Then, the barbarian warrior was gone, running up the dune and back to his tribe. She took the opportunity to pray, standing alone in the sea of dead. She prayed hard for Jak, Maltor, and anyone else who remained in the tribe.

She turned to her friends, who had started a fire. She would not be selfish any longer. She went back through the dead, asking Gella to bless each one and even asking for peace for the fallen undead creatures. After all, they were once members of the tribe.

She eventually made her way to Mateon, who was busy setting up a second tent for her, but she stopped him. "No, Mateon, you and Sitra need to go—it's unsafe."

"What? Where is your friend?"

"He has gone," Sitra answered for her.

"Yes, he has continued, and I want the both of you to go home. I feel you're in danger here."

"We aren't leaving you, Cassandra," Sitra said.

"If we go home now, you're coming with us," Mateon added.

"No, you don't understand. What killed all these barbarians, and the reason Jak was near death when Grog brought him to us, is that some bad people are looking for me. I think they will come for me soon, and if you're with me, they will kill you or worse."

"The prophecy?" both asked in unison.

"Yes, the prophecy," she said, wiping more tears.

"We aren't leaving you, Cassandra," Sitra said, coming and putting an arm around her.

Mateon joined them and took her hand, squeezing it gently. "Yes, we're in the prophecy together."

"If you feel the danger is too great here, we'll pull camp and travel back home immediately," Sitra said.

"Wait," Cassandra said before they could proceed with that line of thinking. "If you are staying with me, I'd like to stay the night here. There is something I need to verify in the morning. But we should leave at daybreak."

"Agreed," Sitra said and hugged her again.

Mateon joined the hug, and Cassandra could feel Gophia's little arms hugging her face. The three were her family, and she felt safe and loved. Cassandra knew that, similar to her life thus far, this family and this group of friends she had made over the last few months would soon disband. She would leave them the next day and probably never see them again. However, she would find Zolmex, Kessi, and Binta. This time, she would go on her terms, not because she disliked these people, but because she missed her friends and family.

"Thank you. I love you all," Cassandra whispered.

They found sleep soon after, with Mateon and Sitra in their tent and Cassandra and Gophia in the other. They weren't disturbed that night by desert creatures or agents of Marnelphion. Cassandra found a deep sleep void of dreams. She welcomed the reprieve.

As the moon was high in the sky and as Cassandra and her three companions slept near the old burial site, the priests of Marnelphion delved deep into their loyalty and fanaticism of the demon lord. It took the combined powers of the remaining six priests, along with Matilda's enhanced powers she had earned at Novafontera, where her body had absorbed some of the tar of Marnelphion's pit. Her heart was made black by the evil substance. Creating wraiths from the devoted was one of the most repulsive and powerful effects the priestess could summon. They began the ritual at nightfall, and by midnight, the power of Marnelphion had started to take shape.

Cass, Ronnis, and Cerus sat right outside the tent that housed the fanatical priests, waiting for the results of their efforts. None knew what to expect, and Matilda had not elaborated. The warriors of Gorl took turns watching the captives, the remaining members of the Serpent Tribe. The men would take shifts, letting three men go at a time to visit the old procreation tent the barbarians used for the female captives. The newest additions to the tent, the four wives of Maltor, were especially popular that night.

As another trio of warriors returned from the tent and another three left their post to reap the benefits of their victory, chanting from inside the priest-filled tent became louder. Some priests even seemed to strain to form the words through gritted teeth.

"I hate to say it, Cerus, but your woman is a bit of a drag," Cass said with a mischievous smile.

Cerus smirked and said, "She has her uses."

Cass got up and strolled over to Cerus, a sexy grin on her face. "And what about me?"

"What about you?" Cerus said, sitting up attentively.

Cass looked over the man, her most recent lover, and the blood that still stained his hands and chest, his hair that was filthy with soot and grime, and the slight hint of body odor that accompanied it all. She ran a finger over his chest and licked her lips.

"Don't I have a use?" she said, pouting.

Cerus smiled and looked like he was about to devour her, but before he could say anything, Ronnis said, "Why don't you two suffer some self-control?" Both looked to Ronnis, who sat in his mask, unmoving with his eyes boring through Cerus.

Cerus stood and asked, "What did you say, Porcelain?"

Ronnis stood as well, though the warrior of Gorl towered over him. He put his hand on the hilt of the Black Adder and stood his ground. "I said, this is not the time or place. We must focus on Cassandra Rho."

At that moment, a purple flashing light erupted in the tent, and the priests of Marnelphion screamed in unison. It was a frightening, inhuman sound that even startled the mighty Cerus. All three took a step back as the screams intensified. The smell of burning flesh accompanied those horrific screams, and the three moved further away. The guards nearby stood agape, trying to take in the unusual scene. The purple light flooded the tent, and the structure violently swayed as if caught in a wind storm. Eventually, the tent caught fire and burned with a purple energy that gave off no heat. Soon, the tent was gone, consumed by the power.

Cerus tightened his grip on his spear, and Ronnis drew the Adder, its black blade dripping with poison. Cass moved to stand behind the two men, unnerved as much as they were at the spectacle. Soon, the flames died away, and there was nothing but darkness. A silhouette appeared where the tent flap had once been, the small form indicative of Matilda. She stretched her arms out to the side of her, and they began to crackle with the purple, fiery energy.

"Behold, the power of Marnelphion!" she said, her powerful voice carrying through the entire tribe.

Behind her six creatures appeared, the remains of the priests, the flesh burned from their bones. A black, smokey substance rolled over them, creating a new protective skin. Their skeletal faces burned with the purple energy that consumed the tent, and each floated about a foot off the ground.

"And now a demonstration of the power of a Marnelphion wraith," Matilda said with an evil smile.

She pointed to the group of barbarian prisoners, and one of the wraiths floated toward them. The women fell over each other, trying to move to the back of the gathered prisoners, and even the Gorl warriors moved aside, wanting nothing to do with the undead creature. The phantom moved to the closest barbarian, an old, blind woman, and reached a clawed hand toward her. She sat there unblinking, knowing she was about to die but accepting her fate. Before the wraith could touch her, a firm hand grabbed the skeletal arm.

"No, unnatural filth, you leave her alone and deal with me," an old barbarian warrior said.

His chest was scarred from many battles, and he was missing an eye. The man stood nearly seven feet tall and showed no fear in the face of the evil creature. The thing turned to look at him, the purplish fire consuming its skull.

"Go back to hell, spawn of a devil!" the barbarian yelled, then punched the undead creature in the face.

The creature barely flinched from the strike, and the barbarian held his broken hand to his chest, shocked that the hit did no damage to the abomination. Then he screamed and fell to his knees, his hand afire with the purple energy. He shook it vigorously, but within moments, the fire ignited his entire body, and the stench of burning flesh filled the air. Soon, the barbarian was a smoldering husk, a charred skeleton, face down in the Yaddaton sand.

The creature turned back to the woman, who continued to sit and accept her fate. It reached out with both hands and grabbed her by the head, taking its bony thumbs and pushing them into her blind eyes. The woman was stubborn and did well not to cry out, even after her eyeballs popped and the thumbs found her brain. The purple energy engulfed her skull and she indeed cried out then. She fell, a second burned husk to join the first.

"Any questions?" Matilda asked.

Other than the barbarians whispering among each other, no one spoke up. The undead creature turned and fell in line with its brethren behind Matilda.

"The wraiths will assist in watching over the prisoners until we return," Matilda said.

"Why not send them to fetch Cassandra? They seem formidable; surely they can handle the task," Cerus reasoned.

Matilda pulled him away from the gathered prisoners so none could hear her whispered response. "The creatures are weak during the day and would be powerless while the sun is out. The priests are now powerful undead creatures, a gift from Marnelphion, but they will eventually fade as their life essence slowly escapes their corpses," Matilda said.

"So, they aren't a permanent ally?"

"No, my husband, they will disintegrate at the end of thirty moons. However, they will suffice as a means of intimidation. The barbarian savages are hearty and brave but not stupid. After the demonstration we just had, none will attempt an escape."

"All of your priests gave their lives to be guards over a few prisoners for a month?" Ronnis asked, now holding his mask in his hand, a concerned expression on his face.

Matilda stood before him and said, "Transforming to a wraith is the greatest honor a priest of Marnelphion can have, especially if your service in undeath is to further the Great Summoning. Those men knew exactly what they were doing and will all be rewarded handsomely in the afterlife."

"You mean hell?"

Cass giggled at the remark and put a hand to her mouth to stifle it. Matilda's face turned red, and she gnashed her teeth. Ronnis remained calm, and if he was nervous about provoking Matilda, he did not show it.

"Are you trying to antagonize me, Lord Ronnis?" Matilda asked with a mocking smile.

"No, I'm just ready to find Cassandra. I hope we're close and that the sacrifice of your priests is not in vain."

Matilda relaxed considerably and processed his words. She eventually turned to Cerus and said, "He is right. The trail is hot, and we should go."

"So, don't kill him?" Cerus asked as Ronnis grabbed the hilt of his sword.

She turned to Ronnis and said, "No, he is one of us. He's an ally." She then turned to their scout, Jest, and discussed something quietly with him.

"I guess you're safe for now, Porcelain," Cerus teased Ronnis with a wicked grin.

Ronnis didn't back down. He looked up to meet Cerus's gaze and said, "I guess so, cuckold."

Cerus's eyes opened wide, and his knuckles whitened on his spear handle. Ronnis partially withdrew his wicked blade. Cass, who stepped in the middle of them, was the only thing that stopped the two from trading blows.

"Now, boys, this is not the time to fight. We have a virgin to catch."

She smiled mischievously at Cerus and walked away. Both men watched, and Cass knew she had their attention, so she exaggerated the sway of her hips. When she disappeared into the night, Cerus and Ronnis made eye contact again.

"This isn't over," Cerus growled.

"I look forward to continuing our discussion later," Ronnis answered.

Matilda interrupted their stare-down and appeared not to even recognize the conflict. She gave Cerus explicit instructions. "Tell the men that you're leaving here to watch over the prisoners that the wraiths are free-thinking, unlike most undead. They don't need to be, and cannot be, controlled. They know their purpose and will only act in Marnelphion's best interest. They are here to guard the prisoners, mainly Maltor, but they will watch over the entire flock.

"Also, Jest informed me that the barbarians had little to no livestock. He found three more horses and a bunch of camels. We'll utilize the horses if you can spare three of your best warriors to travel with us. I assume the new allies Marnelphion has blessed us with will easily suffice to replace those three warriors. The seven of us leave in less than an hour. The trail to Cassandra Rho is close, and we will pick up her filthy scent soon enough."

She made her way to the gathered horses on the south end of the tribe while the wraiths floated into Maltor's tent. Cerus recruited three of his top remaining warriors for the trip and relayed Matilda's instructions to those he was leaving behind and in charge of the prisoners.

Soon, Matilda led them out of the tribe, and the seven riders, including Cerus, Cass, Ronnis, and three highly seasoned Gorl warriors, made haste toward the barbarian burial ground. Luckily, the night was old and nearly consumed. The sun would rise a few hours later, awakening Cassandra and her friends, unaware of the quickly approaching danger.

Illa had led Binta to her home, a small cottage deep in the woods. Binta didn't remember much of the trek there except wading through ash. She sat on a chair, a bucket nearby in case she was sick, and shook from the serum Illa had made her drink. It was a detoxing liquid that would draw the milk from her pores. Currently, the milky substance spotted on her skin in many places, drawn to the surface by the concoction. It would also occasionally leak from her eyes and mouth. She held a plush towel to wipe the stuff away as it appeared.

Illa sat on the other end of the table, sipping some tea. The smell of it had Binta nearly dry-heaving, and it took all her willpower not to throw up in the bucket. A side effect of the intense serum was that it made Binta very cold. She only wore her tiny dress from Poppy's Inn and suffered from the chills. She couldn't wrap up because she had to be vigilant in wiping the excreted milk away as soon as possible. Her hopes of surviving relied on it. And so she sat, cold and shivering, as Illa looked on with a smile.

"Wh-what?" Binta asked through chattering teeth.

"Nothing, except you should already be dead," the demoness answered.

"What d-do y-you know?"

"I know that you drank enough of my milk to die, and yet here you are," Illa said, standing and walking over to gently pet Binta. "The only explanation is that you have ingested nepalin milk before. Is that true?"

Binta wanted to ask more questions, especially about why Illa had let her drink so much poisonous milk. The answer was clear: X'lor had initially planned to kill her. Anything to let him gain the information he desired was acceptable to him. The hint that Amphoria had somehow assisted Binta made him change his mind. Binta wanted out of Vasym before he changed it back. She was shaking so severely that she couldn't speak, so she nodded as her teeth began chattering again.

"I thought so! You are full of surprises, Binta Mulay, and I sure hate to see you go," Illa said, then knelt so she was eye level with Binta. "We could have lots of fun together."

Binta had already sensed the tingling in her stomach when Illa touched her hair, but as the beautiful demon knelt before her, it took Binta's breath away.

"You see how you feel right now, how I so easily manipulate you into thinking of sex?" Illa asked, standing with a victorious smile. "You see, we nepalin excrete pheromones that have absolute power over you once you drink the milk."

She walked back over to her chair and sat down, and Binta couldn't help but admire her long legs that were visible due to the excessive slit in her dress. Illa smiled as she began sipping her tea once more. She was correct; Binta was losing control, and she didn't doubt the demon used her natural pheromones to manipulate her. She felt the milk running from her right eye and used her soft towel to wipe it away.

"Now that you have consumed the milk of two nepalin, a feat I have never heard of a human accomplishing, you will now be completely helpless against the pheromones." Illa studied her for a moment, a suggestive look on her face. She eventually sat up and said, "We have time as The Mystic locates your friend. What do you say you and I have some fun while we wait?"

"N-no, Illa. I-I do not f-feel well."

"Call me selfish, but I've kissed you and want more. Besides, you can't resist me with as much milk that remains in you. You are mine to play with as I see fit until The Mystic comes calling. Besides, it's not like you don't want it."

Illa stood next to Binta, a hand extended for her. She knew that if she grasped it, that would be it. If she wanted to resist the demoness's advances as she had practiced before coming to Vasym, she would need to do so then. A whiff of her scent had Binta thinking of Cass and had her squeezing her legs together in a failed attempt to keep her arousal under control. She looked into Illa's dark, smiling eyes and took her hand.

CASSANDRA AWOKE BEFORE ANYONE THAT STRANGE MORNING. SHE blinked away the sleep and gained her bearings, remembering she was camping in a tent at the barbarian burial ground. The thought of all those dead bodies yards away and the fact that they died because of her broke her heart. Sure, she held no love for the savages, but those innocent people had perished because of her. The sun hadn't risen yet, but the first hints of dawn began to lighten the sky. She found Gophia sharing her pillow as she often did. Cassandra rose, dressed, and exited the tent quietly so as not to disturb Gophia. Once outside, she found that Mateon and Sitra were still asleep, a fact given away by Mateon's light snoring.

She sat on a nearby rock, facing the mountain ridge, and waited. Soon, she would have her answer. Her heart raced in her chest, and she pondered what she would do if the skull-shaped top were not visible. No matter what, she would have to say goodbye to her friends, which made her sad. As the sun began to crest the eastern sky, Mateon and Sitra woke and came out to sit with her.

"And what is it that you seek this morning?" Sitra asked.

"Something from my dreams."

"Having to do with the prophecy?" Mateon asked, yawning and taking a large swallow from his canteen.

"Yes, possibly. I haven't told you much about my dreams, but this burial ground is the centerpiece of one of the recurring ones. In the dream, I turn from this burial ground to the mountains in the south. At the top is a room with two windows that give the illusion of a giant skull sitting atop the ridge. In that room lies my birthright."

"Wow, that is some dream." Mateon chuckled.

"Yes, I am nervous about what I'll see when the sun rises."

"How close are we to sunrise?" Sitra asked.

"Just a few moments until I can see. The outline of the mountain is already visible," Cassandra said.

"Mateon and I have hiked that place. It is called Witch's Rise, and a path leads up to the top," Sitra explained. "Supposedly, it's named after a witch who made the trail by walking up and down the mountain, going mad because of some spell that went wrong."

"Yes, it's been a while, but I remember the trail. It's a nice hike that will get you to the top in a few hours. But I don't remember a room with two windows at the top," he said, scratching his head.

Gophia joined them, fluttering to land on Cassandra's shoulder with a giant fairy yawn. That brought a smile to Cassandra's face. She looked around at the gathered friends, three of the best she had ever had. It broke her heart, but this would be the last day she would be with them. It was time to become legendary, as Cedric had suggested.

"Sitra, will you take off the blindfold?" Cassandra asked.

"What? Why?"

"The sun is nearly up, and I want you to view this with me. I have waited a long time for this moment, even though the last few months haven't indicated that."

Sitra smiled, placed her hand on the blindfold, and said, "Ready?"

"Gophia, you understand not to look at Sitra?"

"Yes, Gophia not look, I promise," the fairy said, moving to the shoulder opposite Sitra. There, she hid in Cassandra's hair as usual.

"We're ready, Sitra," Cassandra said after Gophia settled in.

Cassandra focused her gaze on the mountain ridge as Sitra removed her blindfold and did the same. She took Cassandra's hand and squeezed it. Although Mateon couldn't see, he came over to stand on Cassandra's other side and similarly took a hand. Gophia poked out her tiny head just as the sun rose, bathing the large mountain with light. And that was how the four friends watched the sunrise that fateful morning.

Cassandra gasped when she saw the familiar view from her dreams. The rocky mountain wasn't tall, but unmistakably, sitting atop the ridge was the same vision from her dreams: the skull-shaped room! The two holes that comprised the eyes she knew to be windows. She knew what was behind those windows—Zolmex!

"I can't believe it," she whispered.

"I'm sorry, Cassandra, I'm sure you're disappointed," Sitra said, careful not to take her gaze from the mountain.

"What? Do you see the skull, Sitra?"

"No, do you?" she answered, squinting through the morning sun and studying the ridge harder.

Cassandra watched her friend peripherally, her heart racing. Was she imagining the scene before her? She rubbed her eyes and looked again, and once more, she saw the skull.

"Gophia, do you see the skull?" Cassandra whispered.

The fairy ducked back into the tangle of her hair and imparted a telepathic reply: "*Gophia sees no skull. Gophia wishes not to see it. They are death.*"

"So, no one sees it?" Cassandra whispered as Sitra put her eye covering back on.

"I'm sorry, Cassandra. Perhaps you're the only one who's supposed to see it. After all, it wouldn't be much of a hiding spot if everyone looked up and saw a skull-shaped room on top of ole Witch's Rise," Mateon said with a smile.

Cassandra nodded and faintly smiled. She turned back to the mountain range and fixated on the skull on top. Memories from her first expedition into one of Kane's mystical caves haunted her. She'd failed miserably then when she was with her friends. She would have to go this one alone, and she expected it to be as deadly as the last adventure. With a sigh, she sat on the rock and just stared, thinking that perhaps when the sun crested the mountain, the skull illusion would disappear. It didn't.

The others ate a quick breakfast and then started breaking down the tents. Cassandra didn't eat but helped with breaking camp the best she could. She couldn't get her mind off the pending trek she would soon make. Perhaps this time, she would find Zolmex. If her dreams were any indication, she surely would.

"Notel X," she whispered, wondering how that phrase would play into all this.

Soon, they were on their way home, and Mateon used the limbs of a nearby desert bush to cover their tracks as they left the area. He had them walk in a straight line, Cassandra leading the way, with Sitra behind her with her hand on her shoulder to stay in line. Mateon followed suit, his hand on

Sitra's shoulder and dragging the bush behind him. After a few hours, he discarded the bush, and they strolled.

"That should be good enough to keep us safe from any possible trackers," Mateon said with a smile, wiping the remnants of the bush from his hands.

Matilda and her band made the old burial site with only a few hours of sunlight remaining. A few vultures dotted the dune that they leisurely trotted their horses down. They ignored the birds and even trampled over the dead, not having a way of dodging them. Once across the ravine used as a burial place for the barbarians, they stopped. The scene before them stood out to even the most novice tracker. Someone had been at the burial ground recently, and Matilda smiled despite herself.

"She was here," she said.

"You can't know that, Matilda. Someone was here recently," Cerus argued, then dismounted to investigate.

Matilda followed, eager to investigate the area. The others dismounted and tethered the horses. Matilda turned back when she noticed and said, "Do not dismount; we are leaving now. Cassandra Rho has been here!"

"No," Cerus said, shaking his head. "We've ridden through the night and most of the day, and the horses must rest. We'll break here, feed and water them, and grab a quick meal ourselves. We'll leave in one hour."

"My husband, the trail is hot, and I know it is her! We must leave immediately," Matilda said, nearing a panic.

Cerus grabbed the reins of her horse and said, "If we don't stop, the horses will perish, and that would take away our advantage. The desert sun is unforgiving, and we cannot push them. From what I can tell, whoever made this camp is on foot; there is no sign of livestock. If it is indeed Cassandra Rho, we will have her soon."

"It is her," Ronnis said from off to the side.

"How do you know?" Matilda asked excitedly.

"When the incident with the wolves and the ravens occurred, she was five. I scrutinized that day with all my heart; I knew something magical and unnatural was at work."

"And now? Do you scrutinize me?" Matilda asked.

Ronnis chuckled. "No, what you have displayed in raw magical power far exceeds whatever that little girl did when she was five. However, she lived in my facility then, and Oldorburg outlawed magic. So, I took the proper precautions. I watched her, knowing someday she would mess up again."

"Yeah, it looks like she messed up your face," Cerus said.

Cass giggled, and Matilda fixed Cerus with a hateful glare, which did nothing to diminish his bluster. Ronnis slowly removed his mask so his scarred cheek was on full display. Cass stopped her giggling once she saw the look on the lord's face. Even Cerus's smile diminished slightly.

"I have pledged my allegiance to Matilda and her cause because of this scar. I will stop at nothing to make sure Cassandra dies a horrific death, even if that means I cannot kill her myself. I will see it through. I tend to do that with people who annoy me."

"Is that a threat?" Cerus asked, moving to tower above Ronnis.

"Absolutely," Ronnis said, not backing down from the more prominent man.

"Enough of this!" Matilda screamed, then turned calmly to Ronnis once more. "Please finish your explanation."

"As I was saying, as Cassandra grew, I kept a watchful eye on her. I grew suspicious of her, but her mother distracted me with sensual pleasures, which I allowed without complaint. However, as I kept one eye on her mother, Sera, I kept one on Cassandra."

"Mother?" Matilda asked, concerned.

"Surrogate mother. The orphanage used to assign workers to children to act like a mother. Do not doubt that Cassandra is an orphan and fits the description of your desired sacrifice."

Matilda smiled and nodded, becoming secure in her belief that the child of Kane was indeed within her grasp now.

"When she reached eighteen years of age, she revisited the site of the wolf attack. She went alone, without even her sister's knowledge. However, I knew, and I watched."

"How does that make you believe Cassandra was recently here?" Matilda asked.

"It's simple. She journeyed back to the spot of the wolf attack, and so she has returned to the spot of another traumatic experience: being buried alive. Whether to relive the nightmare and make sense of it or to look for clues, I cannot guess. However, if your intuition tells you she was here, I agree the chances are good."

"It is not intuition, dear Ronnis, but Marnelphion who guides me. I feel this is correct; my god acknowledges that belief."

"And I agree with both of you," Cass said with a grin that enveloped her face.

Matilda turned a curious glance her way and wrinkled her brow in confusion. "What do you know, girl?"

"Not much, but I can tell you that this thing is working again," Cass said, holding up the medallion attuned to Cassandra.

Matilda's eyes widened, as did her evil smile. "It works?"

"Faintly, but it's unmistakable. She's that way." Cass pointed to the southeast.

"That's the same direction in which the tracks we followed the first time led," Cerus said, even the large Gorl warrior growing a little excited with the developments.

"The device's power has diminished to nearly nothing. However, it must work if you're close enough to the little witch," Matilda guessed, pointing to the medallion.

Cass shrugged, and they quickly ate and cared for their steeds. Soon, they were on the trail again, galloping at full speed to the one person who could make their plans a reality—Cassandra Rho.

CASSANDRA AND HER FRIENDS WERE NEARING HOME, AND THE SMALL structure was in their sights as the sun began to set. The bright orange sky behind them was brilliant as always during the Yaddaton summer. The group was cheerful, and only Cassandra felt the impending dread, knowing she wouldn't stay the night and that she had to leave for her friends to be safe. She was about to have that difficult conversation when Mateon stopped them with a raised hand. He cocked his head as if listening. Cassandra heard nothing but the beating in her chest.

"I hear it, too," Sitra said.

"What? I don't—" Cassandra began.

"Run! To the house, quick!" Mateon yelled.

All three ran, with Cassandra running between them so they could touch her and stay oriented toward their home. A frightened Gophia flew from Cassandra's hair and quickly made for the house.

"What approaches?" Cassandra asked between labored breaths.

"Horses, or camels, at least half a dozen and running fast," Mateon answered.

"They're coming right for us as if they hone in on our location," Sitra added.

"I need to leave. I'm putting you in danger," Cassandra said.

"When we get home, Cassandra, I want you to go downstairs to the hydro garden. At the last row of yucca roots is a tangle of falinca vines and a door behind that. Take it, and it will lead you to the base of Witch's Rise," Sitra instructed as they neared the home.

"Here they come, Sitra. Fetch my weapon, quick!" Mateon said.

He stopped about fifty feet from the door and removed his gear and shirt. Cassandra didn't know what weapon he referred to, and Sitra ushered her along, not letting her see who or what was coming. Soon, they were in the weapon storage, and Sitra activated the lever near the second shelf, and the trap door opened. Sitra activated another lever Cassandra didn't know about, and a hidden door opened into a room with many weapons.

"Now, go, and don't look back. We will hold them off as long as we can," Sitra said.

Cassandra was scared, and tears welled in her eyes. "Thank you," she said, giving Sitra a tight hug.

"You're a friend, Cassandra, and we fight for you. Go, and don't make our stand in vain," Sitra said.

Gophia flew from the other room and perched on Cassandra's shoulder. "Gophia go with," the fairy said.

"May Gella protect you both," Sitra said, ushering Cassandra and Gophia into the hidden lower level of their home.

Cassandra wasted no time running to the large garden comprising most of the cavern. The falinca vines gave off enough light for her to see clearly. She made her way to the last row of the garden. There was no time to pack her belongings or even take food. She plucked a couple of items from the plants they passed and stuffed them in her pack. Soon, she found the tangle of vines and, after some work, discovered the secret wooden door behind them, built into the stone wall.

"Gophia, I must leave. My road is dangerous, and I don't want you in harm's way, my little friend. Do you wish to stay here and hide in the garden?"

Gophia flew from Cassandra's shoulder and fluttered in front of Cassandra's face. "Gophia stays with her friend," the fairy said, wringing her little hands nervously.

"Very well, let's go," Cassandra said, opening the old door.

Gophia found her perch once more on Cassandra's shoulder, and when the door was opened, she hid in Cassandra's long hair. The two friends stepped out of Sitra's garden and into the next phase of their lives.

Binta was dressed in her skimpy outfit, her regular clothing lost in the ash of Vasym. Her back now had a plethora of scratches and her neck was bruised from multiple bites. Illa lounged in her bed, stretching and smiling at her handiwork.

"I don't suppose you can retrieve my dress I came here in?" she asked Illa.

"Don't be silly. You're much sexier in this one," Illa purred.

"I don't wish to be sexy, Illa."

Illa threw the covers off, revealing her nakedness, the fake manhood she had used to please Binta still strapped to her. "It's nothing you can help, my lover. You're sexy whether you want to be or not."

Binta sighed as Illa came to stand behind her. The demoness brushed Binta's hair aside and gently kissed her tender neck. Binta closed her eyes and, without meaning to, cooed. The demon milk was mostly expelled now, and Binta was in more control of her primal urges. But she couldn't deny Illa, having consumed the demon's essence through the milk. She was powerless against her advances.

"X'lor still searches for your friend," Illa whispered in Binta's ear while reaching around and playing with her nipples.

Binta gasped at her touch and whispered, "I don't have time for this. I must be going."

"Nonsense, there is nowhere to go until The Mystic is ready," Illa said, gently pushing Binta over so her hands rested on the bed. "So, until he finds your friend, we will play," she added, moving behind Binta and entering her.

Soon, Binta was lost in her lustful tryst with the demoness once more. Her resolve against X'lor was lost as well, and The Mystic could devour her thoughts if he so chose. Binta knew he wouldn't; she had beaten him fairly, and he respected her victory, especially since his true love was behind it. She soon forgot about X'lor as her current lover quickly brought her to climax. Illa was relentless, however, and used Binta for a long while as they waited together for word from X'lor. It was the longest yet most enjoyable few hours of Binta's life.

CERUS WAS THE FIRST TO SPOT MATEON STANDING IN FRONT OF THE small stone house. The party made a line in front of Mateon about twenty yards away from the blind man, who now stood naked from the waist up, his muscular chest on full display.

Matilda could tell that Cerus was in a fighting mood, so she quickly spoke before her unpredictable husband could react to the sight of the lone, unarmed man. "Hello, good sir, we come in peace," she said.

"You most certainly do not," Mateon responded.

"I assure you, we mean you no harm. We just ask that you give us what is ours and we will be on our way," Matilda explained.

"She's inside the house," Cass whispered beside Matilda, concentrating on the magical medallion.

"I'm searching for Cassandra Rho. We need to speak with her. There are people trying to find her that want to do terrible things to her. We have come from Pelesea in the hopes we can keep her safe," Matilda lied.

"I see, and so does the prophecy mention your death at the hands of her friends?" Mateon asked.

Matilda turned a surprised glance Cerus's way and whispered, "This simple man knows about the summoning?"

Cerus shrugged and said, "You mean man and woman."

Matilda turned back, and now a blindfolded woman stood beside the man, handing him a silver mallet. Matilda found the woman beautiful and thought it strange that she wore a blindfold. She was armed only with a staff. The pair made an unusual couple but gave off a hint of confidence that Matilda didn't like.

"Take care of this, my husband. We need to enter that house," Matilda whispered.

"Gladly," Cerus said, dismounting and motioning for his three warriors to follow.

Mateon and Sitra separated as if they had rehearsed the scenario many times.

"I'll take the woman," Cerus said as he walked briskly toward Sitra, and the warriors began to circle Mateon.

"Let's enter the house and find our prey," Matilda said to Ronnis and Cass and prepared to dismount.

Before she could do so, Grog lurched up from the sand, the giant lizard buried and waiting beside Matilda's steed. The lizard bit hard into the horse's side, and it reared and flipped Matilda off its back. Grog's mate and offspring also burst through the sand, startling the horses. The riderless ones ran off, which included Cass's steed after it had bucked and flung her. Ronnis was the only one to remain on his horse, but the attack spooked it so severely that it took off at full gallop, moving him quickly away from the ensuing battle.

Grog's bite partially included Matilda's leg, and her thigh showed a garish wound as she lay on the ground, writhing in pain. Nearby, the lizard shook her horse violently, ending the creature's suffering. It tossed the dead horse aside, locked its gaze on Matilda and Cass, and advanced on them with a hiss.

Matilda rummaged around in a pouch and brought forth a vial of a dark, sticky substance she used for one of her most potent spells. The pain in her wounded leg made fishing out the vial difficult, but she eventually had it and poured a few drops on her fingertips. The pain was unbearable, and her fingers smoked and hissed as the substance ate at her. She whispered the proper command words, and her pointer and middle fingers turned black, absorbing the foul liquid.

"Come along then, lizard," she bade with an evil grin.

Cass had to summon a spell to protect herself from the remaining three lizards, a mother and two babies. The juvenile lizards were as long as she was tall and had sharp teeth. She decided to focus on one of them, hoping she could quickly kill it and only have two to deal with. Soon, two sizzling, magical darts shot forth from her fingers and slammed the smaller lizard in the face. Luck was with her as one of the missiles hit the creature in the eye, exploding the eyeball and severely hurting it. It roared in pain and thrashed in the sand a few feet from her. Cass stood and readied another spell in case she needed it.

CERUS ENGAGED THE WOMAN AND IMMEDIATELY KNEW THAT SHE WAS well-trained with her staff. She fought valiantly and knocked away his thrusts as if she could see. He found it humorous more than exciting, and he toyed with the woman, feigning attacks and trying to move behind her to see if she could hear or sense him. He was impressed, but he knew she was no match for him. He found her attractive and entertained taking her before her husband.

He was so confident in his pending victory he called out to his men, "Don't kill him. I want to rape his woman as he watches." The Gorl warriors confirmed their leader's intention and laughed as Mateon growled.

"This fool is blind," one of them said, amused at the apparent disability.

His comment was met with an aggressive attack as Mateon swung his mallet proficiently and accurately. The man, no novice to battle, parried the attack, but the tingling in his arm indicated that he was fighting no ordinary man and no ordinary mallet. His mirth was soon lost and the three Gorl warriors moved in simultaneously, spears blurring.

IT TOOK RONNIS A FEW MOMENTS TO STEADY HIS HORSE AND CALM IT. He had been raised on a horse and was a proficient rider, which was the only reason he could stay mounted during the sneak attack. Turning the steed back toward the battle, he peripherally noticed movement to his right and instinctively glanced that way. His heart thumped in his chest at the vision—less than a few hundred yards away, a young, blond-haired woman ran up the base of a small mountain. It was dusk, so he couldn't see well, but the woman carried a lantern, and its light gave him a glimpse of her features. She looked very similar to Cassandra Rho! He squinted in the waning light but couldn't make out any details before he lost sight of her behind the rocks lining the base. He couldn't hope to know if it was Cassandra, but his heart told him it was. Who else would be running away, alone in the desert, and fitting her description?

"Well, well, at long last, Cassandra Rho. I have you now," he whispered to himself.

He had the notion to gallop at full speed to her and trample her with his horse. However, he knew the consequences and refrained from that course of action. After all, the tortures he and Cass had discussed would be exquisite, and the ultimate death Cassandra would face at the end of Matilda's dagger pleased him. So, he made a note of the area where he last saw her, and although he was not sure, it appeared as if a path led up the mountainside. If they could find that path, they would find Cassandra. He reluctantly turned his horse back to the battle to tell Matilda his discovery.

THE LIZARD GRABBED MATILDA UP IN ITS VISE-LIKE JAWS AND BIT down. She felt the sharp teeth sink into her side, and more than one rib cracked under the immense pressure. She quickly set her black fingers on the lizard's head and unleashed her spell before the beast could shake her around like it had the horse. She knew the spell would quickly kill it. The tar seeped from her fingers and into the lizard. It spat her out and started rolling in the sand, bellowing pitifully as its skin blackened and spread across its head and upper back. Soon, the thrashing ceased, and the creature lay motionless, the blackness eating away its skin even after death.

"GROG!" MATEON YELLED, HEARING HIS OLD FRIEND DYING JUST A FEW feet away.

He fought with a rage then, swinging the mallet proficiently and efficiently blocking the coordinated attacks of Cerus's well-trained men. They couldn't score an opening, and he was enraged. The attackers soon became defensive as they began to dodge Mateon's attacks. He wanted to at least knock one of them out of the battle. Grog and his lizard family were no match for these vile people, and he needed to finish with the warriors before him and concentrate his wrath on the leader, the female battling Grog.

He knew he was too late when he felt his muscles tightening up from a spell, no doubt from the very leader he wanted to engage. He slowed and felt the pain of multiple stabs to his arms, making him drop the mallet, then to his hamstring, making him fall to his knees. A spear stabbed through his collar bone and he screamed in pain and frustration. Another assailant came behind him, grabbing him by the hair and holding a deadly spear tip to his throat.

"Don't move, or I'll impale your throat, blind man," the warrior whispered in his ear.

Mateon complied, knowing he had no choice. He just hoped they'd given Cassandra enough time to escape.

MATILDA SAW THAT THE MOTHER LIZARD HAD HER BABIES, ONE INJURED badly by Cass's magic, and was herding them to a nearby hole in the sand. The fight with the lizards had ended, so she focused a powerful hold spell on the crazed blind man who seemed to be doing an excellent job against Cerus's seasoned warriors. He resisted most of the effect but slowed enough for them to overwhelm him.

With a sigh, she began casting a healing spell on her torn side and ribs. Once the soothing effects of the spell mended those wounds, she healed her torn leg. As she finished, Cass was beside her and helped her stand. Not for the first time, Matilda understood the strength that the young woman possessed.

CERUS TOOK A SMACK ON HIS KNUCKLES AND SURMISED THAT ONE finger might have broken with the strike. He yelled out in pain and shook that hand. "You will pay dearly for that one," he said.

Sitra didn't respond but settled into a defensive posture. Cerus growled and came on in a flurry of strikes. The woman did well to block his attacks, and even dished out her own counters, cracking him on the wrist and neatly breaking it, but Cerus's rage was uncontested and his spear eventually cut her arm, severing a tendon and making the staff nearly useless. She fell to her knees, similar to how Mateon knelt not far away, now at the mercy of their tormentors. Cerus jerked the staff from her hands and tossed it aside, then backhanded Sitra so hard, she fell to her side.

"Sitra!" Mateon screamed. His outburst met with pressure from the spear at his throat, the razor tip cutting slightly into his tender skin.

"If I were you, I'd hold real still. Your woman friend is going to be doing a lot more screaming shortly," the man said.

"You bastards," Mateon said through gritted teeth.

"Exactly," the man said, and the three shared a laugh at his expense.

Once on her feet, Matilda made her way with Cass toward the humble abode, seeing that both the man and the woman who were defending it were subdued. Matilda noticed Ronnis racing his horse back toward them and understood everything was under control. They only had the one horse left, but they would now have their prize—Cassandra was hers!

She watched as Cerus pulled the woman up by the hair so she knelt in front of him. She knew his intentions and understood they were warranted. But before she entered the house, something about the woman's hair caught her eye. She knew something was amiss, and her voice caught in her throat. She looked on with horror, knowing what was about to transpire.

Cerus pulled the woman back to her knees by the hair and received several tiny bites for his effort. Sitra's hair, tied in a ponytail, came to life when he grabbed hold. The little snakes bit at him, and although the bites caused no real damage, he was surprised by the sudden attack.

"Well, now, what do we have here? A sleeth? I hear sleeth make fine lovers. Is that true?" he asked, removing the blindfold.

Sitra's eyes were still closed, and one would soon turn black from Cerus's backhand. The worst of the swelling was yet to come and she could see perfectly well out of it. More importantly, others could see her eyes clearly if they looked at her.

"Yes, it is true, and it's a fact that you will never discover," Sitra said.

"We'll see about that," Cerus said with a chuckle.

He vaguely heard Matilda cry out a warning not so far away. Sitra opened her beautiful green eyes, eyes that few had looked upon and lived to tell about. Cerus found them exquisite, and the last thought that ran through his mind as he looked upon them was how unique they were. He would so enjoy looking into them as he forcefully took her.

Cerus froze, and slowly, his entire body and his belongings, including his magnificent spear, began to turn to solid stone. He had a moment to react as he felt his body quickly solidify. He wanted to look at Matilda and warn his wife, but his petrified neck wouldn't respond. Soon, he was immobile. His men watched the spectacle unfold, and Matilda warned everyone that Sitra was a gorgon. Cerus hadn't heard it in time, but the three warriors of Gorl did, and when they witnessed their leader become petrified, they all looked away or closed their eyes.

SITRA WAS UP QUICKLY, LOOKING AROUND, KNOWING SHE COULD FIND more victims with her gaze, but the men expected her attack, and they all stumbled around blindly, making their way from her. One had a spear to Mateon's throat, and before he moved away, he impaled her husband's neck with one quick thrust.

"Mateon!" she screamed and ran to him as he fell face first to the sand, which quickly turned red around him. Something washed over her, and she knew it was a spell because her muscles stopped moving and froze. She stood perfectly still and could only watch as the blood pooled around her husband.

She heard the evil woman who seemed to oversee the group yell, "She is held! Find her blindfold and reapply it. Then take her eyes. I want her left alive, and I want those eyes!"

Sitra could only watch as the blind warriors moved slowly toward her. It took them some time to feel around aimlessly in the air, and she saw peripherally that the two women had entered her home just as a new rider had dismounted. He didn't enter the house but instead made his way to Mateon. Her heart ached at the scene, and luckily, before she had to witness the evil man's intentions with her dying husband, she was mercifully blindfolded. Soon after, they bound her hands behind her and dragged her inside, the men punching her in the sides or smacking her head, cussing at her for what she had done to their leader. If she hadn't just witnessed Mateon's demise, she would have smiled.

RONNIS RODE UP AND DISMOUNTED JUST AS MATILDA AND CASS entered the house. They wouldn't find Cassandra in there, and so he used their search as a distraction. Cerus's men seemed to have the woman under control, a woman that was far more dangerous than any of them had realized. He had witnessed Cerus's demise and was quite pleased with it. As the warriors dragged the woman inside, cussing and threatening to pluck her eyes from their sockets, he went to the felled man.

The man was bleeding out and unmoving. Ronnis noticed the mallet nearby and quickly went to work. He fished around his pack and found the potion of healing, one of three he had brought along. He checked Mateon and found him barely alive, his breaths coming in gurgling gasps. He turned him over and gently eased the liquid down. The nasty wound on his throat partially healed and Mateon cracked open his eyes.

Ronnis ceased administering the potion and said, "Your mallet is to your right about ten feet away from where you lie. Your wife is dead, but not before she turned one of our leaders to stone. He is petrified and about twenty feet past your mallet. I hate him as much as you do, and so, I have healed you enough to carry out your task of vengeance. You won't live much longer, but you will have the opportunity in just a moment to rid the world of the man who is responsible for your wife's death. We take our leave shortly."

Ronnis dropped him face down in the bloody sand, precisely as he found him. He went to the small house, where he could hear Matilda screaming in rage, followed by frequent smacks and subsequent moans. When he entered, he found the pretty woman on her back, Matilda on top of her, slapping and punching her face.

"Where is she?" Matilda screamed, but the woman would not answer.

Matilda cried, tears streaming down her cheeks. It was the first time Ronnis had seen her out of control, and even Cass, who stood nearby, seemed to carry a worried expression. Matilda truly loved Cerus, which was exactly why he didn't dare pick up the mallet outside. Even so, if Matilda found out he had healed the dying blind man, he knew he would be punished in the cruelest way.

He cleared his throat, and Matilda looked up from her bloody victim, who seemed not to be conscious. "What, Ronnis?" Matilda asked.

"I found Cassandra. We must hurry."

"What? Where?"

"She's climbing a mountain ridge not far from here. Come, I'll show you."

Matilda rose and said to the nearest Gorl warrior, "Do with her what you want, but collect her eyes and wait for me here. If we don't return soon, make your way back to the tribe and wait. We'll eventually return with the prize."

"Yes, my lady," one said and bowed.

"And keep her alive. I want her to live without her husband… exactly as I have to," Matilda added, wiping away tears and kicking Sitra hard in the ribs. Sitra moaned and curled into a fetal position. Blood poured from her busted mouth, and she seemed unaware of her surroundings.

"As you wish," the warrior replied with another bow.

Outside, it was dark, so Matilda lit a lantern and handed it to Cass. "We only have one horse, and we must ride quickly. Are you sure you saw Cassandra?" she said, turning to Ronnis.

"What does the amulet say?" he replied.

They both turned to Cass, who took it in her hand and concentrated for a moment. Soon she nodded her agreement.

"Excellent! The two of you take the horse," Matilda said.

"What will you ride?" Ronnis asked.

"I won't ride," Matilda said. "Go, now. I will follow your lantern as a beacon."

Ronnis nodded and helped Cass onto the horse. Then he urged his mount to full speed. Soon, they were galloping quickly through the desert and toward the mountains.

Matilda watched them go and made her way to Cerus. She found him in the dark, petrified and cold. She ran her fingers over his beautiful face and kissed his lips.

She stifled more tears and said, "I will avenge you, and more importantly, I will find a way to remove this curse. I will come back for you, I promise."

They had been through a lot together, and now that their goal was near, he was gone. Her heart ached, but she knew she had to be strong. Perhaps Malikai would find a way to cure him; she had heard of old spells that could do that. She put the thought out of her mind. She had to focus, or the brat would elude her again.

She began casting a spell, one she had not cast since she first visited Novafontera all those months ago. The spell normally sprouted mighty demon arms from her sides, which could carry her at speeds equal to a horse's. However, since the last time she had cast it, she had absorbed the tar of Marnelphion on the cobblestone street of Novafontera and she had become powerful. She expected something entirely different this time.

As the spell took hold, she fell to her knees, screaming. She was in so much pain that the three warriors stopped beating Sitra long enough to investigate. As they watched from the doorway, Matilda sprouted appendages, not the demon arms as before, but very long and slender spidery legs, four on each side. The pain was excruciating, and she blacked out several times during the four-minute transformation. Once it was over, she stood on eight-foot-tall spider legs. They were magnificent! They held her body well off the ground, her true legs a few feet above the Yaddaton sand. She tested out the new appendages, and once satisfied she could use them, she nodded to Cerus's men and sped toward the diminishing light offered by the lantern Cass held. She was even faster with her spider legs and caught the horse quickly. She slowed her pace then and ran easily beside Ronnis and Cass, focused on the looming mountain and the prize that awaited them.

NOTEL ✠

MATEON CRAWLED TO HIS MALLET, WHICH WAS THERE JUST AS the man said it would be. His leg wouldn't work and he couldn't walk, and breathing was a chore as he felt himself drowning in his blood. None of that mattered. The only thing in his mind were the horrible words the man had whispered to him: Your wife is dead.

He sobbed as he crawled. His senses were failing, where they usually far exceeded an average person's. His hearing wasn't as acute in those awful moments, or perhaps he would have heard the beating Sitra was receiving, and he would have gone to her instead. In his despair, he could only focus on staying alive long enough to destroy the man who had taken his precious Sitra away.

He used the hammer, swinging it out in front of him as he crawled in the direction indicated. Eventually, the hammer hit something solid, and he was delighted to discover a petrified man exactly like his healer had described. Mateon struggled to his knees, spitting out blood as he did, trying desperately to clear a way to breathe. He hadn't much time left, but he would avenge his Sitra. Not trusting the source of the information, he felt the statue to make sure it was indeed an enemy. He grabbed hold of one of the large, petrified arms and pulled himself to a standing position.

He used his hammer as a crutch and stood before the statue. He ran his hands along the face and the body, feeling as many details as he could, and making a mental note of the large spear the statue grasped.

"You bastard, whoever you are, you took my Sitra. You don't deserve an eternity of petrified silence. Instead, you deserve the pleasures of hell, and I am here to set you free so that you can experience those things that await you in the afterlife," Mateon said, spitting up more blood.

It wasn't easy for him, but Mateon grabbed the mallet with both hands, nearly falling several times as he tried desperately to keep his balance with a cut hamstring. He took the weapon above his head for an overhead chop to demolish the statue. Tears streamed down his face as blood poured from his mouth and the wound on his neck.

"Sitra! I love you!" he screamed, and he brought the hammer down as hard as he could.

The swing wasn't nearly as powerful as it could have been due to his injuries, but his aim was true, and the weapon had more than a bit of magic. When it hit directly atop the statue, Cerus's head, shoulders and upper chest shattered into many pieces. Mateon fell on his back, hearing the deadly strike and knowing he had avenged his love. He smiled and lay still, waiting for death to take him, waiting to reunite with his one true love.

Binta was spent, and Illa milked her stamina for all she was worth. She stood on wobbly legs, still leaning heavily on Illa's bed as her lover finally released her from the constant lovemaking. Binta collapsed face first on the bed, breathing heavily and sweating profusely. She closed her eyes, and sleep quickly took her. A good while later, she awakened to Illa's touch, the demoness brushing her sweaty hair from her face.

"No more," Binta pleaded, turning her head in the other direction and feeling the burning between her legs at Illa's touch.

"Nonsense, my little slave. You are my plaything, and if I desire you, I will have you. Unfortunately, our time here is ending as The Mystic has relayed to me that he has narrowed down your friend's location."

"Cassandra!" Binta said, turning to face the demon and sitting up.

"Yes, that got your attention, now, didn't it?" Illa said with a smile.

"I need to get dressed. I must go to her."

"As I said, The Mystic is *close* to finding Cassandra but has not yet done so. We must get you cleaned up; you look and smell like a whore, Binta. This doesn't smell much better," she said, sniffing Binta's discarded dress that Cass had given her.

Illa drew a bath and Binta soaked in the refreshing water. Her female parts hurt all over and she keenly felt the scratch marks on her back and buttocks. She closed her eyes and relaxed just a bit before she felt Illa's hands on her. She tingled all over and her eyes flew open at the touch.

"I will bathe you, my love," Illa said, caressing Binta under the water.

The demoness's touch was pleasurable but also painful. Binta wanted to refuse her touches, but she couldn't begin to move the strong woman's arm away. And so she became putty in Illa's hands once more, the demon quickly bringing her to another powerful orgasm before bathing her.

Afterward, an exhausted Binta slept naked in a chair near a fire, a blanket wrapped around her shoulders. Binta could sense Illa standing over her and she cracked open an eye to see the demoness smiling evilly and standing just a few feet away. Binta was too weary to even ask what she wanted, so instead, she dozed off.

Binta awoke next to the fire and had difficulty shaking the slumber. It took her a few moments to find her bearings and understand she was clean and rested, and soon she discovered she wore her tiny dress, which had also been washed. She also realized she wore the collar and leash now. She picked up the thin chain of the leash and puzzled over why she wore it.

As her fuzzy mind tried to recall the events before her sleep, Illa's voice made her jump. "The Mystic has found your friend."

Binta turned to see Illa standing near the threshold leading outside of her home. Binta could see the vines slithering over the windows, evidence X'lor was present. Binta steeled her focus, putting up barriers to block The Mystic from accessing her thoughts. She stood and made her way to Illa, anxious to find Cassandra.

Illa moved to block the door and said, "You look lovely. I'll take this," grabbing the leash and pulling Binta out the door.

Outside, the ash poured and the zombie-like victims of the tome walked around removing the deep piles. There was a small covered porch that protected Illa and Binta from the filthy precipitation. In front of the porch was the plant monster Binta knew to be X'lor. Binta could faintly make out the image of the once-god inside the tangles—a normal-sized man, deep within the monstrous plant creature.

"And so, I have found your friend, the one you risked your life for by coming here," X'lor said.

"Where? Take me to her, please!" Binta said.

Illa pulled gently on her leash as one would to calm an excited pet. Binta gave her a hateful look, but Illa only smiled and blew her a kiss.

"I am ready to make the trade, X'lor. Please, take me to Cassandra."

"In time, Miss Mulay. First, you rescue the tome, then Illa will see you to your friend."

"No, I won't give that information. You take me to Cassandra first, then I tell Illa where the tome is."

"Do not disappoint me and make me regret letting you leave here alive," X'lor said. "With all the whoring you were doing the last few hours, I easily discerned the location of the tome. You can thank Illa for that."

Binta turned again to the demoness, who shrugged and continued to smile. It was as if she knew something, perhaps a dark secret that Binta would not enjoy.

"But we still have a deal?" Binta asked, nearing a panic.

"Of course, I cannot deny that I'd love to break your will and keep you here, and Illa would enjoy you as a plaything for a while. However, you bested me at my own game, which no human has ever done. I will keep my word because of it. I will send you and Illa to the tome first, and once it is secured, I will take you to Cassandra.

"But mark my word, Binta Mulay, if you so much as step a toe in my woods again, I will kill you, or at least let Illa play with you for a while before you meet your ultimate demise. Understand?"

"Of course," Binta said, swallowing hard.

"And never speak of this place. No one should come here. If they do, I will kill them, then hunt you down in retribution. Is that clear, Miss Mulay?"

"Yes, I have no reason to come back. Now, please take us."

"As you wish. Goodbye, Miss Mulay," the plant creature said as vines began to creep along the porch.

Illa pulled Binta to her, using the leash, and stood close to her as the vines wrapped around them. Binta's heartbeat was in her ears, and she felt the familiar sensation as if she were hurled across the universe. When the feeling subsided, she felt the pull of the leash as Illa guided her out of the large rose bush that grew near the pond in Pelesea.

Binta looked around to gain her bearings and saw Daro's cottage nearby, the place she had lived in for a few weeks. She was standing near the bench that she had sat on many a night dreaming of Greyson's return and mourning the loss of Cassandra. She looked past the bench to the loose rock, which Illa easily lifted. There lay the tome, as Binta had left it when she had switched it for the slutty dress she now wore. The tome was wrapped tightly in cloth, protected from the elements.

Illa tossed the rock down as if it weighed nothing and smiled. "Well, you are lucky The Mystic trusted you. This is where we say our goodbyes, my little plaything," Illa said, taking the leash in her hand and rubbing a finger on the small chain.

"You are taking me to Cassandra first, right?" Binta asked, grabbing Illa's arm.

The demoness looked at Binta's hand on her arm, then back to Binta as if in warning not to touch her. Binta understood and removed her hand. "Please," Binta whispered.

"I'm not taking you anywhere. The Mystic will take you to your friend, and I will take the tome to him," Illa said, unbuckling Binta's collar and taking the leash in her hand. "A souvenir of our time together." She held up the collar and leash and stepped toward the rose bush, where vines began to entangle her.

"When ready, step into the bush, and you will find your friend. Goodbye, my pet," Illa said, and soon, the vines obstructed Binta's view of the woman.

Binta sucked in her breath, not knowing if she could trust either X'lor or Illa. She had no choice. She looked around at the familiar place, knowing Jamison was probably in the castle just a few hundred feet away. She wanted to run to him, fall into his arms, and be safe. Instead, she thought of Cassandra and followed Illa into the bush.

The vines wrapped her quickly and she was soon teleported to the other side of the world, to the Yaddaton Desert. An instant later, she stepped out of a cactus. It was dark, and the heat of the desert overwhelmed her for a moment. It was drastically cooler than it had been before the sun set, but still much hotter than the pleasant weather Pelesea offered this time of year. She turned and watched the vines slink back into the cactus, and they were soon gone. She couldn't see well, but she knew they were forever gone. Wherever she was, she was there to stay.

A man's screams made her jump, and she turned in the direction of the sound, which was very close. The man's words reverberated off the many boulders: "Sitra! I love you!"

She made her way quickly toward the sound and soon discovered a light spilling from the doorway of a small home. A man stood in the doorway, and his appearance made him look evil. He wore black leather armor, and the little she saw of his face reflected pure rage.

"Shut up, fool! Your woman is getting what she deserves. Hurry up and die!" The man then ducked back into the house, and Binta could soon hear muffled voices and loud smacks followed by soft moans.

"Cassandra!" she whispered.

The frightened Binta gave way then to the powerful Binta, who had mastered the Tome of X'lor. She heard the man moaning softly not far away in the shadows. He made a wheezing, gurgling sound, and her heart went out to him. He would have to wait, though; Cassandra was in trouble!

As she neared the threshold, she heard a woman moaning and could make out the distinct sound of a fist striking flesh, followed by another moan. She peeked in to see three men, two holding a limp woman who had her arms bound behind her back and was blindfolded, while a third one was hitting her. Binta had to put a hand to her mouth when she saw the bloodied pulp the woman's face had become. Her lips were torn and blood poured from her mouth and nose, which looked to be broken. A blindfold, once white, was crimson with blood. The man hit the woman in the mouth. Blood flew all over the nearby table, then ran down her chin and trickled down the front of her shirt. She would have fallen over long ago, but the evil men held her up. To Binta's relief, it wasn't Cassandra.

The man mercilessly beating her stopped and drew a knife. He handed it to one of the men and said, "Lay her on the table. You guys extract her eyeballs while I teach this bitch not to mess with a Gorl warrior."

The mention of the god Gorl had Binta's mind wandering back to Greyson's journey. He had sailed to Varish to investigate the existence of a Gorl army. How was this related to Cassandra? Her thoughts were interrupted as the woman was slammed down on the table. The third man began undoing his pants, and Binta had seen enough of that in recent times to know exactly his intent.

"You hold her head still, and I'll do the carving," one of the other men said. He produced a small sack and added, "We'll put them in here for Matilda. Just don't look at them; they may function even after we remove them."

Binta had heard the name Matilda as well. Greyson had bragged about an excellent lover he had taken in Tara, one that worshipped the demon lord Marnelphion. A chill ran down her spine. She had heard enough; it was time to end this. She walked into the room, her powers of the mind already reaching out to the three men.

The man undoing his pants noticed her first and said, "Hello, what do we have here?" looking Binta up and down.

Binta was vaguely aware of how she was dressed, but she quickly put that out of her mind. She walked right up to the man, who put on a large smile at first, before Binta was in his mind. His face twitched, and he eventually opened his mouth nice and wide and stood there with his hands at his sides and his pants around his ankles. Binta walked by him and muttered a spell, the only one she really knew from her time at Victoria's School of Magic. As she passed the motionless man, she put her finger in his gaping mouth and released the magical energy that had built up on her fingertip. The dart exploded out the back of his head and he fell over dead.

"Get her!" one of the other men shouted, and he picked up his spear.

Binta looked at him and said, "Run that way, and don't stop until three days have passed or you fall over dead, whichever occurs first." The man dropped the weapon, ran out the door, and was never seen again.

Binta turned to the third man, who still held the knife and no longer looked very confident. "You stay back, or you'll get what she got!" he said, pointing to the table.

He froze then as Binta imparted a new course of action for him. He slowly brought the knife to the edge of his eye and began cutting it out. Binta blocked out his screams and he fell into the corner of the room, carving around his eye with the knife. She went to check on the woman, who was softly moaning.

"It's all right, you're safe," Binta whispered in her ear, slowly removing the blindfold.

The woman's eyes were swollen shut to go along with her broken nose and busted lips. Binta gasped, having never seen anything so brutal. She refocused on the lone warrior's screams as he pulled one of his eyes from its socket. She had seen enough. Binta sent the one-eyed man a new suggestion. The man stopped screaming and plunged the knife into his remaining eye. Soon he was silent.

"Rest easy. I'll get you some water," Binta said.

She went to the kitchen and luckily found a pail of water. She dunked a cup into it and soaked a towel she saw on the counter. She came back to the woman and helped her drink. The woman could do little with her swollen lips, and most of it ran down her chin. Binta cleaned her wounded face the best she could, and the woman eventually sat up. Binta helped her into a chair.

"I'm Binta Mulay. I've chased off those bad men."

The woman then said something that Binta did not expect, and it made her smile. "Binta? Cassandra's friend?"

CASSANDRA WAS EXHAUSTED, BUT SHE KNEW SHE SHOULDN'T STOP. SHE was about halfway up the mountain ridge and paused just long enough for a drink. Gophia wanted some, too, so she let the fairy drink some from her cupped hand.

"Oh, Gophia, I hope Sitra and Mateon are all right. Something tells me they're dead, and it's all my fault."

The fairy wiped the water from her mouth and gave Cassandra a hug.

"Thank you, my friend," Cassandra said.

Cassandra shivered and realized for the first time that the desert night was taking over and they were in a higher elevation. She was about to start moving again when she spotted the light at the base of the mountain.

"A lantern, Gophia!" she whispered.

Her heart raced, and she knew that if she could see their lantern, they could see hers. She knew it was the people who had decimated Jak's tribe and had probably done the same to her friends. They would be the ones who worshipped Marnelphion, and she surely didn't want to get caught.

"We have to make it to the top quickly," Cassandra said, craning her neck to find the top of the mountain. It was impossible to locate the top or judge how much more ground they had to cover because of the darkness. Soon, she was running as fast as she could. She couldn't extinguish her lantern or she wouldn't be able to see, so she kept it open and ran for her life.

"There!" Cass said, pointing to a light halfway up the mountain.

"Cassandra," Matilda whispered from above them. She still maintained her unnatural spider legs, allowing her to move over great distances very quickly.

"Your horse can't make it up the trail. Leave it and follow me as quickly as you can," Matilda said.

They had been fortunate to find Cassandra's prints in the sand that led right to the path Ronnis had glimpsed. Unfortunately, it appeared too narrow for the horse. Ronnis and Cass dismounted, and the horse wandered off. Matilda grabbed the lantern from Cass and started up the mountain. She was still very quick on the narrow path, and they knew Matilda would overtake Cassandra well before they could reach her by foot.

"I have an idea, snake man," Cass said.

"What do you have in mind?" Ronnis answered, already putting a hand on the hilt of the Black Adder, as if reading her thoughts.

He watched with glee as Cass released her inner demon. She sprouted two tiny horns on her forehead, her eyes turned black as night, and she sprouted a large pair of bat wings. Ronnis instinctively called on the powers of his sword and changed into a large black adder. Cass bent down so that the lord could slither up her body and wrap around her shoulders.

"We should have done this long ago," Cass said with a giggle.

Ronnis responded by lightly flicking his tongue along her neck. Soon, the two were airborne, following Cassandra's light.

***

"MATEON, MY HUSBAND, HE NEEDS HELP," SITRA SAID DESPERATELY.

Although Sitra couldn't see with her swollen eyes, she donned a new blindfold and quickly found her medical kit, consisting of herbs, ointments, balms, a needle and thread, and a bottle of curing powders. Binta was amazed at how easily the woman could find her way around without using her eyes.

"You know, you should use some of this healing on yourself. You don't look well," Binta said.

"No, Mateon is hurt badly. Please grab a lantern and help me find him," the stubborn woman replied.

Binta did as instructed and led Sitra outside. The battered woman walked as if more than a few ribs were bruised or broken, but they made their way to Mateon, who somehow clung to life. Sitra fell near him and whispered words into his ear. He seemed to respond with a raspy cough.

"Let me help you get him inside," Binta offered.

"No, there's no time," Sitra said, and she began sprinkling some of the powders on his neck.

She worked quickly, Binta identifying the wounds and Sitra applying her primitive healing to those areas. It took them nearly an hour to stabilize him enough that he seemed to breathe easier. He slept, and Sitra sat down in the sand next to him. Binta went into the house and brought a blanket for each of them.

"Shall I build a fire?" Binta said.

"No, Binta, you have done enough. You have given us a chance to live," Sitra said. "If you build a fire now, they may come back."

"Who?" Binta asked.

"The evil people chasing your friend."

Binta's eyes widened. "Where is she?"

"There is a mountain ridge south of here. She's trying to make the top to find her birthright."

"Zolmex?"

"Yes, yes. However, those pursuing Cassandra are evil, as you've seen. You must stop them."

Binta looked to the south into the pitch-black night. There, she saw two little dots high above the horizon that looked like fireflies from that distance. They were close together—too close. Binta grabbed a lantern, said her goodbyes, and was soon on her way. She didn't know much about the people she had just met other than that they had kind hearts and cared for Cassandra. She ran with all speed toward the mountains. She knew there was little time.

Cass flew over the two lantern dots that were very close now as Matilda gained quickly on Cassandra.

"Oh Ronnis, we will have such fun at play. I can't wait to see her face when she runs right into us," Cass said, flying up the mountain a good way and setting down near the path.

Ronnis slithered off her and quickly changed out of snake form. Cass willed her demon features away, and they hid in a small cove of rocks, watching Cassandra's lantern slowly make its way toward them.

Cassandra watched in amazement as the lantern grew closer on the trail behind them. She thought of hiding off the path and waiting for her pursuers to pass. Instead, she formulated another plan.

"Gophia, meet me at the top of the mountain. Fly away from the path so you'll be unnoticed."

"No, Gophia stay with friend," the little fairy said, wringing her hands.

"I'll be there shortly. Go, and be quick. Trust me," Cassandra said with a smile.

Gophia eventually flew off, and Cassandra immediately changed her focus. She saw the arcane symbols Gophia generated flitting in the air behind her as she flew away. Cassandra grabbed the ones she needed and quickly pieced together a spell. She wasn't sure about her ability to cast it but had practiced it during her time in the Pelesea jail. She had never succeeded then, but she had to try again. It was a complex magical door that would take her short distances. She had first saw Baxter use it to save her while trapped in Kane's caves. She had stolen the magical door then, but now she attempted to cast it from memory. Her chances were slim.

She fell within herself and ignored the closing lantern now less than a few hundred yards away. She weaved the symbols together quickly and, in her haste, failed to hold them together, and the door blinked into existence only to blink out just as fast. She doubled her efforts and thought she heard the telltale sound of spider legs closing quickly. It was a flashback to the caves when hundreds of giant spiders descended upon her while she was trapped within. It sounded the same now, except instead of many spidery legs clicking on stone walls, one giant set seemed to be approaching, making a similar sound on the stone path. Whatever the thing was that hunted her, it was close.

She cast the spell again, amazed and delighted that it held long enough for her to step through. She willed a second door to appear high on the mountain ridge and exited through it. Her door spell blinked out of existence as soon as she stepped through, but now she was much higher up the mountain.

CASS AND RONNIS CAME OUT OF HIDING, PERPLEXED BY THE TURN OF events. They looked down the trail from where Cassandra had been traversing a short time ago and saw nothing.

"There!" Ronnis said, pointing to a spot far up on the mountain.

Cass turned just in time to see Cassandra walk through a portal near the very top of the mountain.

"Clever girl," Cass whispered.

"Take us to the top this time," Ronnis said, melding back into an adder.

Cass nodded and sprouted her wings. Soon the two were back in the air.

BINTA FELT OUT OF SORTS RUNNING ALONE IN THE DESERT, HER LANtern providing minimal light. She tried to keep her coordinates locked on the two tiny lanterns that seemed so far away. They would flicker in and out of view as the terrain allowed. It was surprisingly cold, and she wasn't dressed appropriately for travel in those conditions. She stopped to catch her breath and hugged her arms to her chest, and her teeth chattered. She didn't dare stop for long because time was of the essence, so she kept walking toward the mountain, but the sand seemed endless.

As she reached the darkest part of the journey, the one between the mountain and the home where Sitra and Mateon lived, she felt a sensation, almost a smell. It was all too familiar, like someone who wore too much perfume. A shiver ran down her spine and at the same time a touch of excitement coursed through her body. She held the lantern up to get a look at who could be in the dark with her. She knew before the shadowy figure appeared out of nowhere.

"You," she whispered.

CASSANDRA FINALLY MADE HER WAY TO THE TOP, USING BAXTER'S DOOR spell three times to take her to the peak, covering long distances at a time. Gophia was already there and flew onto Cassandra's shoulder when she arrived. Cassandra smiled and said, "I'm glad to see you too, my friend."

Her smile was short-lived, however. She looked around and found no room shaped like a skull with two windows for eyes. Instead, the top had a flat, almost polished surface lined by two smooth rock walls to her left and right. On the far side of the peak was a cliff face, which opened up to nothing. The trail ended there, but in her estimation, the room from her dreams should be where the cliff was. She went to the edge and peered over. The cold desert air blew in her face, and although in the dark she could see nothing, she knew the barbarian burial ground and Sitra's home were there, very far down, just like she knew the skull room was supposed to be right where she was standing.

"This can't be," she said, feeling the large rock wall that made the right side of the path.

"Uh-oh!" Gophia said.

Cassandra turned to see their pursuer's lantern approaching quickly. "Oh, Gophia, we haven't much time! What am I missing?"

She calmed herself and tried to recall the skull room from her dreams and where it was located. There was no way to figure it out now that she stood at the top. She tried to recall Cedric's words on how to find Zolmex. She was too panicked to think straight. Her lantern happened to wink out then, having burned most of the night, leaving her in darkness. That made the approaching lantern light that much more eerie.

She felt trapped with obstacles on all four sides: two stone walls on either side of her, the trail leading down to her pursuers, or the open cliff face. There was nowhere for her to hide. She could hear the spider legs again and understood it wasn't a dream—whatever pursued her had spider legs! She panicked, a million thoughts running through her mind. She took a deep breath just as some of the lantern light began to spill into the rock prison where she now found herself.

"What am I missing?"

A thought came to her then as Gophia ducked into her hiding spot in Cassandra's hair. She thought of the old coffin she had found, the resting place of Leo, the wizard. That had to be a clue! "Notel X!" she said, louder than she intended.

She looked around, expecting maybe a door to open like the last cave she was in, but nothing happened. More lantern light from her pursuer poured into the area, nearly catching her, and she could hear the spider-creature coming around the bend.

"Notel X!" she said, loudly again, and started banging on the rock wall in front of her.

She glanced toward the lantern bearer to see what looked like a human woman with long, spidery legs sprinting toward her. She looked once more to the rock, hoping a door was there. What she saw made her gasp. There in the rock, barely visible in the moonlight, reflected a third wall where the cliff face was, with a doorway in it. She looked over her shoulder at the new wall and doorway, but nothing was there except an open cliff. She turned back to the rock wall, and the reflection was gone.

"Cassandra Rho, I presume," the spider-woman said, running faster, tossing the lantern down and casting a spell.

She was only fifty yards away and coming fast. Cassandra desperately turned to the rock wall and said, "Notel X!"

The image appeared again, and Cassandra didn't look back at the cliff this time. Instead, she focused on the reflection, her eyes wide and unblinking as she backed toward the cliff face, one hand reaching out behind her.

"I have you now, Cassandra!" the spider-lady said, and Cassandra could feel the waves of a spell washing over her just as she backed into the invisible wall.

She felt a smooth stone wall behind her instead of open air! Her hand felt around, and using the reflection as a guide, she found the opening. "A door," she whispered, never taking her eyes off the reflection.

The spider-lady was a mere twenty yards away, the bright moon revealing a gleeful look plastered across her surprisingly pretty and innocent-looking face. She reached out with her hands as if she planned to scoop Cassandra up like a baby. The spell took hold, and Cassandra could barely move. It was a spell she understood priests used to hold their prey if they were evil or to run from attackers if they were good. This woman was definitely the former.

Cassandra tried to ignore the spell, but it was powerful, and she barely moved now, fighting the effects. She pushed through it the best she could, knowing that if she let this priestess grab her, the prophecy would come to fruition. Cassandra was vaguely aware of a large bird-like creature, the size of a human, landing behind the spider-woman. She couldn't look away from the reflection in the stone wall and only viewed the newest arrival peripherally. Whatever it was, it was an ally to the priestess. She managed to take one more shaking step backward toward the wall. Cassandra watched herself in the reflection step into the doorway.

⚬⚬⚬

To Matilda, Cass, and Ronnis, it appeared as if Cassandra had stepped backward over the cliff. But instead of falling, she had simply blinked out of existence.

"No!" Matilda screamed and ran to the spot where Cassandra had just disappeared.

She reached out, trying to find some secret door or invisible ledge, but she found nothing but cool air. Cass and Ronnis joined her, Cass with her wings still stretched out wide and Ronnis now in human form. From what they could tell, Cassandra Rho had simply vanished without a trace.

Epilogue

To Cassandra, the doorway was a leap of faith and she had survived that leap. Her heart beat out of her chest as the spider-woman rushed up to the door and towered above her. She even seemed to reach in and touch Cassandra, but that didn't happen, as her hand simply slipped through her as if she were insubstantial. Unfortunately for Cassandra, the woman's spell had taken hold and all she could do was stand perfectly still. Her heart raced and her breathing was quick, but all of her other muscles tensed up and would not answer her call. The spider-woman was powerful!

As the paralysis took hold of her, Cassandra could only watch the strange woman and her two friends standing in front of the doorway. The new arrival wasn't a creature or a bird, although Cassandra swore she saw wings when it landed. To her surprise, it was Cass Ruben! And not just Cass, but there before her, only a few feet away, stood the biggest villain she had ever known—Ronnis D'Breeth. She was furious that these were the people chasing her. She would have gladly welcomed a fight with Cass and Ronnis if she'd known. Still, the spider-woman was the real mystery. Who and what was she?

Cassandra stood there for a long time, unable to move from the spell effects. She stood in that doorway, which served as a soundproof window, one step over the cliff face. Cassandra could see the three evil beings conversing but couldn't hear them. She watched as the woman released her spell and lay on the ground in what appeared to be excruciating pain as the spider legs retracted back into her body. When it was done, Ronnis helped her stand once more.

That was when Cassandra noticed Gophia flittering about above the three. Cassandra's breathing increased, and her eyes looked all around. Had the door repelled her friend? She could only see blackness from the corners of her eyes and had no other explanation. Perhaps, just perhaps, this cave had been made for Cassandra only. She could feel its energy, almost like the floor pulsed with it. This one felt very different from the cave she had navigated near Godhomme.

Her three adversaries were in a heated discussion, and Cassandra saw Gophia fly off into the darkness undetected. She felt a sense of relief at that. Cassandra wanted her friend with her and didn't want to be in this dangerous place alone, but she was also concerned for the fairy's well-being. She didn't want her hurt—the further away from these three, the better off Gophia would be.

After a very long while watching the spider-woman nearing a complete panic and Ronnis and Cass shrugging in response, just as puzzled as she was, the spell finally began to fade. First, her fingers began to twitch, then her left foot continued its trek, taking one small step backward. Soon she was able to move again and take in her surroundings. Then something caught Cassandra's eye that had her mind reeling—Cass had the medallion that Cedric had used to track her. How did she come into possession of the device? Cass handed it to the strange spider-woman, and she closed her eyes, turned directly toward Cassandra, and then opened them again, looking straight at her. Cassandra needed to break the spell and be away from this place. They could sense her through the medallion!

Before she thoroughly beat the effects, she saw something else that made her heart sink—Cass produced the cottage token that Cedric had carried. Again, Cassandra wondered how Cass could have obtained the magical items. Had she robbed Cedric after he had died? Her anger with Cass was already great, but she vowed to take those items from her when the day finally came, and she could confront her rival one on one.

The spell fully broke then, and she nearly fell out of the doorway and back into the presence of the three evil beings. She regained her balance and watched them for a while. The spider-woman seemed to be the leader, and from her skull-covered robe, Cassandra determined she was probably a priestess of Marnelphion, which explained a lot. How her two rivals had met and then traveled with the vile woman was a question for another day.

She ignored them. She was safe for now and confident they couldn't enter the magical space. She turned to take in the surroundings. Pure blackness met her. There was no light source, and she would indeed need one. On a whim, she summoned the abundant magical energy in the place and called forth a tiny flame on her palm.

Its appearance startled her, not because it worked but because it was different. Typically, the cantrip produced an orange flame about two inches tall, enough to produce the same light as a candle. This flame was about six inches tall and seemed to consume her entire palm. It was blue, just like the topaz that adorned Zolmex. She watched the heatless flame burn in her hand and felt its energy as if the cave amplified the spell.

When she could finally draw her eyes away from the spell and take in her surroundings, she discovered she was at the top of a stairwell leading down. There was an arcane symbol etched into the wall to her right. She recognized it as a familiar rune usually used to aid with light spells. She stuck her burning hand into the etching, and the flame transferred from her hand into the rune. The wall seemed to absorb her spell, and it grew dark again.

Just when she was about to recast the cantrip, there was a humming sound and lines of blue energy shot through the wall to her right. It quickly descended the stairs like a lightning strike, tiny fingers of blue light etching in the wall. There were only about two dozen steps, to her relief, as she recalled the trap with the spiders in the last cave contained a stairway with thousands of steps. The small hallway at the foot of the steps lit up in bright blue light. It flickered like a torch, and she descended to take in the strange place. She watched as the lightning continued down the right wall, and every fifty feet as the lightning passed, a torch held by a sconce flared to life with the strange blue light. Cassandra watched as the hallway slowly lit up, stretching as far as she could see.

She sighed. "Please let there be no water this time."

She began to walk down the steps. She was more prepared this time. She had her spells, which were far more powerful than before; she had her faith, feeling closer to her goddess now than on her first adventure; and she had the two scimitars hanging from her hips. She was ready but not nearly as confident, knowing exactly how dangerous one of her father's caves could be.

A FEW HOURS AFTER THEY HAD LOST CASSANDRA, MATILDA, CASS, and Ronnis sat around a fire on the flat rock atop Witch's Rise. Cass had shown Matilda the cottage and explained that Cassandra was probably nearby in a similar extra-dimensional space. The medallion confirmed that to be the case, so Matilda decided to wait right where they were, hoping Cassandra would eventually come out of her hiding spot. The cottage enthralled Matilda, but she insisted they all sleep out in the open so they could catch Cassandra if she tried to sneak away.

The desert air was cold, especially at that altitude. Ronnis and Cass sat near the fire, neither able to sleep, the adrenaline at being so close to catching Cassandra keeping them restless. Matilda eventually drifted off, wrapped in a blanket on the other side of the fire. Her sleep was fitful, and she would turn and mumble occasionally.

"I guess she did love that giant warmonger," Ronnis said as Matilda moaned loudly in the throes of a horrific dream.

Cass nodded with a smile. "Yes, even a demon-worshipping bitch has love in her heart," she said, and they both stifled a laugh.

Ronnis poked the fire with a stick, sending embers into the air between them. He didn't wear his porcelain mask, and the hole in his cheek that started at the bottom of his right eye and stretched down to the bottom row of his teeth was on full display. It was a gruesome scar, and Cass couldn't stop staring at it.

"Don't stare at me," Ronnis finally said, not taking his eyes from the fire.

"Cassandra did that?" Cass asked, ignoring his request.

"Yes, she did," Ronnis said, turning an icy stare from the fire to meet Cass's wide-eyed gaze.

"She's more powerful now, you know that, right?" Cass asked, absently rubbing the scar that Cassandra had put under her left breast.

"Maybe, but so am I."

"So are *we*," Cass corrected.

She got up and moved over to sit by Ronnis. She produced the Tooth of Leo, the golden knife she had found during her quest with Cassandra. She held it up near the firelight, and the blade reflected the light majestically.

"What is that?" Ronnis asked.

"The magical knife that I stabbed her in the back with," Cass said nonchalantly.

"You stabbed her in the back?"

"Yes, and the exhilaration I felt from doing so was exquisite," Cass purred. "Its bite also paralyzes, leaving its victim immobile. We can use it to keep Cassandra still and receptive to whatever tortures we desire."

"I like the way you think, but she'll be watching," Ronnis said, nodding to Matilda.

Cass turned to regard the woman and said, "We won't break her rules, only Cassandra. After all, we don't need to deflower her to have sex with her, correct? I mean, a girl has many holes to enjoy, which won't take her virginity."

A wicked smile creased Ronnis's lips at the thought. His sexual domination of Cassandra had been a priority since he lost Sera. He had given up hope on that when he met Matilda, but what Cass suggested would work nicely.

As he thought about the possibilities, the Adder warned him: "*Careful.*" Ronnis stood and drew his sword, startling Cass, who backed away a few steps.

"What do you know?" she asked.

"The sword issued a warning."

Ronnis concentrated on making mental contact with the sword, asking for more information. The Adder was silent, letting the vague warning serve as its only communication. Ronnis hated the sword sometimes because it wanted to be the one in control of their new relationship. To prove that, it offered vague words to keep Ronnis guessing.

"And?" Cass prodded.

"And that is all I know. I believe something approaches."

Cass moved to awaken Matilda but stopped and looked to the trail leading up the mountain and into their camp, her eyes wide. Ronnis followed her gaze to find the intruder, a tall, beautiful woman dressed in a thin black dress, which was very low cut and with slits on both sides, revealing most of her legs. The attire was entirely inappropriate and couldn't possibly keep the woman warm in the cold desert air. The fact was evident by her nipples, which clearly showed through the thin material of her dress.

"Who are you?" Cass asked, suddenly forgetting Matilda.

"I am Illa, messenger of the powerful Mystic from Vasym," the woman said with a bow.

She was standing partially in the shadows, which made her appear striking and mysterious. Still, Ronnis didn't bring his weapon to bear, but kept the tip toward the ground as Cass walked closer to Illa.

"Messenger?" Cass asked.

"And who is this Mystic you speak of?" Ronnis added.

"Do not fear; he is no enemy and wishes you the best on your hunt for Cassandra Rho."

Ronnis and Cass shared a concerned glance, and Ronnis's grip tightened on his sword. Still, it didn't communicate anything further.

"How do you know who we seek?" Cass asked suspiciously.

"The Mystic knows everything; he is a god. But fear not; he has an offering, something that will assist you in your quest for the Rho girl."

Illa stepped out of the shadows, and it became evident she was holding a small chain. She tugged at it, and Binta came stumbling out of the darkness to stand beside the demoness. Cass's face brightened with recognition, and Ronnis's eyes widened. Binta wore her collar and leash and still donned the skimpy little dress Cass had given her all those months ago. Binta couldn't hold Cass's gaze, so she shamefully looked at her feet instead. Ronnis's lustful stare took in shapely legs of the beautiful captive, the tiny dress barely covering her crotch.

"Binta Mulay," Cass breathed.

"Who?" Ronnis asked.

"Cassandra Rho's girlfriend," Cass explained.

"And Cass's plaything," Illa added.

Binta knew right away from the disfiguring scar on his cheek that the man standing before her was Ronnis D'Breeth. She didn't understand how he and Cass knew each other, but Illa couldn't have delivered her to anyone more despicable than those two. She wanted to reach out and infiltrate their minds, to control them and torture them into submission for what they had done to Cassandra. Binta could do it now with her new powers, but something about being close to Illa made her weak, and seeing Cass again only amplified that feeling. She was smart enough to know that the milk was the culprit and the pheromones that both women secreted would be her downfall. She was totally helpless, only able to concentrate on suppressing her sexual urges.

"Why? How?" Cass asked in amazement.

"She came to Vasym looking for Cassandra. She bested The Mystic at his mind games, which he took personally. So, this is his payback for that insult; he is handing her over to you to do as you wish. No human truly bests The Mystic," Illa said, smirking at Binta.

"This simple whore beat a powerful god-like being with her mind?" Cass asked with amazement.

"It's true, and her powers are genuine. She's no longer simple, but definitely still a whore," Illa said.

"Binta, I am so glad you made it. You will give us something to do while we wait for your girlfriend," Cass teased.

"No. I'm not that person anymore, Cass, and you will leave Cassandra alone," Binta managed to say, but with no conviction.

Cass and Ronnis shared a look, and Cass laughed. "Yes, yes, it looks like you're no longer a whore, just a slutty adventurer in a slinky dress."

"She's still as promiscuous as before, but now even more so," Illa said. She produced a vial of white liquid and added, "She has partaken of more nepalin milk. Mine, to be more exact."

"Nepalin?" Ronnis asked.

"Demon milk," Cass replied.

Ronnis took a step back, and it appeared he understood precisely what Illa was.

"Yes, and she is quite naughty when she drinks the milk. So, if she gets out of control and starts threatening you with her powerful mind abilities, which I assure you are real, give her a drop of this, and she will quiet down."

"Enough of this! I'm not a plaything, especially to you, Cass!" Binta said with as much authority as she could muster.

Both Illa and Cass laughed at Binta, which infuriated her, but she couldn't focus on that; she was already distracted by the possibility of sex. She wanted to please Cass and give herself to that ogre, Ronnis. Binta barely kept her thoughts in order long enough to speak, much less use her new-found powers. She wanted to scratch Cass's eyes out, yet she also wanted to please her. She tingled all over with the thoughts of what terrible things Cass would force her to do with Ronnis. She licked her lips in anticipation, giving away her true feelings.

She felt so powerless at that moment, despite what she had gained from the Tome of X'lor. She had fought this side of her, the sexual deviant that threatened to spoil all her work. She thought she had won that battle back in Pelesea, but Binta had been hopelessly lost since she had met Illa.

Illa said, "I wish I had time to play, but The Mystic expects me back. I will leave your pet with you, and I hope you enjoy her as much as I have during the last few hours."

Binta was furious and wanted to scream out that she was not a slave, not a plaything. But all that came out was a whisper: "No."

Illa laughed, saying, "You cannot resist, Binta; it's who you are. Now come here and taste the milk once more."

The demoness slid the shoulder strap of her dress down to reveal her right breast, and Binta's breathing became labored, and the tingling sensation grew to a boiling point. Cass walked over and watched, taking the vial of milk from Illa and smiling at Binta's dilemma.

"You cannot resist. Now come here and prepare yourself for your new mistress," Illa said, pulling the leash hard enough that Binta nearly fell.

The demoness pulled her in close. Binta locked eyes with Illa for just a moment, and all her senses dulled except the aching between her legs. She looked at Cass and licked her lips, her mouth and throat suddenly parched. Cass wore that evil smile, and she wanted nothing more than to wipe it off her stupid face.

"Go ahead, dear. We don't have all night," Illa said, offering Binta her breast.

Finally, not able to resist any longer, Binta moved to the demon's breast and began to suck. Illa gasped as the milk trickled into Binta's mouth. It amplified all the tingling sensations and fueled the fire between her legs. She closed her eyes, savoring the taste and the feeling of pure ecstasy, moaning lustfully.

Illa pulled her away before she could receive much of the irresistible nectar and said, "Careful, my pet, we don't want you poisoned again; that's not The Mystic's goal."

Illa handed the leash to Cass and said, "She is yours. Do with her as you wish."

With that mischievous smile, Cass pulled Binta close, said, "You know what to do," and gently pushed Binta to her knees.

Binta hated Cass, but at that moment, all she wanted to do was obey, to open herself up to control and abuse once more. The tingling between her legs left her no choice, and the milk worked its way through her system, making her vulnerable. So, she went to work, licking her mistress's sexy boots, just as Cass had taught her to do. Thoughts of saving Cassandra floated to the recesses of her mind. Her sole objective was to please Cass, and so she did.

GOPHIA SPOTTED THE FIRE AT SITRA'S HOUSE AND MADE HER WAY there. The little fairy was exhausted, having flown most of the night from the top of Witch's Rise. Sitra stood by the fire, a pyre with two bodies burning near her front door. She was deep in thought, so it startled her when Gophia landed on her shoulder.

"Is that you, Gophia?" she asked after she collected herself.

"Gophia, yes," the little fairy said, panting and near exhaustion.

"And Cassandra?"

"She hides from the bad people. She left Gophia, so here I came."

"So, she's in trouble?"

The fairy whimpered, nearing tears, and nodded. Sitra couldn't see the reaction but understood what the fairy was doing. Sitra didn't wear her blindfold, but her eyes were swollen shut, so there was no chance of petrifying the little creature.

"What of Cassandra's friend, Binta?"

Gophia shrugged at first, then, no doubt remembering Sitra couldn't see her, said, "Who?"

"A strong woman who went to the mountain behind you and Cassandra. She is a friend and has come to help Cassandra. You didn't see her?"

"No," Gophia said, and all was quiet as they watched the fire. "Mateon," Gophia whispered lightly, pointing toward the pyre.

"No. It's just a distraction. Mateon is down below, at the garden, healing."

Gophia clapped her hands and batted her wings in joy, and Sitra smiled. The movement shot waves of pain through Sitra's torn mouth, and she brought a hand up to her busted lips. Sitra had never received such a vicious beating, and she couldn't imagine what the evil people would do to Cassandra if they caught her. The two bodies burning on the pyre were two of those warriors who had beaten her, two that Binta had killed. Binta had saved her from the savage beating and certain death. She owed it to the woman to help as much as she could. She also would die for Cassandra, whom Sitra considered a genuine friend.

"We'll go to Mateon and hide below the ground where the evildoers can't find us. When my face heals and Mateon recovers from his injuries, we'll find Cassandra and Binta. It may take weeks, but we will go, I promise."

Gophia hugged Sitra around her neck as the sleeth's snake hair gently caressed the fairy. Gophia giggled, and it sounded like tiny bells to Sitra. She laughed, and the two friends went to the hidden underground tunnels beneath Sitra's home. They would heal, and then they would find Cassandra. Sitra hoped that they wouldn't be too late.

It was a late summer morning in Pelesea. Kringus and Penelope stood on the temple's highest balcony, along with the other members of the New Order. Also in attendance was the new steward of the city, Jamison Oland, and his three advisors, Franklin Ruben, Sam Velt, and Raul Franz. They were five stories above the gathered crowd of city folks, who cheered the appearance of their king and queen. People packed the streets from the temple yard to the docks, the school of magic, and the north gate. Some found a better seat on top of the buildings across the street, while those lucky enough to live or work in those buildings opened windows for a magnificent view of the royal couple.

The priests used the balcony for grand ceremonies and holidays. Thousands had gathered to listen to Kringus because they knew the speech was of the utmost importance. Lady Victoria had cast a spell of amplification so the king's voice would carry.

After the initial cheering died down, Kringus waited a few moments, taking in the magnificent scene. The city was a product of his and Penelope's hard work, and the subjects that lived there made it the grandest city on Torlia, in his opinion. He was so proud at that moment. He glanced at Penelope, who stood at his left, and she smiled genuinely. His heart filled with love, matching his pride at being the king of the great city. Something told him this would be the last few moments of life as they knew it. Things were about to change, and he would never be at this point again.

After that realization sunk in, he finally spoke. "Dear citizens of Pelesea. I appreciate you gathering here today to listen to my words. What I have to say is extremely important, not just to Pelesea but to all living beings. A time has come in our history when the goodly people of the world must stand together to defeat a potential evil we have not endured in nearly seven hundred years. The demon, Marnelphion, stirs and has his eyes set on Novafontera, the very city he cursed all those centuries ago."

There was murmuring, and Kringus continued so the panic wouldn't set in. "The New Order is called to duty, my people, not just to defend Pelesea and the neighboring communities but the entire world. This threat comes from a valid source, but it is just that, as of now—a threat. We formed the New Order to smite threats like this before they take shape. And we will see it done."

He paused and watched as people spoke in hushed tones, some with shocked faces and others holding hands over their mouths in disbelief. He didn't like sharing such awful news but needed to instill confidence, so he looked to his queen for support, and Penelope nodded with a smile.

He continued, "The New Order does not take threats to our freedom lightly, so we must answer the call. We leave in three days to journey to the west to Varish to stop the prophecy that is taking hold on the world, which predicts the arrival of Marnelphion."

The mutterings in the gathered crowd grew louder, and people began to panic. Kringus patted his hands in the air, asking for silence. Eventually, the whispers died, and the people looked to their king for reassurance.

"That is the bad news. The good news is we will defeat this evil that threatens to invade our world, just like the original New Order did all those years ago. We are confident, and you should feel safe knowing the world is in good hands. For you see, dear people, the prophecy that predicts the demon lord Marnelphion will rise and conquer the world also predicts the New Order will defeat the evil, destroying it before it manifests."

The murmuring was there still, but Kringus could see hope replacing the fear on the people's faces. The sight gave him the courage to continue. "At times such as this, the world's free people must take a stand, which starts with the New Order. It does not stop there, as Pelesea must remain vigilant in our absence and have a ruler with the same desire for justice and integrity as the queen and I would demand. Therefore, Penelope and I have found a steward for Pelesea who will rule with dignity in our absence."

There was light applause, mixed with the mutterings this time, and Kringus saw many heads nod in approval. "So, as the New Order ventures out to destroy this threat, we ask that you live your lives, not in fear as the demon lord would want, but as free people, because free people you remain. The New Order will see to it!"

There was a massive cheer as Kringus's words broke the dour mood and turned it more positive. The people believed in him and accepted his statement that they would be all right.

"And now, before I introduce you to the New Order members who have courageously stepped up to fill this oath—some new to the group, others long-time members—I want to introduce your new rulers for the foreseeable future. These men have been hand-selected by Penelope and me, along with input received from our typical advisors and from the New Order. People of Pelesea, I give you the new steward of our city, Jamison Oland."

There was little fanfare as Jamison made his way to stand beside Kringus. Most of the city knew who Jamison was, but little knew of his integrity, like the king and queen. There was minor applause from those who knew his reputation, but it wasn't the standing ovation that Kringus had hoped for. Jamison waved and smiled, and Kringus patted him on the back. Still, the reception was lukewarm for the new steward.

Jamison asked if he could say a few words, and Kringus thought it would be a grand idea, so Victoria cast a spell on Jamison to amplify his voice as she had done with Kringus.

Jamison nervously cleared his throat and began. "Good people of Pelesea, some of you may know me, but I imagine most of you do not. So, I think it is appropriate to introduce myself. The king and queen could have asked anyone to be a steward, but of all the options they had, they chose me. So, I'm hoping you will put your faith in Kringus and Penelope and, in turn, me to perform this job adequately.

"First and foremost, I am a citizen of Pelesea, and I will act to put the citizens' interest first. Life will go on as you know it. Businesses will open, we will collect taxes, we will hold church service, we will punish crimes, and I hope to do this with the same efficiency as your king and queen. I want your lives to continue unscathed. Sure, we will increase security and keep a watchful eye out for the dangers Kringus spoke of. And in the end, I will gladly step down when Kringus and Penelope return to resume their rule, whether in a month, a year, or two years. I believe they will complete their task, and we will live uninterrupted by the evil lurking beyond our walls."

There was cheering then as Jamison's words and humble demeanor struck a chord with the citizens. They cheered slowly at first, but as the moments passed, more joined in, and soon, there was a roaring applause, to the relief of Kringus and Penelope. The people of Pelesea accepted the steward of Pelesea, and Kringus could focus on the New Order business, knowing Jamison was in control of his precious city.

Jamison waved and smiled, and when the cheering finally died down, Kringus introduced his advisors, Franklin, Sam, and Raul. The citizens cheered them as well, their mood becoming increasingly more pleasant. The city readily accepted all four men as the new ruling council for Pelesea. Kringus allowed the cheering and the applause to continue for a long while, and then Jamison and the advisors took their seats.

After a few formalities, Kringus swore Jamison in as steward, and the other three took a similar oath. The good people of Pelesea witnessed the ceremony and sealed it with more applause. Afterward, Kringus introduced the New Order members.

"So, as we sail over the Nepress Sea and end the threat to our freedom, I want all of you to know who the men and women of the New Order are.

These individuals are not only my dear friends but also heroes, willing to put their lives on the line for the free people of the world."

More cheering ensued, and when it died down, Kringus introduced each person one at a time, starting with the older members. "You know Penelope and me," he began but was immediately interrupted by a loud and long cheer.

Penelope and Kringus waved and patiently waited, and once it had died down, Kringus continued. "Arrin, the captain of our army." Arrin stood and waved, to more cheering.

"The brothers Von and Lenore, cousins to the queen." The elves rose and bowed, to more cheers.

"Lady Victoria, the grandest wizard in the lands," Kringus said, waving a hand her way. Victoria curtsied, and people cheered and whistled.

"And finally, Daro, Keeper of the Woods, ranger, and dear friend." Daro rose slightly and waved quickly, not wanting or liking the attention. After the cheering died once more, Kringus continued introducing the newest members.

"And now, my faithful citizens, I have introduced all the original members except one. Alleah Mansuell, the high priestess of Sinnis, is our group's eighth original member."

There was another round of applause, but when it was evident Alleah wasn't coming forward, it died down, and Kringus continued, "Alleah is currently on Varish on a reconnaissance mission. The first order of business will be to reunite with her." Kringus left out the part about how long Alleah had been gone and how they didn't know where she was or if she was still alive.

"This strange prophecy that has befallen us is precise about our little group. Just as the original New Order, we are to travel light, only the New Order members, no army or other allies. It also stipulates that there must be exactly twelve members, just as in the original New Order. So, as Penelope and I searched diligently for a steward over the spring and summer, the New Order searched for new members. I am glad to introduce those new members now."

More applause followed, and Kringus allowed it to play out. The crowd's joy was contagious, and the ceremony had gone just as smoothly as he had hoped. Once it was quiet, he continued, "Each member will take a vow, pledging their lives to protect Pelesea and the world's free people. That will come at the end of the introductions. Please meet the amazing heroes who have agreed to join the cause of the New Order.

"First, there is Baxter Von Glord, High Wizard of Victoria's school." Baxter stood and bowed slightly, glancing at Jamison, who returned a troubled smile. Baxter quickly sat down, and the applause eventually died down.

"Then there is Max Smithston, former sheriff of Oldorburg." Max stood and waved nervously. People clapped and shared whispers, as Oldorburg was a town most had heard of.

"Lastly, in attendance is Sasha De'Formen, an ice carofex from the world of ice."

There was stunned silence at first as Sasha stood to be recognized. Her beauty was like none other, and the little applause that had begun quickly quieted down as men and women alike gasped at the true beauty Sasha represented. She was already uncomfortable in the sweltering heat of the summer morning, but the silence amplified that discomfort. She quickly sat down, and the gathered mass murmured, trying to understand her incredible beauty.

"Another new member, and one who has not accepted the offer yet, is Greyson Kavince, the young prodigy of Plath." There was applause once more as some people had heard of Greyson's exploits and how he had miraculously arrived in the city.

"He has not accepted yet because he has not received the offer. Greyson is with Alleah, and when we reunite with her, we will ask for his pledge. And, as I've stipulated, the New Order must maintain a membership of strictly twelve as we travel. Since we are missing two members, the knights Erik and Marcus will travel as temporary members."

The two knights of Pelesea stood and received another round of applause. Afterward, Kringus swore the new members into the New Order, witnessed by all those gathered.

Kringus ended the ceremony with a final declaration. "We leave in three days and intend to return by next summer. However, we will not tire or stop until we complete our quest. If it takes longer than a year, so be it. This mission is our destiny. We do it for you and the other good people of the world, and we also do it for ourselves because we believe in freedom. So, stand tall and proud, people of Pelesea, and fear no evil. Rest assured, the New Order will prevail."

There was one final roaring cheer as the king and queen of Pelesea, along with their fellow heroes and the new steward of Pelesea, made their way back into the temple. It took a while before the cheering subsided, and the crowd began to disburse. The crowd's mood was good, and Jamison and his advisors' wide acceptance gave Kringus and Penelope great comfort. A feast awaited the New Order, Jamison, and his advisors. They would share a private meal before the adventure began. Everyone was seated and being served, except for Kringus and Penelope, who remained outside the banquet hall.

"What is it, my husband?" Penelope asked as if reading his thoughts.

"I don't know, my queen. I have a bad feeling that we'll lose friends on this quest, good friends. I do not doubt that we will prevail, but knowing that Cassandra Rho could indirectly be responsible for those deaths does not sit well with me."

"What are you saying?"

"I'm saying that perhaps my leniency with the girl was a mistake. I could have executed her and foiled the prophecy."

A fire lit in Penelope's eyes, and she put her hands on her slender hips. "You must not say things such as that, Kringus. It defeats the whole purpose of our mission and the meaning of the New Order."

"I agree, my love, but I promise you this: if I have to decide to sacrifice Cassandra to save my friends, especially you, I will do it in the blink of an eye."

Penelope could only nod her agreement and offer a weak smile. She took Kringus's hand and led him into the hall to join their friends. Soon, they were lost in food and conversation as the celebration lasted most of the day. However, Kringus silently vowed then to make good on his word. He would readily sacrifice the young woman to save the lives of many. The New Order was coming, not to save Cassandra, but to save the world.

About the Author

A fan of fantasy and science fiction from a young age, Phillip Martin dreamed about writing stories. He's used that desire to run roleplaying games and even develop them. His roleplaying stories have created countless adventures and worlds for the benefit of his closest friends. Finally, some of his vivid imaginings have been immortalized in print for others to enjoy. Phillip lives in Christiansburg, Virginia, and can be found at www.cassandra-rho.com.